When Time Runs Out

Part 3
of
The Ambition & Destiny Series

By
VL McBeath

When Time Runs Out
By VL McBeath

Editing services provided by Wendy Janes at WendyProof and
Susan Buchanan at Perfect Prose Services.
Cover design by Michelle Abrahall

ISBN: 978-16978257-8-7 (Large Print Edition)

Main category - FICTION / Historical
Other category - FICTION / Literary Collections

Legal Notices

This story was inspired by real-life events but as it took place nearly two hundred years ago, parts of the storyline and all characterisation are fictitious. Names have been changed and any resemblance to real persons, living or dead, is purely coincidental. Although the story took place in and around the Summer Lane area of Birmingham, and Handsworth, exact locations have been changed.

Explanatory Notes

Meal Times

In the United Kingdom, as in many parts of the world, meal times are referred to by a variety of names. Based on traditional working-class practices in northern England in the nineteenth century, the following terms have been used in this book:

Breakfast: The meal eaten upon rising each morning.

Dinner: The meal eaten around midday. This may be a hot or cold meal depending on the day of the week and a person's occupation.

Tea: Not to be confused with the high tea of the aristocracy or the beverage of the same name, tea was the meal eaten at the end of the working day, typically around five or six o'clock. This could either be a hot or cold meal.

Money

In the nineteenth century, the currency in the United Kingdom was Pounds, Shillings and Pence.

- There were twenty shillings to each pound and twelve pence to a shilling.
- A crown and half crown were five shillings and two shillings and sixpence, respectively.
- A guinea was one pound, one shilling (i.e. twenty-one shillings).

It can be assumed that £1 at the time of the story is equivalent to approximately £100 in 2018

Politics

During the second half of the nineteenth century, two parties dominated politics in the United Kingdom: The Conservatives and The Liberals.

Conservatives:

Originally derived from the Tory party, during the time of the story they were lead by Benjamin Disraeli and latterly by Lord Salisbury (otherwise known as the Marquis of Salisbury).

Their main aims were to support the monarchy and the British constitution, the British Empire and the Established Church of England.

They also believed that the landowning aristocracy were the given rulers of the country.

Liberals:

Initially a party called The Whigs, they evolved into the Liberal Party in 1859.

They saw themselves as a party of reformers and called for the supremacy of parliament over the monarch.

They offered the opportunity for non-conformists (ie those whose religions were outside the Church of England) to have greater status in society and supported the abolition of slavery and the expansion of votes for men.

MP stands for Member of Parliament

For further information on Victorian England visit:
https://valmcbeath.com/victorian-era

Please note: This book is written in UK English

It is recommended that *When Time Runs Out* is read after Parts 1 & 2

**Previous books in
The *Ambition & Destiny* Series:**

Short Story Prequel: *Condemned by Fate*
Part 1: *Hooks & Eyes*
Part 2: *Less Than Equals*

Join my mailing list for further information and
exclusive content about The *Ambition & Destiny*
Series.

Details can be found at **www.vlmcbeath.com**

The Family Tree shown on the next page represents
the family at the start of this story.

For larger versions please visit:
https://valmcbeath.com/time-runs-family-tree/

To Stuart
Sometimes the seemingly insignificant events of life
can have the most profound consequences...

The Jackson and Wetherby Family Tree

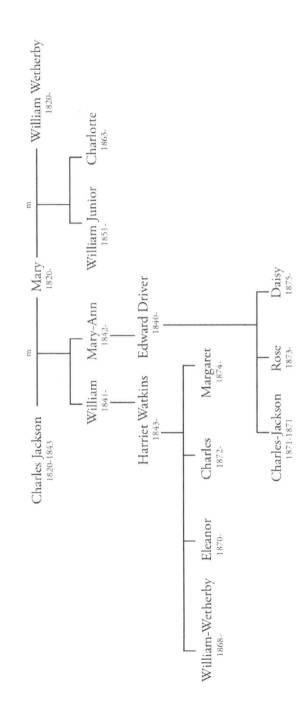

Chapter One

Birmingham, Warwickshire. January 1876

With the light fading, Mr Wetherby leaned forward on the edge of his seat and peered through the window of the carriage. He let his eyes run along a row of terraced houses as they came into view, but the one he was looking for was in darkness. *She has to be here. Where else can we look if she's not?*

As the carriage pulled up outside the house, his stepson, William, broke the silence of their journey.

"There doesn't appear to be anyone at home," he said. "I can't see any light from the window."

Without waiting for the coachman, Mr Wetherby pushed on the door and jumped out. "I hope you're wrong. If she's not here, we've no idea where she might be."

"I don't know why she would come here in the first place," Mr Wetherby's son, William Junior, said as he prepared to follow William from the carriage. "Aunt Alice hasn't lived here for months and from what I can gather, all her possessions are in Handsworth. If Mother had wanted a memento of her sister, she'd have been better off at Aunt Susannah's."

"None of us here are in a position to understand how a woman's mind works." Mr Wetherby checked his pocket watch. "Now, let's see if she's here before we decide what to do next."

With William and William Junior beside him, Mr Wetherby opened the front door and stepped inside. The small room was almost dark and William lit a candle in the middle of the table. "Shall I go upstairs and see if she's there?"

"No, I'll go." Mr Wetherby took the candle from the table, but as he approached the bottom step he heard a noise. "Mary, is that you?" He strained his neck as he called up the stairs. "Mary ... speak to me." When he got no response he started up the stairs, but as he approached the top the bedroom door creaked open and Mary gazed down at him, her eyes wide with horror.

"What are you doing here?" She squeezed around the door, pulling it closed behind her.

"What are we doing here?" Mr Wetherby's mouth fell open. "I could ask you the same thing. The last time we saw you we were at your sister's funeral but when we came back from the grave you'd disappeared."

"Yes ... I'm sorry." Mary watched her fingers playing with a tassel on the shawl covering her mourning dress. "How did you know I was here?"

"We didn't for certain, it was a hunch Susannah had. She said you were upset and needed some time."

Mary nodded. "Yes, she's right. I did ... do. I'm sorry. This week hasn't been easy."

"Of course it hasn't." Mr Wetherby moved closer and put his arms around her. "We've got you now. We were worried about you. Come on, let's get you home." He released his grip and turned to go back down the stairs, but Mary remained fixed to the spot.

"I'll follow you, but first I want to clear out the last of Alice's things."

Mr Wetherby stared at her, a frown etched across his face. "What are you talking about? I'm not leaving you here on your own. I'll arrange for a couple of men to empty the room this week and bring the personal property to Handsworth."

Mary hesitated. "There are one or two things I'd like to fetch myself. I'll be with you in a minute."

Mr Wetherby turned to face William who stood behind him on the stairs before he shrugged and they both made their way back to the living room.

"Don't be long," he said, but the sound of the bedroom door closing behind him suggested that Mary hadn't heard.

As soon as she was inside the room, Mary leaned against the door and tried, without success, to control her breathing. Richard stepped towards her.

"You must go," he whispered, cupping her face in his hands. "He can't find me here. I'll make my own way out once he's gone."

Mary closed her eyes and took a deep breath.

"Mary, please," Richard said. "You need to go."

The sound of Mr Wetherby calling her name, and his feet once more climbing the stairs, brought her to her senses and she fumbled in her pocket.

"Take my key, I don't need it. Pass me the clock too. I said I'd come back for something."

"Just go." Richard wrapped her cloak around her shoulders. "I'll write when I know he's back here in Birmingham."

Richard kissed her cheek as the footsteps stopped on the landing. A moment later, the door swung open, forcing Richard to dart behind it and press himself against the wall.

"What's taking you so long?"

Mary flinched at the sight of Mr Wetherby. "I'm coming." Her heart was beating so loudly, she worried he would hear it. "I was checking there was nothing else I wanted to take." Mary picked up the clock and glanced around the room, forcing her eyes to ignore Richard who stood less than a foot away from Mr Wetherby, hidden only by the door. "I always liked this clock, I thought we could put it in one of the bedrooms."

Mr Wetherby glanced at the battered clock and gave her a doubtful stare. "It's a dreadful thing. You can put it in the servants' room, but nowhere else." Willing herself to stop shaking Mary froze as Mr Wetherby stepped into the room and glanced around before his eyes rested on the rumpled bedcovers.

"I-I needed to lie down ... it's been a difficult day."

Mr Wetherby studied her before he took her arm and walked her to the dresser. "There's nothing but rubbish in here." A second later he blew out the candle, plunging the room into darkness.

Chapter Two

As the cold evening air hit Mary's face, the carriage drifted in and out of focus and she caught hold of Mr Wetherby's arm to stop herself falling. If she could only sit down, she'd be fine. Her heart pounded as she thought of Richard and how close they had come to being found together.

"In you get," Mr Wetherby said as he helped her into the carriage. "You've had a difficult day, you need to rest."

Mary nodded but said nothing. Her husband had no idea.

Once in the carriage, Mary sat next to her son William and took his hand, thankful he was there. If anyone could understand how she was feeling, it would be him. Not that she could tell him. She glanced at her other son, William Junior, and wondered why he was there.

"What were you thinking of?" Mr Wetherby said as the carriage pulled away. "We've been searching everywhere for you. With the four of us missing there was hardly anyone at Alice's wake."

Mary turned to the window and smiled. *It served her right.* "I needed to be on my own."

"But why come all the way down here ... and where did you get the money for a carriage?"

Mary closed her eyes and rested her head on the hard interior of the carriage. "Please, I'm exhausted. Just take me home."

～

Handsworth, Staffordshire.

MARY WAS late down the following morning but Mr Wetherby was still sitting at the breakfast table.

"I thought you'd have gone by now," she said.

"I'm not leaving you on your own after yesterday."

Mary picked up the pot of tea and poured herself a cup. "Don't be silly. You have to go to work."

"William's taking care of things in Handsworth and William Junior's in Birmingham."

Mary raised an eyebrow. "Is that wise? You can't leave William Junior in charge for too long."

Mr Wetherby put his hand on hers. "I'm more concerned about you at the moment. You've not been yourself since Alice died."

"I'm fine, honestly. Now the funeral's over I just want to get back to normal. It won't help if you keep fussing over me." She withdrew her hand from under his and sat down.

Mr Wetherby gazed into her eyes. "I've been neglecting you, I'm sorry. Things are going to change from now on. I'll travel home from Birmingham every night, like I used to, and I'm going to spend a couple of days a week in Handsworth with William."

"You don't need to do that." *That's the last thing I want.*

"Yes I do. It'll mean I'm around to keep an eye on you. It also means William doesn't have to travel to Birmingham every week. I need to know what's going on in both workshops."

Mary felt the colour drain from her face. *What about Richard? How will I see him?*

"I don't want to see you doing anything around the house today. You're still delicate. I'd say you thought more of Alice than you realised."

Mary's eyes flicked in Mr Wetherby's direction, but she said nothing. How could she tell him she hated her sister more than she hated anyone she'd ever known? How could she explain such hatred to the man who had married her and brought up her two children as his own, when the truth was she had never stopped loving her first husband? The husband she had lost because of Alice's selfishness. How could she explain that the only man who could make her feel whole again was Richard, the brother of her dead husband? That his likeness to her beloved Charles, with his dark, unruly hair, and deep brown eyes, was the cause of all her emotions?

"I didn't care that much for Alice and you don't need to stand guard over me." Tears pricked at Mary's eyes. "I'm sorry about yesterday, but I'm not going to disappear again. Please, go and see William. He needs you more than I do."

Mary left the table and went back upstairs for a lie-down. She had only been there for an hour when she heard a knock on the front door, followed by footsteps on the stairs.

"Mrs Wetherby." The maid spoke softly as she tapped on the door. "Are you awake?"

Mary sat up on the bed. "Yes, come in."

"Sorry to disturb you, ma'am, but Mr Diver is

here. He asked if he could speak to you. He said it's urgent."

"Oh my, yes of course he can." Mary hurried to the dresser to fix her hair, before she went down to greet her son-in-law in the back room.

"I'm sorry to disturb you," he said. "It's Mary-Ann. The baby's coming but I need to be in Birmingham. Will you come and sit with Rose and Daisy?"

"My dear Mr Diver, of course I will. Anything to spend time with my granddaughters. Please lead the way."

MARY SETTLED herself in the back room of Mary-Ann's house, waiting for Mr Diver to leave. The girls hadn't woken from their mid-morning nap and Mr Diver asked the maid to make a pot of tea while Mary busied herself with her knitting. She waited a full five minutes after he had gone before she stood up and went to the window in the front room. It was still like a building site out there. Not satisfied with what she had seen, she crept up to the back bedroom on the second floor. That was more like it. Beyond the wall at the back of the garden sat some allotment gardens with a path running diagonally through the middle of them. There were several older men working their plots, but other than that it was empty.

They weren't the sort of men Mr Wetherby would associate with.

As she made her way back downstairs she heard a noise from the nursery. Popping her head around the door she saw Daisy sitting up in her cot.

"Come to Grandma," she said as she bent to pick her up.

"Where's Mother?" a small voice said from behind her.

"She's busy at the moment. You come downstairs with me and I'll find you some dinner. You can see Mother later."

As the afternoon wore on, the sound of crying from the bedroom told her she had a new grandchild. With a smile on her face she took the girls back to the nursery and asked a maid to stay with them while she waited for the doctor to call her.

"Another daughter," Mary-Ann said as Mary was shown in. "I so wanted to give Mr Diver a son."

Mary studied the round, usually cheerful, face of her daughter, her long brown hair falling loose about her shoulders. "Don't say it like that, look at her." Mary held the blanket away from the baby's face and gazed at the button nose and light covering of dark hair. "You can't be upset with such a lovely, healthy baby. You of all people should be thankful."

"You're right." Mary-Ann smiled as she held one

of the tiny fists. "I'd just hoped ... you know, after Charles-Jackson was taken."

Mary sighed. "You can't think like that. I didn't want any more children after I lost Albert and Edwin, but do you think I'd be without Charlotte now? Of course I wouldn't. You'll love this baby as much as you love the other two."

MR DIVER ARRIVED home shortly after five o'clock and drove Mary back to Wetherby House. Mr Wetherby was waiting for her in the hall.

"Where on earth have you been?" He spoke before she had taken her cloak off. "I thought I was going to have to come looking for you again."

"Didn't Emily tell you I went to Mary-Ann's?"

"No, she didn't!"

"Well, I have and we have another granddaughter. Lillian or Lilly for short." A smile beamed across Mary's face.

Mr Wetherby's anger softened as he turned to Mr Diver. "Well, congratulations. I suppose you're used to all this by now."

Mr Diver smiled. "There's always something special about it, but if you'll excuse me, I'd better be getting back. Thank you, Mrs Wetherby."

"I need a word with that maid," Mr Wetherby

said when they were alone. "She didn't say anything to me. After everything that happened yesterday as well."

Mary walked into the back room. "Be fair to her. I don't suppose she knew you were looking for me yesterday and I didn't specifically ask her to tell you where I was."

"Well you need to start telling her where you're going. I don't want to be worrying every time I come home and find you not here."

"I'm sorry, but with you being in Birmingham so much of the time we're used to going out and not thinking about it."

"Well, you need to start thinking. I won't be in Birmingham for the foreseeable future and in case you've forgotten, you're in mourning. You're not supposed to go out socialising."

"My daughter was having a baby, it wasn't a usual afternoon visit. Besides, I might be in mourning, but it doesn't mean I can't visit my daughter, or my daughter-in-law for that matter. They are both the mothers of my grandchildren and I won't keep myself away from them."

"If Mary-Ann and Harriet want to see you, why can't they come here?"

Mary unravelled the knitting she'd brought in with her. "You've no idea, have you? Mary-Ann has three children and Harriet four. It's not a simple task getting them all out of the house at once. I'm not going to make life difficult because Alice has died."

"You were distraught about her yesterday and now anyone would think you didn't care."

Mary's eyes narrowed as she glared at Mr Wetherby. "I'm more upset about Alice than anyone will ever know, but I'm not going to let her ruin the rest of my life. If I want to visit my family I will."

Chapter Three

Harriet paced back and forth across Mary-Ann's living room, the short train of a new lilac-coloured dress trailing on the floor behind her.

"What do I have to do to persuade William to move house?" she said. "After all the trouble I had getting him to move last time, I thought it would be easier now, but he's so stubborn."

Mary's brow creased. "What did you do last time?"

Harriet stared at her mother-in-law, her mouth gaping, before she answered. "I was in the asylum! I'm not doing that every time I want to move house."

"Oh yes. I'm sorry, I'd forgotten." Mary rubbed her temples.

"Forgotten? How could you possibly forget? It was the worst six weeks of my life." Harriet's voice pierced the room.

"Harriet, calm down." Mary-Ann stood up to peer into the cots of her youngest two daughters. "We know how dreadful it was, but you'll wake the babies. Sit down and we'll help you think of something."

Harriet's shoulders slumped and she checked her own young daughter before she sat next to Mary.

"Where do you want to move to?" Mary asked.

"I haven't got anywhere in particular in mind, although something like this would be ideal." Harriet let her eyes wander around the room.

"The house next door's still empty," Mary-Ann said. "If we could persuade William to buy it, we could be neighbours."

"What a splendid idea." Harriet clasped her hands under her chin. "It'd be lovely to have you next door and William should be able to see the benefits. How many times has he been around here?"

"Only once or twice I would say. He's not been lately. He doesn't need to when we always meet at Wetherby House."

"Well we need to get him here." Harriet was on her feet again. "Have you shown him around? Has he been upstairs ... or seen the stabling?"

Mary-Ann hesitated. "I don't think so. He was with Mr Diver and so possibly not."

"That's it then. We need to show him what he's missing."

"Why don't you and William call here one Sunday?" Mary suggested. "You often go walking when the children are at Sunday school. You could come here."

A smile lit up Harriet's face. "We could. Mary-Ann, we can both try and talk some sense into him. He might listen to you ... or Mr Diver at least."

HARRIET SAT at the dining table in their cramped downstairs room, oblivious to the rain lashing against the window. William didn't know it yet, but she was taking him to Mary-Ann's house on Sunday and she needed to be ready. She could already hear him telling her that they didn't need a bigger house, and that they couldn't afford one, but she was going to prove him wrong. She studied the housekeeping book she had open in front of her. With the exception of the two months Mr Wetherby had reduced William's wage, she had managed to put a bit of money aside each week. To start with it had only been a few shillings, but since William's wage had almost doubled, she had accumulated a decent amount of money.

Once upon a time, she might have been happy to rent somewhere, but not now. If Mr Wetherby and Mr Diver could buy their own homes, William could too. Her savings weren't nearly enough, of course, but banks were lending money to people like them nowadays. She had no idea how much they would charge, but looking at the figures, they should be able to pay back at least a pound a week.

IT WAS two o'clock the following Sunday when Harriet and William arrived at the Divers' house. Before they walked up the drive, Harriet stopped and stared at the buildings beyond her. They were in various states of readiness, but they looked magnificent. Those with roofs were three storeys high with large bay windows to the front. Some stood alone while others were joined to one other house. They all appeared to have stabling and room for a couple of carriages in the back gardens.

"Wouldn't you like a house like this?" she asked William. "Can you imagine how splendid it would be for the children?"

William gave her a sideways glance. "Is that why I'm here? Have you any idea how much they cost?"

"Not yet, but you can speak to Mr Diver about it. If he can afford one, so can we."

Harriet pushed the baby carriage up the drive before William could argue and left Margaret asleep by the front door. She kept tight hold of Charles's hand.

"What have you done with the girls?" Harriet asked Mary-Ann as they walked into the back room.

"They're upstairs in the nursery. One of the maids is with them."

A smile spread across Harriet's face. "Oh William, wouldn't it be wonderful if we could do that?" She nodded her head at Charles. He gave her more trouble than the rest of the children put together and she dreamed of being able to send him to the top of the house. "Can we take him up?"

Mary-Ann led the way and at Harriet's insistence, William joined them.

"Look at the space," she said to William as they neared the top of the stairs. "There are two good-sized rooms up here. We could have one for the boys and one for the girls ... or they could have the rooms on the first floor. There are another three bedrooms there."

"How would we find the money to furnish it?" William asked.

"We will, trust me. Come and see downstairs as well." She pushed Charles into the nursery and took

William's hand again. "They have an inside bath-room, with hot and cold running water. Imagine, no more getting the tin bath out in front of the fire. And, even better," Harriet said with a final flourish, "the house next door is still for sale. We could all be neighbours."

William said nothing as Harriet showed him from room to room, only smiling when Mr Diver joined them.

"Have you come to rescue me?" he asked.

Mr Diver laughed. "Is it that bad? I thought you were a willing viewer."

"Only in so far as it makes for an easier life."

William moved towards Mr Diver and lowered his voice, but Harriet strained her ears to listen to what they were saying.

"We don't need to move yet."

"You need to invest your money somewhere though," Mr Diver said. "You'll end up with a better return than if you left your money at home or gave it to the bank. It's a good time to buy as well. If you sign the paperwork before the whole road is finished, you'll get a discount. That's why we moved when we did."

"I did wonder," William said.

"Let me show you around outside," Mr Diver said. "We can talk while we're out there."

Once they had gone, Harriet and Mary-Ann returned to the back room.

"Do you think he'll buy one?" Mary-Ann asked.

Harriet laughed as she watched William through the window. "He will by the time I've finished with him. I want the house next door more than anything else. Do you think we could go and look around?"

Chapter Four

Mary put her pen back into the holder on her writing desk and reread the letter she had written. It was addressed to her sister-in-law, Sarah-Ann, but she was uncomfortable about it. She needed an excuse to go to Birmingham and Sarah-Ann was her best option. The problem was, as ever, Mr Flemming. Although Sarah-Ann would undoubtedly enjoy a visit, he was never happy to see her.

She had put the letter in an envelope, and was about to seal it when she heard a knock on the front door. She wasn't expecting anybody and stopped to listen as the maid answered it. When she couldn't hear voices she picked up a stamp and placed it on the envelope.

A moment later, Emily knocked on the door. "I'm sorry to disturb you, ma'am, but there's a new coalman at the door. Says he wants a word with you."

For an instant Mary froze before she scrambled to her feet and hurried across the room. With her heart in her mouth, she stopped by the door and took a deep breath.

"That will be all, thank you, Emily. I'll see to it."

She waited for the maid to disappear into the kitchen and close the door, before she hurried down the hall and went outside.

"Richard!" She didn't know whether to scold him or throw her arms around his neck. "What on earth are you doing here? Mr Wetherby could be home at any time."

Richard smiled. "I saw him on Frankfort Street about an hour ago and decided it was safe to call."

"We've still got to be careful. Let me show you the coal bunker." She closed the front door and led Richard down the side of the house. "We'll be less conspicuous here, just try not to disturb the dogs."

Once they reached the back of the house, Richard reached for her hands. "Where've you been? I've been worried about you."

Mary's shoulders slumped. "Since the funeral, he's barely left me alone. I made the mistake of going to Mary-Ann's house the day after without telling him. Now, if ever I go out, he thinks I won't come back. He's not stayed overnight in Birmingham once for nearly two months."

Richard let out a heavy sigh and raked his hand through his hair. "He didn't see me then?"

"No, I'm sure of it. He'd have said something."

"So what do we do?" Richard gazed into her eyes. "I need to see you."

Mary could feel her heart thumping. "I'm about to post a letter to Sarah-Ann to ask if I can visit for a few days. There isn't anyone else in Birmingham I can ask."

"Not Sarah-Ann. Please. I don't trust her."

"She's your sister!"

"Maybe she is, but she's too friendly with Mr Wetherby for my liking."

Mary caught her breath and stared at Richard. "What have you heard? He's not seeing her, is he?"

"Not that I'm aware of, but you know they're close ... besides, you won't be able to go out as you please if you stay there. She'll want to be with you."

Mary nodded. "You're right, but what else can I do? Since Mr Chalmers died I don't like imposing myself on Martha and it doesn't help that I have to wear this." Mary pulled at the black crepe of her mourning dress. "How can I go anywhere without people pointing me out as being disrespectful."

"What about me coming here?"

Mary walked a little way down the drive to study those passing the house. "You'd better go and fetch a couple of bags of coal. I don't want anyone talking about us."

Richard did as she requested, but when he returned with the second bag, he asked the question again.

Mary shook her head. "We can't risk you coming here. Not only have I got Mr Wetherby to think of, there are the staff as well. There is another option though." Mary's eyes shone as she smiled. "I visit Mary-Ann regularly. She's near Birchfield Road and it's quiet around there. The houses are still being built and they back onto a field of allotment gardens. If I ask the coachman to drop me off on the corner of Livingstone Road, I could meet you there."

Richard smiled. "You've been thinking about this. Are you sure we won't be seen?"

"I've checked the last few times I've been to Mary-Ann's house. There are walls with secluded alcoves around the edge and the only people I've seen are a few old gardeners. Mr Wetherby won't talk to men like that."

"It sounds like a plan. I can be up here from Birmingham by around two o'clock. Shall we say the same time, same place every week? Keep things simple."

Mary grinned. "I'm visiting tomorrow, we could start then ... if you're not too busy."

"I've told you before, I'm never too busy for you."

Chapter Five

Harriet pulled up Charles's knee-length socks and wiped his face with her handkerchief as William knocked on the door of Wetherby House.

"I want you three to behave yourselves, do you hear me?" Harriet pushed William-Wetherby and Eleanor closest to the door. "No repeat of last week."

As she lifted Margaret from the baby carriage, Emily opened the door and took the children into the morning room. Harriet hurried to take her cloak off and went into the front room where she sought out Mary-Ann.

"You're here," Mary-Ann said. "Why do you persist in going to the Congregational Church? You'd be here a lot quicker if you came with us to St Mary's."

"You know very well why we don't, but you can't upset me today." Harriet flashed Mary-Ann a broad smile and clapped her hands together. "William's agreed."

"Agreed to what?"

"He's going to see about buying the house next door to you."

Mary-Ann's face lit up. "That's wonderful. When?"

Harriet didn't have a chance to reply before William joined them. "What are you up to? Not building Mary-Ann's hopes up of getting new neighbours, are you?"

"Yes, she is," Mary-Ann said. "And quite right too. It'll be marvellous."

"There's the small matter of seeing the bank manager first." William's smile faded. "I can't say I'm looking forward to it."

"What's all the excitement?" Mary asked as she saw them.

"We're going to buy the house next door to Mary-Ann and Mr Diver," Harriet said. "Isn't that wonderful?"

"Well, yes, of course." Mary smiled and turned to William. "Have you mentioned it to Mr Wetherby? He might be able to help you. He knows the right men to talk to."

"Not yet. I was hoping to catch him once dinner was over."

Mary glanced over at her husband. "Why not speak to him now before William Junior arrives?"

William glanced in the same direction. "Yes, that's not a bad idea."

HARRIET WATCHED as William and Mr Wetherby left the room and was relieved to see a smile on his face when they returned five minutes later. She desperately wanted to ask him what Mr Wetherby had said but before William joined her, Mary was ushering everyone into the dining room. It wasn't until they came to walk home that Harriet was able to talk to him.

"Mary-Ann and I have the whole house planned out," she said as they set off. "We're going to need to buy some more beds for the children, and chairs for the living room, but other than that ..."

"Harriet, calm down. I haven't seen a bank manager yet. I'm going to have to open an account first and he could say no."

"Of course he won't say no. I've gone through the figures and we should easily be able to afford it. What did Mr Wetherby say?"

"He was all for it. He's even offered to set up a meeting for me with his bank manager."

"Marvellous." Harriet couldn't keep the smile from her face. "He wouldn't do that if he didn't think you'd get the loan."

"Perhaps not, but please don't tell anyone else. You know I'm uncomfortable talking about money at the best of times."

"You'll be fine. All you need to do is show him the figures I give you. I'll write it all out so you understand it."

"What if he asks me questions?"

Harriet took hold of William's hand. "Stop worrying. We'll go through everything until you're comfortable with it."

~

Birmingham, Warwickshire.

WILLIAM STOOD outside the railings enclosing the bank and studied the exterior. It was a formidable stone building, which incorporated ornate roman pillars giving it an appearance similar to Birmingham Town Hall. His heart pounded as he pushed open the gate and walked up the path to the front door. With a final glance at the papers in his hand, he stepped into the cavernous banking hall. The voices of bank tellers and customers echoed around the walls and he heard his every footstep on the stone floor as he made his way towards the counter.

With a slight cough to clear his throat, he waited for the clerk to look up before he spoke. "I'm here to see Mr Ashford." While the clerk flicked through the diary, William wiped the palms of his hands on his trousers.

"Follow me," the clerk said after several seconds. He led William down a small corridor and asked him to take a seat outside the manager's office. With its mahogany-panelled walls, and lack of windows, the seating area couldn't have been more different to the bright expanse of the main hall and as he sat down William sensed the walls closing in around him.

Twenty minutes later, when he was still waiting, William was struggling to breathe. For the umpteenth time he wiped his hands on his trousers before he took out his handkerchief to mop his brow. He was so hot, he needed air, but he doubted his legs would carry him. Feeling himself swaying in the chair, he was thinking about making his escape when the door opened and a clerk asked him to step into the office.

With a deep breath, William steadied himself before he walked into a small, formal room. It was set with a mahogany desk across one corner that matched three of the walls. The fourth wall was made entirely of shelves and contained row upon row of books.

"Mr Jackson." Mr Ashford leaned across his desk and held out his hand. "Take a seat."

As William sat on the small wooden chair looking up at Mr Ashford, an image of his younger self, sitting in front of the headmaster after he'd failed a mental arithmetic test, flashed before his eyes. He blinked to be rid of the image but felt a bead of sweat trickle down his back.

"So, Mr Jackson, you want to borrow four hundred and twenty-five pounds. Is that correct?"

"Yes, s-sir," William stammered.

"A large sum of money for one house. It must be impressive."

"Yes, sir ... we need a bigger house."

"Do you have a big family?" Mr Ashford sat with his hands clasped in front of him, peering at William with steely eyes.

"Yes, sir. I have a wife and four children. Two boys and two girls."

"And you expect to make the weekly repayments and support a family of six at the same time? Do you earn a large wage?"

"Yes, sir. It's all in here." William handed Mr

Ashford the paperwork Harriet had prepared. "My income and all costs are listed."

The room fell silent as Mr Ashford read the papers. William's heart thudded and he willed himself to keep breathing.

"How old are you and your wife?" Mr Ashford spoke without raising his head.

The question caught William off guard and he froze before Mr Ashford stared at him.

"Your age, Mr Jackson?"

"Yes ... sorry. I'm thirty-five, nearly thirty-six. My wife will be ... thirty-four."

"And your youngest child?"

William wiped his forehead. Why did he never pay attention to these things? "Two ... I think."

The expression on Mr Ashford's face didn't change. "So, still time for you to add to your number."

"I suppose, but ... no, I don't think so. There's only two years between each of the others, and there's no sign of another one. We've finished now."

"So the eldest will be ...?"

William squeezed his eyes together. "He's nearly nine."

"Will you send him to school?"

"I imagine so."

Mr Ashford turned back to the document.

"Well," he said when he had finished. "I'd say that borrowing such a large amount of money will be too much for you."

As he felt himself swaying, William became aware that he had stopped breathing and let out a small cough. "But ..."

"But what, Mr Jackson?"

"The figures show we can afford it ... it's all written down."

"I think you could afford the repayments now, but imagine what would happen if you had another couple of children. You're both young enough."

William shook his head. "We won't."

"You also have to ask where the school fees will come from for your sons."

"If they pass the admission exam ..."

"You can't live on 'ifs', Mr Jackson." Mr Ashford stared at William before he turned back to his finances.

"You work for Mr Wetherby, I believe."

"Actually I'm in partnership with him."

Mr Ashford lifted his head in disbelief. "A partner? A junior partner I would say looking at this. I'm sure Mr Wetherby takes home more than five pounds a week. No, I'm sorry; on this sort of income it would be reckless of me to lend you such an amount."

"Please," William said. "We could afford it, we don't waste money."

Mr Ashford studied him before he turned back to the paperwork. "I'll tell you what. Mr Wetherby is a personal friend of mine. Let me speak to him. If he'll act as a guarantor, I may be able to show some discretion."

Chapter Six

As Mr Ashford stood up to escort him from the office, William was shaking from head to foot. He leaned on the desk to ease himself up and after a brief handshake, he stumbled down the corridor and into the banking hall. With the back of his shirt sticking to him, he ran his finger around his collar. He had to get out of here. As soon as he was away from the bank, he headed for the steps of a neighbouring building and with a deep breath sat down and put his head in his hands. How was he going to tell Harriet? She had set her heart on that house. She'd put so much effort into making the figures add up, and he'd ruined it. She'd be furious with him.

It was a full fifteen minutes before William was

able to stand up again, but he couldn't go home. Not yet. He knew Mr Wetherby would be at the work-shop on Frankfort Street and he needed to talk to him.

William found Mr Wetherby sorting through some papers in the office.

"I wasn't expecting you today." Mr Wetherby put down the papers he was holding and walked to the front of his desk. "Have you been to see Mr Ashford?"

Still exhausted from his visit, William sat down in one of the visitor chairs. "I have. That's why I'm here. He thinks we might be overstretching ourselves."

"How much do you want to borrow?"

"Four hundred and twenty-five pounds."

"I thought you said you had some money saved?" Mr Wetherby said.

William sighed. "We have, but clearly not enough. He wasn't impressed with my five pounds a week either, even though it's considerably more than most men earn."

"Most men don't want to buy such a big house."

William shot him a disbelieving glance. "I thought you were in favour of it."

"I am, but I didn't realise you'd need to borrow so much. Perhaps he's right."

"No, he's not. It was like he was deliberately trying to get out of it. Making excuses." William put his hands on his knees and pushed himself up. "He said he's going to come and see you. If you'll act as a guarantor he'll reconsider. Would you do that for me?"

Mr Wetherby walked to the window and stared out across the road. "If I did, it would mean I'd be liable for all your debts if you miss any repayments. That's quite an undertaking."

"Please. I'm not going to default and it wouldn't be for long. Once I have a pay rise he should release you from the clause. Perhaps you could give me a pay rise now?"

Mr Wetherby turned round slowly. "I'm going to need to think about it. Leave it with me."

IT WAS STILL early afternoon when William left Mr Wetherby. He decided to make the journey to Handsworth on foot to give him time to find the right words for Harriet, if such a thing were possible. On top of everything else, he knew she'd be mad at him for not taking a carriage and going straight home.

It was past three o'clock when he opened the front door and he fully expected her to be in the hall as soon as she heard him. When there was no sign of her he took off his hat and coat and went into the living room. Immediately his frown changed to a smile when he saw his mother.

"Mother, what a lovely surprise." He offered a silent prayer of thanks. "Is this a social visit?"

"No, not really. I knew you were going to see Mr Ashford and so I thought I'd call and see how you got on."

"Yes, do tell us, dear." Harriet's tone caused the hairs on the back of his neck to stand on end. "I've been waiting for you." The anger in her eyes was barely hidden by the serene expression she wore for Mary's benefit.

"He hasn't made a decision yet," William said. "He said he'll let me know."

"When?" Harriet asked. "We need to confirm with the builders that we want it."

William studied his hands. "In a week or two. He needs to make a few enquiries first."

Harriet was on her feet. "A week or two! We can't wait that long. What sort of enquiries?"

"He needs to check how much I earn, make sure we can afford the repayments that sort of thing."

"You should have shown him your wage slips; it tells him on there."

"I did, but ... I don't know, he wants to check me out with Mr Wetherby."

Harriet seemed to be about to say something but her glance at Mary suggested she'd thought better of it.

"I'm sure he'll vouch for you," Mary said. "He was pleased when he heard you wanted to buy something and so I'm sure he'll help you. Let me have a word with him."

"Would you?" William let out a sigh of relief. "If he could give me a pay rise, I'm sure it would help."

MARY WAS WAITING in the back room when Mr Wetherby arrived home that evening. She was wearing her favourite dress and had used a little more perfume than usual in the hope of putting him in a good mood. So far he didn't appear to have noticed.

"You've been quiet this evening," she said as he finished his tea.

"Yes, I'm sorry, I was thinking."

Mary put down her china teacup. "I saw William today."

Mr Wetherby looked up at her. "He hasn't asked you for any money, has he?"

"No, of course not. Why would he?"

"What did he want?"

"He didn't want anything; I was visiting Harriet when he came home. Is he in trouble?"

Mr Wetherby pushed back his chair and stood up.

"What's going on?" Mary persisted. "What aren't you telling me?"

Mr Wetherby held her gaze. "Mr Ashford's not going to lend him the money for the house."

"How do you know? William said he hadn't heard."

"Because Mr Ashford came to see me this afternoon."

Mary's heart skipped a beat. "And ...? You're hiding something. What is it? Please don't lie to me."

Mr Wetherby took a deep breath. "He asked if I'd act as William's guarantor ... in case he couldn't repay the loan ... and I refused."

Mary sat with her mouth gaping before she rose to her feet. "You refused to help my son ... our son ... buy his own house?"

Mr Wetherby walked towards her and took her hands. "It's not like that; it would mean I'd be liable for all his debts."

"And what's wrong with that? You have enough money. You could buy the house outright for him if you wanted to. If it were William Junior or Charlotte they wouldn't need to ask ... and don't say it's different, because it isn't. Why won't you help?"

"He's got to learn to stand on his own two feet."

"And will William Junior and Charlotte have to do that as well? I doubt it."

Mr Wetherby said nothing.

"You can't let them lose that house," Mary continued. "Harriet has her heart set on it and the one they're in now isn't nearly big enough. You have to help them."

There was a long pause before Mr Wetherby responded. "I won't act as their guarantor. William has to learn to be responsible for his own actions. I won't always be there for him."

"I don't want you to act as his guarantor, I want you to treat him as if he were William Junior. I imagine you'd buy him a house without him having to ask." Mary couldn't hide her contempt.

Mr Wetherby walked back to the table and sat down. "Leave it with me. I'll sort something out."

Chapter Seven

Handsworth, Staffordshire

Having put the children to bed, Harriet came down the stairs with a face like thunder.

"Why didn't you come straight home earlier?" she asked as she shut the living room door. "You knew I was on tenterhooks before you even left."

William stood up and put his arms around her. "Please don't be angry with me. I did my best, I promise."

Harriet stepped back. "He's not going to lend us the money, is he?"

"I don't know, he might, but..."

"But what?"

"He was worried about you having more children, and how much it would cost to send the boys to school."

"Why the boys?"

"He assumed we'd only send the boys and I didn't want to mention there could be fees for the girls too."

Harriet gave a weak smile. "Yes, of course. That would have made things worse ... but these things are years off yet. Why is everything so difficult? You earn the money; we're careful with it; we need a bigger house. It's not fair." Harriet sat down and put her head in her hands. "I really want that house."

William pulled up a chair and sat beside her. "He hasn't definitely said no yet. There was one other option."

Harriet's eyes shone as she took hold of his hands. "What?"

"If Mr Wetherby agrees to act as a guarantor, which means he'll help with the repayments if we can't pay them ourselves, then Mr Ashford will reconsider."

"So Mr Wetherby has to be involved? Isn't there any area of life where we can be free of him?"

William squeezed her hand. "Don't you think it would be worth it? It needn't be for long. Just until I have a pay rise."

"He could give you a pay rise now if he wanted to, but being a guarantor gives him that bit more control, doesn't it?"

William sighed. "Would you turn it down if he offered?"

Harriet's eyes glistened. "Of course not. We have no choice, do we?"

WILLIAM STOPPED by the door of the workshop and gave the room one final glance before he reached for the keys to lock up. He was about to leave, when Mr Wetherby arrived. William's stomach somersaulted when he saw the expression on his face.

"Mr Wetherby. I wasn't expecting you. Have you spoken to Mr Ashford?"

Mr Wetherby nodded. "I have. Come into the office."

William took a deep breath and started walking. "What did he say?"

"He took me through the figures and I fully understand his reluctance to lend you the money. If I'm honest, I wouldn't either. It does mean though that I can't act as a guarantor for you."

William couldn't speak as he imagined how Harriet would take the news.

"I won't be liable for any debts that you or your wife may incur either now or in the future."

William's shoulders slumped and he sat down in the visitor's chair. "So we can't have the house?"

Mr Wetherby looked down at him. "I can see how much you want it and I also realise that the place you're in now is far too small."

William nodded but said nothing.

"I've come to an arrangement with Mr Ashford. He believes you should be able to manage a loan of three hundred pounds. That will leave you one hundred and twenty-five pounds short. I'm going to put the money forward so you don't miss out on the property."

William's face lit up. "You'll give us the money?"

"I will."

William jumped up and shook Mr Wetherby's hand. "I don't know what to say. Thank you. You've no idea what this means. You won't regret it. I promise."

Chapter Eight

With the last of the crates unpacked, Harriet walked into the back room and sat on one of the new chairs. She glanced around in wonder and smiled. This one room was almost the size of the whole downstairs of the old house, but now she also had a front room, a morning room and a good-sized kitchen as well. The sound of shrieking from the garden caused her to stand up and go to the window. The children were having a wonderful time.

She was about to sit down again when the maid knocked and ushered Mary-Ann in.

"You've unpacked! It looks fabulous." Mary-Ann did a turn in the middle of the room. "I love the settee and chairs, the red matches the curtains perfectly."

Harriet smiled and walked around the backs of the new chairs, the velvet feeling soft under her touch. "I love the writing desk in the corner. I haven't had one since we left my aunt and uncle's house. I wasn't sure everything would fit with having the new dining table as well, but I needn't have worried."

"And the maid's started too. You won't know you're born. I love having help in the house."

"I'm looking forward to being able to have visitors," Harriet said. "I'm going to start sending out invitations as soon as I can."

Mary-Ann's eyes lit up. "Why don't you have everyone round for Christmas? It'll be here soon enough."

"What a wonderful idea." Harriet clasped her hands together under her chin. "We could invite whoever we wanted and still have room to spare."

Mary-Ann raised an eyebrow. "Does that include your aunt and uncle?"

Harriet's smile disappeared. "No. Not my aunt and uncle. I don't want their names mentioned in this house."

"I'm sorry," Mary-Ann said. "I didn't mean to

spoil the fun, I just thought ... well it's been a long time."

"If I see them in another twenty years it'll be too soon, but enough of them. Let me fetch some tea and we can write a list of who to invite."

THE FOLLOWING AFTERNOON, as her carriage made its way down Livingstone Road, Mary saw the coal waggon parked near the allotments. She knocked on the roof to indicate for the driver to stop, and waited for him to let her out. Once she'd paid him, she made her way to the corner and glanced around. Nobody. She was about to enter the allotments when Richard appeared by her side and gave her a kiss on the cheek.

"You're going to get me into trouble," he said. "Visiting twice in two days. Has William moved into the new house?"

Mary grinned. "I hope so, that's where I'm going when I leave you."

Richard took her arm and they walked around the edge of the gardens. "Will we be able to meet on Tuesday and Thursday every week, or is this week special?"

"Now William and Harriet live here I've two reasons to visit, so why not?" Mary's eyes twinkled as she smiled. "Are you complaining?"

"Certainly not," Richard said as they reached the familiar seat nestled between the wall and two shrubs. "I have been wondering though, do you think Mr Wetherby will ever go back to staying in Birmingham all week?"

"Not at the moment. He keeps insisting on coming home of an evening, but at least he's down there most days. I've been thinking though, it's going to be getting cold soon. What will we do then?"

"We've a few weeks left yet, but the bushes will be losing their leaves too. It could be a long, lonely winter."

Mary snuggled into Richard's chest as he put his arm around her. "Have you ever considered getting an allotment? If you had a plot with a hut on it we could meet in there."

Richard laughed. "No I haven't, but you have a point. Perhaps I should make a few enquiries."

As HARRIET POURED a cup of tea for herself and one for Mary-Ann, there was a knock on the front door and a moment later, Mary was shown in.

"I hope I'm not disturbing anything." Mary's eyes flickered about the room.

"Of course you're not disturbing anything. Violet," Harriet said as the maid was leaving the room, "can you bring another cup and saucer for Mrs Wetherby?"

"I wasn't expecting you today," Mary-Ann said to her mother.

Mary's cheeks flushed and she turned to face Harriet. "I can visit if I want to, can't I? I came to see the new house."

"I thought you'd come on Thursday," Mary-Ann said. "That's when you normally visit me."

"I wanted a change. Is there anything wrong with that?"

Harriet smiled as she took the crockery from the maid. "No, there isn't. In fact, I'm glad you're here. Mary-Ann suggested we invite everyone here for a celebration at Christmas. Not Christmas Day, but maybe Boxing Day. We've drawn up a list of who to invite." Harriet picked up the paper she'd been writing on and handed it to Mary. "What do you think?"

Mary scanned the list but said nothing.

"Do you think we should invite Mr Flemming and Aunt Sarah-Ann?" Harriet continued. "William wasn't sure. He says there's often trouble with them at Christmas and last time I saw them together she didn't go home for months afterwards."

Mary took the tea Harriet offered her. "They're fine now. If you're inviting everyone else, you can't leave them out."

"Do you think Uncle Richard will come?" Mary-Ann asked.

Mary jolted and spilt some tea into her saucer. "How on earth should I know?"

"I was only asking. Why are you so jumpy?"

"William would like him to be here," Harriet said. "For reasons I can't fathom, he still hasn't seen the children. He probably doesn't even know where we live."

"Mother, are you listening?" Mary-Ann asked when Mary remained silent.

"Yes, of course. You'll invite Uncle Richard ... What about your aunt and uncle? You've not put them on your list."

"After the way they treated me, you shouldn't be surprised." Harriet's voice was icy. "We're asking all William's aunts and their families, both from your side and Mr Wetherby's; my friends from Birmingham; several of William's acquaintances and the neighbours. Such as they are."

"Are you sure you can deal with everyone?" Mary said.

"We're only likely to do it once, and we're mostly family. It shouldn't cause any problems, should it?"

Chapter Nine

Sarah-Ann pulled her daughter's cloak tightly around her shoulders and fastened it securely. There was a biting wind and the drive to Handsworth would be uncomfortable. At least the gathering was in the afternoon and they wouldn't be late getting home.

"Now, where's your bonnet?" Sarah-Ann spoke to herself as Elizabeth stood silently in front of her. "Here it is, let's get you wrapped up." She finished with Elizabeth and fastened her own bonnet while she shouted up the stairs to Mr Flemming. "Are you coming? The carriage will be here any minute."

"Do we have to go?"

Sarah-Ann patted Elizabeth on the head before she hurried up the stairs. Once in the bedroom she found Mr Flemming lying on the bed. "What are you doing? I thought your headache had gone."

"I'm not going."

"Yes you are. If you choose to drink too much, you can suffer the consequences. If you don't want to come with us, we'll go on our own."

"You're not going up there ... to see *him* ... without me." Mr Flemming tried to stand up but fell back onto the bed.

"If you're not downstairs by the time the carriage is here, that's exactly what we'll be doing. Now I suggest you throw some water over your face and make yourself presentable. I want you on your best behaviour."

HARRIET SAT in front of the mirror and brushed her hair one hundred times before she fastened it into a chignon on the back of her head and decorated it with a selection of beads. Once finished she walked to the wardrobe and surveyed the gowns before her. She sighed as she reached for her favourite, a deep blue dress with a fitted bodice and bustled skirt. She'd only worn it a couple of times, but it was no use to her now. She doubted she'd wear it again such was the swelling around her waist. How she'd managed to find herself expecting her fifth child she didn't know. At least it hadn't happened before they'd bought the house, although it could have been the excitement of the move that had led to her current predicament.

She reached into the back of the cupboard and took out one of her looser-fitting garments. It was a dress she'd worn when she was carrying Margaret, three years ago, and the fuller skirt was so dated. Why didn't men understand the importance of having new clothes? With the dress fastened she studied her bulging shape in the mirror and pulled a face. There was still another five months to go.

She hurried downstairs to find William dozing in front of the fire. "Are you ready?"

William studied his familiar trousers and shirt, and grunted. "Of course I'm ready."

"Well you're lucky. Look at me in this. I don't think I'll fit into any of my old clothes ever again."

William sat up and inspected the dress. "I hope you do. You've had about six new dresses in the last few months. Anyway, what's wrong with that? It's nice enough."

Harriet pulled out the sides. "Look at the material. It makes me look even bigger than I am. Can I have a new dress, please? I won't have anything to wear otherwise."

William was about to respond when there was a

knock on the door and they heard the maid open it to Mary-Ann, Mr Diver and the children.

"Are you all ready?" Mary-Ann asked as she walked into the back room.

"We are. You look fabulous. Is that a new dress?" Harriet asked.

Mary-Ann did a slight courtesy and swished the skirt of her new bustled dress. "Mr Diver bought it me for Christmas. He thought the emerald green would suit me."

"And he's absolutely right. You make me feel even more dowdy than I did before you arrived."

Mary-Ann laughed. "It's about time I was more glamorous than you."

Harriet pouted. "Why don't you take the children upstairs? Violet's going to keep them entertained upstairs for the afternoon. If you want to take them up, William will pour you some mulled wine."

Mary-Ann had no sooner gone upstairs than she was back accepting the glass from William.

"Here's to a long and happy stay in Havelock Road." Mr Diver raised his glass. "And may you always be on good terms with the neighbours."

Harriet laughed. "Let's hope so!"

"I thought Mother would be here by now," Mary-Ann said. "It's not like her to be late, although she has been acting strangely over the last few months."

William's brow furrowed. "In what way?"

Mary-Ann paused. "It's difficult to say, but she's often flustered when she comes to visit and she's getting later. She says she's misjudged the time, but I'm sure she shouldn't be doing that every week."

William shrugged. "Mr Wetherby's still keeping an eye on her since she disappeared, so perhaps he's the problem."

As if she'd heard her name being mentioned, Mary arrived with Mr Wetherby, William Junior and Charlotte.

"Oh good, we're not late," Mary said as they walked in. "We'd have been here earlier except the driver was late harnessing the horses."

"What is it today with everyone looking so elegant?" Harriet said to Mary. "I'd say you've had a new dress too, and you look lovely with your hair taken back like that."

Mary smiled as she ran her hands over the hair that rolled back around the edges of her face. "Emily helped me do it. My, what a lovely Christmas tree. I wasn't expecting one in here with you having one in the front window."

"It was my idea," Harriet said. "I wanted a tree in the front to show off the house, but it seemed silly to have one in there and not in here, seeing this is where we spend most of our time."

"Very sensible. We should do that, shouldn't we, dear?" She turned to Mr Wetherby.

"It's a bit late now."

"Can I get you all a drink?" William said. "We've made mulled wine to warm everyone up. We're hoping Uncle Richard will remember to bring some coal for the fire too, to give the house a real warming."

The veins in Mr Wetherby's neck twitched as his face reddened. "What's he coming for?"

"He's my uncle. We've invited all my father's family. I wanted to show them that we've done all right for ourselves. Thanks to you."

"They can't all come," Harriet said. "Aunt Louisa isn't well and Aunt Adelaide's not free, but the others should be here. In fact, that sounds like Aunt Martha and her family now."

WITH THE NEXT knock on the door, Mary felt Mr Wetherby take hold of her hand as Richard's voice boomed down the hall. A moment later he strode into the back room with Mrs Richard behind him.

"Uncle Richard." William extended his hand to

him. "Thank you for coming. We don't see nearly enough of each other."

Richard accepted the greeting and smiled at Mary with a twinkle in his eye.

"Don't you smirk at my wife like that." Mr Wetherby tightened his grip on Mary's hand causing her to wince.

Richard turned to face him. "Mr Wetherby, Merry Christmas to you too. Don't tell me nobody mentioned I was coming."

"I did tell you, dear." Mary smiled at Richard as she prised her hand from Mr Wetherby's and stepped away. "Perhaps you weren't listening. William, will you pour Richard some mulled wine, so we can propose a toast to your new house."

Mr Wetherby glared at Richard as he accepted his drink and raised his glass.

"To William and the new house," Richard said.

"And Harriet and the children," Mary added.

"Of course." Richard spun round on the spot. "Where are the children? Don't tell me you're hiding them from me again."

William smiled. "No, of course not. They're in the nursery. Harriet, shall we take Uncle Richard upstairs?"

"You don't need to do that," Mary said. "You'll

be expecting the rest of your visitors soon. Let me take him."

"Don't forget me," Mrs Richard said. "I'd love to meet them."

Mary forced herself to smile. "Of course, I wouldn't dream of excluding you."

TAKING A LARGE MOUTHFUL OF WINE, Mr Wetherby watched them leave, checking Mrs Richard was firmly placed by the side of her husband. He couldn't bear to think of Mary alone with that man. He was about to refill his glass when another knock on the door caused him to stop. *Mr Flemming! What on earth's he doing here?* He quickly poured more mulled wine into his glass, spilling a little as he overfilled it, and took another gulp.

"Sarah-Ann," he said once William had greeted them. "How lovely to see you. Come and stand by the fire, you must be cold."

"You leave my wife ..." Mr Flemming started.

"I don't want to hear a word from you. Understood?" Mr Wetherby glared at him.

"Frederick, please ..." Sarah-Ann said.

"Don't you Frederick me."

Sarah-Ann stared at her husband. "No arguing.

It's William and Harriet's day as well as Christmas. Can't you be civil?"

Mr Flemming glared back before he levelled a glowering stare at Mr Wetherby and took a seat by the fire.

"What do you have to do to get a drink around here?" He nodded at Mr Wetherby's glass.

Mr Wetherby took another large mouthful of mulled wine. "Stand up and get one yourself."

Two floors above them, Mary introduced Richard and his wife to the children.

"Look at them all," Mrs Richard said, her eyes glistening. "How I wish we had some grandchildren. You'd think with four children, at least one of them would have done us proud by now."

"I'm sure they'll come," Mary said. "The two boys and these two girls belong to William, and the other three belong to Mary-Ann."

"My word, they've got the Jackson eyes," Richard said, looking at the boys. "Especially this one, he's just like his grandfather Charles."

Mary laughed. "His name's Charles too. He has the same impish nature as well. I'm not sure Harriet would agree though. He wears her out."

Richard laughed. "I think my mother was often worn out with our Charles too. He always got his own way though."

Mary smiled as she recalled her first husband's cheeky smile.

"Come on, don't go all sad on me," Richard said.

Mary smiled and glanced over at Mrs Richard who had become engrossed in stacking a pile of wooden blocks with the children. Richard followed her gaze.

"I've just remembered," he said to his wife. "I brought some coal with me to warm the house but I didn't bring it in. While you're here, I'll go and fetch it."

Mrs Richard acknowledged him but made no attempt to move. Mary followed him from the room and led him down the stairs.

"In here," she said when they reached the bathroom door on the first floor. "If anyone finds us I'll tell them I was showing you the new plumbing."

Richard smiled and glanced around the landing before following her into the bathroom. "I've missed you these last few weeks."

"Not as much as I've missed you." Mary relaxed as Richard took her in his arms and kissed her tenderly. "Have you managed to rent one of the allotment gardens yet?"

"They're all taken but I've put my name down on a list." He kissed her again. "I'll keep trying until they're fed up of me."

Mary let his hands move up her back and caress her neck before he cupped her face in his hands, kissing her cheeks, her nose and her lips before he gazed longingly into her eyes. "I can't wait until the spring before I see you again." He kissed her once more. "We need to think of something ..."

The sound of a door slamming downstairs made them jump to opposite sides of the bathroom. A moment later they heard footsteps coming up the stairs.

"So, there you are, an inside bathroom," Mary said as she walked out onto the landing. "I couldn't imagine going back to an outside privy now."

Once on the landing, Mary saw Mr Flemming reach the top of the stairs. "Are you looking for the bathroom?"

Mr Flemming stared from Mary to Richard but said nothing.

Mary felt her cheeks colouring. "We've been to see the children and I was showing Mr Jackson the bathroom. You can go in now."

Chapter Ten

With the delivery of her baby imminent, Harriet had been confined to bed every afternoon for the last fortnight. Although she hated it, it did have its advantages. Mary had insisted on hiring a nursemaid to take care of the other children, William was buying her extra magazines to keep her occupied, and she had plenty of time to think. It was thinking that was taking most of her time at the moment.

Mary had paid her a visit earlier that afternoon, and a comment about Aunt Sarah-Ann and Mr Flemming took her back to the Christmas party at their house. It may have been months ago, but the memory of the events still entertained her. She had enjoyed watching the interaction between Mr

Wetherby, Uncle Richard and Mr Flemming. Uncle Richard had spent most of his time with Mr Flemming. She hadn't known they were particularly close, but they were brothers-in-law, so maybe they were. The interesting thing was that Mr Wetherby appeared to dislike both of them. Why was that? And then there was Aunt Sarah-Ann. She had barely spoken to Mr Flemming and only acknowledged Uncle Richard when she disagreed with him, but she'd been all smiles with Mr Wetherby. Much to Mr Flemming's indignation. Was Mr Flemming jealous of Mr Wetherby's friendship with Aunt Sarah-Ann?

Whatever it was, something wasn't right between Aunt Sarah-Ann and Mr Flemming. Harriet had assumed their problems had been sorted out a couple of years earlier, but clearly not. She always prided herself on knowing what was going on, but this had stumped her. Mary had suggested Mr Wetherby was responsible for them being back together again, but if that was the case, Mr Flemming should be thanking him. Shouldn't he? She replayed the evening again and thought of Mr Flemming's excessive drinking. Then there were the looks shared between Aunt Sarah-Ann and Mr Wetherby when they thought nobody was watching. She knew the idea was ludicrous, but it was as if they were having a secret affair. Maybe Uncle Richard had found out about it. That would explain why Mr Wetherby didn't want to see him. Harriet smiled at the thought. *Someone with something they could use to manipulate Mr Wetherby. Wouldn't that be nice? I need to find out what's going on.* Mary must know. Perhaps a little gin once the baby was born might loosen her tongue.

THE FOLLOWING DAY, with the elder children at school and Charles and Margaret with the hired nursemaid, Harriet flicked through her magazine. Seeing nothing of interest, she flung it onto the bed beside her. The weather had gone warm and she couldn't concentrate. She wasn't going to endure this again and if it meant keeping William at arm's length, then so be it. Five children was more than enough for anyone.

It was after six o'clock when William arrived home and he gave her a broad smile as he entered the bedroom. "No sign of a baby yet?"

Does it look like it? Harriet rolled her eyes and took a deep breath. "No. Will you help me up? I need to walk around. It can't do me any good lying around all day."

"But the doctor said ..."

"I don't care what the doctor said. He's never carried a baby, and I need to move. Besides, if it makes the baby come quicker, it can't be a bad thing."

William helped Harriet to the bathroom before they made their way downstairs.

"You know what I'd like?" she said as she settled in the back room. "A glass of gin. It's been hot all day and if I'm going to have this baby tonight, it might make it more bearable."

William smiled as he poured the drink and took it to her. "Here you are, my dear. Is there anything else I can do for you?"

"Perhaps," Harriet said with a smile. "Why do you think Mr Wetherby dislikes Mr Flemming and Uncle Richard so much?"

"What's brought this on?"

"I've been thinking and decided you must have some idea. You've known them all long enough. Have a guess."

William's brow furrowed as he sat down. "I always wondered if he disliked the fact that Mother had been married before. He's never said anything, at least not to me, but I wonder if Uncle Richard reminds him that my father existed."

Harriet thought for a moment. "That's a good point. Your mother does seem fond of Uncle Richard. I wonder if he's jealous."

"It would be rather silly if he was. My father's

been dead for over thirty years and Uncle Richard's not a threat."

"Why do you say that?"

William's frown deepened. "Because he's not. There are so many reasons. He's married to Mrs Richard for one, Mother's married, Uncle Richard is Father's brother. Do I need to go on? The Church wouldn't allow him and Mother to marry even if they wanted to. Do you think Mother would dream of doing anything against the Church?"

Harriet cocked her head as she thought. "Maybe not... What about Mr Flemming? What's going on there?"

"You tell me. I've no idea."

"Do you think your mother knows?"

"What's got into you tonight?" William stood up to go to the kitchen. "Where's Violet? Are we not getting fed?"

"She'll be here in a minute, come and sit down. I'm going to ask your mother."

William shook his head. "Ask her what?"

"About Mr Flemming. I don't believe she knows nothing. If ever I try to raise the subject she shuts me up as if she's trying to hide something. I need to try a new tack."

Chapter Eleven

Harriet sat up in bed nursing her new daughter. It was another warm day and the sunlight streamed into the room. As she lifted the baby onto her shoulder to pat her back, Violet knocked on the door and showed Mary into the bedroom. Mary had a broad smile on her face.

"Let me see her," she said as she sat by the side of the bed. "What a beauty, and so dainty."

"Will that be all, madam?" Violet asked.

Harriet turned to Mary. "It's so hot today I wondered if we should have some gin rather than tea. What do you say?"

Mary took the baby from Harriet. "You know me, never one to turn down a glass of gin."

Violet nodded and left them before Mary continued. "William said you're going to call her Florence."

"Florence Mary. Do you like it?"

"I've never heard it before."

"You will before long. I was reading about it. It's a town in Italy that's becoming popular as a name. We chose Mary after you."

Mary laughed. "I worked that last bit out, and I'm honoured."

Harriet rearranged the bedcovers across her legs. "I should be able to get out of bed tomorrow. Not before time either."

Concern crossed Mary's face. "It's only been a couple of days."

"I won't be going far. Only to the chair. At least it's over and this time, when I say never again, I mean it."

Mary raised an eyebrow, but Harriet continued. "William agrees with me. We don't want to give the bank manager any reason to ask for his money back. He suggested to William last year that we could have more children and William promised him we wouldn't. Well, this time we mean it."

As she was speaking, Violet knocked on the door and placed a silver tray complete with two glasses, a bottle of gin and a small bowl of sugar on the table.

"Since when have you been putting sugar in your gin?" Mary asked.

"Only for the last few weeks. I went off it a couple of months ago but I read that putting sugar in made a pleasant alternative. They were right." Harriet smiled as she poured out the drinks.

"You and those magazines. I think it's about time you started doing more housework and less lying around."

Harriet laughed. "Give me another week and I will. I need to start receiving visitors again, too. I'm out of touch with everyone. Who've you seen recently? Anyone interesting?"

Mary hesitated before she spoke. "No. No one of interest. I still visit Susannah, and some of the other neighbours. And Mary-Ann obviously."

"Don't you see Aunt Sarah-Ann any more?"

Mary pulled a face. "No, not really. Why do you ask?"

"No reason. You used to be friendly, but since she went back to Birmingham, you've stopped seeing her. You can travel to Birmingham easily enough nowadays. I just wondered ..."

"We write regularly, but Mr Flemming likes her to stay at home."

"All the time?"

The high pitch of Harriet's voice dragged Mary's

gaze back from Florence. "Are you prying again?" Harriet was about to protest when Mary smiled. "You never give up, do you? If you want the honest truth, I don't know any more than you about why Sarah-Ann and Mr Flemming are constantly arguing. It's a question I've asked myself for a lot longer than you, but she won't tell me."

Harriet grinned back. "Well that's told me. If you ever do find out, please tell."

A WEEK later Mary climbed down from her carriage and made her way through the summer sunshine to the allotments. She waited for Richard on their usual seat, reflecting on the letter she had received from Martha that morning.

A couple of minutes later, Richard joined her. "My, you look deep in thought. Is Mr Wetherby troubling you again?"

Mary smiled as he took hold of her hand. "No, no more than usual. I had a letter from Martha this morning telling me Louisa's poorly. I was wondering if I should pay her a visit. After all, she was my best friend for a time when she lived with Charles and I in Birmingham."

Richard sat forward in his seat and turned her

head to face him. "I'm sorry to be the one to tell you, but you're too late."

"She's gone?"

Richard nodded. "I called earlier today. I hadn't seen her for months and so I thought I should, but when I arrived the family were there and she'd passed."

Mary stared in disbelief. "Martha only wrote two days ago. I'd no idea it was so serious. Why is it your family either love or hate Mr Wetherby? Things were never the same between Louisa and I, once I married him."

Richard smiled. "She clearly had sense. She was always close to Charles though, she didn't like the idea that you'd forgotten about her little brother."

"If she'd taken the time to talk to me, she'd have known that would never happen."

Richard stroked her hand. "Don't upset yourself. You were there for her when she lost that illegitimate daughter, and she had a few happy years once she married Mr Robson and had a family. You can come to the funeral with me and Mrs Richard if you like."

Mary laughed. "Do you think Mr Wetherby will entrust me to your care? I wish I could, but I think I'll have to decline."

Chapter Twelve

Harriet rubbed her hands together as William knocked on the front door of Wetherby House. This time last year, when she'd given birth to Florence, the weather had been too warm, but now, after a twenty-five-minute walk from church, it still felt like winter. She pushed the baby carriage, containing a sleeping baby, into a nook between the porch and bay window, and collected the other children to her. Emily, the maid, opened the door and after taking their coats offered to take the children into the morning room.

As they entered the front living room, Mr Wetherby was pouring out glasses of sherry.

"Here you are." He handed them both a glass.

"Why you can't go to St Mary's and get here at the same time as everyone else I don't know."

"We had a wonderful service at the Congregational Church. Is everyone else here?" Harriet surveyed the room as she spoke and didn't wait for an answer before she headed straight for Mary-Ann.

"Who's that over there?" she asked Mary-Ann as soon as she was close enough to whisper. "The girl with the blonde hair. I've not seen her before."

Mary-Ann laughed. "I've been dying for you to arrive so I could ask you the same thing. Have you seen the dress she's wearing? It must have cost a fortune."

"She'll have to be careful no one trips up over the train at the back."

Mary-Ann put a hand to her mouth to stifle a laugh. "You are terrible."

"Well, it is a bit extravagant for Sunday dinner. Maybe she's trying to impress."

"I've been watching her and I think she's with William Junior." Mary-Ann nodded towards her stepbrother.

Harriet's mouth dropped open. "You don't suppose he's found himself a girlfriend, do you? Surely not."

Mary-Ann bowed her head to hide her amusement. "Stranger things have happened, although I'm sure I can't think of any at the moment."

"We'll find out soon enough." Harriet nodded in the direction of Mr Wetherby and Mary as they walked to the centre of the room. A moment later Mr Wetherby banged the side of his glass for quiet.

"My dear family," he said, "thank you for joining us today. It's been a while since we were all together for dinner and although we shouldn't need any justification for it, there is a reason for the invite." He turned to the young lady standing behind him and encouraged her into the centre of the room. William Junior followed her. "I'm delighted to introduce you to Miss Olivia Havers, soon to be a new member of the family. Miss Havers is the daughter of a dear friend of mine from Stonehouse and I'm thrilled to tell you she's accepted a proposal of marriage from William Junior." As the room broke into applause, Harriet turned to Mary-Ann, unable to conceal her amazement.

"She's agreed to marry him! She can't be that desperate!"

"She's got to be nearing thirty, so maybe she is."

Harriet giggled but William grabbed her wrist forcing her to face him. "Behave. He had to get married sooner or later."

"But she's so ..."

"Enough." William wasn't smiling. "If you haven't got anything nice to say, don't say anything."

Harriet smirked at Mary-Ann and rolled her eyes. "I wasn't going to be nasty, she just doesn't seem William Junior's type."

With the noise levels in the room still high, Mr Wetherby held up his hand to indicate he wished to continue. "They'll be married early next year and plan to live in Handsworth, which I'm sure we're all delighted about. Can we raise our glasses in a toast to the happy couple. William Junior and Miss Havers."

"William Junior and Miss Havers," everyone repeated, before emptying their glasses and waiting for the maid to replenish them.

"Will they live here?" Harriet asked William once the formalities were over.

"I've no idea, this is as much news to me as it is to you. I recognise Mr Havers though. He was in the workshop with Mr Wetherby and William Junior years ago. In fact it was the day I took Mother to Birmingham when it had been heavy snow. Mr Wetherby was quite short with me and told me to come back to Handsworth. Do you remember? I thought they were up to something at the time. Maybe this explains it."

"That was years ago. You don't think he'll make him a partner, as a sort of dowry payment, do you?"

"He'd have said something if he was."

"Are you sure?" Harriet raised her eyebrows. "I don't trust him one bit. We need to find out what's going on. Make sure you listen to everything they say over dinner, especially when they get the port out. I'll see what I can find out from Miss Havers."

DINNER WAS A LUXURIOUS AFFAIR. Cook had prepared a large piece of beef, which had been cooking for most of the morning, along with a selection of potatoes and vegetables. As soon as everyone was seated, Mr Wetherby said grace and stood to carve the meat. William was next to William Junior, and once he was sure Mr Wetherby and Mr Havers weren't talking about anything of significance, he turned to his brother.

"She seems pleasant," William said. "Where did you meet?"

"Father introduced us. He thought it would make sense for us to be married."

William's eyes bulged. "Didn't you have any say in the matter?"

William Junior shrugged. "She's nice enough, but you know Father once he's made his mind up. I could do worse, so there wasn't any point arguing."

William took a mouthful of gin punch. "Does she know how you feel?"

"Good heavens no, and please don't tell that wife of yours or everyone will hear about it." William Junior glanced up the table to Harriet who was in deep conversation with Mary-Ann. "As far as she's concerned we're getting married despite the fact our fathers have known each other for over fifty years."

"So what does her father do?"

"Don't you know? He buys our products from us and sells them around the south of Birmingham and Worcestershire. Mr Havers and Father have set up a business relationship so he can supply our goods. After the wedding, Father's going to let him have the goods on consignment so he can take more from us at less risk to himself."

William's eyes narrowed as he glared down the table at Mr Wetherby. "So much for being kept informed."

As the ladies left the dining room to go back into the living room, Harriet jostled to walk with Miss Havers and invited her to sit beside her.

"Welcome to the family," Harriet said with a smile. "We need to get to know each other since we're going to be related. I'm Harriet, William's wife, and this is his sister Mary-Ann."

"Yes, I've heard about you. William Junior's told me about most of the family."

Not necessarily a good thing, Harriet thought. "Have you known William Junior long?"

"Just over a year. I did meet him several years ago when he came to visit my father with Mr Wetherby, but I didn't speak to him then."

"Is that how you met each other, through Mr Wetherby and your father?"

"That's how we were introduced but William Junior came to stay for a few days last year and it was love at first sight. Our fathers were delighted, naturally."

"So it's your choice you're getting married." Harriet ignored Mary-Ann's foot as it struck out at her.

"Yes, of course. William Junior's such a caring, sensitive person. Father would never make me do anything against my will."

Harriet put her hand to her throat as she choked back a laugh.

"Are you all right?" Miss Havers leaned forward on her chair and patted her back. "Let me fetch you a drink."

Harriet couldn't talk for the continuous coughing, and nodded her agreement.

"You need to get that seen to," Mary-Ann said as Miss Havers left them. "Being unable to smile politely while resisting the urge to laugh is socially unacceptable nowadays. I thought you knew that."

Harriet batted Mary-Ann on the arm as she struggled to laugh and choke at the same time. "Stop it," she managed between gasps. "Did you hear what she said?"

Mary-Ann smirked. "Maybe Mr Wetherby told him to be nice. It's the only reason I can think of that would cause such a change."

Chapter Thirteen

William-Wetherby stood in the back room in his underclothes as Harriet unpacked the school uniform she had bought.

"Arms out." She picked up a shirt and fed his arms in, before buttoning it up. Next came the collar and trousers. Once she was finished she stepped back to admire him. "Don't you look smart. Let's put the jacket and cap on and see the whole thing."

"They're a bit big." William-Wetherby hitched up the trousers.

"There's no point buying clothes that fit on day one." Harriet brushed a mark off the jacket. "You'll grow into them. Now, shoes."

After he had tried on the various shoes, Harriet started the process of undressing him again. "Are you looking forward to going to the grammar school? It's not long now."

William-Wetherby wriggled as she took off his jacket. "Part of me is ... but what if the other boys don't like me?"

"Of course they'll like you. You'll get to know them soon enough. A lot of them will be on their own."

"I suppose." William-Wetherby's stomach churned.

"Don't suppose anything, you're lucky to be going. It didn't come cheap getting you help with the entrance exam. It would have been more if Mr Wetherby hadn't known the tutor through the Conservative Association."

"I'm sorry. I am looking forward to it, but it's scary."

"I'd have given anything to carry on at school when I was your age." Harriet pulled at his trouser legs as William-Wetherby sat on the floor.

"Why didn't you?"

"I lived with my aunt and uncle at the time and he wouldn't let me. He made my life miserable."

"That's not fair if you wanted to go."

Harriet sighed and stopped what she was doing. "Life's never fair for women, you'll find that out soon enough. You must promise to teach me all you learn at school though, so that I can be as clever as you."

William-Wetherby laughed. "You're already cleverer than me."

"But I won't be for long if the teachers in this school do their jobs properly. I hope Eleanor can join you one day too. Mr Wetherby told Father that the council may expand the school for girls soon. It's too late for me now, but not for her. I read in my magazine that the University of London is going to let women study the same courses as men and take the same exams. Can you imagine? How I wish I'd been born now and not so many years ago. Perhaps one day you and Eleanor can go to university, wouldn't that be something?"

William-Wetherby smiled but said nothing. He had a feeling that neither he nor Eleanor would be going to university.

MARY SAT at the table in the morning room staring at the plate of bread and cheese in front of her. Mr Wetherby sat opposite, eating his at speed.

"What's up with you?" he asked as he finished another round of bread. "You're not normally slow."

"I'm not hungry. I don't normally eat for another half an hour."

"You'd better hurry up. I'll be ready to go out soon. Are you going to eat that bread?"

Mary shook her head as Mr Wetherby reached across the table and took it from her plate. "You don't need to wait for me. I can get a carriage myself."

"I'm not paying for a carriage when I'm going in the same direction as you."

Mary topped up her cup of tea. "Mary-Ann won't be expecting me so early. She likes the children to be down for their afternoon nap before I arrive."

"It won't hurt if you're early for once. Now hurry up. I don't want to be late."

Ten minutes later, with her food left unfinished, Mr Wetherby helped her into the carriage. The sky was blue with only wisps of clouds. *Why did Mr Wetherby have to come with me today? It would have been a lovely day for a walk.* "You can drop me on the corner of Westminster and Livingstone Roads if you like. A short walk will do me good."

"I'm not going that way. I'm going to the far end of Livingstone Road. I've asked the driver to go straight down Havelock Road and drop you off outside Mary-Ann's. It's too hot for you to be walking."

"The far end of Livingstone?" Mary took a deep

breath to control her voice. "What are you going there for?"

"There's someone I need to see."

"Who?"

"I'm not sure at the moment, but I'll know when I see him."

The colour drained from Mary's face and by the time they pulled up outside Mary-Ann's house her heart was pounding. If Mr Wetherby was going to the end of Livingstone Road, there was a chance he'd meet Richard.

"Will you pick me up at about four o'clock or will you arrange a carriage for me?" Her voice was too high.

"I'll pick you up. I might be earlier than that, but I'm sure Mary-Ann won't mind making me a cup of tea."

ONCE THE FRONT door closed after Mary, Mr Wetherby banged on the roof of the carriage. Seconds later the horses started to move. They didn't travel far before they came to a halt outside the allotments. As Mr Wetherby climbed down, he studied the coal waggon waiting close by. It didn't belong to one of the locals. He took a moment to study the scene.

There were several older men working the land, but other than that the place was quiet. *Where is he?* Mr Wetherby looked around before heading into the allotments.

As he marched up the makeshift path the gravel crunched under his heavy footfall and he slowed his pace. He didn't want it announcing his arrival. After about one hundred yards, he stopped. Two feet extended out from behind a bush, feet that could easily belong to a coal merchant. Stepping off the path he crept forward until he was adjacent to the bush. Richard sat with his head back and eyes closed, taking in the late summer sun. Mr Wetherby's face twitched as he clenched his fists. He could so easily finish him off and no one would ever know he'd been there. He took a step forward and raised his right arm, just as Richard opened his eyes and sat bolt upright. Taking a second to glance behind the towering figure of Mr Wetherby, Richard's eyes widened as he saw the fist aimed at his head. A second later Mr Wetherby's hand crashed into the wall behind the seat as Richard lunged to his left, rolling onto the floor. Mr Wetherby fell onto the bench clutching his wounded hand, as Richard jumped up behind him.

"What the hell are you playing at?" Richard yelled.

"I could ask you the exact same question." Mr

Wetherby's eyes narrowed as he stared at Richard. "What are you doing here?"

"It's none of your business."

"It is my business when it involves my wife." Mr Wetherby inspected his bloodied hand.

"What have you done to her?" Richard looked down the path, back to the entrance.

"I haven't done anything. I was saving that for you. How long's this been going on?"

"Wouldn't you like to know. Perhaps if you were at home more often, she might not need me."

A vein bulged in Mr Wetherby's neck as his face reddened. "If you've laid a finger on her ..."

"What if I have? What are you going to do about it?"

Mr Wetherby stood up and drew back his left arm, ready to strike, but Richard grabbed his wrist and twisted his arm behind his back. He kept his mouth close to Mr Wetherby's ear as he spoke. "For your information, we sit on this bench and talk. Occasionally, if the weather's fine, we'll take a walk. I care too much about Mary to do anything to disgrace her, unlike you with my sister. Don't think Mr Flemming hasn't told me what's been going on." Richard pushed Mr Wetherby towards the bench as he let go of his arm.

Mr Wetherby screamed and grabbed his arm as

he crashed onto the seat. "Mr Flemming's a liar. I haven't laid a finger on Sarah-Ann."

"Maybe not recently, but that doesn't excuse you from putting her in the family way years ago. It also means you have no right to say anything about my friendship with Mary."

"I have every right!" Mr Wetherby was on his feet. "Mrs Wetherby's my wife and I will not have you seeing her again. In fact, if I so much as see you in Handsworth again, you won't get off so lightly."

A sneer crossed Richard's lips. "Mr High and Mighty Wetherby, coming at me with threats again. I could floor you, here and now if I wanted to, but I won't stoop to your level. I will see Mary again, but for her sake, not here and not like this. All I can say is you'd better not punish her. You're not the only one who can make threats and I know where to find you."

Mr Wetherby glared at Richard, hate radiating from his eyes. "Get out of my sight. I don't ever want to see you again."

"The feeling's entirely mutual." Richard pulled back his arm and punched Mr Wetherby in the stomach, causing him to bend over double. "And if I hear you've laid a finger on Mary, there's more where that came from."

Chapter Fourteen

In the back room of Mary-Ann's house, Harriet took Florence from Mary and put her in her baby carriage.

"You have the magic touch today. She's been restless all morning, I've not been able to do anything with her."

Mary stood up to stretch her back. "She was overtired. All I did was hold her at the right time."

"Whatever you did, come and have a cup of tea." Mary-Ann placed a china cup and saucer on a small table next to Mary's chair. "You didn't say why you were so early. What's Mr Wetherby up to?"

Mary walked to the window. "I wish I knew, he ..." She froze. Mr Wetherby was striding up the front path his face like thunder. "He's ... here."

"Already?" Mary-Ann checked the clock. "It's not quarter to three yet."

Mary's face drained of all colour. "I think I'd better go. He seems to be in a hurry." Her stomach churned when she heard the hammering on the front door, but she was momentarily distracted by Harriet.

"What's he playing at?" She jumped up to go to the baby carriage. "He'll have Florence awake again. I'll give him a piece of my mind."

"Harriet, please. Leave it. I'll go before he comes in."

The maid was about to knock when Mary opened the door and stepped into the hall, pulling it closed behind her. "Quiet please. Harriet's just got Florence to sleep." She turned to Mr Wetherby. "If you're in a hurry, we'll go."

With a glare that dismissed the maid, Mr Wetherby grunted and wrapped Mary's cape around her shoulders.

"Goodbye, dear," Mary said to the maid. "I'll see you next week."

Mr Wetherby took her arm and settled her in the carriage before he spoke. "No you won't see her next week or any other week for that matter. I'm not having you coming down here on your own again. Richard Jackson won't be waiting for you either."

Mary turned to Mr Wetherby, and the blue of her

eyes pierced him like a shard of ice when she saw his hand. "What have you done? Stop the carriage." She stood up to bang the roof. "I need to go back. I'll never forgive you if you've hurt him."

"Sit down this minute." He pulled on her arm and shouted to the driver to continue.

Mary pulled away. "What have you done to him?"

"I didn't touch him."

"Then why's your hand covered in blood? It wasn't like that when you left me."

"I banged it on a wall."

"Don't be ridiculous." Mary stood up again to bang on the roof. "You've been fighting."

Mr Wetherby pulled her back down. "What did you expect me to do? You humiliated me."

"How? We weren't doing anything wrong."

"Weren't doing anything wrong? How do you think I felt when people told me they'd seen you with an unknown man?"

"We only sat and talked. Never for long either ... He's my friend."

"Not any more he's not. I've told you often enough, I don't want you having anything to do with him and now I've told him. You can forget about ever seeing him again. If you want to see Mary-Ann or Harriet, they can come to Wetherby House."

~

HARRIET KNOCKED on the door and entered the morning room of Mary-Ann's house, where her sister-in-law was feeding her daughters.

"I wasn't expecting you at this time," Mary-Ann said.

"I've just received this." Harriet waved a letter in the air. "It's from your mother. Have you had one?"

"There are a couple of letters on the sideboard but I haven't had time to open them. Take a look."

Harriet flicked through the letters on the console table. "Yes, you have one too. It's an invitation to visit her tomorrow at Wetherby House."

Mary-Ann frowned. "Why would she do that? She didn't mention anything about a change when she was here last week."

"My thoughts exactly, although thinking about it, she did leave in a hurry when Mr Wetherby turned up. Didn't she say anything to you at church on Sunday?"

Mary-Ann shook her head. "I didn't speak to her. She was acting strangely and Mr Wetherby escorted her from the building almost as soon as the service was over."

Harriet digested the information. "How strange, he normally likes to hold court."

"I noticed his hand was heavily bandaged, maybe he didn't feel up to it."

～

THE FOLLOWING DAY, Harriet and Mary-Ann arrived at Wetherby House with their youngest children in their baby carriages. Mary had a bottle of gin and three glasses waiting for them.

"What's all this about?" Mary-Ann asked as they sat down. "You didn't say anything about us coming here last week."

Mary took a mouthful of gin. "No. I didn't know."

"Are you going to tell us what's going on?" Harriet asked.

Mary closed her eyes and squeezed back the tears that were forming. "Mr Wetherby suggested it. He said he'd prefer it if you came here."

"All the time?" Mary-Ann asked. "It's not easy to get four children ready at the same time."

"I'm sorry, I tried telling Mr Wetherby but he wouldn't budge. As soon as he starts going to Birmingham again, things will change."

Mary-Ann shrugged at Harriet before she continued. "What's Mr Wetherby done to his hand? He seemed to have damaged it when I saw him on Sunday."

"The doctor says he's broken some bones. He's telling everyone he did it at work."

"Don't you believe him?" Harriet asked.

"Y-Yes ... yes of course. I just don't know precisely what it was he did. I'm obviously just a stupid woman who doesn't know anything."

Chapter Fifteen

Harriet stood in front of the mirror, her hands on her hips, as the maid pulled on the laces at the back of her corset.

"What possessed me to think I could get my waist back to twenty-four inches? Florence is almost two and when it hadn't happened by Christmas I should have known it was never going to get any smaller."

"It is a lovely dress though, especially the detail down the back. This shade of blue really suits you too and you've only worn it once." Violet released her grip and started again.

"There's a reason for that. It doesn't fit. I wouldn't mind, but I don't even want to go to the wedding. How would he like it if he had to get out of bed especially early, see to the children and then strap himself into this?" She pulled on the front of the corset. "Not only that, once I'm ready, we have to get to Wetherby House and then take a one-hour carriage ride to Balsall Heath. I won't be able to breathe by the time we arrive."

"It will be lovely though, I'm sure. I imagine there'll be no expense spared for Mr Wetherby Junior's marriage."

"Don't get me started." Harriet thought back to her own wedding and how completely inadequate it had been. "There's one rule for them ..."

"At least Eleanor and Margaret travelled yesterday. That will make life easier for you."

Harriet dropped her shoulders. "Thank you, Violet, you try so hard to cheer me up. And thank you for taking care of Florence and the boys while we're gone. I do appreciate it."

"Are you ready?" William knocked on the bedroom door and shouted in.

"Five more minutes," Harriet said, straightening up again. "But if you want me to go to any more weddings, I'm having a new dress."

When they arrived at Wetherby House at five minutes to eight, Mr Wetherby was in full control. Without being offered a cup of tea, Harriet found herself in a carriage with William, Mary-Ann and Mr Diver.

"He's going to drive me mad today if he carries on like that," Harriet said as she perched on the edge of the seat.

"He's only organising people," William said. "If he didn't do it we'd never get there."

"That might not be a bad thing, I mean, why are you his best man?"

William gave a deep sigh. "You know why. He's my brother."

"You're not even close."

"On a day like today, that doesn't matter. Mother wanted me to be involved and I'm honoured. What's wrong with that?"

"The rest of the time it's as if we're separate families. All this is only for show. Mr Wetherby treats William Junior and Charlotte so much better than he treats you two."

"That's what Mother wants to stop," William said. "You should be pleased."

"I would be if I thought it would make any difference, but it won't. By tomorrow, all of this will be forgotten and he'll be back to his usual ways. Has he introduced you to Mr Havers yet?"

William turned to her. "For heaven's sake, I'll meet him at the wedding."

"See what I mean, William Junior knows everything about him and you've not even met him."

"He's marrying his daughter; of course he knows him."

"And quite what she sees in William Junior, I've no idea."

Mary-Ann laughed. "What is up with you today? The fact he has money and his father's a successful businessman may have something to do with it. Why don't you relax and enjoy the day like the rest of us?"

Harriet took a deep breath. "They'd better have the gin on tap at the wedding breakfast. I'm going to need it."

By the time they arrived at the church, a small crowd had started to gather. Harriet took another deep breath and let William help her from the carriage.

"How am I supposed to smile all day when I feel like this?" she asked Mary-Ann as they walked up the path to the church. "How do you manage?"

"I smile and don't go on about it so much." She grinned at Harriet.

"You've had over a year longer than me to recover from your last baby. I've got more to squeeze in than you."

"And you look fabulous, so stop moaning. Think of poor Miss Havers and how she'll feel when she realises what William Junior's like. She won't be able to take him off and throw him over a chair every evening."

Harriet burst out laughing.

"What are you two doing?" Mary asked as she joined them. "You're in church not at a social event."

"Sorry." Mary-Ann straightened her face and sat down. "Has Miss Havers arrived?"

"Not yet, but she should be here soon. I hope so anyway, William Junior's very anxious."

"She'll be here. She won't get a better offer at her age," Harriet said.

"Harriet. What a terrible thing to say," Mary said.

"I didn't mean it to be unkind, I'm just being honest. They're both a bit on the old side to be getting married for the first time."

"That's as may be, but there's no need to voice it."

MISS HAVERS WORE a long gown of ivory silk with matching hat and gloves. As she walked down the aisle she gave William Junior a broad smile, which he repaid with a slight bow of his head before turning away to face the vicar.

He doesn't look like a man pleased to be getting

married, Harriet thought. I'm going to have to pay some attention to this at the wedding breakfast.

The marriage ceremony lasted for almost an hour and as the main party retired to the side chapel to sign the register, Harriet turned to Mary-Ann. She nudged her and was ready to share her thoughts when Mary shot her a glance. She turned back to face the front, her hands twitching. What was keeping them so long? Finally, William Junior and his bride led the group down the aisle and Harriet followed as soon as she could. She met William by the church entrance as the new Mr and Mrs Wetherby posed for a photograph.

"That took a long time," she said.

"There were a number of us who needed to sign."

She took a step closer to William and lowered her voice. "How was William Junior? He didn't seem happy in church."

"He was pleasant, to be honest. Not like his usual self. I put it down to Miss Havers, or should I say Olivia."

Harriet's face dropped. "Maybe he's on his best behaviour. I get the feeling he didn't want to marry her."

"Why are you always suspicious of everything?

It's a nervous time getting married, having so many eyes on you. Maybe he felt self-conscious."

"Him! Are we talking about the same person here? He's never been shy in his life."

William took hold of Harriet's arm and led her from the church. "Keep your voice down. I told you, he's being decent today. Perhaps having a wife will be a good influence on him."

Harriet rolled her eyes. "If you say so."

"Behave. As best man, I have to sit with him and I don't want you causing a commotion."

William led the way to the carriage and before Harriet could answer he held the door open while Mary-Ann and Mr Diver followed Harriet inside.

William Junior and the new Mrs Wetherby were waiting for them at the top of the stairs in the tavern. Three long tables had been placed in a U-shape and set for almost fifty people.

"You'll be sat with me, William," his brother said. "Mary-Ann, you and Mr Diver will be sat lower down the table on the right-hand side. You'll be with them, Harriet. Naturally we needed to put more of Olivia's family on the top table seeing that her father's paying for it."

Harriet opened her mouth, but with one look from William she closed it again and walked across the room, taking a glass of sherry from a waitress as she passed.

"Since when has the groom's sister not sat on the top table?" Harriet didn't wait for Mary-Ann to sit down before she started. "Not to mention the best man's wife. I don't envy William being stuck with William Junior and half of Olivia's family."

"At least he'll be sitting next to Mother," Mary-Ann said. "I'd have thought you'd be glad not to be with them."

"Part of me is, but did you notice William Junior in church? He didn't look as if he wanted to be there. I wanted to listen in on the conversation. As it is, I have my back to them so I can't even watch them."

Mary-Ann giggled and turned to Mr Diver. "Would you care to swap seats with Harriet? You appear to have a prime view but I suspect you won't do it justice."

Mr Diver laughed and shook his head as he stood up. "I know when I'm not up to a job. Don't let it be said I got in the way of Harriet on a mission."

"Do you think Mr Havers paid for all this?" Harriet asked as platters of roast meats were served around the table. "I didn't think he was that wealthy."

"He's not poor, but he's not particularly wealthy

either," Mr Diver said. "I've met him through work and if you ask me, he hasn't paid for all this."

Harriet raised an eyebrow. "I don't remember Mr Wetherby helping out my uncle at our wedding."

"Your uncle had enough money of his own, he just didn't want to spend it," Mary-Ann said.

"I'll never forgive him for it either. It should have been the happiest day of my life and he ruined it."

As the food was eaten, Harriet kept her eyes on William Junior. He was seated between his new wife and her mother, but not once did he turn to either for conversation. Instead, he leaned across Mrs Havers so he could talk to Mr Wetherby.

"Nothing like getting to know the family." Harriet nodded in William Junior's direction as the plates were collected. "Let's wait and see how long it takes before he swaps seats with Mrs Havers."

"William seems nervous though. Has he written a speech?" Mary-Ann asked.

"Only a short one, wishing them well and proposing a toast."

"Isn't that what Mr Havers is supposed to do?" Mr Diver said.

Harriet shrugged. "I don't think William cares, he just wants to get it over with."

With William and Mr Havers keeping their

speeches short, all eyes turned to William Junior as he took to his feet.

"My dear family and friends. Thank you for joining us today." He turned and gave a cursory nod to Olivia before returning to his notes. "I'm sure you'll agree that in marrying the new Mrs Wetherby here, I've done all right for myself. I'm sure she'll make an excellent mother when the time comes."

Harriet stared at Mary-Ann, her eyes wide. "I've done all right for myself? What a thing to say."

Before Harriet could continue, she was cut short by William Junior's next words.

"I'm sure you've all heard that after Father's gift to us, we'll be making our home in Handsworth."

Harriet turned to Mary-Ann, her eyes and mouth wide as she struggled for the right words. "He's bought them a house?"

"It looks like it," Mary-Ann said. "Have you seen the smug look on Mr Wetherby's face?"

"William practically had to beg the bank manager for the money to buy our house, and William Junior gets it handed to him on a plate. Besides, why does he need a house in Handsworth when he works in Birmingham?" Harriet tried to catch William's eye, but when he continued to look down the table at William Junior she turned back to Mary-Ann. "They'd better not be planning on moving him to the Handsworth business as well."

"He's used to living in Wetherby House and travelling to work in Birmingham and so it shouldn't make any difference."

"I hope you're right." Harriet tried to catch William's attention again. "You mark my words, I think William knew all about this but chose not to tell me. That's why he won't look at me. Wait until I get him home."

Chapter Sixteen

The trees on Wellington Road provided much-needed shade for Harriet and Mary-Ann as they walked to Wetherby House, each pushing a baby carriage. The sun was high in the sky and Harriet was thankful for the wide brim on her new hat.

"I hope we're on gin punch today rather than a pot of tea," Mary-Ann said as they approached the driveway. "I'm too hot as it is."

Harriet laughed. "We've been on gin ever since we started coming here. I don't think your mother will change on a day like today."

When they arrived, the maid showed them into the back room. The curtains had been pulled across the window and they both stopped to allow their eyes to adjust.

"Why are you sat in the dark?" Mary-Ann went to the window and pulled back the curtains. "It's a beautiful summer's day."

"I had a headache earlier and it was too bright. I'm fine now."

"You look like you've been busy though." Harriet admired the scones and sponge cake on the table.

"I was up early this morning and thought I'd do them. After the terrible weather we've been having I didn't expect it to be so warm and baking made me hotter still. I've had two cups of gin, but they haven't cooled me down. I've made some gin punch for this afternoon, that should be better."

"Is Mr Wetherby in Birmingham again?" Mary-Ann asked.

"Yes." Mary smiled. "He's not back until tomorrow. He's got a meeting at the Conservative Association after work."

"I thought he only went to the occasional meeting."

"He did, but things have changed. With people turning their backs on Prime Minister Disraeli, he's taken personal responsibility for recruiting more members before the election's called. He'll be furious if the Liberals win again."

"I can imagine," Mary-Ann said. "Mr Diver won't be pleased either. Why does he have to spend so much time in Birmingham though? He could be part of the Conservative Association here."

"Oh, I don't mind and he thinks there's greater need for his services down there. With it being more affluent around here he says people are more likely to have sense."

"People aren't happy with the foreign policy though," Harriet said. "It has nothing to do with common sense."

"Please don't say that." Mary put the back of her hand to her forehead. "He'll be unbearable to live with if the Conservatives don't get elected next time."

"I'm so glad William doesn't bother with politics," Harriet said. "He supports Mr Disraeli of course, but I don't think he'd lose much sleep if he didn't win."

"He takes after his father." Mary smiled. "William Junior on the other hand now gets dragged to the Conservative Association, whether he likes it or not."

"Has he got the vote?" Harriet suddenly sat up straight.

"No but he's made a claim to be on the electoral

register and there's no reason why he should be rejected. Hasn't William applied?"

"He hasn't mentioned anything." Harriet's relief at William having no interest in politics was gone. How had she missed the notice calling for prospective voters? If William Junior was going to get the vote, she had to make sure William got it as well.

WILLIAM HADN'T BEEN HOME MORE than a minute before Harriet raised the subject. As hard as she tried, she couldn't keep her voice calm.

"Did you know William Junior's applied to be on the electoral register?"

William said nothing and carried on buttering the piece of bread he was holding.

"You did, didn't you? Why haven't you applied?"

"Can't I eat my tea in peace? I've had a busy day and I'd like some quiet."

"No, not tonight. You knew, didn't you? Why didn't you tell me?"

William gazed at his bread and placed it purposefully on his plate. "Because I knew you'd react like this."

"But there's a reason I react like this. Every time I find out something about William Junior, it turns out that you knew about it and haven't told me. You should be applying for the vote as well. He doesn't deserve it. He hasn't saved like us to buy his own house. Being given a house as a gift shouldn't count."

William sighed and picked up his bread again. "If it means that much to you, why don't you do the application for me? There's still time."

"Don't worry, I'll do it now." She went to the dresser and lifted out her writing set. "It's the principle as much as anything else. Haven't you noticed there's status attached to having the vote. The last thing you want is for William Junior to have another reason to think he's better than you."

As William finished his tea and wiped his lips on a napkin, Harriet handed him a letter to sign.

"All you need to do is sign the bottom and put it in the post."

"Does it have to go tonight?" William asked. "I was hoping for a quiet evening."

"Of course it has to go tonight. If you go now, you'll be home before I've tidied up. Off you go."

WITH THE LETTER sealed in an envelope, William collected his hat from the stand in the hall and left the house. As he approached Westminster Road Mr Wetherby's carriage drove past him; a moment later it drew to a halt and Mr Wetherby opened the door and climbed out.

"I'm sorry I've not been into the workshop for a few days. We've had a few issues in Birmingham, which have kept me busy."

"Anything I should know about?" William asked.

"No, just a couple of orders that needed extra attention. Where are you off to at this hour?"

"Only to the post box. I'm registering for the electoral register."

"Excellent. I've been meaning to tell you to do that. Where are you applying?"

"Handsworth, why?"

"We need more Conservative votes in Birmingham than we do around here. William Junior's applied to St Stephen's ward. You should too."

"On what grounds? The house I own is here."

"Yes, but you're a partner in the business. Using the Frankfort Street address would mean you can apply there. You'll need to be seen in Birmingham more often, at least until the application's approved, but that shouldn't be difficult. It would be sensible for you to start coming to the Birmingham office more often anyway."

William's brow furrowed. "What about the business here?"

"I've been thinking about that, as it happens.

Now William Junior's married, I want him to be in Handsworth with Olivia."

"Won't he need to be in Birmingham as well if he's applied for the vote?"

"He will, but if you split the week, he can run Handsworth for three days and you for the other three."

"But ... but, that's my business. Mr Watkins gave it to me."

"Come now, William, it's all one big company. It won't do you any harm to work in button manufacturing again."

William's face fell as he imagined Harriet's reaction to the news that William Junior would be running their business. "Can I think about it?"

"There's nothing to think about, it's an excellent idea." Mr Wetherby took the letter from William. "I'll send the application off for you tomorrow and tell William Junior."

A lead weight settled in William's stomach as he watched Mr Wetherby continue his journey to Wetherby House. He hadn't wanted the vote in the first place and now he was going to have to share his business with William Junior. He walked home slowly, rehearsing what he would say to Harriet, but even as he opened the front door he was unsure how to approach it. He was relieved to find William-

Wetherby sitting by the fire in the back room. Harriet was nowhere to be seen.

"I wasn't expecting you to be here. I thought you'd be at school."

A frown crossed William-Wetherby's face. "I've just got home for summer."

"Yes, of course, good ... and how is school? Are you enjoying it?"

"Yes, I like it better than my other school and most of the boys are friendly. I try and stay away from the horrible ones."

William didn't get a chance to ask what his son meant before Harriet came in. "I didn't hear you come home, why didn't you say?"

"I was talking to William-Wetherby."

"You could have shouted when you came in. Did you post the letter?"

"No ... no I didn't." William looked at his son before he turned back to Harriet. "I saw Mr Wetherby while I was out and he wants me to apply to be on the register in Birmingham rather than here."

"Why on earth does it matter, a vote's a vote, isn't it?"

"Apparently not. He says they need more Conservative votes in Birmingham than up here."

Harriet put her hands on her hips. "So I have to rewrite the letter?"

William turned to William-Wetherby. "Would you mind leaving us for five minutes? I'd like to talk to your mother in private."

William-Wetherby shrugged and walked out of the room before William closed the door behind him. "Mr Wetherby's going to do it. He also wants me to work in Birmingham for a few days a week, so that the application appears authentic."

"You go down to Birmingham occasionally anyway. It shouldn't make much difference, should it?"

"He wants me to stay down there for three days a week."

"You can't do that." Harriet's eyes were wide as the high pitch of her voice cut through the room. "What about the children?"

"It's only Margaret and Florence. The others are at school all day."

"I have to deal with Eleanor and Charles of an evening and it's Charles who's the trouble. You know what he's like. Tonight I caught him using the wall at the bottom of the garden as a tightrope. He was halfway down next door's garden, with his arms outstretched to balance himself. That wall must be ten feet tall; he could have killed himself."

"It's not that high, six feet at the most. He's only having a bit of fun."

"It's easy for you to say. You're not the one who has to put up with him. He'll have me in an early grave if you're not here for three days a week."

"It will only be for two nights a week until the vote is granted. I'm sure you'll be fine."

Harriet raised her eyebrows and sat down. "You can have a week's trial and then we'll see. Besides, where will you stay?"

William shrugged. "In one of Mr Wetherby's houses, I would imagine. There's something else I need to tell you ... but please don't be angry."

Harriet raised an eyebrow but said nothing.

"William Junior's going to do the same as me; but for the other three days of the week. He'll be in Handsworth when I'm not there."

"You mean William Junior's going to manage my uncle's business?"

William nodded.

"You have to do something. We can't let him poke his nose in where it's not wanted."

William went to his seat by the fire and sat down. "It's not that simple, as you well know. Mr Wetherby's made up his mind and he won't be swayed."

Chapter Seventeen

Birmingham, Warwickshire

As William made his way down Summer Lane he rued its deterioration. The streets were filthy and in places it appeared that the only thing holding the houses together was the dirt. When he reached Frankfort Street, Mr Wetherby's workshop and the houses he owned appeared to be in better condition than those around them, but if he was being honest, it wasn't much of an achievement.

Mr Wetherby had given him keys to one of the houses and when he arrived in court nine he headed for house number two. It appeared empty and so without knocking he went straight inside. It was warm enough to leave the door open and once he'd removed his hat and jacket he went upstairs to unpack. He was back in the living room within five minutes and sat by the unlit fire with the evening paper. *How nice to have some peace and quiet.* He was never alone at home.

Within an hour the solitude had become unbearable and he stood up and walked to the door. Most of the children had disappeared from the court for the evening, and besides the stragglers, the only people he saw were women rushing to the water pump. He smiled at the thought that Harriet would never need to collect water. He would never admit it, but he was glad she had pushed him to buy the house. He would never have done it on his own.

The following evening, he shuddered at the thought of going back to the empty house and called in at the beerhouse on the corner of the street. He ordered a pie and a pint of ale and sat down to watch a game of dominoes. Was this going to be a regular occurrence? He hoped not. Beerhouses weren't places he liked at the best of times, and this one had seen better days. The locals were friendly enough though, and as the alternative was sitting on his own he could probably get used to it.

Leaving the beerhouse shortly before nine o'clock, he turned the corner into the court to find the door to his house open. He stopped and looked around. Nobody seemed concerned, but then he was a newcomer himself and no one had questioned him yesterday. Taking a deep breath he crept towards the door. What would he do if there were a stranger in the house? He reached the door sooner than he would have liked and was about to go in when he heard the distinctive sound of Mr Wetherby's voice.

"It's you." William breathed out a sigh of relief as he walked in. "You had me worried for a minute."

"What time do you call this?" Mr Wetherby asked. "I've been waiting half an hour for you." He walked to the bottom of the stairs and shouted up. "Betsy, he's here."

"What's going on?" William asked.

"You've met my sister Betsy, haven't you?" Mr Wetherby was talking as Betsy arrived at the bottom of the stairs.

"Yes, of course." William gave her a broad smile. "It's nice to see you again."

"Well, as you know she lost her husband earlier this year and she's been having a difficult time since. I've suggested she moves to Birmingham to be closer to the rest of the family."

William looked from Mr Wetherby to Betsy and back again. "She can't stay here. Not just the two of us. That would be wrong."

"That's what I came to tell you. She is going to stay here but she'll have the children with her. I can't have a whole house with a tenant who's only here for two nights a week."

"We can't do that ... share that is," William said. "No disrespect, Betsy, but I'm a married man."

"Nonsense, everything'll be fine," Mr Wetherby said. "Besides, it's not only the two of you. Her daughter Edith's nearly eighteen and her twin boys are sixteen. It'll be like a family living together. The boys are going to be working with us, making buttons, and Edith will work in the warehouse with Betsy. What is there to object to?"

William shuffled his feet as he studied the floor. He could think of plenty Harriet might object to, after all, Betsy, or Mrs Storey as he must get used to calling her, was only a few years older than he was. "You seem to have it all planned. When will they move in?"

"She has to go back down to Gloucester to give notice on her house and collect the children but she doesn't have to stay. How does Monday sound?"

"Mr Jackson, if it helps," Betsy said, "I've suggested to my brother that the children and I have the top floor. Edith and I will share one room and the boys will have the other. We'll keep out of your way as much as possible, but if we become a burden, you must tell me."

William's face started to colour. "I'm so sorry, the thought of you being a burden hadn't occurred to me. I just worry about the gossip."

"That won't be a problem," Mr Wetherby interrupted. "Anyone who matters will know the truth and if I hear any gossiping, I'll sack the women involved. This is a positive situation for everyone and I won't have it jeopardised by people with nothing better to think about."

Handsworth, Staffordshire.

THE FOLLOWING Saturday afternoon William travelled back to Handsworth with Mr Wetherby. It was after five o'clock when they arrived at Wetherby House but he knew he couldn't go home without seeing his mother.

"You're late," Mary said as she met them in the hall.

Neither man had time to respond before there was a knock on the door and William Junior arrived.

"William," he said as he took off his hat. "I didn't expect to see you here."

"We've just got back from Birmingham and I came to see Mother."

"Well, don't rush off." William Junior walked into the back room and waited for everyone to join him. "I've some news and you might as well hear it with everyone else, I'm going to be a father."

A broad smile spread across Mr Wetherby's face as he shook his son by the hand. "I'm going to be a grandfather! Congratulations, my boy; that's wonderful news, in fact the best news I've had in a long time. Let me find some sherry."

"We already are grandparents ... to eight grandchildren," Mary called after him as he disappeared into the dining room.

"But they're not Wetherbys, are they?" William Junior said. "This one will be different."

William flinched at his brother's words, but offered his hand in congratulations. "That didn't take long."

"Well, no, naturally." William Junior rolled back his shoulders and puffed out his chest. "The doctor says he'll be born early next year. Probably February. I'm sure Father's delighted we'll be able to keep the family name going and have an heir for the business."

"This is splendid news," Mr Wetherby said, as he came back with four glasses. "Let's drink to the future of Messrs Wetherby and Sons."

William felt the blood draining from his face as he took a sip of his sherry. *Do my sons count for nothing now? Did they ever count?*

"As much as I'm delighted with the news, don't get carried away," Mary said. "Olivia may have a daughter yet. Besides, you have William-Wetherby and Charles to keep the business going."

"And they'll be able to join the business years before any sons of yours," William said.

William Junior glared at his brother but Mary took William's arm. "I thought the same thing. You won't have any shortage of heirs. Perhaps you should rename the business Wetherby, Jackson and Sons."

Chapter Eighteen

Temperatures had barely risen above freezing since the start of the year and as Harriet and Mary-Ann pushed their baby carriages towards Wetherby House the clouds appeared ready to release more snow. The wind cut through Harriet's knitted gloves, biting into her face and bringing tears to her eyes. Mary-Ann reached the front door first and by the time Harriet joined her, Emily had opened it and invited them both into the warmth of the hall. With the children sleeping, they left them in the hall and went into the back room, where they were surprised to see Aunt Sarah-Ann sitting with Mary.

"What brings you here on a day like this?" Mary-

Ann said to her aunt. "It must have been awful travelling in a carriage with this cold."

"I needed to speak to your mother." Sarah-Ann pulled her shawl more tightly around her shoulders and glanced at the fire. "Fortunately she's invited me to stay overnight, so I can warm myself up before I have to go back to Birmingham."

"Is it a social visit?" Harriet asked.

"Yes, it is," Mary said. "Now, there's some mulled wine over the fire, would you pour some for us?"

Mary-Ann moved to pour the drinks, but Harriet stayed where she was, staring from Mary to Sarah-Ann and back again. *A social visit in weather like this? I don't think so. What am I missing?*

"Harriet, why don't you sit down?" Mary extended her arm to the empty chair next to her. "You must be cold too after your walk. I wasn't sure if you'd come today."

"We always come unless there's so much snow we can't push the baby carriages," Mary-Ann said handing out the drinks. "Do you want us to go?"

"Of course not; don't be silly. Come and sit down."

The room fell silent and Harriet wrapped her hands around the glass as she raised her eyebrows at Mary-Ann. *Why doesn't somebody say something? Mrs Wetherby isn't usually lost for words.*

"Well, isn't this pleasant," Mary said, glancing around. "Oh ... while I remember, I have some news that's worthy of a toast."

"If it's such good news, how did you manage to forget about it?" Mary-Ann said. "What is it?"

"Charlotte received her school exam results this morning." Mary's face shone with pride. "She got a first class, first division in scripture, history, French and political economy."

Harriet gasped. "I always knew she was clever. She's so fortunate. Where is she now?"

"Visiting a friend."

"Will she go to university? Oh I hope she does. It would be such a waste for her to finish school and sit at home doing nothing."

"No, I don't think so ..." Mary hadn't finish her sentence before there was a knock on the door. A moment later William Junior walked in.

"Good afternoon, ladies." Despite the smile, his expression was unreadable. "How fortunate to find you all together. I came to give Mother some news, but it appears I can make an announcement. I have a son and heir. Olivia's been delivered of a baby boy. Henry Wickham Wetherby."

"What marvellous news." Mary clapped her hands under her chin.

"Yes, congratulations," Sarah-Ann said. "You must be thrilled."

"Of course we're thrilled. I went down to tell Father first thing this morning. Naturally he was delighted we now have someone to carry on the family business."

"What do you mean?" Harriet spluttered as Mary jumped to her feet and took William Junior by the arm.

"Let's not talk about it now. Come and have a drink. We were celebrating Charlotte's end of school exam results. She did very well."

William Junior sniggered. "I'm sure she did."

"You should be proud of her," Harriet said.

Mary held up her hand to stop Harriet saying any more. "Let me refill everyone's glasses and get one for William Junior. We've got a lot to be thankful for." Once she'd passed William Junior his glass, Mary raised a toast. "To Henry Wickham Wetherby."

"To Henry Wickham Wetherby," they all repeated.

"It's an unusual name. Where did it come from?" Mary continued.

"Henry was the name of Olivia's grandfather. Wickham is from a book she's been reading. You know what she's like."

"What's wrong with her reading?" Harriet's

voice was shrill but she was silenced by a glare from William Junior.

"Tell us about the baby," Mary said. "Was he a healthy weight? And Olivia, has she come through unscathed?

"He's a decent size and by all accounts everything went smoothly. I don't suppose there's much to it."

Harriet's mouth opened and closed several times before she picked up her glass and emptied it of the mulled wine. "I think I should be going. Will you stay a little longer?" she said to Mary-Ann.

"No, I'll come with you. I'm sure Mother and Aunt Sarah-Ann have a lot to talk about."

William Junior emptied his own cup and followed them out. "Yes, I need to leave as well. I need to check on the workshop to see who's not getting paid today."

Once Mary and Sarah-Ann were alone, they continued the conversation they had abandoned earlier.

"Do you want me to tell Mr Wetherby about Mr Flemming?" Mary asked.

Sarah-Ann bit down on her bottom lip. "I don't know. In many ways, yes, I want to tell him about the drinking and violence, but I know how angry he'll be. If he approaches Mr Flemming again, my life won't be worth living. When he's drunk he doesn't care who he lashes out at. I just thank God that Elizabeth is out of it all. I'm dreading her coming home for Easter in case he turns his attentions to her."

Mary's eyes lit up. "Why doesn't she come here? That way Mr Flemming can't touch her."

"Could she? That would be a huge weight off my mind ... although it would mean we'd have to tell Mr Wetherby why she was here."

"We can say she wanted to see the children ... and the new baby. She's always been fond of them and she rarely gets to see them."

Sarah-Ann paused to think. "Would she be able to stay with William or Mary-Ann, do you think? That way I could tell Mr Flemming she was there rather than here. It would be easier to explain."

"I don't see why not. It's a shame the girls have gone, we could have asked them."

"You don't think Harriet will want to know what's going on, do you? She's never been one for keeping out of other people's business."

Mary laughed. "I didn't think you knew her so well. Leave her to me, I'll think of something to tell her."

Chapter Nineteen

Birmingham, Warwickshire

The winter air froze William's every breath as he made his way down Frankfort Street, back to the house he shared with Mrs Storey. He slipped through the door into the living room as fast as he could, trying to restrict the amount of cold air he brought in with him.

"My, it's bitter out there tonight," he said as he walked straight to the fire to warm his hands. "I think it could snow."

"I hope you're wrong. I've had enough of it." Mrs Storey poured boiling water into the teapot and set it on the table. "Come and sit yourself down."

William rubbed his hands one last time before he

took off his coat and sat down. "Where are the boys tonight? And Edith?"

"They'll be along soon enough, but there's no need to wait for them. Let me get you some soup." Mrs Storey was quiet as she spooned the broth into a bowl and put it down in front of William. "You're not going out again, are you?"

"I wish I wasn't, given the weather, but I've arranged with Mr Wetherby to go to the Conservative Association."

"You're quite taken with it now, aren't you? I remember the first night I was here you told me you only went for something to do. Now I'd say you enjoy it."

William smiled. Since he'd gained the vote he'd taken more of an interest in politics and to his surprise, he did enjoy the meetings. Not that he was ready to admit it. "I like going out and meeting people socially. It's not something I do much of in Handsworth."

"Well, this soup will warm you through before you go out. Get it eaten while it's hot."

With his tea finished and his overcoat fastened on top of his heaviest jacket, William strode briskly to Mr Wetherby's house on Summer Lane. Within a minute, Mr Wetherby was out of the house leading the way to the Conservative Association. As they arrived in the hall, there was an unusual air of excitement.

"What's going on?" William asked, casting his eye over groups of men huddled together.

Mr Wetherby didn't wait around to be told and went straight to the chairman at the front of the room. William followed him.

"An election? Now. In this weather? What's he thinking of? We'll never get the voters out." Mr Wetherby's face was red.

"A general election?" William asked when he joined them.

"It shouldn't be a surprise," the chairman said. "It is nearly six years since the last one and it won't take place until the week after Easter. We've got time yet. The weather will be much warmer by then."

"Easter's at the end of March this year," Mr Wetherby said. "That doesn't give us long at all. I presume you have a plan."

Within minutes, Mr Wetherby was called to a meeting with the chairman and organising committee. As William watched them leave he spotted Mr Diver entering the room.

"I didn't expect to see you tonight," William said as he joined him. "You've heard the news, I take it?"

"Only as I came in," Mr Diver replied. "I can't say I'm pleased."

A frown settled on William's face. "Why not? We're due an election."

Mr Diver lowered his voice. "I probably shouldn't be saying this, but I'm not convinced the Conservatives can win. I think we're going to have a proper fight on our hands."

"I don't think many around here will agree with you."

"Maybe not, but if you want my opinion, we were fortunate when we won the last one. Since then the foreign policy's been a disaster. People don't want us spending money in Turkey when they can't afford to eat here. The trade figures aren't helpful either. I think the Whigs are going to make mincemeat out of us."

William sighed. "I hope you're wrong. Mr Wetherby'll be unbearable if we lose."

"Unfortunately people don't vote based on Mr Wetherby's moods. We're going to have to give the party as much help as we can."

Chapter Twenty

Sarah-Ann sat at the table, staring at the clock. Quarter to ten and still no sign of Mr Flemming. She knew the reason for his lateness. It was the fifth time this week he had gone to the ale house rather than coming home, and each time he returned home more inebriated than the time before.

The previous evening, she had been in bed long before he arrived home, but that hadn't stopped him from waking her up and demanding to know why Elizabeth wasn't home from school. Telling him she was staying with William and Harriet hadn't been enough to satisfy him and when she refused to say any more, he had picked up every ornament in the bedroom and hurled them at her. She'd buried herself under the bedcovers and once he ran out of things to throw at her, she worried he would start beating her. Instead, much to her surprise, everything had gone quiet. Unsure of what to expect, she peered over the top of the blankets and saw him sitting on the floor at the bottom of the bed, weeping. Overwhelmed with guilt she had gone to him and cradled his head on her shoulder until he slumped into unconsciousness.

When she awoke the next morning he was still on the floor, snoring loudly. Rather than wake him she went downstairs to make up the fire and prepare some breakfast. An hour later when he had still not appeared she went back to the bedroom.

"Frederick." She shook him gently. "Wake up." When she received no response she shook him harder until eventually he grunted and opened his eyes.

"Frederick, it's time to open the shop. Would you like me to do it for you to give you more time?"

He started to stand up, but was too quick and fell back to the floor. He sat for a minute before opening his eyes again.

"What happened here?" He looked at the debris of broken pottery. "Have we been burgled?"

"No, we weren't." Sarah-Ann straightened up. "You had too much to drink last night and decided to throw them at me."

Mr Flemming moved once again, this time more slowly, and pulled himself onto the bed.

"I'm sorry." He put his head in his hands. "I don't know what came over me. I don't want to hurt you."

"Frederick, we need to talk. Neither of us can carry on like this for much longer. Why don't I make a special tea for us tonight and we can discuss everything?"

"All I want to do is see my daughter, why won't you let me?"

"Because I'm frightened of what you'll do to her. She's only fourteen ..."

"But I want her here, now. How can we celebrate Easter when she's not here?"

The thought of celebrating Easter had passed Sarah-Ann by. If she could manage to survive it she'd be happy.

"Come home straight from work and we can spend some time together, just the two of us, like the old days when we used to get along so well. I've bought a piece of ham for dinner tomorrow and we can spend the afternoon doing whatever we want, with nobody else to worry about."

Mr Flemming studied her with a glint in his eye and nodded his consent. "And then Elizabeth can come home?"

Sarah-Ann hesitated. "We'll talk about it."

"We'd better do more than talk." He staggered to his feet and went downstairs. Sarah-Ann let him reach the living room before she followed him. *What have I let myself in for?*

Now she sat at the table once again staring at the clock. Despite his promises, she had eaten tea alone and everything was now tidied away. As the clock struck ten, she stood up and peered through the window. The moon was full, but with so many clouds the streets were dark. *Where is he?* Before long she gave up trying to see anything and gave the table one last wipe. *He's going to be in a right state when he gets in. I might be better off in bed.* With another glance out of the window, she picked up the candle and went upstairs. The room was once again tidy and at least there was nothing left for him to throw at her.

The next morning she was woken by the sound of birds and rolled over in bed to find she was still alone. Relief swept over her as she realised she had spent a peaceful night, before a cold chill ran down her back. It wasn't the first time he hadn't come home and although she'd never challenged him, she knew it meant he'd spent the night with another woman. *If they're that desperate, they're welcome to him,* she thought as she dragged herself out of bed.

With it being Easter Sunday, she was ready for church earlier than usual. She sat at the table wearing her hat and coat, debating whether she should go alone. As five past ten approached, and there was still no sign of him, she stood up and walked to the front door. The meat was already at the baker's for cooking so if he did come home she could keep him quiet with a decent meal. That was the plan at least.

When she arrived at church, she paused at the back and surveyed the pews before her. There was no sign of him. With a heavy sigh she took her usual seat, halfway down the right-hand side, and as soon as the service was over she hurried from the building. She hadn't gone far when she saw a figure in front of her, stumbling carelessly along the pavement.

My goodness, what's he doing? Sarah-Ann turned to see if anyone had seen him. *How will I ever explain this to the neighbours?* Lifting the front of her skirt from the ground, she hurried to his side and put her arm through his, trying to steady him. As soon as he felt her touch he stopped and glared at her.

"Get away from me, you harlot." He pulled his arm away, almost falling in the process.

"Frederick!"

"Don't you Frederick me, I've had enough of you, sneaking up on me like that. Are you spying on me or coming back from your fancy man's house?"

"I'm doing no such thing, I'm on my way home from church."

"Was he in church as well?" Mr Flemming wiped his arm across his mouth.

"I was expecting you in church, although I'm glad you didn't arrive smelling like a brewery."

Mr Flemming coughed as he choked on his own saliva. "Me in church, not any more. There's more compassion in the beerhouse than from that lot, the bunch of hypocrites. What have they ever done for me?"

"You don't go to church for what they can do for you." Sarah-Ann tried to take hold of his hands but he backed away from her.

"No point going then. I've finished with God. Has he brought Elizabeth back to me when I've been asking him all week? No."

"I thought we were going to discuss it yesterday. Why didn't you come home?"

"No point is there. No bloody point. If Elizabeth isn't there then I might as well not be there. I need her."

"No you don't and until you promise you're not

going to lay a finger on her you won't be seeing her again."

A fire blazed in Mr Flemming's eyes and seconds later he swung back his right arm and struck Sarah-Ann on the side of the face. Fortunately, his aim was poor and there was little power in it.

"What are you doing?" Sarah-Ann's eyes were wide as she grabbed his hand and glanced up and down the street to check nobody had seen them.

"Don't talk to me like that. She's my daughter and I can see her when I like. You've no right to come between us. I'm going to go to Handsworth to find her. Get out of my way." As he spoke he pushed Sarah-Ann backwards and seconds later she landed on the pavement, her head spinning. As she lay there, she heard footsteps hurrying towards her before a voice spoke from above.

"Mrs Flemming, are you all right?"

Sarah-Ann opened her eyes to see two of her neighbours and their husbands standing over her. "Thank you, yes," she said, forcing herself to sit up. "It was an accident. I must have stepped into a hole in the road."

The gentlemen offered her their hands and helped her to her feet while Mr Flemming watched with a poorly concealed smirk on his face.

"Thank you both," Sarah-Ann said. "Good day to you. We're not going straight home, so we'll perhaps see you tomorrow." As the neighbours retreated, Sarah-Ann glared at her husband.

"What do you think you're doing, embarrassing me like that?"

"It makes a change for me to embarrass you. Serves you right, you old hag. Now, I'm going to get Elizabeth." Without another word, he turned his back on her and walked away.

"It's Easter Sunday, there are no omnibuses running today," she shouted after him. "And the family are all going out, so you won't find anyone at home."

Mr Flemming stopped and turned back to her. "I don't believe you, not a single word, but I'll tell you what, I don't think I will go to Handsworth today. I'll go tomorrow instead. You can manage the shop. What irony, I go for my daughter and you can do nothing about it but cover my back."

Sarah-Ann was about to tell him what he could do with the shop but stopped. Why tell him? She would do nothing of the sort? "So what will you do today?"

"I won't be spending it with you, that's for sure." He looked up and down the street. "There must be an alehouse open by now."

"It's Easter Sunday," she said, exasperation in her voice.

"I don't care, there are plenty of people who enjoy my company and so if you'll excuse me, I'll go somewhere I'm wanted."

Chapter Twenty-One

Sarah-Ann stood in the street, her mind racing. She desperately wanted to get to Handsworth, but she hadn't been lying when she said there would be no transport today. She turned towards home, but had only gone a hundred yards when she turned round and headed back to the town centre. She had no idea how to get to Handsworth but she vaguely knew the direction. If Mr Wetherby could walk there, so could she.

Once she reached the main road she was surprised that there were in fact a number of carriages on the road. They were private carriages, not for hire, but surely one of them must be going to Handsworth. Beyond caring what anyone might think of her, she crossed the road and waved down the first carriage that passed.

It took several attempts to find someone who was going to Handsworth, but eventually she found a couple who were happy to take her. She told them her husband had been taken ill and she needed to see her daughter. They accepted her story without question and she was thankful they made no further enquiries.

~

Handsworth, Staffordshire.

ONCE THE CARRIAGE arrived in Handsworth, she bade a quick farewell to her travelling companions and hurried the short distance to Wetherby House. She was about to knock on the front door when she stopped. *What do I say?* She'd been so intent on getting here, she hadn't considered what she would tell everyone. To Mary and Mr Wetherby she would tell the truth, but she didn't want to tell the rest of the family about her humiliation. With her heart pounding she reached for the door knocker, but before her fingers clasped it, she dropped her arm back to her side and turned away. *I can't do this. What will they all think of me?* She stepped back onto the driveway, but hadn't gone two steps before the front door opened.

"Sarah-Ann, is that you?" The voice behind her was familiar and she turned to find Mr Wetherby staring at her. "I thought I saw you coming up the path. What are you doing here?" The sight of him looking at her with such concern was too much and tears rolled down her cheeks. "You're usually pleased to see me, whatever's the matter?" He reached for her hand and led her into the hallway before he closed the door and put his arms around her. "Talk to me, what is it?"

Sarah-Ann sobbed. It was too long since she'd felt those arms around her. How she wished she could stay here, safe and protected. Eventually she found her voice. "He's after her."

"Mr Flemming?"

Sarah-Ann nodded.

"Is he on his way?"

She shook her head. "Tomorrow."

Mr Wetherby held her tighter and kissed the top of her head. "How I wish I'd never introduced you to him. We need this sorted out once and for all. Go upstairs and I'll ask Emily to bring you some water to wash your face. I'm sure you don't want to join us but I'll send Mary up to see you. In fact, I'll tell her to bring you a brandy, I'd say you could do with one."

Mr Wetherby let go of her and gestured in the direction of the stairs. "Off you go, second room on the right."

It was another ten minutes before Mary joined her, by which time she'd washed her face and tidied her hair.

"I'm sorry I was so long," Mary said, breezing into the room. "Susannah's announced she's going back to live in Birmingham. She doesn't like being on her own and Clara's asked if she'll move in with them. I can't say I blame her."

"Mary, stop, I can't talk about Susannah." Tears once again fell down her cheeks. "I don't know what to do. Mr Flemming's furious with me for letting Elizabeth stay here and he said he's going to come and get her. He's drinking more than ever, and he's become violent again. He doesn't bother to hide the fact he has other women any more and I've got to the point where I'm frightened for my own safety, never mind Elizabeth's."

Mary pulled up a chair and sat down. "I'm sorry, I was being thoughtless. Has he hurt you?"

Sarah-Ann shook her head.

"And what about Elizabeth? Do you think he's ever touched her?"

Sarah-Ann wiped her eyes. "I don't think so, but whenever she's around he never takes his eyes off her.

I've never known him like this before, even after I lost the baby he wasn't this bad."

"You must stay with us again, for tonight at least. Elizabeth should stay here tonight as well. If Mr Flemming arrives, Mr Wetherby will be able to sort him out."

"What will I tell Elizabeth? She has no idea about his drinking and I can't tell her. I don't want her to see him like that."

"Neither of you need see him. You can stay out of sight until Mr Wetherby's dealt with him. He'll calm him down."

Sarah-Ann shuddered. "What will he do?"

"He'll think of something, and once he's spoken to him we'll decide what's best for you."

Sarah-Ann started sobbing again. "What have I done to deserve this? I must have done something really bad."

Mary took hold of her hands. "It's not your fault. Drink has made the devil out of many a man. You did the right thing coming here and at least we can keep Elizabeth safe. Let me go downstairs and see out the guests and then I'll come back and bring Elizabeth with me."

Thirty minutes later Mary returned with Elizabeth.

"What are you doing here?" she asked her

mother, her pale blue eyes shining from her innocent face. "I thought you'd be at home with Father."

Sarah-Ann took her daughter in her arms. "I was missing you. You've been away at school for too long and then you came straight here; I was worried I might not see you."

"What about Father? Will he be all right on his own?"

"He'll be fine. He was the one who suggested I came," she lied. "Apparently I've been miserable all day."

Elizabeth smiled and returned her mother's embrace. "I'm glad you're here, I've missed you too, but I thought you'd think me silly if I said anything."

"Don't ever think that. I love you more than you'll ever know."

Chapter Twenty-Two

Sarah-Ann was awake early the next morning and lay in bed staring at the silhouette of her daughter in the bed beside her. A wave of nausea passed over her as she thought of her husband. *Will he really come here today?* If she wasn't there to take care of the shop, maybe he wouldn't. *Please, Lord, don't let him come.* Mr Wetherby was too much of a gentleman to have to deal with him. She knew he would try to talk some sense into her husband, as he had in the past, but Mr Flemming was a physical man. What if their meeting turned into a brawl? She would never forgive herself if anything happened to Mr Wetherby.

She was disturbed from her thoughts when Mary

knocked on the door and came in carrying a cup of tea.

"How are you this morning?" she whispered. "Did you sleep?"

Sarah-Ann dragged her gaze from Elizabeth. "Not enough."

"Here, drink this. I put some extra sugar in for you. With it being a public holiday Mr Wetherby will be at home today and so if Mr Flemming turns up, he'll be able to deal with him. You never know, he might not come. There won't be many omnibuses running."

"I've just thought." Sarah-Ann sat bolt upright and stared at Mary. "He thinks Elizabeth's at William's house. He'll go there first. I need to go and warn them."

"You'll do no such thing. I don't suppose Mr Flemming will arrive early, if he comes at all. I'll send Mr Wetherby once he's had breakfast. He can tell William that Mr Flemming's visiting today and you gave him the wrong address. William isn't one for asking questions."

"Harriet is though. Mr Wetherby won't tell her, will he?" Sarah-Ann's eyes were wide.

Mary shook her head. "I can say with some certainty that he won't tell her unless he absolutely has to."

~

AFTER BREAKFAST, Mr Wetherby put on his hat and coat and walked to Havelock Road. William was reading the newspaper when he arrived.

"I didn't expect to see you today," William said.

"I've brought you a message. As you know, Elizabeth stayed at Wetherby House last night, but your aunt's realised that Mr Flemming's joining them today and thinks she's still here. He may come here to pick her up. If he does, can you send him in our direction?"

"I think I can manage that. I could probably have done that without a message."

"I'm sure you could, but you know how women worry. I wanted to put your aunt's mind at rest. In fact, could you answer the door yourself and speak to him directly, rather than asking the maid to do it?"

"Violet always answers the door. I'm sure she can give him a message."

"Please, on this occasion could you make an exception? I can't tell you why, just trust me."

William sighed. "Very well. I don't suppose we'll be expecting anyone else this morning. Will you have a cup of tea?"

"No, I must be getting back." Mr Wetherby studied his pocket watch. "There's work to do before

Wednesday's election. Everyone's worried about the impact Gladstone's having and we need to make sure his campaign in Scotland doesn't affect our supporters down here."

"Yes, of course. I don't know how he's managed to get all his speeches into the national press. We need to learn a few lessons from him."

WILLIAM ESCORTED Mr Wetherby to the front door but as they stood on the doorstep Mr Flemming walked round the corner heading directly towards them. William instantly knew why Mr Wetherby hadn't wanted Violet to open the door. The man was obviously drunk and wore the expression of someone you wouldn't want to upset. Sensing trouble, William pulled the door closed behind him.

"Where is she, Wetherby?" Mr Flemming shouted, clearly breathless. "Where've you hidden her?"

Mr Wetherby walked to the end of the driveway, and waited for Mr Flemming. "Good morning, Mr Flemming. You've made it here in good time."

"Don't mess me about, Wetherby, where is she? She's coming home with me."

"I thought you were coming for a visit, I wasn't aware she'd be leaving today."

Mr Flemming turned to William. "You, Jackson, give me a straight answer, where is she?" William wasn't sure whether Mr Flemming was referring to his wife or his daughter, but given Mr Wetherby's reluctance to say anything, he was sure he shouldn't either.

"Who are you looking for?" he asked.

"Are you serious? Who d'you think? My daughter."

"Elizabeth?"

"Of course Elizabeth, how many damn daughters do you think I have?"

William glanced at Mr Wetherby. "She's not here."

"Stop the lies, I know she's here." Mr Flemming pushed William on the shoulder.

"Mr Flemming, I can assure you she's not here," Mr Wetherby interrupted. "We knew you were coming and took the opportunity to move her."

"Is that pathetic wife of mine here?" Mr Flemming's eyes were like slits as he spat his words out. "Is that how you knew?"

Mr Wetherby grabbed Mr Flemming by the lapels of his jacket. "I will not have you talking about your wife like that."

"No, you wouldn't, would you, given she's your mistress. I know you see her while you're in Birmingham ..."

"I most certainly do not, how dare you."

"Does Mr Jackson know the sort of man you are? You're scum, you are, no better than anyone else."

As William watched, everything happened in slow motion. The voices were talking in the background but all he heard were Mr Flemming's words repeating themselves. *His mistress? Was Aunt Sarah-Ann the reason Mr Wetherby stayed in Birmingham so often? What about Mother? Did she know? Surely Mr Wetherby wouldn't do such a thing.*

He was distracted from his thoughts by movement to his left. Mr Wetherby was holding Mr Flemming's jacket and shaking him violently.

"Mr Wetherby, stop. What are you doing?" William moved to grab Mr Wetherby's arm, momentarily distracting his attention from Mr Flemming. A second later, Mr Flemming landed a punch on Mr Wetherby's temple.

Mr Wetherby stumbled and released his grip before he regained his composure and charged at his opponent with his shoulder. Mr Flemming tried to move out of the way, but he wasn't quick enough and the force of Mr Wetherby's frame sent him spinning to the floor. Mr Wetherby instinctively jumped on top of him, pinning him down with his legs while he repeatedly pounded his head with his fists.

"What are you doing?" William screamed. "Stop. Can't you see he's not moving?"

Mr Wetherby paused for breath while William knelt down and lifted Mr Flemming's eyelids. "Good God, I think he's dead."

Mr Wetherby stared at William before he returned his wild eyes to Mr Flemming. "Don't be ridiculous."

"Look at him. He's not moving," William said. "There's a pool of blood on the road as well."

Mr Wetherby slapped Mr Flemming's face from side to side. "Come on, man, what are you playing at? Wake up, damn you." He continued to slap his face.

"Mr Wetherby, stop. Did you hear me? He's dead. His lips and tongue are turning blue. What shall we do?"

Mr Wetherby looked around before stumbling to his feet. "First of all, we thank the Lord it's a public holiday and none of the builders are around. Secondly, we get him out of the street as soon as we can. You grab his shoulders."

"We can't move him. What about the blood?"

"Leave it. Grab hold of him and stop arguing." Mr Wetherby started to lift Mr Flemming's feet but immediately dropped them and gripped his right hand.

"What's the matter?" William asked.

"This damn hand, it's never healed properly; Mr Flemming must have caught it."

William stared at Mr Wetherby. "You hit him."

"Stop arguing, pick up his shoulders and I'll pick up one leg with my good hand."

William shook his head before he positioned his hands under Mr Flemming's arms and manoeuvred him into the front room.

"Now what do we do?" William said as they laid him on the floor. "We can't leave him here."

Mr Wetherby slapped Mr Flemming's face again. "Nothing. Do you have any smelling salts?"

"What good will they do?"

"Have you got any?"

"No, I don't think so. I'd need to ask Harriet." William stepped towards the door.

"Good God, man. Don't ask Harriet. The less she knows about this the better. We don't know he's dead. I'll go and get Dr Hopkins."

William's heart was pounding. "What will you tell him?"

"We'll tell him the truth. That we saw him coming down the street towards us and he was so drunk he could barely walk. He was cursing and swearing at us before he collapsed and banged his head on the road."

"But you pushed him ..."

"I did nothing of the sort. If anyone asks, he punched me, and then collapsed. Look, I have a mark on the side of my head, I shouldn't wonder."

"He has bruises on his face ..."

"Didn't you see them when he staggered towards us? He must have been fighting someone else."

William squeezed his eyes shut, to imagine the scene. "I saw you hit him ..."

"I did nothing of the sort. This has been a terrible accident, brought on by his drinking. Is that clear? I want you to stay here, I won't be long."

The door slammed behind Mr Wetherby as he let himself out and William sat down and put his head in his hands. He was still shaking when Harriet walked in.

"Has he killed him?" she asked, her voice calm.

"Harriet!" William jumped up. "What are you doing here?"

"I was in the bedroom and saw what happened." Harriet walked over to Mr Flemming. "Is he dead?"

William took out his handkerchief and wiped his brow. "I think so. Mr Wetherby's gone for Dr Hopkins."

"He's taken a chance doing that. What if the doctor can tell he's been beaten?"

"Mr Wetherby said he didn't touch him. He said Mr Flemming fell and that someone else must have hit him."

The pitch of Harriet's voice rose. "William, you were stood next to him. You must have seen him charge at Mr Flemming and beat him around the head once he was on the ground."

William sat down again. "I wasn't concentrating."

"How can you not have been concentrating? Two men you've known for most of your life were fighting in the street and you weren't paying attention."

"It was Mr Flemming's fault. He accused Mr Wetherby of ... of ... being overfamiliar with Aunt Sarah-Ann."

Harriet's eyes widened. "No! Is that why they dislike each other so much? I'm not surprised your mother knows nothing of it." She turned and studied Mr Flemming. "I almost feel sorry for him now. Imagine having to deal with that for all these years."

"What do we do about Mr Wetherby though? I thought I saw him hit Mr Flemming but he's trying to convince me he didn't. Do you think he'll get arrested?"

Harriet thought for a second. "No, not at the moment. Right now he thinks you and him are the only ones who know about it, and if he keeps you quiet he'll get away with it. He doesn't know about me."

"Please don't let him see you in here when he gets back. He told me not to tell you."

Harriet smiled. "You didn't tell me, I saw everything myself. You're right though, he shouldn't find out. Not yet. We can keep it to ourselves for the time being, but I've been thinking. Now might be an excellent time to ask for a pay rise. It would give you the money you need to buy a few houses to rent out."

William swallowed down the lump in his throat. "I'll need to pick my moment."

"Well don't take too long about it. In the meantime, I'll write everything down ... just in case we ever need to remind him of what happened." Harriet smiled. "Perhaps the days of him treating you as a second-class citizen are over."

Chapter Twenty-Three

Less than fifteen minutes later, Mr Wetherby arrived back with the doctor. Dr Hopkins bent down over Mr Flemming and put his head over his chest as he gripped his wrist.

"He's still alive," he said after a minute. "I've found a pulse." William gave an audible sigh, while Mr Wetherby took a handkerchief from his pocket and wiped his forehead.

"Is he going to be all right?" William asked.

"It's too early to say. The pulse is weak and his breathing's shallow." The doctor waved some smelling salts under Mr Flemming's nose. "These aren't having much effect. By the smell of him, I'd say he liked his drink a bit too much. That won't help his recovery."

"I did tell you, Doctor, that was why he fell in the first place," Mr Wetherby said. "Mr Jackson and I saw him staggering down the road, but as he reached us he passed out and banged his head. I'd say he'd been brawling before he met us as well, judging by the marks on his face."

Dr Hopkins nodded and examined the marks on Mr Flemming's head.

"What will we do with him?" William asked.

"We need to bring him round and make him comfortable," the doctor said. "Can he stay here?"

William hesitated. "It might be difficult ..."

"Who's his next of kin?"

"That would be my sister-in-law," Mr Wetherby said. "She's at Wetherby House."

"If he regains consciousness, could we take him there? I'm sure he'd be more comfortable with his wife taking care of him than he would be in a hospital."

"No." Mr Wetherby answered a little too quickly. "She's ... she's not feeling well herself at the moment. Mrs Wetherby's tending to her."

The doctor rubbed his beard as he studied his patient. "I'll have to send him to hospital."

Mr Wetherby walked over to Mr Flemming and stooped down beside him. "Look, his eyes are flickering. He'll be fine in a minute. Can you try the salts again? I'm going back to Birmingham this afternoon. If he's awake it might be best if I took him home."

Dr Hopkins took out the smelling salts and held them under Mr Flemming's nose again. "I don't think you should move him too far. He needs rest."

William saw the perspiration on Mr Wetherby's temples. "I'm sure he would be happier going home, he won't want to go into hospital."

"But if you take him home, who'll care for him? He won't be able to manage by himself."

"He has a lot of friends in Birmingham, especially amongst the ladies," Mr Wetherby said. "I'm sure there'll be no shortage of women to offer their services."

William and the doctor both turned to Mr Wetherby.

"Nothing untoward, you understand. His wife is well aware of the fact. Look he's coming round now. Let's make him comfortable and he can stay here for a few hours. I'll collect him in my carriage later today."

Dr Hopkins took a deep intake of breath. "I don't think so ..."

"Please, Doctor. I'm sure that's what he would want."

. . .

163

IT WAS another fifteen minutes before the doctor left. As William closed the door behind him, he breathed a sigh of relief and went back into the front room. Mr Flemming was once again asleep and Mr Wetherby had collapsed into an armchair.

"I'll pour some brandy," he said. "I'm exhausted."

He went to the cabinet and poured two drinks, but his hands were shaking so much that he poured out more than he intended. He handed Mr Wetherby a glass, but didn't speak until he felt the warmth of the brandy landing in his stomach.

"He gave me a fright and that's for sure," William said, breaking the silence.

"Damn man, why couldn't he have stayed in Birmingham? I need to leave shortly and I have to go home before I do."

"Are you still going to Birmingham?"

"Of course I am. We have the election this week and I can't afford to waste any more time when there's still so much to do. I should be there already." Mr Wetherby downed his drink and stood up. "I'll come back here for you in an hour, assuming you're still coming with me?"

"Yes of course ..."

"Right, I'll see you later. In the meantime, keep

this door closed and if you have to say anything to that wife of yours, tell her it was an accident. Understood?"

Chapter Twenty-Four

Despite the laudanum, Mr Flemming groaned as William struggled to lift him into the carriage. It was parked near the back door, to keep it from prying eyes, and he laid Mr Flemming along the rear-facing seat before he sat beside Mr Wetherby in the seat opposite.

"He doesn't look well," William said. "I'm not sure we should be moving him."

"What else could we do? We couldn't leave him at your house for Harriet to find and we certainly weren't taking him to Wetherby House. Did you manage to keep Harriet out of the front room?"

William felt his cheeks colouring and he turned to face the window. "She was upstairs for most of the morning, tidying the bedrooms. We had dinner in the morning room."

Mr Wetherby grunted. "Don't say a word to her about this. What about the children, where were they?"

"Margaret and Florence were upstairs with Harriet, the other three were out somewhere. They came back for dinner, but once they'd finished, they disappeared as quickly as they'd arrived. Did you tell Mother and Aunt Sarah-Ann?"

"I had to. I couldn't go to Birmingham for the week without saying anything, as much as I might have liked to."

"How did Aunt Sarah-Ann take it?"

"Quite well, all things considered."

"Didn't she want to go home with him?"

It was Mr Wetherby's turn to stare out of the window. "There wasn't enough time for her to sort herself out, and she has Elizabeth with her. I told her I'd check up on him."

"Did you?" William couldn't hide his surprise. "I doubt you'll have the time."

They travelled the next few miles in silence before William took a deep breath. "Can I ask you something? I-Is it true what Mr Flemming said ..." He turned back to the window. "About you and Aunt Sarah-Ann?"

Mr Wetherby's face darkened. "Of course it's not true, what do you take me for?"

"He said ... he said she was ... you know, close to you."

"The man's deluded. He's been jealous ever since we met. He thinks every man he meets has his eyes on your aunt. I'm surprised he's not accused you."

"Me? Don't be ridiculous," William said.

"Well, exactly ... and it's the same with me. I like your aunt of course but I'd never dream of any improper behaviour."

William breathed a sigh of relief. "Good ... that's what I hoped. It's just that he said it with such conviction he made me doubt you. I'm sorry."

"Very well, we'll say no more about it. The man's not worthy of your aunt. At least she'll be free from him for a few more days."

William stared at Mr Flemming. "Did you mean to hurt him?"

"Of course I didn't. He fell. It was nothing to do with me."

"But you pushed him. You hurt your hand too."

"I was acting in self-defence; didn't you see him hitting me? It was an accident, nothing more. Besides, he'll live; I just hope the bang on the head will knock some sense into him."

"Did you ask the doctor to look at your hand?"

"There was no need, it's fine now." Mr Wetherby cradled his injured hand with his good one and turned back to the window. "I think we should just forget any of this happened."

By the time they got Mr Flemming home and found someone to take care of him, it was turned two o'clock.

"That damn man's lost us hours with all that messing about," Mr Wetherby said as they arrived at the Conservative Association. "Has he no idea that Birmingham's amongst the first wave of polling in this election and we still have a lot to do? I hope William Junior and Mr Diver are here. If we lose by a small margin, I'll hold him personally responsible."

"At least he was awake when we dropped him off," William said. "I didn't like the sound of his breathing though."

"Stop concerning yourself with him. He always sounds like that nowadays. He's got no one to blame but himself. Now, I've got work for you to do this afternoon. First thing is for you to find Mr Diver and get out on the streets to make sure folks are going to vote Conservative this week."

WITH MR WETHERBY GONE, Mary and Sarah-Ann settled in the back room at Wetherby House. The maid had left a pot of tea, which Mary poured and handed to Sarah-Ann.

"I've put an extra sugar in for you. You seem a bit peaky," Mary said.

Sarah-Ann gave her a weak smile. "I'm fine, I just can't stop wondering what happened earlier. It sounds like Mr Flemming was looking for a fight. Thank goodness he was too drunk to do any damage to Mr Wetherby."

"Thank goodness, indeed. I don't know how Mr Wetherby would cope in a ..." Mary's words trailed off as she recalled the sight of Mr Wetherby's hand after his fight with Richard. It had never healed properly.

"What's the matter?"

"Nothing, I just had an image of them fighting." Mary shuddered. "Not something I want to think of."

Mary offered Sarah-Ann some freshly baked cakes before she helped herself to one and sat down. She was about to take a bite when there was a knock on the front door.

"Who on earth can this be? I'm not expecting anyone."

A minute later, Emily knocked on the door and showed Harriet in.

"Good afternoon ... oh. Aunt Sarah-Ann. I wasn't expecting you to be here. I assumed you'd have gone back to Birmingham with Mr Flemming."

Mary and Sarah-Ann both stared at her. "How do you know about Mr Flemming?" Mary asked. "Mr Wetherby said nobody knew about it except William and Dr Hopkins."

"Well, he was lying unconscious in our front room for half the morning so I could hardly miss him."

Mary and Sarah-Ann exchanged glances.

"How badly hurt was he?" Sarah-Ann's eyes were wide. "Mr Wetherby said it was only a knock and that he'd be fine."

"He did," Mary said. "He didn't mention anything about him being unconscious."

Harriet's eyes flicked between the two older women. "I wonder why not. Perhaps he didn't want to worry you."

"Yes, that must be it." Mary breathed a sigh of relief as she offered Harriet a cup of tea and a cake.

"I don't understand why he wouldn't want to worry you though." Harriet's brow creased as she accepted the cake. "Mr Flemming didn't look well and I wouldn't have thought he'd be able to manage at home by himself. Not for the next few days anyway. That's why I expected someone to have gone with him. Has Elizabeth gone?"

"No, she's gone for a walk with Charlotte," Mary said. "Mr Wetherby gave no indication that he'd need help."

"If it was only a bang on the head, and he's come round again, he should be all right ... shouldn't he?" Sarah-Ann's eyes fixed on Harriet.

"If that was all it was, then yes, probably, but he lost a lot of blood as well. There's a huge bloodstain outside our house that won't wash off."

Sarah-Ann put down the plate that was holding her half-eaten cake and turned to Mary. "Why would Mr Wetherby tell us it was only a knock, if it was more than that?"

Harriet stood up to leave and put her empty plate back on the table. "I think it's time I was leaving, but to answer your question, perhaps he didn't want you to go back to Birmingham."

Chapter Twenty-Five

With Harriet gone, Mary and Sarah-Ann sat back in their chairs and looked at each other.

"What do you make of that?" Sarah-Ann said.

"I've no idea."

"Do you think Harriet made it up? She's never liked me, and so perhaps she was trying to get me to go back to Birmingham."

Mary shook her head. "I don't think so. She did seem genuinely surprised to see you."

"Mr Wetherby wouldn't lie though, would he?"

Mary let out a long sigh. "For reasons I've not been privy to, Mr Wetherby and Mr Flemming have never seen eye to eye. I'm worried that Mr Wetherby may have hurt Mr Flemming, but he didn't want to tell us."

"No, he wouldn't ..."

"He might surprise you. It's a side of him you don't see, but he does have quite a temper if someone crosses him. I've seen him angry with Mr Flemming before when he's upset you."

Sarah-Ann studied the embroidery lying idle in her lap. "He's a gentleman trying to protect me, that's all."

"I think there's more to it than that. Do you think we should pay Mr Flemming a visit? If he's as bad as Harriet suggests somebody needs to make sure he's being taken care of."

"I can't go back to the house." Sarah-Ann's head shot up. "He'll be furious with me."

"I'm sure he wouldn't do anything to hurt you if I'm there."

"After everything that's happened? I'd be taking my life in my hands whether you're there or not. What if he's been drinking again? I can't trust him."

Mary stood up and paced the floor. "Well what do we do?"

Sarah-Ann shrugged. "Could we ask Martha to call? He's always civil to her."

"We can't send her on her own," Mary said.

"Why don't I go and speak to her and perhaps we can go together."

"You can't do that; Mr Wetherby would never allow it."

"He's too busy with the election to notice. Besides he's happy enough for me to go to Birmingham if he thinks I'm visiting Martha."

Sarah-Ann bit her bottom lip. "Promise me you won't go into the house if he's drunk. I wouldn't forgive myself if anything happened."

Birmingham, Warwickshire.

THE FOLLOWING DAY, Mary was in Birmingham by noon. She stood by the wall of St Martin's Church hoping against hope that Richard might join her, but they hadn't arranged to meet today so it was unlikely. When the clock struck half past the hour, and it was clear he wasn't coming, she bowed her head and returned to the carriage. She arrived at Martha's house as she was tidying up after dinner.

"What are you doing here?" she asked as Mary took a seat. "You're not often in Birmingham."

"It's not a social visit. I wondered if you'd visit Mr Flemming with me this afternoon. He's had an accident and I need to see how badly hurt he is."

Mary explained all she knew, before Martha interrupted.

"Why isn't Sarah-Ann visiting? Don't tell me they've fallen out again."

"They have. She turned up at our house on Easter Sunday terrified of what he might do. She was too frightened to come with me."

Martha put her hand to her head. "Are you sure we should?"

"Yes, I'm sure. We need to know he's safe and we don't have any argument with him."

Thirty minutes later, Mary and Martha arrived outside the house in Latimer Street and waited for the coachman to help them from the carriage. Mary smoothed down her pale grey dress before banging on the brass door knocker. A minute later the maid answered.

"Would it be possible to see Mr Flemming?" Mary asked.

"He's not here," the maid said. "He had a nasty bump on the head so he's staying with a friend who's nursing him."

"How is he?" Martha asked.

"Not very well. He was struggling to stay awake and he's lost the use of his right arm."

An icy tremor ran down Mary's body. "Could you tell us where he is?"

"Cregoe Street. Number thirty-two."

Mary thanked her and asked the driver to take them round the corner.

"What do you think we'll find?" Martha asked as they pulled away. "Do you think he has another woman?"

"Let's not jump to conclusions. There could be a perfectly good explanation."

When they reached the house in Cregoe Street, a buxom woman in her mid-forties opened the door. She didn't wait for any introductions before inviting them in.

"He's in the back room but he's in a bad way. It's a wonder that husband of yours didn't kill him."

Mary stared at the woman, her mouth open. She had never seen her before in her life.

"I'm sorry," Mary said after a moment. "I think you must be mistaken. I'm Mrs Wetherby and this is my sister-in-law, Mrs Chalmers. We're here to see Mr Flemming. Mrs Chalmers is widowed, but I'm sure my husband wouldn't have hurt him."

"That's not what Mr Flemming says." The woman pushed open the door to the living room. "Are you awake, Fred?"

Mr Flemming opened his eyes and looked first at Mary and then Martha.

"I knew you'd come." His voice was barely a

whisper. "He couldn't live with his conscience, could he? Needs you to tell him I'm all right."

"Mr Flemming, please, I don't know what you're talking about." Mary took a seat next to him.

"Your husband. It's his fault I'm in this state. Set upon me, he did. Charged at me so hard that I fell into the road. Then he punched me ..." Mr Flemming closed his eyes.

"I'm sure you're mistaken," Mary said. "Mr Wetherby would never do such a thing; the bump on your head must have confused you."

"You don't know a thing about him, do you?" Mr Flemming said with a sneer. "You think he's a perfect gentleman. Perhaps you wouldn't be so keen to defend him if you knew what he was really like." Mary glanced at Martha, while Mr Flemming continued. "Shall I tell you why he hates me so much? I bet you've wondered."

"I'm sure he doesn't hate you, he just wants to see Sarah-Ann happy."

"Oh yes, he wants to see Sarah-Ann happy all right, but not with me. He's hated me since the day I married her ..."

"Come now, Mr Flemming, I'm sure all this talking can't be good for you. You need to rest."

"I'll rest when I've told you the truth. Did you know he couldn't keep his hands off my wife? I came home and found them together ... at our house ..."

"I'm sure there's a good explanation."

"Like him and her doing things they shouldn't? Getting intimate together ..."

Mary took a sharp intake of breath. "No, that's a lie ..."

"Then why was she carrying his baby ...?"

"No ... Mr Flemming, stop," Martha said. "This is nonsense."

Mr Flemming ignored her and spoke as if he was watching the scene in his head. "I had to get rid of it of course ... the baby ... for everyone's sake. You see that, don't you? But she hated me afterwards."

"I don't believe you." Mary stood up to leave. "Mr Wetherby would never do such a thing."

Mr Flemming fixed Mary with a glassy stare. "Mr Wetherby stood and watched while she lost the baby. Never lifted a finger to help her either. I tell you, he'll do whatever's necessary to protect his reputation. Don't ever forget that. He'll be getting a visit from the police soon though; I've reported him for attempted murder."

"How can you be so nasty?" Mary sobbed. "He didn't try to kill you, he took care of you. He was the one who brought you home. Why are you saying these things when all he wanted to do was help?"

"He wanted to help himself to my wife, more like. Haven't you wondered why she spends so much time at your house? He knew you couldn't leave him and so with me out the way he could have the best of both worlds. I hope you believe me, Mrs Wetherby, because everyone needs to know what he's like."

Mary stamped her foot. "I won't believe you, Mr Flemming. The bang on the head has obviously clouded your senses and I won't let you vilify an innocent man. Sarah-Ann was right about you, and the police will be told what a vile and vindictive man you are. For your information, Mr Wetherby doesn't know I'm here. I called here today because I wanted to check you were recovering. Now I'm sorry I did. Good day to you."

As she climbed back into the carriage Mary was shaking. She wiped her eyes with a handkerchief before she turned to Martha. "Do you believe him? About Mr Wetherby and Sarah-Ann, I mean."

"Of course not." Martha patted her on the hand. "Sarah-Ann would never do such a thing."

Mary felt sick. She knew full well that Sarah-Ann was more than capable of such a thing, but she'd trusted Mr Wetherby. "What about the fight? Do you think anything Mr Flemming said was true?"

"I wouldn't think so, but it does look like the

bang on the head was worse than Mr Wetherby told you. We need to get him help."

"I can't go back there, Martha, not now."

"Leave it to me. I'll make sure he gets better and when he does, I hope he apologises."

Chapter Twenty-Six

As Thursday afternoon turned into evening, and the polling stations closed, William and Mr Diver stood by the door to the Conservative Association.

"Are you going to the count tonight?" William asked Mr Diver.

"Do we have any choice? Mr Wetherby will be expecting us."

"Where is he? I thought he'd be here by now."

"Goodness knows. He's not been still for the last three days. He may have gone to the Town Hall already. Shall we make our way there?"

The Town Hall was busy when they arrived, but there was no sign of Mr Wetherby. William and Mr Diver watched while the ballot boxes were opened, but as the votes were sorted into piles, they exchanged worried glances.

"How's it looking?" Mr Wetherby asked when he arrived half an hour later.

"Disappointing, I'm afraid," Mr Diver said. "I'd say the Whigs have run rings around us. We heard this afternoon they've had a carefully controlled campaign to make sure the votes were divided between all three candidates. It appears to have been successful."

The veins in Mr Wetherby's neck grew more visible. "How've they managed that? They'd have to tell all the voters who to vote for."

"I'd say that's what they've done," Mr Diver said. "You have to admire their organisation."

Mr Wetherby's shoulders sagged as he went off to inspect the piles of voting slips on the tables. By the time the results were announced, William thought Mr Wetherby had aged ten years.

"All three Members of Parliament for Birmingham will be Liberal," Mr Wetherby said, "including that damn fool Chamberlain. It'll be all over the newspapers tomorrow. We'll be a laughing stock throughout the rest of the country. We could lose the whole election because of this."

"That's a bit harsh," William said.

"It's the truth." Mr Wetherby glanced at his pocket watch. "It's too late to go back to

Handsworth now, but I can't stay in Birmingham a moment longer than I need to. If either of you want to travel with me, I'll be going at first light."

∾

Handsworth, Staffordshire.

AT EIGHT O'CLOCK THE following morning, Mr Wetherby dropped William and Mr Diver on the corner of Havelock Road before he went back to Wetherby House. William hadn't eaten and so before he went to the workshop he sat with Harriet for breakfast. As they were finishing, there was a knock on the door. Violet answered it and a minute later came into the morning room.

"Excuse me, Mr Jackson, but there's a policeman outside wanting a word with you."

William jumped up. "A policeman ... wanting to talk to me, whatever for?"

"He didn't say, sir."

"No, I don't suppose he did. Show him into the front room. I'll be with him in a minute."

Violet nodded and closed the door behind her.

"What am I going to say?" he asked Harriet. "It's bound to be about Mr Flemming."

"First of all you need to calm down. It might not

be about Mr Flemming, but even if it is, you've done nothing wrong."

"No, you're right." William wiped his hands on his napkin and took a deep breath. "I'm just not used to them calling. I'd better go and see him."

The policeman stood by the window when William walked in.

"Good morning, Officer. What can I do for you?"

"Mr Jackson, I presume. I won't beat about the bush. I understand you were here on the morning of Monday 29th March and witnessed a fight between a Mr Flemming of Latimer Street, Birmingham and a Mr Wetherby of Wetherby House, Handsworth. The fight, as I understand, led to Mr Flemming needing medical attention."

William's heart pounded. "Why do you ask?"

"I understand Mr Flemming received a nasty bang to the head as well as bruising to the face. He's still in a poor condition and I wonder what you can tell me about the incident."

William took another deep breath. "Not much. Mr Flemming turned up here rather drunk on the Monday morning and after a few words with Mr Wetherby he collapsed and banged his head on the road. When he didn't regain consciousness we called the doctor. That was it."

"We have reason to believe Mr Flemming's fall was more than a simple accident. Did you see Mr Wetherby fighting with Mr Flemming and physically hitting him or pushing him to the ground?"

William shook his head. "No ... no, absolutely not. Mr Wetherby would never do that. He's a gentleman."

"Is there anyone who could verify that?"

"Well, yes plenty of people could give a good account of him."

The officer bounced up on his toes. "That's not what I meant. Is there anyone else who can confirm Mr Flemming's fall was an accident?"

William shook his head. "We were alone as far as I'm aware."

"But you can't be certain?"

"What makes you think there was a fight?"

"It's been reported to us and we need to follow it up. I'll have to visit some of the houses nearby and ask if anyone saw anything."

William reached for the back of a chair as his heart skipped a beat. "There's no need for that. The builders weren't working, with it being the holiday, and knowing what they're like around here, if anyone had seen anything they'd have been out on the street as soon as Mr Flemming fell. Nobody came, not one person. We had to carry Mr Flemming into the house on our own, which was no easy task."

"I see. Well, thank you for your help. Perhaps I'll leave it for today."

As William showed the police officer out, Harriet joined him in the hallway. "What was that about?"

William reached for his coat as he talked. "He's heard there was a fight and needs to check up on it. I have to warn Mr Wetherby. I'll see you later." Grabbing his hat from the stand he raced round to Wetherby House. Mr Wetherby was putting on his hat and coat when he arrived.

"Thank goodness you're still here," William said. "Can I have a word with you in private?"

"You'd better be quick, I need to be at the workshop." Mr Wetherby led the way into the front room and closed the door. "Can you stay and see your mother when I've gone? I don't know what's got into her. I've not had a civil word out of her since I came home."

"She's the least of your worries. I've just had a visit from the police. The officer was asking about you and Mr Flemming. They've been told there was a fight and think there was foul play."

Mr Wetherby put his head in his hands. "Hasn't this week been bad enough as it is? Where did they hear that from?"

"He didn't say, but the only other person who was there was Mr Flemming. It must have come from him."

Mr Wetherby's face paled. "It'll be his word against mine. Surely they won't believe anything from a man who was drunk, especially now he has a serious head injury."

"I would hope not, but I wanted to tell you so you can be prepared. I said it was an accident and that Mr Flemming collapsed and hit his head on the road ... like we agreed. I didn't mention that you charged at him ..."

"I hardly touched him."

William had turned to leave, when there was a knock on the front door. A moment later he heard the voice of the police officer.

"It's him," William whispered to Mr Wetherby, but there was no time for a reply. Seconds later, the officer was shown in.

"Well, well, Mr Jackson. It didn't take you long to get here." The officer took out his notepad and proceeded to write in it.

"I was on my way here when you called, Officer. Mr Wetherby and I are business partners; we had work to discuss."

"You didn't mention that earlier, Mr Jackson."

William hesitated. "I-I didn't think it was relevant."

"Is there anything else you should have told me?"

"Can I ask what this is all this about, Officer?" Mr Wetherby asked. "William hasn't had the decency to tell me."

"I'd like to ask you some questions about Mr Flemming."

"The poor man. Is he all right? It was terrible to see him fall like that. I blame the drink. Ten o'clock in the morning, but he reeked of the stuff. Talking of which, where are my manners, can I offer you a drink, Officer? I've got some rather special Scotch whisky here; would you care to take a sip with me?"

"I shouldn't ..."

"Surely one won't hurt and I bet you've never tasted real Scottish whisky before. I have it delivered from London, you can't buy it round here."

"Well, if you're sure, just a small one ..."

"That's the spirit." Mr Wetherby smiled. "William, will you join us?"

William's hands were shaking as he accepted a glass, and he set it on the table and sat down. Mr Wetherby knocked back his drink in one and returned to the officer.

"Now, where was I? Yes, Mr Flemming's problem with drink. It started years ago ..."

William stared at Mr Wetherby, his mouth gaping as he listened to this new version of events. *How does he make it sound so convincing? I wouldn't be able to think straight.*

The officer took a mouthful of Scotch. "He remembers things differently. He told us that you pushed him and he's reported you for attempted murder."

Mr Wetherby's gasp was audible. "What a preposterous thing to say. Of course I didn't try to kill him, not least because it would mean my sister-in-law would become a widow. She has a young daughter to care for so why would I want to leave her destitute?"

Mr Wetherby picked up his glass but as soon as he saw it empty, he jumped up. "Let me top up your drink, Officer. It goes down rather too well, don't you think?"

"I really shouldn't, but it is excellent ..."

"I'm glad you like it. I'll make a note so I can pop a bottle into the station Christmas box this year. Now, where was I?" Mr Wetherby took another gulp of his drink. "Unfortunately, Mr Flemming has issues only he can sort out. The problem is, he always wants to blame somebody else. I see many people like him in my line of work, those who won't take any responsibility for their own lives. I'm sure you see it all the time too, Officer. Not everyone is as responsible as we are."

"You're right there, Mr Wetherby, and I'm sorry to have troubled you. It was just procedure, you understand. Once it was reported we had to follow it up." The policeman gazed at his glass and drained it. "That really is good," he said, licking his lips, "I look forward to Christmas."

Chapter Twenty-Seven

Birmingham, Warwickshire

The following Monday morning, once he had opened up the workshop, Mr Wetherby left William Junior in charge and walked the two miles to Latimer Street. He wouldn't let Mr Flemming spread malicious rumours about him. *If only William hadn't been with me, I'd have finished him off. It would have served him right.*

The maid answered the door when he knocked.

"I'm here to see Mr Flemming. Is he home?"

"No, he's not here. He's staying in Cregoe Street until he recovers from his recent fall. Number thirty-two if you're interested."

Mr Wetherby raised his hat in farewell and

walked round the corner. When he reached the house, he hammered on the front door. A woman opened it, but as soon as she saw him her eyes filled with hate.

"Come to gloat, have you, or did you want to make sure you finished him off properly? Well, you won't be disappointed."

Mr Wetherby momentarily hesitated. "I've come to speak to Mr Flemming, not the domestic. Just go and tell him I'm here."

"No I won't," she yelled at him. "He wouldn't want to see you even if he could." She took out her handkerchief and wiped her eyes. "You should be hung for murder."

"What are you talking about, woman? I didn't touch him. It was him who was hitting me."

"Don't you lie to me. Didn't you notice he could hardly breathe? He wouldn't have had the energy to hurt anyone."

"Out of my way." With a swing of his arm, Mr Wetherby pushed the woman to one side.

"I must say, you haven't got the manners of your wife," the woman said.

Mr Wetherby stopped in his tracks. "How do you know my wife?"

"Didn't she tell you? She called to see Mr Flemming the other day. He found it quite calming to tell her about you and Mrs Flemming. He seemed at peace once he'd got it off his chest."

"Mrs Wetherby's been here?" The colour drained from Mr Wetherby's face.

"I'm surprised she didn't tell you. If I'd been told my husband was responsible for getting someone in the family way, I'm sure I'd have had something to say about it."

Mr Wetherby's face changed from white to purple. "Where is he, the lying cheat? Let me at him."

"Come back, you can't go in there." The woman tried to grab Mr Wetherby's arm but he was too quick and barged into the back room. He'd not taken two steps in when he stopped dead. Before him, stretched out on the dining table was Mr Flemming. Stood behind him was a man he presumed to be a doctor.

"Oh ... I'm sorry," Mr Wetherby said as the man looked up. "I was expecting Mr Flemming to be alone."

"I'm sorry to disappoint you. Mr Flemming passed away about an hour ago and I'm in the process of completing the death certificate."

"He's dead?" Mr Wetherby shut the door in the face of the woman. "He can't be. What did he die of?"

"That's what I'm about to determine and so if you'll excuse me ..."

"He ... he had a bad chest, I believe," Mr Wetherby said. "I expect that was what killed him. Or the drink."

"He did have emphysema although it was relatively mild. I'm inclined to believe the cause of death was a bang to his head."

"No, I'm sure you're wrong."

The doctor gave Mr Wetherby a questioning look. "Are you a medical man?"

"I was with him when he fell," Mr Wetherby said. "I can assure you it wasn't a heavy fall. I got a doctor to him before I drove him back here. He was fine when I left him."

The doctor returned to the patient. "Judging by the gash on his head and the bruising to his face, I'd say the fall was particularly nasty. Mrs Tucker's told me how ill he's been while he's been here."

"You can't believe a woman like that. I tell you, when I saw him it was obvious he'd been drinking and he was struggling to breathe. In fact, he was gasping for breath when he collapsed and banged his head."

The doctor stared up at Mr Wetherby. "Are you the man who pushed him to the ground and punched him?"

"The man was deluded. I didn't touch him."

The doctor stood up straight and stared at Mr Wetherby. "It all makes sense now. If I write *trauma to the head* as the cause of death, you could be tried for murder."

"I've told you, I didn't touch him. He had the bruising to the side of his face when I saw him and the police are satisfied that the fall was an accident. Do you think you're above the law? I'll have you know, I'm a highly respectable member of society and I don't go around brawling. I also have a lot of friends in high places. Very high places, in fact. For the sake of your reputation, Doctor, I suggest you record the cause of death as emphysema. If it turns out you weren't able to detect a serious breathing condition, well ..."

"Are you threatening me?"

Mr Wetherby moved to the table and leaned across Mr Flemming's body. "Not at all, but I don't want you to make a mistake. I'm aware of how valuable a good reputation is ... and how easily it can be destroyed."

The doctor hesitated as he eyed Mr Wetherby and then turned back to Mr Flemming. "Do you know if the other doctor prescribed him laudanum after the fall?"

"Yes, he did. In fact, he gave him a dose as soon as he regained consciousness."

"I don't suppose he would have known about his breathing difficulties," the doctor muttered to himself. "The laudanum could have precipitated respiratory depression. You're right, Mr Wetherby, perhaps I should put emphysema as the cause of death."

~

Handsworth, Staffordshire.

MARY HADN'T BEEN able to speak to Mr Wetherby since he'd returned from the election, but knowing he was due home tonight had knotted her stomach to the point where she felt sick. All she could think about was Sarah-Ann, the baby she had lost, and what Mr Wetherby had known about it. She had just sat down by the fire when there was a knock on the front door. Seconds later, Emily showed Martha in.

"What's the matter?" Mary asked once they were alone. "You look as if you've seen a ghost."

Martha's eyes were moist as she took hold of Mary's hands. "Mr Flemming's dead and I think it might have been my fault. I went to see him this afternoon, to talk some sense into him, but when I challenged him about what he'd said, he got rather agitated. The next thing I knew he was dead."

"My dear Martha, the man was ill. I'm sure it wasn't your fault."

"But I think I pushed him too far when I told him to apologise." Martha wiped her eyes with a handkerchief while Mary poured two glasses of gin. She passed one to Martha.

"What did he say? Did he apologise?"

"No, he was still confused and repeated what he said last week. He clearly wanted to cause trouble for Mr Wetherby."

Mary paced the room. "Do I believe him, Martha? Could Mr Wetherby and Sarah-Ann ... you know ... could they?"

Martha shook her head. "No. I've been thinking about this. I would say that Mr Flemming only wanted to upset you so he could hurt Mr Wetherby. Mr Flemming was always jealous and he probably didn't like Sarah-Ann and Elizabeth staying here. If you overreact you'll let him win and you can't do that."

Mary let out a long sigh. "You're right. He always was jealous. It won't be easy to keep quiet though. Mr Flemming was so convincing."

"What good would it do if you did ask Mr

Wetherby?" Martha asked. "It would only make things worse here and you can't change anything."

Mary sat down on the edge of a chair. "I need to forget everything he said, don't I, and carry on as before? This might be a horrible thing to say, but I'm glad Mr Flemming's dead. He's been nothing but trouble over these last few years."

"It'll mean Sarah-Ann can go home as well, which is for the best. Where is she? We're going to have to tell her."

"She just nipped upstairs. Will you tell her, Martha? After everything that's happened, I'm struggling to have a civil conversation with her at the moment."

Chapter Twenty-Eight

Birmingham, Warwickshire
Eighteen months later.

William walked down Summer Lane with a sinking feeling in the pit of his stomach. It was approaching seven o'clock in the evening and he was due to face the Revision Court. He hadn't had the vote two years, but this was the second time the Liberals had challenged his credentials. He put his head down and frowned. *Why do they always pick on me? They never challenge William Junior.*

Mr Wetherby was waiting for him as he arrived at the house on Summer Lane.

"Right, let's get the story straight," Mr Wetherby

said as they set off. "You're a partner in the company and we're based in Frankfort Street."

"I know that."

"Well, yes, but that's what they're challenging. They don't believe you're a partner and so we need to emphasise it."

"But I am. Part of the business was given to me by Mr Watkins."

"Yes, we both know that, but we need to make sure everyone else does. Mr Barton's representing you, and I suggest you let him do the talking."

William nodded and thought back to the conversation he'd had with Harriet before he left Handsworth. "Can the partnership be made legal, so that this sort of thing doesn't happen again? We probably should have done it when we merged the businesses ..."

Mr Wetherby grunted. "The arrangement works perfectly well as it is. It would be spending money unnecessarily to involve solicitors."

"But it doesn't work well enough if they're going to challenge my right to vote every year. They haven't objected to William Junior."

"Let's get this over with and see what they have to say. I've no idea what goes on in the heads of those Liberals."

William sat in the court alongside Mr Wetherby

for over two hours, listening to other defendants, before his case was called. His hearing only lasted for five minutes before the barrister adjourned the case overnight, pending further details.

Mr Wetherby put his head in his hands before he leaned over to William. "What an idiot that fellow is. I'd swear they just want to waste our time. Come on; let's go. We have to be back here by ten o'clock tomorrow morning."

By the time William and Mr Wetherby returned, the Liberals had withdrawn their previous objections.

"How much time have we wasted this morning only for him to change his mind?" Mr Wetherby said as he stormed from the court building. "I told you he was being bloody-minded. He had no more reason to object than I did. Anyway, congratulations, at least you still have the vote."

"Thank you, but I'd still like to make it official. I'd rather not have to go through this again."

Mr Wetherby snorted. "After this morning's performance, they won't dare try it again. I'll make sure of that."

～

Handsworth, Staffordshire.

HARRIET WAS PREPARING the table for tea when William arrived back in Handsworth.

"How did it go?" she asked. "Am I still married to one of the chosen few?"

William frowned at her. "I was approved, but not without a struggle, if that's what you mean."

"Thank goodness they saw sense. I hope Mr Wetherby realises he needs to make the partnership official now."

William studied his feet. "I mentioned it to him, and I think he'll do it."

"Well, don't let him forget."

"I won't, but enough of Mr Wetherby. What have you been up to?"

"Nothing exciting. I do have something to tell you." A frown spread across Harriet's face.

"You're not in the family way again, are you?"

"No, nothing like that ... it's your mother."

"What about her?" Concern spread across William's face as he put down the newspaper he had just picked up.

"I went to visit her with Mary-Ann this afternoon and we're worried about her."

"Why?"

Harriet stopped what she was doing. "Over the last couple of months, she's often been in bed when we've arrived. She says she likes to take a nap so that she has enough energy for when Mr Wetherby gets home. I spoke to Emily as we were leaving and apparently she goes to bed for about two hours every afternoon. I haven't asked if she's seen Dr Hopkins. Do you think I should?"

"Does she look ill?"

"Not really, maybe a little tired. She doesn't have the energy she used to and she isn't baking any more."

"That's not like her; she's baked since I was a child. Could it be that since they got a cook she doesn't need to do it herself?"

Harriet shrugged. "It could be, but I do wonder if you should say something to Mr Wetherby. I doubt he'll have noticed. By the time he gets home, she's up again and in her best clothes."

"He's gone back to his old ways of staying in Birmingham again. I do wish he wouldn't leave her as often as he does."

"She's rarely on her own. For one, Mary-Ann and I go round there at least three times a week, and she still manages to go and visit Aunt Martha once a week. Charlotte's there too. I know you think of her as your baby sister, but she's finished school now and has turned into a beautiful young woman. She isn't a child any more."

A bemused expression settled on William's face. "Perhaps you should speak to her then. She'll have noticed if something's wrong."

Chapter Twenty-Nine

Charlotte was reading in the back room of Wetherby House when she heard Emily answer the door to Harriet and Mary-Ann. She was confused a minute later when they were shown in to see her.

"Mother's upstairs," she said to Emily as she glanced up from her book.

"We've come to see you," Mary-Ann said. "I hope we're not disturbing you."

"No, not at all. Take a seat." Charlotte took Florence from Harriet. "I don't see you or the children often enough. I can't believe Florence is the only one who hasn't started school."

"You wait until it's your turn," Harriet said. "You'll be glad of the peace by the time they're at school."

The blue of Charlotte's eyes glistened as she smiled. "I won't mind. I'm looking forward to it, although I've a few years to wait yet."

"Well don't be too eager, that's all I can say." Harriet laughed.

"Can we speak to you for a moment about Mother?" Mary-Ann said.

"Mother? Yes, of course."

"We're worried about her health and wondered if you'd noticed anything."

Charlotte let Florence down onto the floor and put her hands on her lap. "She does spend a lot of time in bed in the afternoons. She does her chores in the morning, such as they are, and she's always immaculately dressed when Father gets home, but the time in the middle, well, I have to confess I've wondered myself. It does seem to have got worse."

"Has she seen the doctor?" Mary-Ann asked.

"I tried to speak to her about it last week, but she wouldn't let me call anyone. She says it's her age. Papa would have Dr Hopkins here in the blink of an eye if he knew, but ..."

"Why haven't you told him?" The pitch of Mary-Ann's voice sounded harsh. "If she's ill, she needs to see someone."

Charlotte shifted in her seat. "She asked me not

to say anything. She said there's nothing the matter and I'm not to upset him. He's busy at the moment too ..."

"But it's for her own good." Mary-Ann stood up. "I'm going to give her a right talking-to."

"Is that all you wanted?" Charlotte asked.

Mary-Ann was about to answer when Harriet interrupted. "Can I look at your books? You have quite a collection there."

Charlotte smiled. "Of course you can, although this is only a small selection. I've got more in my bedroom."

Harriet picked up the book lying beside Charlotte. "What's this you're reading? It's beautiful with its leather cover."

"It's quite good. Father bought it for me last week, *Lord Brackenbury* by Amelia Edwards. I'm only on the first volume but it's quite exciting."

Harriet flicked through the pages. "You're so lucky having a father who buys you books."

"He's always encouraged me, but since I finished school, he buys me at least one a week. He likes to think it keeps me occupied if I'm on my own."

A cloud momentarily crossed Harriet's eyes. "Did you know my uncle tried to ban me from reading?"

Charlotte's eyes widened. "Why on earth would he do that?"

Harriet recounted her life with her aunt and uncle, stopping short of her time in the asylum at Winson Green.

"That must have been horrible," Charlotte said. "I wondered why you didn't see much of them, but now I don't blame you. William lets you read, doesn't he?"

"He does, but it's only magazines. I used to go to the library in Birmingham before the fire, but the makeshift one isn't well-stocked and I don't often buy books. Nothing like this at any rate."

"I never went to the Central Library. We had books in the library at school and Father's bought me a lot over the years. You can borrow them if you like."

"That would be wonderful." Harriet's eyes sparkled with delight.

"I'll tell you what," Charlotte continued. "While you go and see Mother, I'll select some for you to take home. Do you read as well, Mary-Ann?"

"I never have the time."

"Well, you can borrow some as well if you want. I can't read them all at once."

~

BY THE TIME Harriet and Mary-Ann made their way upstairs, Mary was waiting for them.

"Here you are. I thought I heard the door but when you didn't come up I thought I must have imagined it. Haven't you got Florence with you?"

"We stopped to talk to Charlotte and she's happy to entertain her," Harriet said.

"Mother, we're worried about you," Mary-Ann interrupted. "Are you all right?"

"Yes, I'm fine, why do you ask?"

"Well, it isn't usual for people to spend the afternoon in bed, not unless they're ill."

"That's where you're wrong," Mary answered. "I read in a magazine that the aristocracy do exactly that to prepare themselves for going out in the evening."

Mary-Ann's face fell into a scowl. "Mother, in case you haven't noticed you are not a member of the aristocracy and you never go out of an evening."

Mary straightened her shoulders to adjust her shawl. "Don't be insolent. What I mean is, if they can do it, so can I."

"But since when have folk like us gone to bed for the afternoon?"

"Mrs Wetherby, we're worried about you," Harriet said. "This has been going on for a number of months now and you're not getting any better. Have you seen a doctor?"

"Harriet dear, I don't need a doctor. I'll be fine. I'm not as young as I used to be and I need to take things more slowly. Now, can we change the subject and will one of you pour the gin?"

When they arrived back downstairs, they found Charlotte in the back room, with Florence on her knee, surrounded by books.

"My goodness." Harriet's eyes were wide. "I don't know where to start. Have you read all of these?"

"Most of them. There were a couple I didn't finish, but I don't usually do that. Do you like Charles Dickens?"

"I've only read one serialisation in a magazine, but yes, I enjoyed it."

"I have most of his. Why don't you start with them? Father managed to get this little novella signed the last time Dickens was in Birmingham." She opened the cover of *A Christmas Carol*.

Harriet ran her fingers over the covers of the books, caressing each as if it were a precious stone. "Thank you so much. Would you mind if I took a couple of the children's books for Eleanor? Since she finished school she hasn't had much to read."

"Yes, of course, but why doesn't she go to school any more? She's only eleven, isn't she?"

"Hopefully she'll go again one day; but it's not that easy. We have the other children to think of."

A puzzled expression crossed Charlotte's face before she smiled. "You must bring her with you next time you come, so she can choose some books for herself."

Chapter Thirty

Birmingham, Warwickshire

Mrs Storey stood by the fire stirring a pot of soup when William arrived back in Frankfort Street. It had been raining heavily all day and he shook his umbrella vigorously before he came in, almost soaking Mrs Storey's son, Sidney, who was following him.

"What a terrible night to have to go out again," he said, warming himself in front of the fire. "That smells good though."

"A bit of oxtail. I thought it would be tasty enough. Do you have to go out? It's not fit."

"I'm afraid Mr Wetherby's expecting me. There's a public meeting to choose the new candidate for the municipal elections. Mr Wetherby's nominated someone and he wants to make sure his candidate gets the nod. I think he sees him as being his new mouthpiece on the council."

Mrs Storey carried the pot to the table. "Where does my brother get his energy from? How he runs his own business, works for all those other companies, and then spends most evenings at the Conservative Association, I do not know. Not that I should complain, at least he's given Sidney and Samuel jobs."

William took his seat at the table next to Sidney. "Yes, and they're doing well too. You're doing all right with me, aren't you, Sid?"

"Not bad," Sidney said through a mouthful of bread.

"Sidney, please," his mother said. "Have I taught you no manners? Do not speak with your mouth full and go and wash your hands. You should have done them before you sat down"

"He asked me a question," Sidney replied, once his mouth was clear.

"And no lip," his mother replied, "or you'll be sent upstairs without finishing that."

"I'm sorry, it was my fault," William said as Sidney left the table. "He's a good lad. It's a shame I don't know Sam so well. With me being in Birmingham more than Handsworth at the moment, it's not easy."

"Sam doesn't like William Junior," Sidney said as he came back to the table. "He's always telling him what to do and doesn't give him any help."

William allowed a small smile to form on his lips. "No surprise there. William Junior believes he was born to be a gentleman. He won't do any work unless he has to."

"I'm surprised he gets away with it, with Mr Wetherby as he is."

"I think it's because Mr Wetherby does so much that William Junior manages to get out of everything. I just keep my head down and let them get on with it."

As soon as tea was over, William donned his wet overcoat and once again picked up his umbrella before he headed off to Summer Lane. Mr Wetherby was waiting for him and they wasted no time getting to the school. Mr Wetherby opened up the building and between them they lit the candles.

"Mr Wetherby," William said, once they had finished. "I hope you don't mind me mentioning this tonight, but I haven't seen much of you lately and I wanted a word with you about Mother."

Mr Wetherby put down the papers he was

studying and gave William his attention. "What about her?"

"We're becoming increasingly concerned about her health."

"She seems well enough to me; what is there to worry about?"

"Nothing specific, but she's taken to going to bed most afternoons for a lie-down. At first nobody thought anything of it, but now, if Harriet and Mary-Ann don't visit, she sleeps for most of the afternoon. Even Charlotte's worried."

"Charlotte's concerned? Why hasn't she said anything to me?"

William shrugged. "I don't suppose she sees much of you, and Mother told her not to."

"That's not good enough." Mr Wetherby slammed his hand on the table, scattering some of the papers. "If she felt she couldn't tell me, why didn't you mention it sooner?"

"As I said, nobody thought anything of it to start with; Mother had been reading about the aristocracy and decided it was quite usual to have a lie-down in the afternoon. No one questioned her, from what I understand. It's only more recently that she's started sleeping for longer. When I was at home yesterday, Harriet told me there was one day last week when

Mother didn't wake up despite her and Mary-Ann being there."

Mr Wetherby gathered up the papers as the members started to arrive. "Right, that's it. She's always been stubborn when it comes to doctors but I'll send Dr Hopkins a telegram tomorrow and insist he calls."

Chapter Thirty-One

Handsworth, Staffordshire

For her midday meal Mary had managed to eat a slice of cake, washed down with some gin and a cup of tea. Even with the extra spoonful of sugar in the tea, however, it hadn't perked her up. It was only quarter past one, but she needed to go for a lie-down. It would be another hour before Mary-Ann and Harriet arrived and so if she were quick ...

As she eased herself up from the chair, there was a knock at the front door and her heart sank. *They can't be this early.* She straightened herself up, expecting Mary-Ann to come barging into the back room, but instead Emily knocked and let herself in.

"Mrs Wetherby, Dr Hopkins is here to see you. He said Mr Wetherby sent him a telegram asking him to call."

Mary sat back down and put her head in her hands. "Who's been talking to him? I knew this would happen. Can't we tell him there's nothing wrong with me?"

"I don't think he's going to leave, not until you've shown him there's nothing wrong."

Mary sighed. "You're right. If he's had a telegram from Mr Wetherby, he's not going to take no for an answer from me. You'd better bring him in."

Emily showed the doctor into the back room and closed the door behind her as she left.

Mary sat up straight. "I'm sorry this'll be a wasted journey for you, Doctor. I've no idea why my husband wrote to you. I'm fine."

"Let me be the judge of that, Mrs Wetherby, you do look rather tired. I need to examine you."

Mary was about to protest, but changed her mind when she saw the look on his face. "If you insist, but I suggest we go upstairs where it'll be more private."

Mary climbed the stairs slowly and clung to the handrail as she paused on the landing to catch her breath.

"Let me help you." Dr Hopkins took her arm.

"No, I'm fine, thank you." Mary moved ahead again, but turned her back on the doctor as she positioned herself on the bed, hiding her discomfort.

Once she was settled, the doctor placed the flat of his hands across her abdomen. "I'm going to feel your stomach, it shouldn't hurt." He first moved his hands to the left, but as he approached the ribs on her right-hand side, Mary let out a yelp.

"I take it that hurt." Dr Hopkins studied her face.

"Not much," Mary said, angry with herself for shouting out.

He continued to feel around her right-hand side, more gently than before, but despite her best efforts Mary couldn't hide her discomfort.

"Have you noticed this pain before?" The doctor moved his hands to her neck, where he felt for her pulse.

"I've had it on and off for a few months, but I'm sure it's indigestion. I've only just eaten."

"If you've been aware of it for some time why didn't you come and see me?"

Mary averted her gaze from the doctor's searching eyes. "I've told you."

"No, you made an excuse. You don't think it's indigestion any more than I do."

Mary could feel the tears forming in her eyes. "I

don't want to be ill and I worry about what you'll say."

"Has it ever occurred to you that I could make you better? Judging by your symptoms, I'd say you have an inflamed liver. Unfortunately, I can't feel the liver properly due to the swelling of your abdomen."

Mary wiped her eyes. "We hired a new cook this year and she's always baking. I'm eating better now than I've ever done; plenty of meat and cheese, and she makes marvellous cakes."

"I don't think the swelling's because you're eating too much, but I wonder if you should abstain from alcohol for a short period to cleanse your system."

"What would I drink if I can't have gin? The water's undrinkable unless it's made into sweet tea."

"Many folks take cleansing periods two or three times a year and they manage to survive on cups of tea. I've also heard that imbibing too much alcohol can lead to excess bile production. This may affect the liver and so I'd suggest you cut down. I'll write and tell Mr Wetherby and I'll call back to see you next week. In the meantime, please promise that you'll tell me if you feel any worse."

Once he had gone, Mary reached for the gin bottle and poured herself a large measure. She didn't drink that much, but if she did, what harm would it do her? It was safer than water. Dr Hopkins didn't know what he was talking about. She settled back in her chair and was about to take a sip when a thought hit her. If Dr Hopkins told Mr Wetherby that she needed to cut down on the gin, he'd remove it from the cupboards. She couldn't let that happen. Knowing where the bottles were stored, she hurried to move them to the kitchen. He wouldn't find them in there. As an afterthought, she left a couple in the dining room to avoid arousing suspicion. The doctor had only told her to cut back, he hadn't told her to stop drinking it altogether.

As soon as Mr Wetherby heard the doctor's diagnosis he returned to Handsworth. Without waiting to check whether Mary had any visitors, he marched straight into the back room.

"Why didn't you tell me you weren't feeling well? I received a telegram from Dr Hopkins and I've just been to see him. I shouldn't have to find out about something so important from other people."

Mary's eyes pleaded with him. "Please don't be angry with me. You've been busy and I didn't want to concern you."

Mr Wetherby studied the lines he had failed to

notice appearing on her face. Her eyes were still the purest blue, but somehow she seemed different. How long had he been putting the business before her? "Mary dear, no matter how busy I am, you're my first priority. Don't you realise that after all these years? Now, I want all the gin removed from the house."

Mary's eyes widened. "You can't do that. What will I drink? The doctor only mentioned a short cleansing period. Nothing permanent."

"It's for your own good; I want you well again. Now, where's Charlotte? I need to speak to her."

Mr Wetherby found Charlotte in the front room by the piano.

"Papa!" She jumped up to hug him. "I didn't hear you come home. Have you no meetings tonight?"

"I did have, but I heard about your mother and came home to see her."

"Oh." Charlotte returned to the piano.

"Why didn't you tell me? I didn't think we had secrets."

"I wasn't sure she was ill and then you were never here. She asked me not to say anything ... it's hard to be disloyal to someone when you live with them every day."

"My dear girl, I'm sorry you had to deal with this on your own." He put his hand on her shoulder. "I should have been here more often. I've let work and politics get in the way of the two most important people in my life ... again."

"It's not your fault, you need to run the business and I know William Junior isn't much help. I wish I could help you."

"I wouldn't dream of letting you work, but you can help by being here for your mother. I'll come home as often as I can, but I want you to write and tell me how she is. Will you do that?"

The blue of Charlotte's eyes twinkled as she smiled. "Of course I will."

Chapter Thirty-Two

Mary smiled as the rays of the sun from the clear blue sky filled the room. It had been a long, cold winter but it was wonderful to feel the warmth on her hands and face. *How lovely it would be to go out for a walk.* If only she could walk anywhere without assistance. Instead, she sat in a chair between the window and the bed, looking out over the houses opposite. Her energy levels had deteriorated and her joints hurt constantly. She stared at her swollen stomach. How had it come to this? It was little more than six months ago that Dr Hopkins had worried about the pain in her liver, but now she feared the end was coming.

She picked up the glass of lemonade Charlotte had left for her and took a sip. The last of the gin had long gone, and although she felt no better for its absence, Mr Wetherby refused to buy any more. As she put the glass down and rested her head on the chair, she heard the now familiar knock on the front door. It would be Mary-Ann and Harriet. They visited most afternoons and she was glad of the company.

"I can't stay too long today," Harriet said. "Eleanor has tonsillitis. Her throat's red raw and she's very warm. I had the doctor to her this morning."

Mary smiled. "Poor thing. I hope she's back at school soon."

A frown settled on Harriet's face as she studied her mother-in-law.

"Don't you remember? She hasn't been to school since she was ten. There isn't anywhere local to send her."

Mary put her hand to her forehead. "Of course, I'm sorry. I do get confused at the moment. William-Wetherby went to school though, didn't he?"

"Yes, he's at King Edward's."

"The school Charlotte went to was excellent. Why doesn't Eleanor go there?"

Harriet sighed. "Our girls can't be treated the same way as Charlotte."

"Why not?" Mary looked bewildered.

"Mother, we can't do everything for our children the way you do for Charlotte," Mary-Ann said. "Mr

Wetherby has enough money to give Charlotte whatever she wants. We have to be a little more restrained."

"He gave you and William a lot when you were younger, don't forget that," Mary said. "He gave us a home and security ... and he sent you to school. Besides, you have Mr Diver. Don't resent Charlotte when it isn't her fault."

"I don't resent her."

"Well, stop sounding like you do."

Mary-Ann stared at her mother and was about to answer when Harriet interrupted.

"To her credit, Charlotte is generous. She lends Eleanor and I books whenever we like, and I've seen in the paper that she gives money to charity too. I just wish I'd had the chances she has."

"There's no reason why Eleanor can't do what Charlotte did."

"Unfortunately, we can't justify the money to send her to school. Not at the moment."

Mary studied at her daughter-in-law. "I know you'd like William to have more say in the running of the business, but the truth is that Mr Wetherby's always going to be in charge. Can you think of anything he does where he doesn't take full control? It's just the way he is ... and William isn't."

"I know. I want William to start his own business, but he's reluctant and doesn't listen when I tell him to be more assertive with Mr Wetherby."

"You should realise that won't work, but be honest, do you really want him to change? Could you, of all people, live with someone like Mr Wetherby?"

Harriet's eyes flashed wide open. "Good grief, no."

"Well, perhaps you should be thankful for what you've got and not go looking for things that might not turn out as you expect."

Chapter Thirty-Three

Birmingham, Warwickshire

William took a final glance around the workshop before he stepped outside to lock up. It was the fifth day this week he had been in Birmingham, and all he wanted to do was go home to Handsworth. Sidney stood to one side as William put the key in his pocket and they set off down Frankfort Street.

"Don't look so down," Sidney said. "It's Saturday tomorrow. Only one more day to go."

William smiled. "Is it that obvious?"

"You've been quiet all day, but I suppose Birmingham does that to you when you're used to being in Handsworth."

"If only that was all it was," William said. "I'm worried about Mother. I had a letter from Harriet this morning telling me that she was no better. I should be with her. Mr Wetherby doesn't give her enough attention."

"I thought the reason you were here was because Mr Wetherby was in Handsworth taking care of her? Sam said last week that he hadn't seen Mr Wetherby in the Handsworth workshop."

"He has so much going on, he could be any-where, but you're right. At least he is with her. I just wish there were something he could do to help."

"He's got enough money. If there was anything, I'm sure he'd pay for it." Sidney paused, but when William failed to answer he continued. "What do you think he'll do with his money when he dies? Will he leave half the business to you and half to William Junior?"

William glared at Sidney. "I hope you haven't asked that because you think Mother's about to die."

"No, of course not. It hadn't entered my head. I'm sorry. It was just something Sam said on Sunday when he was home."

"What did he say?"

"Nothing much ... but I don't think William Junior teaches him as much as you teach me. We've both been apprenticed for three years so far, but he's a long way behind me with what he knows. It's not because he's less able either. I was thinking that if Mr Wetherby leaves everything to William Junior, the business'll end up in a right mess."

"What makes you think I can run a business any better than William Junior?"

"The way you've been with me for a start and the way you are with other people. I've watched the other men at work when you're in charge. They work for you without you having to bully them. William Junior's not like that. He spends the whole time shouting at everyone, whether they deserve it or not."

"I've no idea what Mr Wetherby'll do, but it wouldn't surprise me if everything goes to William Junior. He is his only son after all."

"Doesn't that bother you?"

William shrugged. "There's no point getting upset about something you can't change. Now, can we change the subject? And no more talk of death."

Handsworth, Staffordshire.

WHEN WILLIAM ARRIVED BACK in Handsworth on Saturday evening, the younger children were in bed and Eleanor was sitting outside the front door, reading.

"I believe you've not been well," William said as he went to open the door.

"No, but I'm fine now, just a bit of a sore throat left. You'd better go in. Mother wants to talk to you."

William went to find his wife and put his arms around her. "I've missed you. I wish I didn't have to stay in Birmingham for so long."

Harriet pulled away and continued to lift food out of the pantry for tea. "You need to visit your mother tomorrow. She asked for you and I said I'd pass the message on." Harriet paused. "She's not looking well. She won't talk about it, but you can tell she's in pain."

William sat down and rested his head on the back of the chair. "When did you last see her?"

"Yesterday, but she slept for over an hour while we were there. Even talking exhausts her. At least she has Emily and Cook to take care of her."

"She needs more than the domestic helps. The doctor should be calling every day. And what about Mr Wetherby? Isn't he there?"

"He is sometimes."

"What do you mean *sometimes*?" William was on his feet. "I'm practically living in Birmingham so that he can be with Mother. Are you telling me he isn't?"

"He's never around when I visit with Mary-Ann,

but I suppose it's a good time for him to do things he needs to do."

"He should wait until you're there, at least. What's he doing that's so important?"

Harriet's eyes bulged. "Do you think he'd tell me? The only thing I know is that he's still furious about the new school board for Handsworth and the plan to remove the influence of the Church from education. It's as if he's trying to get the decision reversed single-handedly."

"Can't he leave anything alone, even at a time like this? He needs to concentrate on getting Mother better."

"William." Harriet took his hand and held it between hers. "This might not be the best time to ask, but don't you think you should be running your own company ... so that you're not dependent on Mr Wetherby?"

"Where's this come from?"

Harriet took a deep breath. "If you remember we spoke about it ... when we were in the old house. Just in case."

"Just in case what?" William glared at her.

"In case anything happens to your mother ... remember?"

"Nothing's going to happen to her. I'll have a

word with Mr Wetherby tomorrow and make sure he gets her seen by the best doctor there is."

WILLIAM WAITED until they had been to church and eaten dinner before he picked up his hat and paid a visit to Wetherby House. He had only seen his mother the previous week, and was confident that Harriet was exaggerating about her decline. When he walked into the bedroom, however, he couldn't keep the shock from his face.

"Mother, what's happened to you? You look terrible."

"You say the nicest things." Mary forced herself to smile. "You look your usual handsome self. How are you?"

William hurried to her side and sat down. "Stop pretending everything's all right when it isn't. How long have you been like this?"

"I'm not that bad. I thought I was having a good day today."

William took hold of her hand. "There's no shame in being ill, it happens to everyone. We just want you well again."

Mary bowed her head before she produced a handkerchief to wipe her eyes. "I don't want to talk about it ... but I'm not going to get well again."

"Nonsense. When did you last see the doctor?"

"Dr Hopkins told Mr Wetherby there's nothing more he can do for me. My liver isn't working any more, and my body's poisoning itself."

William's tone became severe. "I've never had much confidence in him. You need to see another doctor. Someone who knows what he's talking about."

"He's doing his best."

"But it isn't enough. There must be something they can do. You mean the world to all of us and I'm not going to sit by and watch you get worse."

"You'll be fine." Mary squeezed his hand. "You have Harriet and the children and I'll make sure Mr Wetherby's always there for you."

"Do you think that's enough? It's not. I want *you* to be always here for me. We're going to make you well again."

IT WAS over an hour later before William went downstairs in search of for Mr Wetherby. He found him dozing in the back room.

"She's sleeping now," William said when Mr Wetherby opened his eyes. "I'm not happy though. She's got worse this week."

"She has. She's lost a lot of weight and she's getting weaker by the day."

"Will you find another doctor to see her? I don't believe Dr Hopkins is up to the job."

Mr Wetherby stood up. "I already have as it happens. I haven't told her yet, but I'm taking her to the hospital in Birmingham tomorrow. They have someone there who knows more about livers than most. Hopefully he'll have something for her."

William nodded. "Good and not before time."

"Don't come in here telling me what to do. I've loved your mother for as long as I've known her and I don't intend to stop now. I'll do everything in my power to make her well again."

"I'm sorry, I didn't mean to suggest ... it was such a shock to see her as she is."

"I know, but you'll have to trust me. I'll do everything I can."

Chapter Thirty-Four

Birmingham, Warwickshire

M ary opened her eyes to find herself in a strange bed surrounded by three men in formal black jackets. A woman, also dressed in black, stood at the foot of the bed. They seemed to be talking about her, but she had no idea who they were or what they were saying. She turned her head from side to side, and noted she was in a room on her own. *Where am I? Why aren't I at home?*

The doctor closest to her spoke when he saw her move. "Mrs Wetherby, welcome to the hospital."

Mary's eyes were wide as he spoke and she pressed herself into the bed.

"There's no need to be alarmed. My colleagues and I are discussing the best treatment for you. Your husband asked us to do everything possible but before we do that, we need to have a quick look at you." He pulled down the bedcovers and laid his hands on her stomach.

"Ouch!" Mary went rigid at his touch.

"Hmm." The doctor turned to his colleagues. "I put very little pressure on her. It shouldn't have hurt like that."

"It's unlikely she can tolerate much pain," the younger man to her left said.

"Her stomach is extremely distended," the third doctor said. "Should we operate?"

"No. I think not," the first doctor said. "I'd like to try something different on her. A new type of cure I came across in France. We'll need to discuss it ... but perhaps not here."

He pulled the bedcovers back over Mary's torso."

"Let her sleep," the second doctor said. "Nurse, can you give Mrs Wetherby some laudanum and make sure she has everything she needs? We'll be back tomorrow."

～

WILLIAM WAS SUPERVISING Sidney on a new piece of equipment when Mr Wetherby walked into the workshop.

"Mr Wetherby." William left Sidney and escorted Mr Wetherby into the office. "I wasn't expecting you here today. Is everything all right?"

"I hope so. I took your mother to hospital yesterday and they're keeping her in for a few days."

"Can they do anything for her?"

"They didn't say, but I told them to do everything they could. I wasn't doing anything useful at home and so I thought I might as well come here. I need to go to the Conservative Association as well, I haven't been for weeks."

"Did they say when she'd be out?"

"No, but hopefully this week. She hasn't been sleeping well recently and so they gave her a sedative and said they'd start their assessments today."

MARY HAD LAIN in bed for three days but today, as she was expecting the doctor to visit, the nurse came and sat her up in bed.

"The doctor has something for you. You need to be ready," she said. "And don't forget to thank him. He's gone to a lot of trouble to get it."

Mary nodded but said nothing. *What has Mr Wetherby done to make them all so obliging?*

Minutes later the doctor arrived and without any of the usual examinations, he handed her a cup and proceeded to pour a ruby liquid into it.

"Port?" Mary asked, a puzzled expression covering her face.

"After a fashion," the doctor said. "Coca wine. I've seen miraculous results in patients treated with it. I think it'll work wonders on you."

Mary took a sip and smiled as she felt it pass into her stomach. "It doesn't taste like medicine. It tastes wonderful."

The doctor watched as she took another sip. "I'm glad you approve. If you respond to the treatment, I'll need to order some more as soon as possible. It's not easy to come by."

By the following day Mary felt like a different woman. After only three cups of the wine, her energy had returned and the pains in her joints disappeared. The doctor smiled as he led his two colleagues to her bedside.

"What did I say?" he said to anyone who was listening. "I knew it would do the trick. Just look at her. The wine's done you the world of good, Mrs Wetherby. I imagine you're keen to have some more, but before that, we do need to examine you. I hope the pain in your stomach's disappeared."

"It has, Doctor, and I'm eternally grateful. It's as if my prayers have been answered and I've been renewed."

The doctor smiled. "We need to get you walking again. We have some more of the wine ordered and all being well we should be able to let you go home in the next couple of days."

Mary returned his smile. "Mr Wetherby will be pleased."

Once the doctors left her, the nurse came to plump up the pillows behind her back.

"There you are, Mrs Wetherby. Is there anything I can get you?"

Mary thought for a moment. "Not as such, but I wonder ... if I write a letter, would you be able to post it for me? It's rather important ..."

The nurse smiled. "We should be able to manage that. I'll find you some writing paper. The postman calls at around five o'clock."

MARY DRAINED the last of the wine from her cup and put it back on the table. It was better than having her gin back. She picked up the magazine that Charlotte had brought her the previous day and settled back into the pillows. She was still finding her place in the article when there was a knock on the door and Richard walked in.

"You came." Mary's eyes sparkled as she smiled and put the magazine down.

Richard bent over and kissed her cheek. "I did, but what's been happening to you? I've seen more of Martha this last year than I ever have before. She told me how ill you've been but it's been terrible not seeing you."

"I don't know what happened. It started with me feeling a little tired and before I knew it I couldn't get out of bed."

"Well, you look wonderful now, you must have needed to spend some time away from Mr Wetherby." A grin spread across Richard's face.

"It was the gin I needed. The doctor at home thought it might be a problem, but while I've been in here they've given me some wine that's made a tremendous difference. They think I can go home tomorrow, which is why I wrote. I hope you don't mind. Did Mrs Richard see the letter?"

"I'd spoken to the postman months ago and asked him only to give my letters to me ... just in case you wrote. I'm sorry I didn't tell you, but I had no way of contacting you. As soon as I saw your hand-writing though, I knew it had been worth it. Now that you're back to your usual self, will you be able to start coming to Birmingham again?"

Mary's shoulders slumped. "The way he's been these last few days, I don't think he's going to let me out of his sight. That's why I had to write. I thought it might be the only chance I had to see you before ... you know ... I wasn't here."

Richard took her hands. "You mustn't talk like that. Once you're home and up and about again, he'll be back to his old ways. You mark my words. As soon as you find out he's going to Birmingham, write and tell me. I'll pretend I'm the coalman again."

Mary laughed. "Make sure you're not covered in too much coal dust. I had to wash my dress before Mr Wetherby saw it last time you tried that."

"I've missed that smile and those beautiful eyes," Richard said. "You get better soon. I don't want it to be another year before I see you again."

Chapter Thirty-Five

Two days later, Mary walked from the hospital with her head held high. Mr Wetherby escorted her to the carriage and settled her in before he stored the bottles of wine she needed under the seat facing them. It was a slow journey home, with the driver trying to avoid the bigger potholes, and as soon as she arrived, Cook put some water over the range to boil. Mary hadn't finished her first cup of tea before William and Harriet came to visit her.

"Mother, how wonderful to see you so well," William said as they went in. "You have colour back in your checks and your eyes are smiling again. What wonderful news Mr Wetherby's been giving me. Do they expect you to make a full recovery?"

"They don't know whether my liver will recover, but this new wine and coca mixture has taken away all the pain. They say it works like morphine, but because it doesn't have any harmful effects I should be able to stay on it indefinitely."

"I thought you had to stay off alcohol."

"That's what Dr Hopkins said, but it goes to show what he knows. If he hadn't stopped my gin I might never have been so ill."

"You wouldn't have got that tonic from Dr Hopkins," Mr Wetherby said. "We were fortunate the hospital could get some from London when they did. The bottles we brought home came from Paris. but they were well worth the money."

Mary smiled. "I wondered why they were treating me so well in the hospital. Did you give them a donation?"

"Of course I did. I wanted the best for you and I wanted you home. You get what you pay for."

That night, Mary slept soundly and the following morning she got herself up and dressed and found Mr Wetherby sitting in the back room reading the newspaper.

"What are you doing in here?" she asked. "I thought you'd be at work."

"And leave you on your own? Don't be ridiculous. I want to make sure this recovery lasts."

"It's a beautiful day outside," Mary said once she'd eaten a slice of bread. "Do you think we could walk round to visit Mary-Ann and Harriet this afternoon?"

"I don't think so, you haven't walked that far for months."

"Please, it would make me feel so much better. You could come back for the carriage and collect me if I can't manage. I'm sure that sitting here all day isn't helping."

Mr Wetherby thought for a moment. "I'll tell the driver to follow us in the carriage, in case you tire on the way. That would make me feel happier."

Mary nodded. "Before we go, can we talk? I did a lot of thinking when I was in hospital. I thought for the first few days that I wouldn't come home again, and it worried me."

Mr Wetherby took hold of her hand. "Please don't worry. I'd move heaven and earth for you. I'm not going to give up on you that easily."

Mary smiled. "It wasn't me I was worried about, it was William and Mary-Ann. You will still watch out for them if anything happens to me, won't you?"

"Why wouldn't I?"

"I worry that you don't think as much of them as you do William Junior and Charlotte."

"Haven't I brought them up as my own since they were small children?"

"Yes, of course, but I need you to promise you won't forget about them, William especially. He looks up to you as a father and still needs your support."

Mr Wetherby frowned. "He's a grown man."

"I know, but ..." Mary gripped Mr Wetherby's hand as her eyes pleaded with him. "I worry because William Junior acts as if he's your sole heir. He'll push William out if he can."

"I can deal with him."

"But you weren't going to help him buy his house at one point. That upset me."

"That was a misunderstanding and we sorted it out. Now stop worrying. William works for me and I'm not likely to change that."

"Will you treat him more like a partner though? It is partly his business after all."

Mr Wetherby patted her hand. "If it makes you happy I'll see to it as soon as I can, but you have to stop thinking like that. Nothing's going to happen to you. Now, not another word."

Chapter Thirty-Six

Handsworth, Staffordshire

Mary sat in the chair between the bed and the window, looking out over the street below. Harriet and Mary-Ann had just left and she watched them hurrying down the road to get to school in time to pick up the children. She wiped away a tear that rolled down her cheek before she poured herself another glass of wine. *Stupid wine. Why have you stopped working? Why am I sat here on my own ... again?* She studied the bottle. It was nearly empty and she'd only opened it yesterday. Mr Wetherby couldn't keep up with the rate she was going through it. After emptying the cup, she rested her head on the back of the chair and closed her eyes. If she drank enough to ease the pain, it made her sleepy. What a choice that was.

She was roused from her thoughts by the sound of the door closing and she opened her eyes to see Mr Wetherby walking towards her.

"How are you feeling?" His eyes were full of concern.

"I'm fine. I just hate being up here on my own. Will you sit with me?"

"Of course." Mr Wetherby pulled up the nearest chair and nodded at the bottle. "Has the pain been bad today?"

"It's fine as long as I have the wine. I just hope we don't run out. It just goes down too easily."

"Don't worry. I'll order some more. I want you well again. The doctor from the hospital's going to call again tomorrow. I didn't want you to have to go back in there again."

"You are good to me." Mary smiled before she closed her eyes again.

"Would you like me to leave you to sleep?"

"No," Mary said as she opened them again. "I was just thinking. Do you remember all those years ago when we were walking out together?"

"I do. I remember them as if they were yesterday." A frown settled on Mr Wetherby's face. "Not that they were easy times. At one point I thought you were going to leave me."

Mary nodded. "I remember. I also remember you telling me that one day I might say I love you." Her eyes searched his age-worn face, with its grey-blond hair and neatly groomed beard. "You did ... make me love you, that is ... for a time. I'm sorry I never told you. Perhaps if I had, you would have stayed away from Sarah-Ann."

Tears formed in Mr Wetherby's eyes as he squeezed her hand. "It wasn't like that ..."

"Mr Flemming told me."

Mr Wetherby put his head in his hands. "I never meant to hurt you. You were my first love and I love you still. Please don't leave me, I couldn't bear it."

"You have the children. As long as you have them, you'll always have a part of me. Don't ever forget that."

THE FOLLOWING day Mr Wetherby crept into the bedroom and pulled the curtains closed before he turned back to the bed. Mary lay still, undisturbed by the noise. He didn't think she had moved since he had last been in. He sat down by the bed and took her hand, bringing it to his lips. He'd done everything he could. There was enough wine to last her another few weeks, but even taking a few sips was becoming too much for her. How much longer would he have her?

The sound of footsteps on the stairs caused him to wipe the tears from his eyes. A few seconds later, William Junior knocked and came in.

"I thought I'd find you here," he said. "Has there been any change?"

Mr Wetherby stood up and shook his head. "Not today, she just lies there peacefully, which I suppose is a blessing."

"I've come to see if you're going to the Conservative Association dinner tonight."

"What do you think? I can't leave your mother like this."

"I wasn't aware she was permanently in bed."

No, well perhaps you should take more of an interest in your own mother. Mr Wetherby took a deep breath. "I've sent my apologies and Mr Diver's going to take the chair."

"Why did you ask him? I could've done it."

"I saw him the other day and he offered."

Mr Wetherby didn't miss the glare William Junior gave him. The sound of their voices roused Mary from her sleep.

"Is that William?" she asked turning her head towards them.

"No, William Junior," Mr Wetherby answered.

Mary's eyes flicked open. "Where's William?"

"He's in Birmingham."

"I need to see him. Will you ask him to call?"

Mr Wetherby nodded. "Of course we will. William Junior, can you mention it tonight if you see him at the dinner?"

"He won't be there, not if you don't go. He never goes anywhere by himself."

Mr Wetherby glared at his son.

"All right, if he's there, I'll tell him. I'll see you at the weekend, Mother."

Once the door closed, Mary spoke. "You won't let him cause any trouble with William, will you?"

"He'll be fine, he's just upset."

"Maybe. You will ask William to call, won't you? I have to see him again."

"Next time he's back in Handsworth I'll make sure he comes straight here."

Chapter Thirty-Seven

As his carriage reached the outskirts of Handsworth, William rubbed his eyes and sat up straight in his seat. It had been a long week and his bones ached but he knew he needed to visit his mother. The driver took him straight to Wetherby House and as the carriage came to a stop in the driveway Mr Wetherby opened the front door.

"Thank goodness you're here," he said. "She's been asking after you all week."

William climbed down from the carriage. "How is she?"

"She's slept for most of the day and so I'm hoping that she'll wake up now you're here. I must warn you before you see her that her skin's turned yellow. The doctor said it was to be expected."

"Can't they do any more? What about the wine?"

"They don't know what's happened. She's been taking more and more to ease the pain, but it sends her to sleep. They think her body must have got used to it, but they've nothing else to offer."

Mr Wetherby took William upstairs and stood by the window as William took the seat by the bed.

"It's me, Mother. Can you hear me?" When he got no response, he tried again. "I've just got back from Birmingham. It's cold out there. You're in the best place, you must be nice and warm in bed."

When there was still no response, William turned to Mr Wetherby. "Is this what she's been like?"

"It is and it's getting harder to wake her up. If you keep talking to her, she might come around. I'd say that if she doesn't wake in the next half an hour, you might as well go home and try again tomorrow. She rarely wakes up after dark."

The moon was bright as William stepped out of Wetherby House an hour later. His mother hadn't moved in the whole time he'd been there, and there had been times when he'd wondered if she was still alive. If only she would open her eyes, he could speak the words he'd rehearsed. The words he needed to tell her. If he were too late it would only make things worse. If they could be any worse.

. . .

WILLIAM WAS round at Wetherby House by nine o'clock the following morning and Mr Wetherby was waiting for him.

"Will you go to church this morning?" William asked.

"Not today. I've done all the praying I can, and I can't leave her. She was asleep when I went in ten minutes ago. You go up and see if she wakes. I'll follow you up."

As he reached the bedroom door, William took a deep breath. *Stay strong. I have to stay strong.*

The sound of the door clicking shut behind him echoed around the silent room and he stopped where he was, wondering if he might have woken her up. A moment later he saw a movement.

"Is that William?"

"Yes, Mother, I'm here."

A weak smile formed on Mary's lips as she opened her eyes. "I've wanted to talk to you so much. Hold my hand, will you?" Mary's voice was weak as she struggled for breath. "I've things I need to tell you before I go."

"Mother, be still, you don't need to talk."

Mary silenced him with her gaze. "You'll be taken care of ... Mr Wetherby's promised to share more of the business." She paused for breath. "I want you to look after Harriet ... she deserves to be happy."

"She is happy, thanks to you."

Mary ignored him and carried on. "Don't let William Junior bully you ... I know he does."

"Mother, please; don't worry about me. Save the talking until you're up to it. We need you well again."

Mary's gaze rested on him, the blue of her eyes discoloured by the yellow pigments invading her body. "It's too late, William. I love you ... your father would be so proud of you."

As she paused, William blinked back the tears stinging his eyes.

"Tell Mr Wetherby ... tell him ..." Mary closed her eyes. "Tell him ... he has my blessing to be with Sarah-Ann now."

It took a second for her words to register and William leaned forward. "What do you mean? Mother, talk to me, please."

There was no response. Mary's head rolled away from him as sleep claimed her once more. With tears now falling down his cheeks William held her hand and watched the rise and fall of the bedcovers as she struggled for each breath. What did she mean that Mr Wetherby could have Aunt Sarah-Ann now? That was gossip from Mr Flemming. How did she know about it? Mr Wetherby had said it wasn't true.

It couldn't be true. Images of Mr Wetherby with his aunt invaded his mind and he failed to notice the lengthening periods of time between each of Mary's breaths. Periods of time when the bedcovers didn't move. He was only brought back to his senses when Mary started gasping for air. It only lasted a few seconds before she fell silent.

"Mother." William shook her gently. "Wake up. Shall I call the doctor?" He leaned over and turned her face towards him. She remained still and he felt the tears on the side of her face that had fallen down onto the pillow. "Mother, please wake up. Don't go." He took hold of her hand again. "Please don't go."

Instinctively he rubbed her hand, occasionally pausing to bring it to his lips, but with each passing second, the realisation came to him. She had gone. He bowed his head over the bed, clutching her hand, making no attempt to stop the tears. Everything he had was down to her and she had never stopped caring for him. As he wiped his tears with the sleeves of his jacket, he heard Mr Wetherby come into the room.

"She's gone," he said, his voice deep and husky.

Mr Wetherby moved to the other side of the bed and gazed down on his wife. Seconds later he took her face in his hands before he leaned forward and kissed her forehead. "Goodnight, my darling. I love you." He closed his eyes momentarily before he straightened up and tidied the bedcovers over her. Seconds later, he took a deep breath and walked from the room. William was in a trance as he heard Mr Wetherby's bedroom door close and the key turn in the lock.

William wasn't sure how long he sat there before he realised Mr Wetherby wasn't coming back. That meant he was going to have to tell the rest of the family. *How do I do that? I'm not ready for this.* He let the seconds tick by before he moved to draw the curtains and stopped the clock. With one last look at his mother he ventured downstairs and found Charlotte sitting in the back room. He didn't need to say anything.

"Has she gone?" she asked as soon as she saw him. William nodded and, for the first time ever, the two of them held each other tightly. He could feel Charlotte's slender frame as her body shook in his arms, and he held her until her sobbing subsided.

"I'd better go for the doctor," William said as he pulled away. "Will you tell William Junior? Once the doctor's been, I'll have to tell Mary-Ann and Harriet."

Charlotte wiped her eyes. "What about Father, who'll tell him?"

"He knows. I don't expect you'll see much of him this evening. He went to his room."

"He'll take it badly. Everything he did, he did for her."

I T W A S over an hour later before the doctor signed the death certificate and William was free to leave. He made his way down Wellington Road with his head bowed, wondering how he would tell everyone when all he wanted to do was lock himself away.

Mary-Ann jumped up and gave him a hug as soon as she saw him. "Were you with her?"

William could only nod, but Mary-Ann needed to talk. She needed to remember the mother they had both loved and to whom they owed so much. It was only when Mr Diver arrived that William was free to go home.

By the time William opened his own front door and saw Harriet, his resolve had gone. Feeling utterly ashamed he broke down and cried like a baby.

"It's all right, let it go." Harriet held him tightly. "Violet's taken the afternoon off and the children are out. At least she's at peace now. That wine was the best thing she could have had. At least it gave her a couple of happy months when she first started taking it."

"It wasn't good enough though, was it?" William said through his sobs.

"At least she got her dying wish." Harriet wiped her own tears. "The only thing she wanted before she passed away was to see you, nobody else. Did she say anything of any significance?"

"That she loved me and I wasn't to forget it. God, I wasn't good enough for her ... I should have been there more often, talked to her when she wanted to see me, made time for her. It's too late now ... what am I going to do without her."

Chapter Thirty-Eight

Harriet stood in front of the mirror in the hall fussing over her hat while William put on his jacket and overcoat. Once she was satisfied, she remembered she needed a handkerchief and went back upstairs.

"Come on, woman, for goodness' sake, we're going to be late," William called after her.

"I'm sorry, I'm ready now." She hurried back down the stairs. "Is Mary-Ann waiting for us?"

"Not yet, I don't know what's keeping her either. It'll take us ten minutes to walk round to Wetherby House and I bet the carriages are there already. I'll go and get them."

Harriet knew William was exaggerating, but he

had been on edge for days and this was how he expressed it. It had been a long week since her mother-in-law had died, and today was going to be an ordeal. All the family were expected, the Jacksons, the Chadwicks and the Wetherbys, and Mr Wetherby had promised to give his wife the best possible send-off. Heaven knew how many horse-drawn carriages would be waiting for them outside Wetherby House.

It was a full five minutes before William came back with Mary-Ann and Mr Diver, and the four of them set off towards Wellington Road. Not unsurprisingly, in Harriet's opinion, they were the first to arrive, and Mr Wetherby and Charlotte were waiting to receive them in the front drawing room.

"Do you want to say a final farewell to her before they close the coffin?" Mr Wetherby asked. "Charlotte and I have been in this morning but you might like to pay your respects before everyone else arrives."

The body was laid out in the dining room. As they went in, William held on to Harriet before they approached the coffin. Mary was wearing her best blue dress, with matching choker, and her hair was gathered into a knot on the back of her head, the way she always wore it.

"Why was she taken so soon?" William muttered. Harriet watched as his eyes ran over his mother's face, but to her, this wasn't her mother-in-law. Her lips were a little too red and her skin too white where the undertaker had tried to mask the yellowing of her skin.

"She had a good life in the end," Harriet whispered back. "Mr Wetherby cared for her. We should be grateful to him for that."

"I just wish she'd lived to see more of it." William glanced at Mary-Ann who was lost in her own thoughts. After several minutes, Mr Diver put his arm around his wife and guided her away. William and Harriet followed to find Mr Wetherby waiting for them with a glass of sherry.

"You saw the horses?" Mr Wetherby said. "Nothing but the best for your mother. They're all jet black and they've been specially groomed. I hope I've ordered enough carriages."

"Is everyone coming here before the service or will some meet us at the church?" William asked.

"Most are coming here. I've opened a few bottles of sherry to warm people up before we leave. Actually, Charlotte, did you want to have a word with Harriet before anyone else arrives?"

"Yes, of course. Harriet, shall we go over here?"

Harriet glanced at William, before she followed Charlotte to the other side of the room.

"I wanted to warn you." Charlotte took a deep breath. "Your aunt and uncle are coming to the funeral. Your aunt was a friend of Mother's, and ... well, we couldn't not invite them. I hope you understand."

A shiver ran down Harriet's spine. "Yes, thank you, I did wonder. Have you seen them recently?"

"Father has. Do you want me to stay with you so you don't have to be alone with them?"

"That's sweet of you, thank you, but I think I need to speak to them on my own. It takes an event like this to make you realise none of us are here forever. Perhaps I should make my peace with them. It's been over ten years since we fell out."

Harriet stayed with Charlotte for several minutes before she turned to make her way back to William. As she did she saw her aunt enter the room. She hadn't changed much, although maybe her plump figure was a little rounder than it had been. It was hard to tell under the layers of fabric on her dress. She paused momentarily and took a large mouthful of sherry as her aunt walked straight over to her.

"Good morning, Harriet, it's been a long time. You're looking well."

Harriet's voice quivered as she spoke. "Thank you. How are you?"

"My breathing's getting worse, but I'm all the

better for seeing you. I hoped we'd have a chance to talk."

Harriet glanced at the door. "Are you alone?"

"No. Your uncle's coming. We've been to the coffin and he stopped to talk to someone in the hallway. He's missed you, we both have. After you moved into your own house he started to realise he'd been wrong but he was too proud to admit it."

"I'm sure we all said things that we shouldn't."

"Harriet," a deep voice spoke quietly beside her, and she turned to see her uncle. He still wore a neatly trimmed beard, although it was now more grey than brown, but his head was bald, except for a small rim of hair, just above his neckline.

"Uncle."

"You look well. That husband of yours must be taking care of you. I was sorry about Mrs Wetherby, nice lady; always had time for everyone. You used to visit her regularly, didn't you, dear?"

"Did you?" Harriet turned to her aunt. "She never mentioned it."

"It was the only way I could find out about you. She used to keep me up to date with everything, talk to me about the children."

"I didn't think you were interested."

"Of course I was interested." Mrs Watkins almost choked on her sherry. "They're like grandchildren to us."

"I suppose so."

"Are any of them here today?" Mrs Watkins glanced around the room.

"They're still too young. William-Wetherby's only fourteen."

"Of course he is. I should like to see them though. Would there be a chance?"

Harriet studied her aunt. Perhaps it wasn't her fault things had gone so wrong. "Maybe you should come to the house. I'll do afternoon tea."

"Do you mean that?" Tears welled up in her aunt's eyes. "There's nothing I'd like more. Well, maybe there is one thing."

"What's that?"

"Can I bring your uncle with me? We've not even met Charles, Margaret or Florence. Have you any idea how much that's hurt over the years?" Mrs Watkins held up her hand. "I know, before you say anything, we only have ourselves to blame, but can we start again?"

Harriet thought she was going to cry. She'd hated these people for what they'd done to her, but only because she had loved them so much. They were the only family she had and if she was being honest she had never stopped thinking of them. "Yes, of course you can, I think it's about time."

WILLIAM SAW Harriet with her aunt and uncle and was about to join them when he noticed his own Aunt Sarah-Ann enter the room. She was with her two remaining sisters, Martha and Adelaide, but she walked in behind them, her eyes scanning the room. Mr Wetherby saw her at the same time that she spotted him and they headed straight for each other. William couldn't hear what they were saying, but the way Mr Wetherby greeted her made his mother's final words come back to him. *Was Mr Flemming telling the truth? Is there really something going on?* As he watched his aunt gazing at Mr Wetherby, he took a large mouthful of sherry. If there was, he didn't want to contemplate it … ever, never mind today.

He was about to turn away when his uncle Richard walked into the room, and William noticed Mr Wetherby's stance stiffen. Aunt Sarah-Ann took his arm as if to stop him moving but he unhooked himself and went straight over to Richard.

"What are you doing here?" Mr Wetherby tried to keep his voice down, but within a moment, the whole room was staring at him.

"If you thought I'd miss paying my respects to Mary then you were sadly mistaken. I've known her for a lot longer than you and she was a special lady.

She didn't deserve to be left on her own week after week. At least she had other people she could rely on."

"Get out of my house." Mr Wetherby's face was crimson.

"I came to say my farewells and I'm glad I did." Richard gestured towards the dining room. "I needed to see her one last time."

William saw Mr Wetherby's right arm twitching by his side and hurried across the room. "Thank you for coming, Uncle Richard. Mother would have been pleased, it would have meant a lot to her."

"Thank you, you're right. It's just a shame my presence attracts such hostility." Richard glared at Mr Wetherby, forcing William to position himself between them.

"I don't know what it is between you two, but please, we're here today to pay our respects to Mother. She wouldn't want it degenerating into a brawl. Can you put your grievances to one side, for her sake at least?"

"He started it," Richard said.

"Uncle Richard, please."

Sarah-Ann stepped forward to join William and after a moment's hesitation Mr Wetherby grudgingly held out his hand to Richard.

"For Mary's sake," he said, before he gestured to the maid to bring over a tray of sherry.

"For Mary." Richard took the glass offered him and drank it in one.

"Mr Wetherby," the maid said. "The undertaker and pallbearers have arrived. I've shown them into the dining room."

"Good grief, is that the time?" Mr Wetherby took out his pocket watch. "We need to leave. Is everyone here? There's Betsy and Amelia over there, what about Mr Chadwick?"

John Chadwick and his sister Susannah were still with the coffin when William and Mr Wetherby found them. Susannah wiped her eyes with a handkerchief as she watched the lid to the coffin being fastened.

"We need to make a move," Mr Wetherby said, taking one last look at the coffin. "Will you follow me?"

Within minutes, everyone emptied their glasses and made their way to the waiting carriages. Mr Wetherby and Mary's children were in the carriage following the hearse, with the rest of the immediate family in the next two carriages. The rest of the mourners were allocated places in the remaining five. Those neighbours who weren't attending, as well as passers-by, stood to watch the spectacle. The procession made its way slowly down Wellington Road, before turning into Hamstead Road where the vicar was waiting for them outside the church gates.

Chapter Thirty-Nine

The funeral was a full communion service and once it was over, the men and several of the younger women followed the coffin up the hill to the grave where Alice, Mary's sister, had previously been laid to rest. Despite her pleading, Mr Wetherby had refused to allow Charlotte to attend the burial and she stood by the side of the church watching the committal from a distance.

"You must come and visit us if you're lonely in that big house," Harriet said as she and Mary-Ann joined her.

Charlotte gave a small smile. "Thank you, I may well do that. I suspect I won't be seeing much of Father after today."

"I'm sure he won't neglect you."

"Not deliberately he won't, but being at home will remind him of Mother and he hasn't dealt with things well this week. I expect him to go back to Birmingham where he'll end up being so busy with work and everything else that he won't have time for me." The sadness in Charlotte's voice was obvious.

"Do you think he'll try and find you a husband?"

Charlotte's eyes widened. "I hope not ... not yet anyway. I'm still only eighteen."

"Many a girl's been married at that age if it suited the men in her life."

"I don't think he'll have thought to be honest. Besides, he will come home occasionally, and he won't want the house to be empty.

THE WAKE WAS HELD in Wetherby House. Additional servants had been hired, and tables and chairs set up in the three reception rooms to cater for the fifty or more people who had been invited. Once the food had been served, and eaten, Mr Wetherby invited the guests to give their recollections of Mary. William recounted his earliest memories when his mother struggled to put food on the table, then Mr Diver spoke on Mary-Ann's behalf to recount how patient she had been when they lost their son. William Junior spoke for his son when he talked of an affectionate grandmother, while Charlotte talked of a mother who had been her best friend and companion. The longest speech was saved for Mr Wetherby who elaborated on all the stories they had shared, as well as adding anecdotes of his own.

By four o'clock many of the guests were making their way home and Mr Wetherby felt like a footman showing everyone out. After saying goodbye to William and Mary-Ann he closed the front door and leaned back against it, willing the smile back onto his face before he returned to the drawing room. As he summoned up the energy to move, Sarah-Ann found him.

"Here you are," she said. "I'm going to be leaving soon and wanted to say goodbye."

"How are you getting back?"

"Martha's arranged a carriage; it should be here soon."

"I need to sit down for a few minutes. Will you join me in the dining room?" Mr Wetherby gestured to the room on his right. "We should get some peace in there."

"You look tired," Sarah-Ann said as they sat across the table from each other. "How are you feeling?"

"I've had better days, but I'll manage. Today was always going to be a challenge."

"It went well though; Mary would have been pleased."

"She deserved it ... I'm going to miss her. I'm sorry, I shouldn't be speaking like this in front of you."

Sarah-Ann reached out and took his hand. "She was my friend and I'm going to miss her too, you are allowed to grieve."

Mr Wetherby stood up and walked to the sideboard where he poured them both a brandy. "Will you join me?"

Sarah-Ann took the glass he offered and they sat in silence, appreciating each other's presence. It was several minutes before Mr Wetherby spoke.

"Don't go home tonight."

Sarah-Ann gazed at him before returning her attention to her glass. "Isn't it too soon?"

"Perhaps ... but nobody will know. I don't want to be on my own, not tonight."

"Charlotte will be here."

"I won't see much of her tonight. She'll want to be on her own."

Sarah-Ann was about to speak when Martha poked her head round the dining room door. "What are you two doing in here on your own? Mr Wetherby, haven't you got guests to see to?"

Mr Wetherby looked at Sarah-Ann.

"He needed a minute to himself," Sarah-Ann said. "I found him on his own and offered to keep him company."

"Well, it's a strange going on if you ask me. I was searching everywhere for you."

Mr Wetherby stood up. "I'm sorry, Mrs Chalmers. Thank you for coming. Shall I see you out?"

"You'll need to find Sarah-Ann's cloak first. Come on, Sarah-Ann, hurry up. You'll make us late and Elizabeth will be wondering where you've got to. Adelaide's gone outside to speak to the driver."

Sarah-Ann rose and glanced at Martha before she turned to Mr Wetherby. He said nothing but his eyes pleaded with her. It didn't take long for her to make up her mind.

"I'm going to stay a little longer. You go on without me. Elizabeth's staying out overnight."

Martha glared at Sarah-Ann and then Mr Wetherby. "Mr Flemming was telling the truth about you two, wasn't he? How could you? Mary's barely cold."

"Martha, please, it's not like that." Sarah-Ann

took a step forward, but Martha headed for the door and slammed it behind her.

Mr Wetherby walked over and took her hand. "I'm sorry, I've got you into trouble. I wasn't thinking."

Sarah-Ann sighed. "Nothing I haven't heard before."

"Come on, let's see if we can persuade everyone else to go home and then we can have the evening to ourselves. I'll take you back to Birmingham in the morning."

Chapter Forty

Harriet studied the book that lay open on the table in front of her, her hands on her hips. Mary had bequeathed her *Mrs Beeton's Book of Cookery and Household Management*, and she'd decided that baking was something she could do with her now free afternoons. With Christmas fast approaching, it was something that needed doing anyway. She studied the ingredients measured out on plates in front of her: flour, eggs and sugar. Something was missing. With another look at the book, she went to the pantry for the butter and placed it on the table alongside everything else. Right, she was ready.

Fifteen minutes later, after she had beaten all the ingredients together, Harriet was exhausted.

Having a recipe book seemed to make things harder, not easier. With the cake finally in the oven, Harriet wiped the kitchen surfaces and made a pot of tea. At least William would be impressed with her.

She was setting her cake in the centre of the table when William arrived home from work. Since his mother's death, she had rarely seen him smile but tonight he appeared more cheerful.

"You look pleased with yourself," Harriet said as he walked into the back room.

"I am. Mr Wetherby's given me some news I think you'll be happy about. King Edward's are opening a high school for girls next year and they're about to start accepting applications."

A smile lit up Harriet's face. "That's marvellous, Eleanor'll be thrilled."

"Eleanor might be, but Mr Wetherby raised the issue of Charles going to King Edward's as well. I told him he doesn't want to go, but he insisted. He even said he'd pay for him."

Harriet's smile faded. "On this occasion I agree with him, but you're going to have to speak to Charles. He won't listen to me."

"I know, don't think I didn't try to talk Mr Wetherby out of it, but he was having none of it. Where are they now?"

"They're not far away, I told them to be back for tea, so they won't be long."

As William walked into the hall, the front door opened and Charles came charging through it.

"What's going on here?" William asked as he grabbed Charles by the shoulders to stop him going any further. "This is a house, not a playground."

Charles broke free from his grip and put his hands on his knees while he caught his breath. "We're having a race, and I won. I bet you wouldn't stop Eleanor running like that."

"She wouldn't come charging in like that. Now go and wash your hands, tea is almost ready." As Charles disappeared into the kitchen, Eleanor came in with Margaret and Florence. "You don't look like you were having much of a race," William said.

Eleanor rolled her eyes. "Do you think we'd run like that? You have to humour him though."

William smiled. "You all need to wash your hands before tea, but Eleanor, before you do, Mother would like a word with you."

Eleanor's face dropped. "What have I done?"

"You haven't done anything you shouldn't have, now go and see her. It might be good news."

Eleanor wasn't convinced but went into the back room where Harriet was laying out the cutlery. "Father said you wanted to see me."

Harriet smiled. "I did. I've been praying for this day, and it's finally here. How would you like to go back to school?"

Eleanor cocked her head to one side as a frown settled on her face. "School? Where? When?"

"Next year in Birmingham. Mr Wetherby's found out that they're opening a girl's branch of King Edward's. Would you like to go?"

"Really?" Eleanor's face lit up.

Harriet went and took her hands. "Really. Can you imagine it? Going to secondary school and learning something other than running a house. I'm so envious."

"Oh, yes please." Eleanor put her arms around her mother. "I promise I won't let you down."

As Harriet returned Eleanor's hug, they heard a commotion coming from the kitchen.

"I'm not going," Charles shouted.

"You'll do as you're told," William said. "Mr Wetherby wants you to go, and he's paying for you, so you'd better behave yourself."

"Why does it always have to be up to him? I'm going to sea, I don't need to learn about grammar."

"Charles." Harriet walked down the hall towards her son. "Have you any idea how lucky you are? In a few years' time you might change your mind and you'll be able to get a better job than if you didn't go."

"I'm not going to change my mind. Besides, William-Wetherby's told me what some of the older boys do to you if they don't like you. Why do I want to go to a school like that?"

"William-Wetherby's said nothing of the sort," William said.

"You don't know what he tells me when he's home," Charles said. "Even if you force me to go, you can't make me learn, and if those boys think I'm going to take their bullying lying down, they're going to be in for a shock."

Chapter Forty-One

As the first signs of spring approached, William sat in the corner of the living room with his head in his hands. He'd heard the same words so many times before, yet still she persisted.

"It's not fair."

"Harriet, please, we've been over this a thousand times. I'm not going to be part of the reception for the Marquis of Salisbury and that's all there is to it. The invitations have been given out and I didn't get one."

"But why not? Now Mr Wetherby's chairman of the Conservative Association it's up to him who he gives the tickets to. Why did he give one to William Junior and not you?"

"He's only the chairman of one local association, and he was limited in the number of tickets he could offer. Unsurprisingly, he chose William Junior over me. Why do you get so upset about it? He always has and always will favour his own son."

"But you could be meeting the next prime minister, not to mention everyone else who comes with him. Half of the House of Lords will be there by the sounds of it. Don't you want to be seen with the aristocracy?"

"No, I've told you, I don't care. Besides, the Conservatives have got to win an election before Lord Salisbury becomes prime minister, which doesn't seem likely. Now, please will you let it rest? Nothing you say is going to change the situation and I'm worn out with it all."

"He wouldn't have done this if your mother was still alive, she would have ..."

"Harriet, I said enough." William stood up. "I don't want to hear another word about it. I'm going for a walk."

THE MOMENT she heard the front door close behind him, Harriet took out her writing set and sat down at the table. At Mary's funeral, she'd spoken at length with William Junior's wife, Olivia, and suddenly wondered if she might be able to help. An invitation to taste some of her freshly baked cakes might be the perfect opportunity. She wrote a short letter inviting her to visit later in the week, before she asked the new maid to stop whatever she was doing and hand-deliver it immediately.

Once the maid had gone, Harriet lifted out Mrs Beeton's book and thumbed through the pages to the cakes section. What should she make? Something new and exciting. Something worthy of getting a ticket to meet a future prime minister.

WHEN TWO O'CLOCK on Thursday approached, Harriet made sure the water was set to boil and her new creations of queen cakes and a sponge cake were displayed attractively. At precisely two o'clock, there was a knock on the front door.

"I'm so glad you could make it," Harriet said as Olivia arrived. *Another new dress by the looks of it.* Harriet studied Olivia's slim shape, beautifully draped in a pale blue gown. *How does she always look so elegant?* "Come in and take a seat, we don't see nearly enough of you. I wonder sometimes if William Junior keeps you locked up in that house of yours."

Olivia smiled. "Not at all, but with looking after

Henry and practising my recitals, I don't have time for anything else."

Harriet handed Olivia a cup of tea and offered her the plate of cakes, which Olivia waved away. Harriet glared at her before remembering her smile.

"What have you done with Henry this afternoon?"

"The maid's happy to take care of him. I need time to myself in the afternoon."

It took Harriet a second to remember to close her mouth. "Is that so you can practise the piano? You play beautifully, I believe. It must take a lot of time."

"It does, but I enjoy it. You must pay me a visit one afternoon and I'll play for you."

"I'd like that. Are you often left alone of an evening as well with William Junior being in Birmingham?"

"No, I see him most evenings. His father thinks we need to add to the family and so he stays in Handsworth most of the week."

Harriet rolled her eyes. "Why is Mr Wetherby involved in every aspect of everyone's life whether they want him to be or not?"

"I suppose it's the way he is, but I don't mind." Olivia smiled. "He's good to us and I would like Henry to have a brother or sister."

"Perhaps William Junior should stay with you

every night then." Harriet watched Olivia's quizzical look. "Well, he'll be spending time in Birmingham when the Marquis of Salisbury comes to Birmingham presumably. Has he told you he'll be meeting him?"

"Oh, yes, he has, and he's thrilled. He doesn't get excited about much so I couldn't begrudge him that, could I?"

"I suppose not. It's such a shame that my William won't be able to join him, though. He's so disappointed."

"Is he? William Junior didn't think he minded."

"He puts a brave face on things, but underneath I can tell he's upset. I suppose when you see your stepfather and brother attend something like that you wonder why you can't be included as well."

Olivia put her finger to her chin. "I suppose so. Is there nothing Mr Wetherby can do?"

Harriet shrugged. "William won't ask. He doesn't want to admit that he'd like to attend and so he won't ask him."

"Would you like me to ask William Junior if there's anything he can do?"

Harriet fought the urge to smile. "I hadn't thought of that. Do you think he would? I don't want William knowing I've gone behind his back but I know how happy he'd be."

"Leave it with me and I'll see what I can do. Come over to me for afternoon tea next week and I'll tell you how I'm getting on."

Chapter Forty-Two

Birmingham, Warwickshire

M r Wetherby put his pen on the desk and checked his pocket watch. Almost six o'clock; he shouldn't still be at work. Sarah-Ann was expecting him and it would take him at least three quarters of an hour to walk there. He'd have to hail a carriage. He couldn't risk leaving his own carriage outside Sarah-Ann's house again. With a final glance around, he locked the office door and walked the short distance to Summer Lane, where he jumped in the first available carriage.

When he arrived, the table was set, ready for tea.

"I'm sorry I'm late," he said as he handed Sarah-

Ann his hat and coat. "There's too much work to do and not enough hours in the day."

"The fact you're here is enough for me." Sarah-Ann smiled. "I've got a new purpose in life all of a sudden, from Monday to Friday at any rate. I wish you didn't have to go back to Handsworth on a Saturday. It's when the shop's closed on a Sunday that I miss the company the most and it doesn't help that Elizabeth spends most of the day at church now she teaches at the Sunday school."

Mr Wetherby sat down and reached across the table for some bread. "I do need to see Charlotte on a Sunday. I feel guilty enough about leaving her alone all week, but I feel so miserable going back to the house and Mary not being there."

"Why don't you buy a bigger house in Birmingham and move Charlotte down here? That would solve your problems."

"As daft as it sounds, I couldn't bear to part with Wetherby House either. It would be like erasing Mary from my life; Charlotte wouldn't be pleased either. It's her home and her friends are there."

"You pay too much attention to her. She should be glad you put a roof over her head, let alone everything else you give her."

"She doesn't deserve to be left on her own so much though, she's not nineteen yet. I tell you what, rather than you being on your own here, why don't you travel to Handsworth with me each Saturday and stay with us on Sunday? That way, I can repay some of your hospitality and it will save you being on you own. You can get to know Charlotte better too."

"As long as you don't mind. I don't want to intrude."

~

Handsworth, Staffordshire.

WILLIAM JUNIOR and Olivia sat in the front room of their house in Handsworth. Easter was fast approaching and they were practising a new piece of music for a performance they were giving on Easter Sunday. Olivia had spent the last week practising it on the piano, but it was still new to William Junior and he hated it when his wife could do anything better than he could.

"Why on earth did you choose this piece?" He waved his violin bow. "The tempo's far too quick."

"Because it's beautiful; think how spectacular it'll be when we perform it."

"It's all right for you on the piano, but when you're playing this damn thing ..." He held up his violin and threw it onto the chair.

"Perhaps we've done enough for one day. You're always like this when you learn a new piece, but in a week or two you'll wonder what all the fuss was about."

"I haven't got a week or two; we're doing the first performance on Sunday, in case you'd forgotten." He walked over to the violin and picked it up again.

"Of course I haven't forgotten, but it's only for family and I'm sure they'll forgive the occasional lapse. Anyway, by this time next week you'll be preparing to meet the Marquis of Salisbury. Are you excited?"

"Of course not. It'll be an honour to meet him of course, but it's all in a day's work."

"You know I visited Harriet last week ..."

William Junior stopped what he was doing. "What's she up to now?"

"Nothing. Why are you always so unkind to her? She's lovely when you get to know her. She says William's unhappy that he hasn't been invited to the reception next week."

"It isn't William who's bothered, it's her more likely."

Olivia took the violin from her husband and placed it in its box. "I don't think so; she said William was trying to hide it."

"Well he's doing a fine job; I've never seen anyone appear less interested."

"I was wondering if you or your father could get him a ticket."

"I wouldn't waste my time trying." William Junior went to the sideboard and poured himself a whisky. "I'm telling you, she's the one who wants him to go, and I'm not asking Father for her. He already thinks she's a troublemaker."

"No he doesn't; he likes her."

"That's an act; she drives him mad, always wanting more."

Olivia walked to the cupboard and put the violin away. "You're being unfair."

"No I'm not, but whatever you think, I can't get William a ticket; and that's the end of it."

Chapter Forty-Three

Birmingham, Warwickshire

Mr Wetherby and William Junior stood on the platform at New Street Station, surrounded by a delegation of local dignitaries and Conservative Association chairmen. The train bringing the Marquis of Salisbury to Birmingham was due to arrive in less than twenty minutes' time, but so far they were the only people there.

"Where is everyone?" Mr Wetherby asked as he pulled his coat tight against the wind. "This man could be the next prime minister of our country, the place should be thronged with people."

"The weather's probably kept a lot of them

away," a man said to his right. "Either that or the Liberals have done a fine job of putting them off."

"Damn Gladstone and his cronies. The sooner we get rid of them from government the better. At least we have more chance with Salisbury in charge than we did with Disraeli. His foreign policy certainly seems more popular."

"It'll take more than that," the man said. "I can't wait to hear what he has to say tonight."

The train carrying the marquis arrived at a quarter to five precisely. The men lined up on the platform to welcome him before they made their way to a series of carriages that were waiting to transfer them to the Town Hall.

Once the toasts and introductions were complete, the marquis stood up to speak. He focussed on the policies of the Liberals and condemned the damage they had done to the country.

"He makes a fine case," Mr Wetherby whispered to William Junior as he finished speaking. "We need more people to hear him, take the Liberals on at their own game and have open rallies at the next election. If Mr Gladstone can sell the Liberals to the whole country, then I'm sure the marquis can do the same for the Conservatives."

Once the formal part of the evening was over, the Marquis of Salisbury walked the room meeting as many members of the party as he could. Mr Wetherby watched him work his way towards him, waiting for his chance to introduce himself.

"I believe you're doing a sterling job," His Lordship said.

Mr Wetherby nodded to conceal his smile. "Yes, sir. I try my best."

Lord Salisbury patted him on the back. "I'm sure you do. You have a good reputation around these parts, I believe."

"I like to think so, sir, although I didn't presume to imagine you would know the detail of our local politics."

"It always pays to keep an eye on places as influential as Birmingham." Lord Salisbury tapped the side of his nose with his forefinger. "Now, tell me, I believe that fool Chamberlain's washed his hands of the slum clearances, now he's made it to Westminster."

Mr Wetherby nodded. "That's how it appears. Over ninety acres have been cleared and around sixteen thousand people have been forced from their houses, but so far he's only put a row of shops and office buildings in their place. The rebuilding of houses hasn't started. I'd like to give him one on the nose for the mess he's left us in."

The marquis laughed. "I like a man with passion. How's it affecting the people though?"

"It isn't pleasant, sir, and morale is low. I live in Birmingham during the week, to be closer to work, you understand, but I go to Handsworth every Saturday for respite. My late wife, God rest her soul, refused to live here a number of years ago and it's worse now. All the folks who've been displaced from their homes are having to move into areas that are already overcrowded."

"So, why's the work stopped? Don't tell me it was all down to Chamberlain."

"No, sir, I can't lay all the blame on him, although when he was in charge he did take all the glory. I'm afraid the truth of the matter is a shortage of money."

"We need to do something about that," the marquis said. "If you're to change the political views of these people, you have to find the money and improve their lot in life. That includes giving them decent housing. You're not going to get anything from the Liberals. I've heard of several schemes around the country where they've set up limited companies to raise the money to build houses. If you were to do that in this area it could help us greatly at the next election. Can I leave it with you, Mr Wetherby?"

Mr Wetherby stood with his mouth open. He

hadn't for a moment thought about taking on the slum clearance. "Me?" he said. "Y-yes, of course. It would be an honour."

As the marquis moved to another group of men, Mr Wetherby sat down and ran his finger around his collar. How on earth was he going to rebuild Birmingham? He'd no idea where to start. He would have to find help, of course, and at least he had a good selection of contacts.

"Well, that was a turn-up," William Junior said as he sat with him. "Rather you than me. It sounds too much like hard work."

Mr Wetherby glared at his son before he turned away. William always said he wanted to be treated as an equal partner in the business. Well, now he'd have his chance.

Chapter Forty-Four

Handsworth, Staffordshire

Harriet paced the back room waiting for William to come home. He'd been in Birmingham the previous evening and a letter that had arrived yesterday was tormenting her. She knew it was from the school, but couldn't tell whether it concerned Eleanor or Charles. She wouldn't normally open William's mail but she'd been sorely tempted this time.

She glanced at the clock again. Turned six o'clock; he should be home. She went into the front room and stared out of the window. No sign of him. Within a minute of returning to the back room, she heard the front door open.

She hurried into the hall. "Where have you been?"

"I'm not late; I'm always home around now. What's the matter?"

Harriet had the letter in her hand. "This came from the school."

"Is that all? I thought someone was ill ... or worse."

"What do you mean, 'Is that all?' It arrived about ten minutes after you left yesterday. Will you please open it and put me out of my misery."

William walked to the sideboard in the back room and picked up the letter opener. "It's about Charles," he said as he read it. "The stupid boy's failed the entrance exam."

Harriet put her hands to her head. "He did it on purpose, I shouldn't wonder; wait until I get hold of him."

"He can still have a place as a fee-paying student. I'll need to speak to Mr Wetherby again."

"Just when we're trying to become less dependent on Mr Wetherby as well. Charles needs a good thrashing." Harriet paused for a moment. "I don't suppose it says anything about Eleanor?"

"No, nothing. I imagine they sort all the boys' places out first."

"So, what's your news?" Harriet asked. "You looked concerned when you came in."

William walked to the chair by the fire and sat down. "I've been talking to Mr Wetherby and he wants me to take on more responsibility in the business."

Harriet's face lit up. "But that's marvellous; we've wanted that for years."

"You may have wanted it for years. The truth is, I never have."

"Why on earth not? We always said you should be treated as a partner and now I presume you will be."

"I'd be happy enough if it only involved taking on responsibility in the workshop, but this'll be different. He wants me to do all the bookkeeping as well."

"Don't you ever listen to a word I say?" Harriet sat down beside him. "We've been through this before; I can do the bookkeeping."

"This isn't a household budget," William said. "Mr Wetherby's business turns over tens of thousands of pounds a year. There's a big difference."

"But the principles are the same, money in and money out. It's just bigger numbers."

"I'm not sure. Mr Wetherby would be horrified if he knew you were doing the books."

Harriet smiled. "Then he needn't know. I'm not going to tell him, but why this sudden change of heart? He's never wanted to pass the bookkeeping over to you before."

"It was when he met the Marquis of Salisbury ..."

"At the meeting you didn't go to."

William sighed. "At the meeting I didn't go to, the marquis told him to take over the slum re-building work that Chamberlain's abandoned. He's going to set up a new company to raise money to carry on the work. It'll be a full-time job for the next few months and so he needs to pull back from our business."

"Nothing trivial then. Where does William Junior come into all this?"

"It doesn't affect him. He'll carry on in Handsworth."

Harriet clapped her hands under her chin. "Excellent. If Mr Wetherby's off doing other things and William Junior's in Handsworth, you should be able to bring the books home for me to do. That way you can carry on at the workshop. If you bring the papers home one night, I can log them all the following afternoon and you can take them back the next day. Mr Wetherby'll never know."

· · ·

ONE WEEK LATER, Harriet had a feeling of déjà vu. She sat staring at the letter she had placed behind the clock on the mantelpiece, and this time she knew it related to her daughter's future. As soon as William walked through the door, she grabbed the letter and rushed into the hall thrusting the letter at him. "Well, did she pass?"

William smiled as he read. "She did, the clever girl, she got a scholarship."

"Let me see that." Harriet snatched the letter from him. As she read it, tears welled up in her eyes. "I'm so proud of her, I can't wait to tell her. I'll go and find her."

Before William could say anything, Harriet had disappeared, a broad smile on her face.

Chapter Forty-Five

As usual for a Wednesday afternoon, Harriet sat at the table poring over the books for the business. It never failed to put a smile on her face. She had long since finished entering this week's figures; but that wasn't what thrilled her. It was the fact that she could check back through the figures and find out more about the business. Previously she'd had no idea how much money Mr Wetherby made and it was a revelation. She felt like a naughty child spying on her parents, but it was so exciting she couldn't help herself. She smiled when she confirmed that William was earning significantly more money than anyone else in the Birmingham workshop. *Why can't they do the Handsworth ac-*

counts in the same books? I'll never find out how much William Junior earns.

The only downside to having all this information was that she couldn't talk to anyone about what she learned. William wouldn't be happy with her taking such an interest and it was hardly a topic for afternoon tea when her aunt and uncle or Charlotte and Olivia came to visit. In fact it was often their arrival that forced her to put the books away.

With no visitors expected this afternoon, she made herself a pot of tea and was putting some jam onto a scone when Mary-Ann walked in. As soon as she saw her, Harriet froze.

"Have I disturbed something?" Mary-Ann frowned at her.

"No ... not at all." Harriet hurried to close the book in front of her. "What brings you here?"

"I thought you'd like some company, but it looks like I've had a wasted journey."

"No, not at all, I was finished. Let me ask Violet to bring you a cup and some more scones." Harriet picked up the books as she hurried out, but once she returned, Mary-Ann stood with her hands on her hips.

"What were you doing when I came in? I'd say you were up to something you shouldn't have been."

Harriet stared at Mary-Ann, her mouth gaping. *What do I tell her?*

"Well?" Mary-Ann pressed.

"It's not what you think," Harriet said as she poured out a cup of tea.

"I don't know what I think. What were you doing?"

Harriet studied her sister-in-law. "Can you keep a secret?"

"Of course I can, you should know that."

"Well, you know how I always wanted to stay at school and my uncle wouldn't let me; well, with Eleanor about to start school, I've become restless about wanting to do more learning. William said he'd teach me how to do some bookkeeping so I can help him out if he's busy."

Mary-Ann raised an eyebrow. "I don't think you're telling me the truth."

Harriet averted her gaze. "Of course I am, why wouldn't I?"

"Perhaps you want to protect my brother."

"What do you mean?"

"You know what I mean. William once mentioned that he struggled with his arithmetic and I know that you're rather good at it, so it doesn't make sense that he should be teaching you. Are you doing the bookkeeping for the house?"

Harriet sighed. "I didn't think he'd told anyone. Who else knows?"

"Nobody as far as I'm aware. It was only an off-the-cuff comment and he probably doesn't realise I heard him. There's more to it than that though, isn't there? You wouldn't have such a guilty look otherwise. Come on, out with it."

Harriet straightened the cloth on the table before she took a deep breath. "I've been doing the bookkeeping for the Birmingham business."

"Oh my ... Harriet, you've not. Does Mr Wetherby know?"

"No, of course not, and we have to make sure it stays like that. It's only because he's working on setting up this new company. He expects William to do everything, but he can't."

"I did wonder how he managed."

"Well, now you know. Please don't tell anyone else or we'll both be in trouble."

"Of course I won't, as long as you do something for me in return."

Harriet's heart sank. "What do you want?"

Mary-Ann grinned. "You have to tell me about the business. Is it as prosperous as he has us all believe or is he just trying to impress?"

Harriet let out a huge sigh and laughed at Mary-Ann. "Oh, he's wealthy all right. Here, let me show you." She went to retrieve the books and put them on the table in front of Mary-Ann.

"Look at this. Some weeks he is taking in nearly two hundred pounds, but he's only spending about sixty to seventy pounds a week on wages and materials. He takes about one hundred pounds a week for himself. And that's just in Birmingham. Even if he makes half of that in Handsworth, that's a hundred and fifty pounds a week. Then he's got the houses in Birmingham that he rents out."

"What on earth does he do with it all?"

"Well, he spends a lot, obviously, especially on Charlotte, and look at the gravestone he had made for your mother, not to mention the memorial he's commissioned for her in church. It must be costing a fortune. I don't feel guilty that he pays for Charles to go to school any more."

"I bet he gives William Junior a lot too."

Harriet's posture stiffened. "I bet he does. I can't be sure but William Junior always seems to be wearing a new suit and Olivia has some lovely dresses."

Mary-Ann suddenly became serious. "You know he'd be furious if he found out you knew all this."

"He's never in the office nowadays. He won't find out."

Mary-Ann wasn't convinced. "Please promise me

you won't go getting yourself into trouble. There's no telling what he'd do."

"I won't. He's no idea they're here and I'm careful with them. I promise if there's any sign of trouble, I'll stop."

Chapter Forty-Six

It had been a long week and Mr Wetherby sank into the back of the carriage with relief. He wasn't frightened of hard work, he never had been, but he was beginning to wonder if he had taken on too much. His new venture, now called the Artisans Dwelling Company, was gaining momentum and they were ready to start the building work. The problem was, he couldn't just recruit several building firms and let them get on with it. There were plans to be scrutinised, objections to be dealt with, and issues about the land he hadn't expected.

As usual for a Saturday evening, he picked Sarah-Ann up to take her to Handsworth, but unusually he'd let her do all the talking. They were halfway to Handsworth before she noticed.

"You look tired, have you had a busy week?"

Mr Wetherby smiled weakly. "You could say that. I thought things would be simpler once the company was up and running but it's quite the opposite. The way things are going at the moment, it wouldn't surprise me if it takes another twenty years to get these houses built."

"Surely not, we can't wait that long. People have nowhere to live."

"I'm aware of that, but there are obstacles at every step. Anyway, you don't need the details. Let me have a day off tomorrow and I'll be ready to go again by Monday. How was your week?"

"Quiet. Elizabeth's gone to stay with a friend. I hate the fact that she'll come of age soon. She won't need me at all then." The sparkle disappeared from Sarah-Ann's eyes. "You haven't even been there to keep me company."

Mr Wetherby took hold of her hand. "I'm sorry; next week should be better. I'll tell you what ..."

Sarah-Ann turned to him. "What?"

"Nothing." He withdrew his hand. "It was just a thought. It'll keep."

By the following morning, Mr Wetherby had had a decent night's sleep and was reading the paper before they left for church. Sarah-Ann had breakfasted with him, but had since disappeared back upstairs. He folded the paper and was about to stand up when Charlotte joined him.

"Are you on your own?" she asked.

"Yes, Sarah-Ann's getting herself sorted out for church. Are you ready?"

"I need my coat, but perhaps I'll wait until Sarah-Ann comes back down. I don't often see you on your own and I miss you. You must be busy."

Mr Wetherby studied his daughter. She looked beautiful with her fair hair rolled back around the edges of her face, revealing her clear complexion and the pale blue eyes that reminded him so much of her mother. She was still only twenty years old, but for all she'd seen of him lately she may well have lost both her mother and father eighteen months ago.

"I'm sorry. I am busy, but that's no excuse to ignore you."

"It's not just that I don't see you, but when I do, you're never on your own."

"Sarah-Ann, you mean?" Mr Wetherby watched Charlotte nod her head. "Do you like her?"

"She's nice enough, but she's not comfortable with me when you're not around. She's not easy to talk to."

"She was one of your mother's best friends."

"Maybe, but she seems to have turned her attentions to you now."

"She's lonely. Things haven't been easy for her."

"You like her a lot though, don't you?"

"I'm fond of her, yes, but she could never take the place of your mother. Does it bother you that I like her?"

Charlotte shrugged. "Is it any concern of mine?"

"It could be ..." Mr Wetherby took a deep breath. "If she came to live here."

Charlotte said nothing for what felt like an age. "Have you asked her?"

Mr Wetherby shook his head. "No, it was just an idea. I wanted to see what you thought." Mr Wetherby saw a single tear roll down her cheek as she stared into the fire. "Please don't cry. I won't do anything to upset you."

Charlotte wiped her tear away and turned back to face him. "If it meant you'd come home more often, then I'd agree to anything."

Chapter Forty-Seven

Harriet paced back and forth across the living room as William stood by the window, his face flushing scarlet. They'd had an hour to digest the news in the recent letter from school, but it had only served to increase their anger.

"What are we going to do with him?" Harriet asked for the umpteenth time. "I'm sick to death of him. Is he never going to get any better?"

"What else can we do? He's been caned, given detention, separated from the rest of the boys in the school. Nothing works. If anything, it makes him worse."

"Well, we have to do something. This time it sounds serious."

William walked back to the table and picked up

the letter. "Ten o'clock on Monday morning, I have to be at school to see the headmaster."

"Do you think they'll expel him?"

"I've no idea. If I apologise to the headmaster and tell him it won't happen again, maybe he'll give him one last chance."

"You can try but we can't make promises like that. We'd no idea when he started school that he'd be fighting with everyone, let alone injuring them." Harriet was silent for several seconds. "We need to work out what he'd miss the most if we stopped it. That might be the best way to deal with him. In fact, I think I've got an idea."

～

Birmingham, Warwickshire.

FIRST THING ON MONDAY MORNING, William ordered his driver to take him to King Edward's Grammar School. As they approached Birmingham, he took his handkerchief from his pocket to wipe his brow. He hadn't felt this sick since he'd visited the bank manager when they wanted the house. He could feel his heart pounding as the carriage trundled along the uneven road, taking him ever closer. As he climbed from the carriage outside the school gates, he thought of his own schooldays. He'd lost count of the number of times he'd been called to the headmaster's office because he couldn't do his arithmetic, and here he was again.

When he arrived, he was shown to Mr Vardy's office where he was offered a seat and told to wait. Ten minutes later, the headmaster swept in.

"Mr Jackson, I'm sure you're aware of the reason I asked to see you." Mr Vardy sat with his forearms on the desk, his fingers linked before him. "I'll send for Charles presently, but first I'd like to give you more details of his disgraceful behaviour."

William closed his eyes and took a deep breath. It felt as if he personally was being accused and there was nothing he could do about it. He opened his eyes to see the headmaster with a scroll stretched out between his hands.

"The trouble began within a week of him starting school, if you recall, when he was found wrestling with a boy in the dormitory. Fortunately the encounter was broken up before any damage could be done. There were a couple of similar incidents soon afterwards and, as you're aware, he received the cane to both hands on each occasion."

William nodded but said nothing.

"We then move to January of this year when he was found forcing a boy's arm behind his back to the point where the boy was begging to be released. When the teacher broke them up there was no sign of remorse from Charles, who said to the boy, and I quote from the teacher's notes, *Next time I'll break it*."

William sank into his seat and put his hand to his face.

"Then we come to this most recent incident where we now have a boy in hospital with damage to his skull."

William hadn't known the details and sat upright as the headmaster spoke. "Oh my word. What happened? Is the boy all right?"

"I believe he'll recover, but it's no thanks to your son. They were in the school grounds when, once again, your son initiated a fight. Unfortunately this time there were no teachers close by and it went on for too long. Exactly what happened, we're not sure, other than the fact the other boy ended up being punched in the side of the face before he fell to the ground, banging his head. It's this latter detail that we think caused the fracture. At that stage some of the older boys moved in to hold Charles back, which was fortunate, because I believe he still wasn't happy to leave it."

William felt his face turning red, although whether it was due to anger or embarrassment, he wasn't sure. "Headmaster, what can I say other than I'm so sorry and ashamed of my son. He never showed any tendency towards this sort of behaviour when he was at primary school. Whatever punishment you have in mind I'm sure will be acceptable, but may I make one request? You said in your letter you were considering expelling him from the school. While you'd be well within your rights to do so, could I ask that you don't follow through with it?"

William ploughed on, hoping that the headmaster would agree.

"My wife suspects that one of the reasons for his behaviour is because he wants to come home. If she's right, he'd see expulsion as a victory. As an alternative, we'd like you to keep him at school until he learns how to behave himself. With your permission, I'd like to tell him that he won't be allowed to leave the school premises until his behaviour improves. We thought that for every month he keeps out of trouble he could come home on the last Saturday afternoon until Monday morning."

Mr Vardy sat with his back straight, looking down his nose at William. "Mr Jackson, may I remind you that this is a school and not a home for wayward boys. There are plenty of other places that provide that sort of supervision."

"Yes, I'm sure, but I think you'll agree the boy is

317

bright and deserves a chance. We're also paying handsomely for him to come here, which I presume you're happy for us to continue."

"Yes, I'm aware that Mr Wetherby is funding his time here." Mr Vardy thought for a couple of seconds. "As a personal favour to him, I'll allow him to stay. This will, however, be his last warning. If he so much as causes one more problem, he'll be out."

"Thank you, sir, I appreciate it, but can I suggest you don't mention that to him? If he knows he only has one chance left, I fear he'll continue to cause problems until he achieves his goal."

"Very well, it will be between the two of us." The headmaster picked up a small bell from his desk and shook it for the count of three before placing it back on its mat.

CHARLES WAS USHERED into the office by a clerk and ordered to stand in front of the desk. He glanced at his father before he stood and glared at the headmaster.

"What have you got to say for yourself, boy?" the headmaster said without waiting for the office door to be closed.

Charles said nothing but turned his attention to his feet.

"Charles," William said. "I won't have such impertinence. Speak to Mr Vardy when you're spoken to."

Charles looked defiantly at his father before addressing the headmaster. "He asked for it."

"I beg your pardon," Mr Vardy said. "You do not speak to me like that."

"He asked for it, *sir*," Charles repeated, his eyes holding the headmaster's glare.

A second later, the headmaster was on his feet, striding across the office to where the cane hung on the wall. "Right, hands out now." Before Charles knew what was happening, the headmaster was bringing the cane down across both palms with increasing ferocity.

"You," *whip*, "will," *whip*, "not," *whip*, "talk," *whip*, "to," *whip*, "me," *whip*, "like that. Do you understand? If I hear another word of insolence from you, you'll be in here every day for a week and the lashes won't be confined to your hands."

Charles stared at his hands. Both were bleeding and the cuts felt as if they were on fire, but he wouldn't cry. He wouldn't give them the satisfaction.

"I've been talking to your father about the situation," Mr Vardy continued. "He's told me you're not welcome at home until your behaviour improves and that includes this Easter break."

Charles glared at his father with horror in his eyes. He couldn't do that.

"I don't know what game you're playing, Charles," William said, "but your mother and I are extremely angry with you. Mother doesn't want to see you at home until you've learned how to behave yourself. She asked me to tell you that you'll be allowed home for one day a month, providing you stay out of trouble for the whole month before. If we hear anything more from Mr Vardy, your home leave will be cancelled and the clock will start ticking again. If you continually misbehave, you'll be kept here for longer and longer each time. Have I made myself clear?"

Charles stood with his mouth open, shaking his head. "No," he managed, as he wiped tears from his eyes with the backs of his hands. "Tell Mother I'm sorry. I didn't mean to make her mad, but he was tormenting me. I was only standing up for myself."

"I don't care what he did. You can't go around hitting people and even less so breaking their skulls. If they torment you, ignore them, walk away, come and speak to Mr Vardy, anything but don't resort to violence."

Charles bowed his head to hide the tears that

were now falling. *I want to go home, I don't want to be here.*

Charles didn't hear Mr Vardy's final words but accepted a wet cloth to wipe the blood from his hands. The water burned into his cuts and he screwed his eyes together to force the tears to stop. *Stupid eyes; stop it. Only girls cry.*

Charles wiped the bloodied cloth across his eyes and glared at his father. "I hate you. If it wasn't for Mother, I'd never want to see you again."

The headmaster was on his feet, but William put up his hand to stop him. "That's enough. If he doesn't want to see me, he won't mind not coming home, which will suit everyone. Just get him out of my sight."

Mr Vardy nodded at William before he picked up the bell and shook it. A moment later, the clerk returned and taking hold of his arm walked Charles back to his dormitory.

Chapter Forty-Eight

Sarah-Ann stood by the table in her living room folding some clothes. Mr Wetherby was due to pick her up and take her to Wetherby House for the four days over Easter. She put the last of her things into her carrying bag and placed it on the floor near the door. He would be here any time now.

As she thought about the days ahead, a shiver ran down her back. Easter Sunday would be the first time she would be with the whole Wetherby family since Mary had died. Although she knew most of them, she was still terrified. William and Mary-Ann were no problem, but she didn't know Mr Diver well and as for Harriet, for some reason they had never got along together and frankly she found her overpowering. Then there were Charlotte and William Junior. She'd only recently started to feel comfortable with Charlotte; but William Junior was a different matter altogether. He never made any effort to acknowledge her, and he was so condescending. Not just to her, but to everyone. What Olivia saw in him she couldn't fathom, but then she didn't know her either. *What am I doing?* She glanced at the clock. *Is it too late to change my mind?*

A knock on the door, followed by Mr Wetherby letting himself in, confirmed that it was indeed too late.

"Are you ready?" he asked, picking up her bag.

"I suppose so. As ready as I'll ever be." With a final glance around the room, she followed Mr Wetherby outside. "I hope Mr Taylor's all right opening and closing the shop by himself on Saturday."

"He'll be fine. He's a trustworthy sort."

"He is and he's opened and closed for me before, but not on the same day. I hope Elizabeth's all right as well."

"She isn't going to be in Birmingham this weekend and so you're no further from her in Handsworth than you would be here. Now stop worrying." He held the carriage door open for her. "I want you to have a complete break for a few days. You haven't stopped since the death of that good-for-nothing husband of yours, it's about time somebody else took care of you."

Sarah-Ann smiled. "I'd like that. I don't think I've been looked after for so long since before Mother died."

"Do you miss having a man about the house?" Mr Wetherby asked once they were seated.

"Occasionally, but not him. Besides, I see you most evenings. I sometimes think I'd like to settle down again ... but we'll see."

"I miss Mary when I'm in Handsworth." Mr Wetherby said. "I miss having someone to come home to, to talk to, to take walks with ... Charlotte misses the company too."

"You could do many of those things with Charlotte when you're at home."

"I can and I do on occasion, but it's not the same. A daughter can never take the place of her mother."

"She'll be wanting a husband soon too, I should imagine. What will you do when you're on your own?"

Mr Wetherby held her gaze. "That's a question I'm yet to answer."

~

Handsworth, Staffordshire.

As Saturday morning turned into afternoon, Mr Wetherby sat at the dining table with Sarah-Ann and Charlotte. They were finishing dinner and planning an afternoon stroll, when there was a knock on the door.

Mr Wetherby sat back in his chair and turned his eyes to the ceiling. "Who on earth can this be?" His answer came seconds later when Emily knocked on the door and opened it to reveal Mr Wetherby's brother.

"Thomas!" Mr Wetherby leapt from his seat and hurried to shake his brother's hand. "What are you doing here? It must be over twenty years since I last saw you."

"Just passing," Thomas said with a grin. "I thought I'd call on my big brother."

"Come in, come in. How did you even find us? I think the last time I saw you we lived in Frankfort Street."

"You did, and that's where I went, only to find Betsy there. She gave me quite a shock I can tell you."

Mr Wetherby laughed. "I suppose she did, but

it's a good job she was there, otherwise you might never have found us. Take a seat. Do you want anything to eat?"

"Well, if you've anything to hand, that would be splendid."

"Emily, will you ask Cook to plate up another meal for us, and then come and clear the rest of the table, we may be here for some time."

Mr Wetherby turned back to his brother. "It's so good to see you. I was beginning to think you'd never come back. I don't suppose you know everyone here."

Thomas shook his head.

"This is my daughter Charlotte and this is Sarah-Ann, a friend of the family. You two may have met last time you were here?" Mr Wetherby looked between Thomas and Sarah-Ann.

"I think we did meet once in Frankfort Street," Sarah-Ann said. "As I recall I was visiting Mary and you were living close by."

"You have a better memory than I do." Thomas laughed. "All that rum can't be doing me any good."

Concern crossed Mr Wetherby's face. "You got my letter about Mary?"

Thomas bowed his head. "I did, probably about six months after you sent it. I'm sorry I didn't reply, but when you're on a ship, things are different. Such a shame, she was a lovely woman."

"Save your apologies," Mr Wetherby said. "I understand. How long are you here for?"

"I'm not sure yet. At least two weeks, but I might be back for good."

Mr Wetherby's face broke into a smile. "That's excellent news. What's brought that on?"

"Nothing in particular, but it's time for a change."

"Birmingham's not the same place you left. If I was you I'd go and check things out before you commit to anything."

"You might be right, but I want to come home. I've been travelling the world for most of my life and I need to find a place to rest. None of us are getting any younger, and seeing your beautiful daughter for the first time brings it home to me that I've been away for too long." He turned to Charlotte. "When were you born?"

"October 1863."

Thomas let out a long whistle. "That was when I was in America. I've sailed around the world a few times since then. It's delightful to meet you at last."

Charlotte smiled. "And you, I'm sure."

"What are your plans for the next couple of weeks?" Mr Wetherby asked.

"To start with I need to find somewhere to live."

"You can stay here for the next few days at least," Mr Wetherby said. "After that, I'm sure I can find you a room in one of the houses in Birmingham, if that's where you'd rather be."

Thomas's eyebrows shot up. "How many have you got now? You'd only just started buying them, last time I saw you."

"I've got six in Frankfort Street near the workshop and over twenty in Summer Lane."

Thomas let out another long whistle. "Business must be going well, I'd have been back sooner if I'd known. You don't have any jobs going, do you?"

Mr Wetherby laughed. "Not for anyone else, but for you, Thomas, I'm sure I could find something. In fact, maybe you could keep an eye on things for me."

"What, so you can start slacking?"

Mr Wetherby's laugh disappeared as quickly as it had begun. "So that I can work for less than sixteen hours a day. You don't have any idea how hectic life is at the moment."

Thomas held up his hands in surrender. "All right, I'm sorry, don't bite my head off."

"What about William and William Junior?" Sarah-Ann asked.

"What about them? I'm sure they won't mind Thomas watching over everything."

Charlotte raised an eyebrow. "Are you sure? I can't see William Junior being happy."

"Well, he should make more of an effort to do the job himself. He's no one else to blame."

Chapter Forty-Nine

Mr Wetherby sat in the morning room at Wetherby House waiting for the kettle to boil. It was still only half past five in the morning, but he'd been awake for so long he wondered if he'd slept at all last night. Emily didn't start work until six o'clock and so he'd set the fire up himself and put the water on to make a cup of tea. With the tea brewing, he put the teapot onto the tray with his cup and saucer, milk jug and sugar bowl, and carried them into the back room.

Once the tea was poured, he took a seat by the fire, to mull things over again. He'd barely sat down when the door opened, causing him to let out an involuntary groan.

"I'm sorry, I'll go." Sarah-Ann stood by the door in her nightdress. "I'm disturbing you."

Mr Wetherby jumped to his feet. "No, please don't, I thought it was the maid. Take a seat, I can get another cup." He gestured for her to sit down before he went to the kitchen and came back to pour a second cup of tea. "Couldn't you sleep?"

Sarah-Ann rested her head on the back of the chair. "I did, but sleeping in a different bed must have made me wake early. I'm not used to everything being so quiet. The streets of Birmingham are busy by now. What about you? You don't have the excuse of a strange bed."

"No I don't, although I feel like a stranger here at the moment. I just couldn't sleep ... I have something on my mind."

"Do you want to talk about it?"

Mr Wetherby let his eyes wander over the contours of her nightdress before he took in the fair hair, now more grey than blonde, which fell around her shoulders. Finally, his gaze settled on the dusky eyes that stared back at him.

"I was thinking about you." He stood up and walked to the window.

"Me?" Sarah-Ann's eyes were wide. "What were you thinking?"

"Everything, I suppose. I was remembering when

we first met, not long after I'd asked Mary to marry me ... at Adelaide's wedding. Do you remember? We didn't speak to you for months afterwards."

"I'm not likely to forget, it wasn't one of my finest hours ..."

"Then I thought about your move to Birmingham after your father died, when I showed you to your first house. You wouldn't let me show you to your room ..."

Sarah-Ann's eyes glazed over. "I remember. What would have happened if I had let you? Our lives might have been very different."

Mr Wetherby nodded. "But then I went and introduced you to Mr Flemming. Of all the stupid things I could have done ... and then despite everything I gave you away. How could I have done that? I still can't forgive myself."

"Don't think badly of everything he did. We were happy for a time and he gave me Elizabeth. I'll always be thankful to him for that."

"But he was responsible for the death of your son. How can you forgive that?"

Mr Wetherby turned back to face Sarah-Ann and she held his gaze. "I admit he nearly broke me, but I had you and he couldn't change that ..."

Mr Wetherby turned back to the fire and sat on the edge of his chair. "But you didn't have me, not really. I was never going to leave Mary."

"I knew what I was letting myself in for; but having a part of you and knowing that you cared for me was enough. I'd do it again if I had to ..."

"It also crossed my mind that without me you'd have had a much happier life ..."

Sarah-Ann shook her head. "No ..."

"Please, let me finish." He held up his hand. "I want to make amends to you and I've been wondering if you'd like to move to Handsworth. You could sell the shop and move in here. You'd have your own room and you could call the place your home."

Sarah-Ann opened and closed her mouth twice before she could force her words out. "Take a room here? You mean like a lodger?"

"No, of course not a lodger."

"Then what?" Incomprehension covered Sarah-Ann's face.

Mr Wetherby stood up and took hold of her hands, a playful smile on his lips. "Do I have to spell it out to you?"

"Like a mistress?" Sarah-Ann stumbled to the other side of the room. "I'm a respectable woman."

"And it would be a respectable arrangement," Mr Wetherby followed her across the room and stroked her cheek. "With two daughters living here to chaperone us, and with being the age we are, nobody will imagine that you are any more than a companion."

"I don't want to be your companion, I want to be your wife. Is that too much to ask?" As Sarah-Ann turned and fled through the door, Mr Wetherby reached out after her but was too slow.

"It's too soon. Sarah-Ann, come back, we can talk about it."

Chapter Fifty

The Easter Sunday service at church went on for longer than expected and as soon as it was over, William and Harriet headed directly to Wetherby House with the children. William strode ahead with William-Wetherby, while the girls dawdled behind with their mother. Harriet watched as the men walked. Her son was almost as tall as his father, and with his dark hair, he reminded her of William when they had first met. Where had the years gone? He'd be finishing school next.

William waited for her on the corner of Wellington Road, while William-Wetherby went to help speed his sisters up.

"I wish we didn't have to go," Harriet said when she reached him. "I'd much rather go home."

William glanced at her from the corner of his eye. "You normally enjoy seeing everyone. What's the matter?"

Harriet shrugged. "I suppose I'm bothered about Charles not being with us. Does Mr Wetherby know he's still at school?"

William took a deep breath and caught hold of her arm. "No, I haven't told him. I was hoping he wouldn't miss him."

"How can you not miss Charles? He's never quiet."

"Perhaps we can say we left him at home because he was in one of his moods."

"We'll have to. I don't want to tell him the truth with the whole family there. Why is he such an embarrassment?"

"Stop worrying and leave the talking to me. I wish you'd hurry up or they'll be eating dinner before we arrive."

Harriet refused to walk any faster and was relieved that Mr Wetherby was preoccupied when they arrived. As soon as he saw William, however, he excused himself from his conversation and took William by the arm.

"What's this about Charles being kept at school over Easter?"

William glanced at Harriet before he answered. "How did you know? I was going to tell you later."

"Have you forgotten that Mr Vardy's a member of the Conservative Association?" Mr Wetherby spat his words out. "He told me what Charles has been up to and said he'd spoken to you a couple of weeks ago. Didn't it occur to you to have the courtesy of telling me?"

William stared at the floor. "I'm sorry. The timing was never right and I didn't want to trouble you at work."

"Didn't want to trouble me? Instead, you'd rather humiliate me by letting the headmaster tell me himself?"

"I'm sorry, it wasn't meant to be like that."

"I'm sure it wasn't. You were probably hoping I'd never find out, but let me remind you, not much of what goes on around here escapes my attention. In future I expect to be told if there's a problem with any of the children, do you hear me?"

"Yes, sir."

Mr Wetherby left without offering them a drink and Harriet, who was behind William, turned him around to face her.

"Why do you let him speak to you like that? Who does he think he is?"

"Harriet, please ..."

"Please nothing. You let him treat you like a child and as for me, I may as well not be here. He's got worse since your mother died too." Harriet was about to continue when Mary-Ann joined them.

"There you are," she said, "I was beginning to think you weren't coming."

"I wish we weren't. That man ..." Harriet paused. "What's she doing here? William, look over there."

The colour drained from William's face as he spotted his Aunt Sarah-Ann on the far side of the room.

"Did you know she'd be here?" Harriet said.

William shook his head. "Of course not, do you think I'd have wanted to come if I had?"

"What's the matter?" Mary-Ann asked. "Have you seen a ghost?"

"Perhaps I have. So much for me not telling him about Charles, he's been lying to me for years."

"Will you say anything to him?" Harriet said.

"Like what? Have you been keeping my aunt as your mistress?"

"William!" Mary-Ann's eyes were wide. "What's going on? What haven't you told me?"

"Where's that maid with the sherry?" Harriet glanced around the room. "I think we need two each. "I'll tell you later," she said to Mary-Ann who stood gaping at the two of them.

"You don't think she's part of the announce-ment, do you?" Mary-Ann asked, once Harriet had a drink.

"What announcement? What have we missed?"

"I'm not sure yet, but having maids serving glasses of sherry is a bit much for Easter Sunday, even if we are at Wetherby House. I'd say we're going to make a toast to something or somebody."

"He can keep his toast." Harriet took hold of William's arm, worried that he might collapse. "Take some deep breaths. It might all be perfectly innocent ..."

"Ladies and gentlemen." Mr Wetherby tapped a spoon against the side of his glass, interrupting all conversation. "May I have your attention? I trust you've all received a glass of sherry. Before we sit down to dinner I'd like to propose a toast to my dear brother Thomas. As you know, Thomas has spent the last forty years travelling the world. He's been to and seen places most of us don't know exist, but I'm delighted to say that he told me yesterday he plans to hang up his sea legs and live a life on dry land."

Thomas smiled at his sisters who stood to his right-hand side while Mr Wetherby continued. "It's also been decided that he's going to be working for me, helping out at the workshops. He'll live in Birmingham but divide his time between the two sites. Kindly raise your glasses to Thomas."

"Thomas!" A chorus of voices sounded around the room, but Harriet stood with her mouth open before she turned on William.

"Did you know about this? What's he going to be doing?"

William shook his head. "I've no idea. He said himself he only found out yesterday."

"So he's offered him a job in your business and he hasn't bothered to ask you your opinion?"

"Harriet, it is his brother we're talking about, not just anybody."

Harriet's nostrils flared. "I don't care; he should have the common decency to mention it to you before he makes an announcement. I bet William Junior knew."

William looked over at his brother. "I bet he didn't. I'd say he's as pleased about it as you are."

"That man is unbelievable. You've got to find out what he'll be doing; I don't want him interfering with the bookkeeping ..."

"Keep your voice down. Let me talk to him over dinner before we decide if we need to worry."

Harriet took a deep breath. "All right, but this could be the final straw. We have to think about you starting your own business."

Chapter Fifty-One

As the dinner went on around her, Sarah-Ann studied the faces at the table. She had never felt so alone. What had started out as a pleasant break had turned into an ordeal. How she wished she could leave the table and walk away. She was seated next to Mr Diver but he was in deep conversation with William, while Harriet, who sat opposite, was raging over something to Mary-Ann. Further up the table she saw Charlotte talking to Olivia and William Junior while at the head of the table Mr Wetherby entertained Thomas and his sisters. The rest of the table was filled with the older children. Either accidentally or deliberately, he appeared to have forgotten she was in the room.

Once the plates had been cleared and she was

sure no one would miss her, Sarah-Ann slipped from her seat and out of the door. She was halfway up the stairs when she heard a noise and turned to find Harriet staring up at her.

"We didn't expect you to be here today. We thought the rumour about you and Mr Wetherby was a figment of Mr Flemming's imagination ... but maybe not." Harriet cocked her head as she waited for an answer.

"I don't know what you're talking about." Sarah-Ann turned and continued up the stairs.

"He's not worth it," Harriet said as she caught her up.

"Who?"

"Mr Wetherby, he's not worth it. I've seen you watching him all the way through dinner, but I'd say he's deliberately trying to avoid you. Perhaps he only wants the things he can't have."

As she reached the landing, Sarah-Ann glared at Harriet. "You're very observant all of a sudden."

"Not particularly, it was quite obvious. Have you done something to upset him?"

"That's no concern of yours,"

"Maybe not, but when the host puts his house guest at the opposite end of the table and doesn't give her an introduction, it makes me wonder ..."

"Well, you can stop wondering. I have a headache

and I'm going for a lie-down. If you're looking for the younger children they're in the back room, *downstairs*."

～

HARRIET WAITED for Sarah-Ann to lock her bedroom door before she joined Mary-Ann and the other ladies who were moving to the front drawing room.

"There's something going on with your aunt," she said. "I think we can add her to the list of people Mr Wetherby's upset today."

"What did she say?"

"Nothing ... but that's what makes me suspicious. If she's nothing to hide, she'd tell me."

Mary-Ann raised an eyebrow. "Are you sure? I'd say you were the last person she'd confide in. You've never got on with each other."

"That's besides the point. You mark my words, there's something going on between her and Mr Wetherby. I can't work out what it is, but at the moment she's not happy about it."

It was over an hour later before the party broke up and William and Harriet walked home with the children.

"How did you get on?" Harriet asked William

when they were alone. "Did you find out anything about Thomas?"

"I think everything will be all right. He needs to learn the business so he's going to spend time with me and William Junior while we teach him the trade. I don't think there's anything more sinister to it than that. He seems genuinely pleased that he's being given a chance."

"What happens when he's learned the business?"

"It'll take him years to learn everything and so we'll cross that bridge when we get to it."

"We need to make sure it's no concern of yours by then. You have to set up your own business ... I'm not prepared to take no for an answer any longer."

SARAH-ANN LAY ON THE BED, staring at the ceiling. Had she overreacted this morning? He might think so, but she didn't. What did he expect? That she was just at his beck and call? The way he'd spoken had made her think he was going to propose marriage to her. Being a mistress, masquerading as a companion, hadn't occurred to her. He may as well have slapped her across the face for the hurt he had caused her. Did he think she was that cheap? And he expected Elizabeth to lie for him. How dare he. He may have almost ruined her life, but he wasn't going to do the same to her daughter. She had brought Elizabeth up to love and serve the Lord, not to conceal evidence of sin. She felt the heat rising in her cheeks. How she wanted to go back downstairs and slap him across the face. Her thoughts were interrupted by a knock on the door.

"It's open," she said, expecting the maid to enter. When she didn't hear the maid's cheery greeting, she turned her head to find Mr Wetherby staring down at her. She immediately sat bolt upright. "What are you doing here?"

"I've come to see how you are; I heard you had a headache."

"Yes." Sarah-Ann fidgeted with the bedcovers. "I did ... I have; I needed to lie down."

"I'm sorry, I shouldn't have disturbed you but I wanted to see if you needed anything."

Do I need anything? What a ridiculous question. "No, I'm fine, thank you. I think I'll have an early night."

"As you wish," he said. "If you change your mind, I'll be downstairs."

SARAH-ANN DIDN'T TRUST herself to leave her room on Monday and when she went down to the carriage on Tuesday morning, there was no smile from Mr Wetherby. She sat in the carriage with a blanket across her knees and her arms folded tightly in front of her.

"Now the weather's turned cold again, the shop's going to be chilly." The comment was made more for conversation than to inform Mr Wetherby.

"Once you get the fire going you'll be fine."

Sarah-Ann smiled. "That was the first thing I remember about Mr Flemming. He always had the fire made up for me when I arrived on a cold morning ... and a cup of tea waiting."

Mr Wetherby gave her a sideways glance. "You talk as if you miss him. He was an alcoholic, in case you've forgotten."

"It's easier to recall the happier times ... and we were happy for a while."

"You're unbelievable ... after all the trouble he caused."

"It wasn't his fault ..."

"Of course it was his fault, who else's fault was it?"

Sarah-Ann glared at him. "Don't you remember how he walked in and found us together? Do you think he forgot about it?"

"Of course not, but he didn't know anything for

certain. All the problems he had, he brought upon himself."

"You talk as if we were casual acquaintances. Do you honestly believe you had nothing to do with it?"

Mr Wetherby stared at Sarah-Ann. "I know he blamed me, and I do bear some responsibility, but he had no evidence of any wrongdoing. There was no reason to suspect the baby was mine. It was all in his head."

"And how would you have behaved if you thought Mary was carrying Richard's child?"

Mr Wetherby stared at Sarah-Ann, his mouth gaping.

"Don't look at me like that," Sarah-Ann said. "You know they were close."

"How close?" The venom in his voice surprised her.

Sarah-Ann turned and stared out of the window. "We're nearly at the shop."

"Answer me, damn you. What do you know about them? Is William Richard's son?" He turned her face back towards his.

"No, of course not. William was born when Charles was alive, before Mary even noticed Richard, but it proves the point. You wouldn't have liked it if you'd found Mary with another man, and Mr Flemming didn't like it either. That's all I'm saying."

Sarah-Ann was shaking as she climbed down from the carriage. Mr Wetherby carried her bag to the shop, but as soon as she opened the front door, he returned to the carriage. By the time it pulled away from the side of the road, her mind was in turmoil. In the space of four days she had gone from adoring him to being furious with him. She thought back to the time she had first told him about the friendship between Mary and Richard and wondered how he had treated her. If he was anything like he'd been this weekend, Mary was a stronger person than she'd given her credit for.

Chapter Fifty-Two

Birmingham, Warwickshire

As midsummer approached, Sarah-Ann sat in the room behind the shop watching the clock. Not a single customer had been in for over half an hour, and as she was due to close in five minutes it was unlikely anyone would call now. She might as well lock up early. She pushed herself up from the chair and looked around. She'd been so busy rearranging the shop, she'd let her little sanctuary become untidy. That must change. At least it would give her something to do tomorrow if she was quiet.

She was about to enter the shop when she heard the door open and a customer come in. Pausing, she let out a sigh. *Why do you have to come so late? Can't a woman go home of an evening?* With her best smile in place she took a step forward, but before she reached the door she heard the lock being fastened and footsteps walk across the floor towards her. A man's footsteps. As she edged to the door, her heart skipped a beat and she instinctively reached for the walking cane that stood in the corner of the room. The metal handle felt cold and strong between her fingers but it did little to slow her heart rate as she listened to the footsteps coming closer. *They're coming around the counter!*

She waited until they stopped, before she took the shaft of the cane in her hands and prepared to swing it. "Who's there?" She sounded braver than she felt. "I warn you, I'm armed."

"What are you talking about?" In one swift movement, Mr Wetherby burst into the room and took the cane from her.

"What are you doing here?" Sarah-Ann gasped for breath. "You scared the life out of me."

"Are you like this every time a customer comes in?"

"Only when I'm on my own and they lock the door behind them when they come in."

"I thought it was about time you were closing for the night, I was saving you a job."

"That's not for you to decide." Sarah-Ann made to walk into the shop, but Mr Wetherby caught hold of her arm and pulled her back.

"It is when I want to talk to you. I've had enough of this nonsense."

"Trying to defend myself isn't nonsense." She pulled her arm from his grip. "What do you want anyway? We've said all we have to say."

"I want you to move to Handsworth with me."

"As your mistress! You think you can come and order me about and that I'll agree to anything. Once upon a time I might have been delighted to think that Mr Wetherby thought enough of me to want to spend time with me. But not now. Even though my heart still flutters every time I see you, I've got more sense than to let it rule what I do. You used me all those years ago, helped ruin my marriage and may have been responsible for my husband's death. Now all you want me for is a mistress."

Mr Wetherby pulled her towards him. "Nobody would ever know."

"I'd know ... and so would my daughter." Sarah-Ann struggled to free herself but Mr Wetherby pulled her closer, causing the handle of the walking cane to dig into her back.

"I'm going to be spending a lot more time in Handsworth; I want you with me."

"The only way you'll get me to Handsworth is with a wedding band on my finger. If you don't think enough of me to make me an honest woman, then you can go on your own."

Mr Wetherby's cheeks flushed. "It's too soon for that. Mary hasn't been dead two years yet. Give me time."

"You can have all the time you want and when you're ready, you know where to find me." Sarah-Ann freed herself from his grasp and walked to the door. "Now if you'll excuse me, I've got things to do."

Chapter Fifty-Three

Handsworth, Staffordshire

Harriet finished tidying up the dinner dishes and went into the back room as William stood up and put his newspaper on top of the pile in the corner.

"Are you finished?" he asked her. "You've been an age today."

"That's what happens when the maid has a day off, but I'm ready now. I just need to find my bonnet and the girls, then we can go."

Five minutes later they left home to take Margaret and Florence to Sunday school before they continued their walk up Hamstead Road, towards Wellington Road. There were new buildings going up at regular intervals and they often stopped to comment on them. As they passed Wetherby House, Harriet peered through the windows.

"It doesn't look like Mr Wetherby's entertaining today. The table in the dining room's empty."

"They might be finished," William said.

"I doubt it. It's only two o'clock; he'd still be sat with his bottle of port. I wonder what's up; I haven't seen anyone there for a few weeks now."

"You can ask his brother." William nodded at Thomas who was walking towards them.

"Good afternoon," Thomas said when he was within speaking distance. "Have you been to Wetherby House?"

"No, we're just out for a stroll," William said. "It doesn't look like there's anyone there. No visitors at any rate."

"No, my brother hasn't been himself lately; I'm not sure what's the matter with him. Perhaps the thought of moving from Birmingham's affecting him more than he imagined it would."

"What do you mean?" William asked.

"Hasn't he told you? He doesn't want to live in Birmingham any more. He's finally realised he's living in squalor and overcrowding when he could be living here. He's going to travel in when he needs to."

"It's taken him long enough, but I suppose it

means I'll be seeing less of him at the workshop than I do already."

"Yes, he's not going to have much to do with it for the time being. He's asked me to take over in Birmingham."

Harriet opened her mouth to say something, but closed it again for fear of making a fool of herself. Instead she turned to William, but it was clear from his expression that he had no more knowledge of it than she did.

"Ah ... he hasn't mentioned it then," Thomas said. "Please don't worry, I'm not going to be there to tell you how to do your job, you do that well enough, I'll be there to watch over things, make sure the stock is up to date and the orders are delivered on time, that sort of thing."

"I thought you were there to learn the trade," William said.

Thomas grimaced. "It's not really my thing, to tell you the truth. I'm much better suited to the office work."

"William-Wetherby's been taken on to do that for the Birmingham office." Harriet's tone was abrupt. "Will he be out of a job?"

"No, not at all, but he's fresh out of school and still has a lot to learn. I'll be there to help and supervise him."

William and Thomas continued to talk about the business, but Harriet didn't hear a word of it. Why did Mr Wetherby have to go and change things? Would it mean she wouldn't be able to do the book-keeping any more? It was typical; he did everything that he wanted without a thought for anyone else. Well she wouldn't stop keeping the books; she would just have to start doing them for William's new business instead. He just needed a push.

"William, we're going to have to go." Harriet took hold of William's arm to encourage him to move. "We have to pick the children up soon."

"We've got time yet," he said, but then noticed the look on her face. "Actually, yes you're right. I'm sorry, Thomas, we need to go."

Thomas nodded his farewell as William and Harriet changed direction and walked back the way they had come.

"Do you have to be so rude?" William said, once they were out of earshot.

"I hardly said anything. He's lucky he didn't get a lot worse than that, I can tell you. What on earth's going on? I take it you had no knowledge of this until today?"

"None. In fact, I thought things were going quite well. Mr Wetherby even complimented me the other week on how well things were being run."

"I don't blame the brother," Harriet said. "I think he just wants a job and he'll do whatever Mr Wetherby tells him to, but I don't trust Mr Wetherby one bit. I think he's putting him there to spy on us."

"You're being silly again. Why do you always think everyone's watching us?"

"Because more often than not they are. You mark my words, Mr Wetherby's up to something, I just can't work out what it is." Without warning Harriet stopped and pulled William back towards her. "He doesn't have any idea that I do the books, does he?"

"How could he? I'm always careful to make sure nobody sees me with them and he always compliments the work. He wouldn't do that if he knew you did it. You haven't told anyone, have you?"

"Mary-Ann caught me working on them one day, but she wouldn't say anything. No, I think there's more to it. You're going to have to start being alert and tell me everything that happens."

THOMAS WATCHED William and Harriet walk back down Wellington Road and let out a sigh of relief. It was the first time he'd spoken to William's wife and he was glad he didn't have to deal with her more often. He pitied William's ears as they made their way home. Once they rounded the corner he continued on his way to Wetherby House.

"Are you all on your own?" he asked Mr Wetherby as he was shown into the back room.

"I wasn't feeling up to company. What brings you here? I thought you'd be keeping the taverns of Birmingham in business."

Thomas laughed. "I can save that until tonight. I wanted to see you. You've not been yourself lately."

"No ... well, I've got things on my mind."

"One wouldn't be William, would it? I met him and his wife outside. I didn't realise you hadn't told them you were coming back to Handsworth."

Mr Wetherby eyed his brother from under half-closed eyelids. "Did you tell them? I don't suppose they'll be troubled by the news."

"They weren't bothered about the fact you were moving, but I felt some hostility when I told them I'd be taking over the running of Birmingham."

Mr Wetherby shot up from his seat. "Good Lord, I'm not surprised if that's what you told them. I said you'd be minding the office side of the business, not taking charge. William will still run the workshop."

"I told him that, but I don't think his wife was best pleased."

Mr Wetherby put his hand to his head as he paced the room. "No, she wouldn't be. You mark my words, she'll have William round here as quick as you like asking what's going on ... and asking why he knew nothing about it."

"I'm sorry, I assumed they knew, but enough of them. I came to find out why you've been so miserable these last few weeks."

"No reason."

Thomas raised his eyebrow. "Are you sure? Haven't you got anything you want to tell me?"

Mr Wetherby studied his brother before he gave a slight nod of his head. "Let me fetch the port and I'll tell you everything."

Chapter Fifty-Four

Birmingham, Warwickshire

The walk down Summer Lane was a familiar one, but Mr Wetherby was still surprised to reach the end and turn into Constitution Hill. When he arrived at the shop, he stopped to catch his breath. He must have walked too quickly; it never used to make him breathless. He peered through the window while he wiped his handkerchief across his forehead. She didn't have any customers.

As he went inside, Sarah-Ann was nowhere to be seen. *She must be in the back; I'll give her a minute before I go any further.* He only waited a couple of seconds, but when she saw him she hesitated in the doorway to the back room.

"Good morning, Sarah-Ann, I've brought this back." He smiled and gestured to the cane in his hand. "I accidentally took it with me last time I was here."

Sarah-Ann stayed where she was. "I didn't think I'd see it again."

"No. I'm sorry." He glanced back at the door. "We need to talk. Can we drop the latch?"

Sarah-Ann held his gaze before she nodded. "If you must."

With the door fastened, Mr Wetherby walked towards her and placed the cane on the counter. "I've made a mess of things and I wanted to tell you that if I could rewind the clock, I would." When Sarah-Ann said nothing, he continued. "I meant no offence when I asked you to join me in Handsworth. I want to be with you and I thought you wanted to be with me."

Sarah-Ann's tone was curt. "How could you imagine I'd appreciate being a mistress? Have you any idea how I'd be treated if anyone found out? I took the risk when I was younger because I worshipped you, and being married to Frederick made me appear respectable. I couldn't do that now."

361

Mr Wetherby took her hands as they rested on the counter. "I'm sorry, I wasn't thinking properly."

He held Sarah-Ann's gaze for several seconds before she gestured towards the back room and he followed her in.

"So where does that leave us?" she asked.

Mr Wetherby put his arms around her. "I still want you to join me in Handsworth but I've realised I can't let Mary's memory ruin my future. I want you to move into Wetherby House as my wife."

Sarah-Ann's eyes filled with tears as she gazed into his eyes. "Do you love me?"

"Of course I love you. I've loved you for years, despite the fact I knew it was wrong."

"You've never told me before."

"I've been a fool. I know what you've given up for me, but I'm going to make it up to you."

"Can Elizabeth join us?"

Mr Wetherby took her face in his hands and touched her lips with his. "Of course she can. If it makes you happy, I'll be happy."

The tears that had been held in check streamed down Sarah-Ann's cheeks. "Do you mean it?"

"Of course I mean it." Mr Wetherby got down on one knee. "Now please, will you marry me?"

Chapter Fifty-Five

Handsworth, Staffordshire

Even for August, the weather was hot and as William and Harriet left church she opened her parasol and let the shaft rest on her shoulder. With no clouds in the sky, it was the only shade around. As usual the girls walked behind them, but today even William-Wetherby and Charles, who had been allowed home from school for the summer, had slowed to a walk.

"You're quiet today," William said as they turned into Wellington Road.

"I'm thinking about dinner. Why does he insist on having these family gatherings when nobody wants to go?"

"You don't know that nobody else wants to go. I think it's decent of him to try to keep the family together. You'd complain if he didn't invite us."

Harriet pouted. "Maybe."

"Besides, he's been in a particularly good mood this last couple of weeks, but he won't tell anyone why. It wouldn't surprise me if he's got another announcement to make."

"Well, I hope it's something like Thomas is going back to sea and you're in charge again," Harriet said.

"I think he'd have told me if that was the case. Anyway, we'll find out soon enough, most of the guests are here."

The front door was open when they arrived and William stood to the side to let Harriet and the children in. They followed the noise into the front living room and took a glass of sherry from the maid.

"Oh my, look over there." Harriet nodded in the direction of the bay window. "Your aunt Sarah-Ann's here again. I thought they'd fallen out."

"So did I. I hope the smile on his face has got nothing to do with her."

"You don't suppose the announcement will be about them, do you?" Harriet's eyes were wide.

"I hope not. She's my father's sister and was my mother's best friend ... it would be wrong for so many reasons." William's face paled. "It might also confirm that Mr Flemming was right."

"What's the matter?" Mary-Ann said as she and Mr Diver joined them.

William couldn't speak. His heart was pounding and he shook his head to clear his thoughts. He needed to sit down. Taking a gulp of sherry, he sat in the nearest chair as Mr Wetherby arrived in the centre of the room and called for attention.

"Thank you for joining me today," he started, the smile almost splitting his face in two. "It's only four months ago since we were last here, but I have a rather special announcement to make and I wanted to tell everyone together." He held out his hand towards Sarah-Ann and beckoned her towards him. "As you know, Sarah-Ann and I have known each other for many years and indeed she was a dear friend and sister-in-law to Mary, God rest her soul. Today, however, I'm delighted to announce that I've asked her to marry me and she's accepted."

Mr Wetherby was about to raise his glass to propose a toast but the gasps of surprise stopped him.

William turned to Harriet and then Mary-Ann before he put his hand to his head. "He's marrying Aunt Sarah-Ann, of all people. He can't. It isn't right."

"If you think you're unhappy, look at William Junior." Mr Diver nodded in the direction of his brother-in-law. "He's probably worried about his inheritance."

"That should be the least of his worries," William said. "I've just realised that Mr Wetherby's been planning this for years and he's put a lot of effort into it, you mark my words."

Mary-Ann stared at William, but the sound of Mr Wetherby tapping the side of his glass with a spoon forced her to save her question. As silence descended, Mr Wetherby turned to Sarah-Ann who appeared frozen to the spot, her eyes staring out at those around her. Only the touch of Mr Wetherby's hand on her back jolted her to her senses.

"I understand this might have come as a shock," Mr Wetherby said. "After all, we haven't been officially walking out together, but I hope you can be happy for us. We've known each other for many years and as we're both widowed we decided we wanted to spend our old age together."

"Have you set a date yet?" Thomas asked.

"Not yet, but it's likely to be early next year. Sarah-Ann will move in here once we're married but we'll need to sell the shop before she does."

Thomas turned to those nearest to him and

raised his glass. "I think congratulations are in order. To Mr Wetherby and Sarah-Ann."

"What are you talking about?" Mary-Ann whispered to William as the guests repeated the toast. "Mother's not been gone two years, how could he have been planning it?"

Harriet moved closer to Mary-Ann to avoid being overheard. "Do you remember I told you we thought Mr Wetherby and your aunt were being intimate together?"

Mary-Ann nodded.

"Well, there's more. We don't think Mr Flemming's death was an accident."

Mary-Ann's eyes were wide. "Why? What haven't you told me?"

"I was with Mr Wetherby and Mr Flemming when they had their fight," William said. "As soon as Mr Flemming made his accusation about Aunt Sarah-Ann, Mr Wetherby charged at him and knocked him to the ground. I think he was unconscious the moment his head hit the floor, but Mr Wetherby was in a wild fury and started beating him about the head. I think he was trying to kill him all along."

"Keep your voice down," Mr Diver said. "You can't go around saying things like that."

William lowered his voice to a whisper. "The

thing is, I think Mother knew about them. Her last words to me were *Tell him he has my blessing to be with Sarah-Ann*. I've been thinking about it though, and I don't think she meant it. In the seconds before she died, just after she uttered those words, she was crying."

"Perhaps he thinks he's doing nothing wrong because he has your mother's blessing," Harriet said.

William glowered at her. "He doesn't know he has her blessing. I was on my own with Mother and I didn't pass the message on. I'll never pass it on now. He doesn't deserve to be happy, and as for Aunt Sarah-Ann, she should be ashamed of herself. Lying to Mother all those years and after everything Mother did for her."

"I can't believe you didn't tell me all this," Mary-Ann said to Harriet.

"We've only just put everything together. There wasn't much to tell before today."

Mary-Ann glared at Mr Wetherby as he talked to her aunt. "Everyone still feels sorry for him, especially with the elaborate memorial he dedicated to Mother in church ... and the peal of bells to mark the anniversary of her death. They think he's still in mourning, but this feels like the final nail in her coffin."

"I'm going to find out about the legalities of

this," William muttered under his breath. "There must be something we can do to stop them."

"Why don't you threaten to go to the police about Mr Flemming if he doesn't call the wedding off?" Harriet said. "I have everything written down as evidence."

"I can't do that. I still have to work with him. Besides, the police won't take your testimony into account. They'll think you're only repeating what I told you."

"Well, now's the time to break away from him and start your own business. If this isn't reason enough I don't know what is."

"I should have had him locked up years ago." William fought to keep his voice low. "I can still see the look in Mother's eyes. It was the look you get when you've lived a lie for so many years."

"You could contest the banns when they have them read," Mr Diver said. "I've heard of many a marriage ceremony that's been stopped because of that."

William nodded. "Maybe I'll threaten him with it. If he's got anything to hide, it might be enough to make him think again."

"Having said that, you do have to think of the inheritance as well," Mr Diver said. "He may or may not choose to change his will in favour of your aunt, but if you go upsetting him, it might force his hand. You don't want to be cut out of it."

Harriet's eyes were slits as she fixed them on Mr Wetherby. "How does he still manage to have the upper hand when he's so clearly in the wrong? I only hope that one day he gets his comeuppance."

Chapter Fifty-Six

Birmingham, Warwickshire

Sarah-Ann secured the last of her boxes and inspected the living room. She had more personal property than she imagined, but then she supposed she had been in Birmingham for over twenty years. She'd loved it all those years ago, but it hadn't been good to her and now she was glad she was leaving. Handsworth was where she wanted to be, with Mr Wetherby.

The only blot on the horizon was the wedding. It was the one thing she wanted more than anything else and yet it could split the family. Mr Wetherby had told her that William and William Junior had both spoken to him; William had even threatened to challenge the banns. *Why can't everyone be happy for us? Is it too much to ask?* Thankfully, Mr Wetherby was having none of it. At least that was one of the benefits of having money. As soon as William had left his office, Mr Wetherby had applied for a marriage licence and brought forward the date of the wedding. To tomorrow. Not that she would have the wedding she hoped for. Most of the family hadn't been told about it, and they needed to keep it that way. Only Charlotte and Elizabeth had been invited. And Richard.

Richard, her brother, and the man Mr Wetherby hated more than any other. The plain fact was that she needed him to give her away, but when she had mentioned it to Mr Wetherby, he had flown into a rage. Finally, after much persuasion, he'd relented and agreed he could give her away, but only if he stayed away from the wedding breakfast.

She was thinking about the day ahead when Elizabeth interrupted her.

"Are you ready?" she asked. "Mr Wetherby will be here soon and we shouldn't keep him waiting. I'm so happy for you; I hated you being on your own once Father died."

Sarah-Ann smiled and took her daughter's hand. "I'm glad you're moving with me. It's a big step."

"I'm sure you'll be fine. Mr Wetherby will take care of you."

"He will and I can't think of being with anyone better. He's not going to stand any nonsense from William or William Junior either."

Shortly after ten o'clock, Mr Wetherby arrived in a six-seat carriage. The familiar figures of the chestnut horses stood patiently in front of the house while the luggage was loaded. Sarah-Ann and Elizabeth were staying at Wetherby House overnight so they wouldn't have far to travel to the church the following day. Mr Wetherby was staying in a tavern with his best man, and his wife who would act as their second witness.

When they arrived at Wetherby House the smell of cooking filled the hall and Sarah-Ann saw that the dining room table had been set for four.

"I decided a celebratory dinner, with just the four of us, was warranted," Mr Wetherby said with a smile. "I want you to feel at home here, you're no longer a guest."

Sarah-Ann felt a knot tighten in her stomach. She'd never needed to manage more than one maid before, nor run such a big house. How different it was all going to be.

"Don't worry, Charlotte will help you," Mr Wetherby said as if reading her mind. "Mary didn't do much in her last year." He paused. "Why don't you and Elizabeth go and change for dinner and I'll arrange to bring the rest of your boxes in. It won't take long and I'll have them sent to one of the spare rooms so you can sort them out when you're ready."

They arrived back downstairs fifteen minutes later and Mr Wetherby handed them a glass of sherry as a dinner of roasted pork was brought in.

"To Sarah-Ann." Mr Wetherby raised his glass. "May you be happy here."

Sarah-Ann raised her glass and smiled, but she had no appetite. Just sitting at this table, as the future lady of the house, was too much. What if she got it all wrong? What if the staff hated her? What if William and Mary-Ann never forgave her? What if ...?

Mr Wetherby put his hand on hers. "Please stop worrying. You'll get used to everything in no time at all."

Sarah-Ann gave the best smile she could, but it was feeble.

"I want you to wear this." Mr Wetherby held out a package to her. "A wedding present from me to you. A sign that you belong here."

Sarah-Ann took the package and unfastened the lid. Inside sat a beautiful diamond and pearl brooch, which sparkled as she lifted it from its box.

"It's beautiful," Sarah-Ann gasped. "I thought I'd seen all types of jewels in the shop, but we never had anything like this. "Are they real diamonds?"

"They are, all set in eighteen-carat gold. I hope you like it."

"Like it? I adore it." Sarah-Ann's face broke into a smile as she placed it back in the box and passed it to Elizabeth.

"And I've one other thing for you," Mr Wetherby said. "We may not be having the grandest marriage ceremony tomorrow, but I still wanted you to have a new dress. It's waiting for you upstairs once you've eaten."

Sarah-Ann managed to eat most of her meal, and once dinner was over, she went upstairs with Elizabeth and waited while Charlotte brought the package into her new bedroom.

"We had to borrow one of your older dresses for the size." Elizabeth grinned at Charlotte. "I didn't think you'd miss it."

"There's obviously been a lot going on behind my back. Let me see." Sarah-Ann gasped as she opened the package to find an ivory dress, made of silk satin, with layers of material and a train falling down the back.

"Are you going to try it on?" Elizabeth asked, when her mother remained fixed to the spot. "We'll help you."

Five minutes later, standing in the middle of a bedroom that was bigger than the ground floor of her old house, and with the sun streaming through the windows, Sarah-Ann had never felt so special in her life. The dress fitted perfectly and was set off beautifully by the brooch. She walked to the mirror that stood in the corner of the room and studied herself. How wonderful she would look once her hair was arranged and she had some powder on her face.

"I'm so relieved it fits," Elizabeth said, before she noticed the tears on her mother's cheeks. "What's the matter? Don't you like it?"

"Of course I like it, it's beautiful, it's just that ..."

"You think no one's going to see you in it, don't you?" Charlotte said. "You think it will all be for nothing."

"I'm being silly, I'm sorry. The most important people will be there ..."

"Can I let you into a secret?" Charlotte said. "Please don't tell Papa I've told you, but he's arranged for a photographer to capture the wedding

... so you'll be able to show your dress to anyone who won't see it."

Sarah-Ann wiped her tears as she took in Charlotte's words. "Is there anything that man doesn't think of? I love him so much. How I wish everyone else could be happy for us."

Chapter Fifty-Seven

Handsworth, Staffordshire

The following morning, Mr Wetherby sat having breakfast in the dining room of the tavern with his best man. Mr Gregory wouldn't normally have been his first choice, but he knew he couldn't trust Thomas to keep the details of the wedding to himself and so he had made the painful decision not to invite him. Travellers occupied most of the tables, but as eight o'clock approached the room emptied and Mr Wetherby pushed his chair back to stretch his legs. As they were starting a second pot of tea Richard walked in, dressed in his morning suit. After seeing the teapot he asked for a cup and saucer and sat down next to Mr Wetherby.

"I hope I'm not disturbing anything," Richard said.

Mr Wetherby glared at him. "What are you doing here? In fact, how did you know I was here?"

"Elizabeth told me." Richard leaned back in his chair and stretched his legs in front of him. "I went to Wetherby House looking for you but found my sister there instead. I left Mrs Richard with them."

"You have no business at Wetherby House. I expected to see you at the church, and not before."

Richard sighed. "We can make this day as difficult or as easy as you like, but the fact is, you're marrying my sister and I'm the one who'll give her away."

Mr Wetherby said nothing as he added some sugar to his tea.

"You've upset a lot of people with this marriage. Martha is furious, as is William. Mr Flemming told more people about you than I realised. Mary may be gone, but they haven't forgotten how you treated her."

Mr Wetherby turned scarlet. "You keep Mary out of this. I don't want to hear you speak her name."

Richard smiled and poured himself a cup of tea. "My, my. I didn't realise you were still so sensitive."

"Did you come here this morning specifically to annoy me?"

"I didn't, but you make it so easy I couldn't resist." Richard laughed to himself. "As I said to you earlier, you can make today as easy or as difficult as you wish. I came here hoping you would make it easy. For Sarah-Ann's sake if nothing else, although whether she deserves it after the way she's behaved is debatable. Still, she is my sister and you haven't got many friends at the moment and so I'd like her to enjoy her day, even if I think she is marrying a fool."

"Get out!" Mr Wetherby could feel the veins throbbing in his neck as he rose to his feet and pointed to the door.

Richard remained where he was and sipped his tea. "This should make for an interesting day. I only hope I don't bump into William on my way back to Wetherby House. I'm not sure how I'd explain being in Handsworth dressed up like this."

Mr Wetherby's eyes were wide. "You promised Sarah-Ann you'd tell no one." The words roared around the room drawing attention from those who were yet to leave.

Richard shrugged as he stood up. "I think I was expecting a little more thanks for it. Never mind ..."

"Stop." Mr Wetherby took a deep breath. "All right. For Sarah-Ann's sake we'll pretend this conversation didn't happen. At least you won't try and turn her head from me."

Richard grinned. "As if I would ever do that ... but I'd watch that you don't leave her on her own for too long." Richard picked up his hat and winked at Mr Wetherby before he sauntered across the dining room. When he reached the door, he turned to see Mr Wetherby glaring at him. "I'll see you later."

MR WETHERBY and Mr and Mrs Gregory walked to the Parish Church and arrived thirty minutes before the service was due to start. It was almost thirty-five years since he had walked into the same church to marry Mary and he made his way to the memorial he had commissioned for her and bowed his head. He knew she'd understand. She was a wonderful woman. *Why does that fool Jackson always have to turn up and spoil everything? May God give me strength to be civil to him.*

Sarah-Ann arrived promptly at eleven o'clock on the arm of her brother. She no longer had the beauty of youth and her hair was heavily flecked with grey, but it didn't matter. She still looked radiant. As soon as he saw her, Mr Wetherby noticed she had arranged her hair so that it fell over her left shoulder in much the same way as it had when she'd married Mr Flemming. The image of the two of them, sitting in the carriage outside church, flashed across his mind. Where had the years gone? As she reached his side, he smiled and turned to face the vicar. The service was short with no hymns and only two Bible readings, read by Charlotte and Elizabeth, before the reverend gave a short talk.

Once the marriage register was signed, Richard and his wife departed while the rest of the party returned to the tavern. A table had been set for six, but before they went into the dining room, Mr Wetherby took them through to the lounge.

"I knew the dress would look wonderful and so I've arranged for a photographer to come and capture our day." He leaned forward and kissed Sarah-Ann on the cheek. "I hope the diamonds in the brooch don't dazzle him."

Sarah-Ann laughed. "You think of everything. Thank you ... and thank you for being civil to Richard. Don't think I didn't notice."

Mr Wetherby flushed. "Anything for you, my dear. Now let's position ourselves for the photograph, it will take a while."

Eventually the photograph was captured and the group moved into the dining room. Once Mr Wetherby proposed a toast to his new wife he turned to Elizabeth.

"Did you do as I asked and packed a bag for your mother with some spare clothes?" When Elizabeth nodded, he turned back to Sarah-Ann. "I didn't want to take you back to Wetherby House tonight, not with things as they've been, and so I've arranged for us to go to London for a few days."

"London, how marvellous." Sarah-Ann clapped her hands under her chin. "Of all the places I've ever wanted to go."

Mr Wetherby smiled. "We'll catch the three o'clock train this afternoon and travel back on Saturday. By then the family will be aware of our marriage. I've written letters to William Junior, William and Mary-Ann, which I'll post as we leave for the train. They'll have them by tomorrow morning, giving them four days to calm down."

"Thank you." Sarah-Ann's smile conflicted with the tears about to break from her eyes. "I don't think I've met a more considerate man in the whole of my life."

Chapter Fifty-Eight

Although spring was on the way, Harriet was sure it was getting colder. She had asked Violet to make up the fire and once the girls were in bed she pulled the heavy velvet curtains across the window and sat down next to William. William-Wetherby sat on the opposite side of the fire.

"How are you enjoying working in Birmingham?" she asked her son.

"I like it."

"You seem to have settled in well. What sort of things have you been doing?"

William-Wetherby put down his book. "Mainly checking and reordering the stock and invoicing the customers, that sort of thing."

"And what does Mr Wetherby's brother do if you're doing that?"

"He checks my work, and he takes the orders and talks to customers. He's been talking about us doing the bookkeeping as well. It should be done in the office, apparently it is in Handsworth, and Father shouldn't have to bring the books home and do it after work."

William and Harriet exchanged a glance.

"When did you see me bring them home?" William asked.

"I've seen them in your bag when you travel. You must stay up awfully late to do them because I've never seen you."

"It doesn't take long," William said. "I don't like to do them while everyone else is around."

"Mr Thomas will be asking you to take him through them so that he can help you out."

"Your father doesn't need any help." Harriet tried to keep her voice calm. "He's a partner in that business and he should do the bookkeeping, not Mr Thomas."

William-Wetherby frowned. "Don't be angry with him, he's only trying to help."

"Perhaps, but do you think you could discourage him?" Harriet said.

"Why?" William-Wetherby glanced from Harriet

to his father and back again.

"I ... I don't want him getting ideas above his station," Harriet said. "He's not been here five minutes."

William-Wetherby shrugged. "If you say so."

SEVERAL DAYS later as Harriet sat at the table in the back room she heard the front door close and somebody moving about in the hallway. The grandfather clock had just chimed half past two and she wasn't expecting anyone. Come to think of it, she hadn't heard the doorbell ring. She felt a lurch in her stomach as she hurried to close the books spread out in front of her. She dropped the first two onto the floor, but as she reached for the last one William-Wetherby walked in. He stopped in his tracks when he saw her.

"Mother, what are you doing?"

"Nothing." Harriet's voice squeaked. "Just tidying up."

William-Wetherby came closer. "Is that one of the books from the workshop?"

Harriet looked down at the book and then back at her son. "I can explain, please don't be angry."

"I'm not angry, but why is it here?"

"I was helping your father. I often have time in

the afternoons and so he said I could do them for him."

"Is that why you don't want Mr Thomas involved, because you enjoy doing them?"

Harriet sat back in her chair. "I'm sorry you had to find out this way, but we couldn't risk telling anyone. You might not be angry, but if Mr Wetherby found out, he wouldn't be happy."

"Why shouldn't he be? As long as you're doing a good job he should be pleased. He's not even paying you to do them."

"I wish you were right but I'm afraid he thinks that women shouldn't do such work, in fact, I'd go so far as to say he believes women are not capable of working with numbers. He's wrong of course. There are plenty of us with the brains to do this sort of work if we were allowed to. I just wanted a chance."

William-Wetherby smiled. "I know you're clever, you always have been. I won't tell anyone, I promise."

Harriet breathed a sigh of relief. "You're a good boy. Why are you home early anyway?"

"I'm not feeling well and so I was going to sit quietly and hope it passes."

"Here, come and sit by the fire. I'll make you a cup of tea and then, if you don't mind, I'll carry on working."

. . .

THE FOLLOWING afternoon as the clock struck three o'clock, Harriet put the kettle on the range and lifted out a selection of cakes. She was about to carry them through to the living room when the back door opened and Mary-Ann let herself in.

"I hope I'm not too early."

"No, of course not, come on through. Violet can make the tea."

"That's a nice selection of cakes." Mary-Ann eyed them as she sat in William-Wetherby's chair. "Have you invited someone else?"

"I did invite my friends from Birmingham, but unfortunately at the last minute they couldn't make it. Mrs Booth's having trouble with her husband and he wouldn't let her come. It makes me so angry. Men shouldn't be allowed to treat us as prisoners in our own homes."

"William's not like that with you."

"Maybe not, but having lived with my uncle I'm well aware of how it feels to be quite helpless. It makes me angry on behalf of all those women who can't stand up for themselves. I've been reading about it a lot lately. Have you seen that there's a group of women who've started lobbying parliament to get women the vote?"

"The suffrage movement, you mean?"

Harriet nodded. "They're getting a lot of attention and a number of MPs agree with them. Can you imagine what it would be like if we got the vote? It might be the first step to us gaining our independence."

"I do love your optimism," Mary-Ann said with a smile, "but don't get carried away. It'll never happen. We'd be too much of a threat if we could make our voices heard."

"That doesn't mean we shouldn't try. I've been looking in the paper to see if there are any meetings locally; I'm thinking of going along."

Mary-Ann's eyes widened. "You're not! Oh Harriet, please be careful. What would Mr Wetherby say if he found out?"

Violet let herself in with the tea tray, but Harriet continued. "I'm fed up of caring what Mr Wetherby thinks. He doesn't own us. We have to be our own people and it's about time somebody told him."

"I'm not disagreeing with you, but you shouldn't be the one who tells him. From what I understand, it's the Marquis of Salisbury who's opposing this in parliament and you know how Mr Wetherby feels about him."

Harriet stood up to pour the tea. "Someone's got to take a stand. I bet every woman who's spoken up for us has had opposition, but it hasn't stopped them. If you truly believe something's right, you have to fight for it. Don't you agree?"

Mary-Ann could only stare at Harriet. "All I'm saying is be careful. Have you said anything to William?"

"I've read him some of the pieces in the newspaper, but I haven't told him I'm going to join up."

"Well, I suggest you try him first and see how he responds. He's one of the most relaxed men there is and if he struggles with the idea, you know what you'll be up against at Wetherby House."

"If Mr Wetherby ever finds out that is." Harriet's eyes turned to slits. "He's too busy making money from other people's misfortune at the moment."

"What do you mean?"

"With the Artisans Dwelling Company. They're building houses sure enough, but nowhere near as fast as they're making families homeless. He doesn't care as long as the money keeps rolling in."

"Harriet, you don't know that."

"I may not have seen the books, but it's obvious. He's buying a new property every other month at the moment and he doesn't take that sort of money out of our business."

"Maybe not, but you have to stop saying things like that. Please. You'll end up getting yourself in trouble."

Chapter Fifty-Nine

Birmingham, Warwickshire

William-Wetherby liked his corner of the workshop. He had a mahogany desk and chair alongside the window and he could shut the door from the noise of the machines in the workshop. Mr Thomas had the desk next to the door, but he was often out, meaning that William-Wetherby spent most of the time on his own. Not that it bothered him. He enjoyed his own company.

He was still only seventeen but he'd settled into working life well. Mr Thomas no longer checked his work and if he did need any help, he asked his mother once he got home. She liked to talk about work, and on occasion she would show him some of the book-keeping.

One afternoon, while he was writing out an order sheet, Thomas came into the office.

"I wasn't expecting you back today," William-Wetherby said, glancing up. "Did you do everything you needed to?"

Thomas shook his head. "No, not a half of it, but I got sidetracked by my brother. I needed a couple of signatures from him and so I called into the Artisans offices on Bennetts Hill. I was about to leave when he told me he wants to do a complete audit of all the work we've done here since he's not been running the business."

William-Wetherby's eyes widened as his mind processed the implications of an audit. "That's over eighteen months ago. Why on earth ...?"

"I've no idea, although I asked him several times." Thomas put his hand to his head as he paced the room. "He's got a bee in his bonnet about something, but he wouldn't tell me what it is. It seems like a perfect waste of time in my opinion, but I couldn't talk him out of it."

"What do we have to do?"

"To start with we'll have to pull all the paperwork together for the orders and match them to the invoices, go through the stock books, check over the accounts to make sure they're up to date and accurate, pull together all the bank statements, and he wants the details of all our customers, in alphabetical order too, if you don't mind."

William-Wetherby was white. "That'll take weeks."

"We don't have weeks. He wants everything ready by this time next week. I'm going to have to bring your father into the office to work with us over the next few days. He's going to have to take me through the accounts as well so I can show them to my brother."

"Why does he ...?" William-Wetherby coughed to lower the pitch of his voice. "Why does he need to do that? It should all be self-explanatory."

"I need to be sure. We all need to work together here because we're all in trouble if things aren't right."

The two of them made a start that afternoon, but as soon as he was able, William-Wetherby grabbed his coat and ran for the omnibus. He could speak to his father later but he needed to warn his mother.

Handsworth, Staffordshire.

With her younger daughters fed and getting ready for bed, Harriet came back downstairs to prepare the table for William and William-Wetherby. She reached into the sideboard for the tablecloth, but stood up again when she heard the front door slam. Seconds later, William-Wetherby charged into the back room.

"You're early," she said. "Is everything all right?"

"No, everything's not all right." William-Wetherby sat down to catch his breath. "Mr Wetherby wants to do a full audit of the business and wants all the paperwork and accounts going back to when he started with the Artisans Dwelling Company."

Harriet thought for a moment. "That shouldn't be a problem. The accounts are all up to date."

"The problem is that Mr Thomas wants Father to take him through the books, so he can brief Mr Wetherby."

Harriet put her hands on her hips. "Why is he talking to Mr Wetherby? Your father's a partner in the business, not him."

"You're missing the point. I may have misread the situation, but I don't believe Father's in a position to take anyone through the accounts, is he?"

Harriet's face paled. "You're right of course, I wasn't thinking. I'm going to have to make sure your father understands everything in those books."

"It won't be that simple. Mr Thomas has collected up everything we need to sort out, including the accounts, and locked them away. Father won't be able to bring them home."

"But it's his business. He should be the one taking charge."

William-Wetherby shrugged. "He can try but Mr Thomas wants to be in control. I think Mr Wetherby's given the job to him."

"That's not good. Let me think. Is Mr Thomas the only one who has a key to the cupboard?" William-Wetherby nodded. "In that case you'll have to get it off him."

"How will I do that?"

"If he won't give it to Father, you have to tell him you need it so you can do your work."

"He won't be going anywhere between now and next week and so there'll be no need for that. He's in a panic of his own, to be honest."

"Could you ask for a copy of the key? Keep going to the cupboard when he's just locked it to show him you need access too."

William-Wetherby paused. "That could work, but what if it doesn't?"

"You'll have to resort to taking it from him when he's not looking."

"You mean steal it?"

Harriet threw the cloth over the table for tea. "It

wouldn't technically be stealing because you'll give it back to him. Think of it more as borrowing."

William was ashen-faced when he got home half an hour later. "I take it you've heard," he said to Harriet once he'd taken off his hat and coat.

"I have, but don't worry, we have a plan."

"Don't worry!" William gasped. "Of course I'm worried, I've got to take Mr Thomas through the accounts."

"Calm down, I'll help you."

William wiped his forehead with a handkerchief. "It's too late for that, he wants to do it tomorrow. On top of that, we've had a lot of invoices in this week and he wants me to enter them tomorrow while he's watching. I tried to bring the books home with me but he's locked them away and was still in the office when I left."

Harriet paced the room while she thought. "There's nothing for it. I'll have to make up some draft pages and tell you how I fill them in. I'll also need to go through a few issues we have with late payments or returns. It'll be harder but it should work."

Once they'd finished tea, Harriet sat with William and William-Wetherby and gave them a lesson in bookkeeping. William struggled to make sense of it all, but William-Wetherby managed to keep up.

"I'll help you," William-Wetherby said to his father once Harriet finished. "If we can sit with Mr Thomas together, I can tell you what to enter as if I was reinforcing the details for myself."

"I shan't sleep tonight worrying about this," William said. "What on earth is Mr Wetherby up to?"

Chapter Sixty

Harriet sat in her chair by the fire, waiting for William and William-Wetherby to come home. She felt as if she'd seen every movement of the clock since they had gone out that morning. She hadn't been able to focus on anything all day and when she heard the front door open at six o'clock that evening, she raced to the hallway.

"How did you get on?" she asked before William-Wetherby had two feet in the door.

"Father was fine." William-Wetherby smiled. "It was as if he'd been doing it for years."

"That was thanks to you," William said as he followed his son in. "I couldn't have done it otherwise. I knew that education was a good investment."

Harriet's eyes sparkled. "So Mr Thomas was happy with everything?"

"He was, and he commented on how neat everything was, so you can take that as a compliment."

Harriet smiled. "So is that it? We've nothing more to worry about?"

"We still have all the other paperwork to pull together, which will take time, but it shouldn't be a problem."

"What a relief. Come and sit down and I'll serve your tea."

~

Birmingham, Warwickshire.

ONE WEEK AFTER HIS REQUEST, Mr Wetherby arrived in the office at precisely eight o'clock. William and William-Wetherby stood as he entered, but Thomas was already pacing the room.

"Sit down all of you," he ordered as he walked in and placed his hat on the stand in the corner. "Now, let's get started. Thomas, I'd like you to take me through the whole business since January 1883 so that I understand what's been going on. This afternoon I have Mr Carlton from the Conservative Association joining us. He's a trained accountant and I want to take him through everything so he can verify the figures."

Thomas let out an audible yelp, but Mr Wetherby ignored him. "Let's start with the order book. Is it healthy?"

"Yes, it is." Thomas pulled up a chair alongside his brother. "We've had two new customers this week in fact."

"Let me see ... ah yes, I spoke to both of them the other week, but what's this?" His eyes moved up the page. "The orders we're getting aren't from regular customers, in fact, looking back, many are only making one or two orders and not returning. Can you explain that?" Mr Wetherby looked first at Thomas and then to William. When there was no reply, he continued. "All right, let me jog your memories."

Mr Wetherby proceeded to go through every order, discussing the fine details of each and questioning why the clients had not returned. It was two hours later before he finished the interrogation but he was far from happy.

"Let me see the stock list, I want to get to the bottom of this. Why have we changed supplier for the metals?"

"I got a better deal from them," Thomas said. "I wanted to keep costs down."

"Bring some of this new stock to me."

William went into the workshop and returned a minute later to hand Mr Wetherby the sample.

"Is this seriously what we're using?" Mr Wetherby glared at William. "I'm not surprised the customers aren't coming back; this is substandard by any measure. You must have noticed it was making inferior buttons."

For the first time, William looked uncomfortable. "Once they're made up, the quality's almost identical."

"I don't believe that for a minute and if you believe it then you're in the wrong job. Pass me the accounts." Mr Wetherby studied the books before turning to Thomas. "You said we were getting these materials cheaper but it doesn't look like it to me. These prices are almost identical to the prices we used to pay."

Thomas remained confident. "The prices of the other materials went up. By switching suppliers we kept the prices at the original level."

"Nonsense, I was talking to one of the original suppliers last week and he was complaining that he'd not been able to raise his prices for three years. How stupid do you think I felt when I had to admit I didn't know he was no longer a supplier? You'll reinstate him tomorrow with immediate effect, do you hear me?" Thomas nodded but said nothing as Mr Wetherby returned to the accounts.

"What's happened here? Some of these figures have been altered. You're responsible for this, aren't you, William?"

"Yes, but ... I don't know. I didn't change them."

"I changed them," Thomas interrupted. "I spotted some mistakes."

"I don't think so." William-Wetherby's cheeks coloured as everyone turned to him.

"Why do you say that, boy?" Mr Wetherby asked.

"Well ... Father is always so careful ... I often sit with him as he's working and I check his figures as we go along."

Mr Wetherby gave the boy an unconvinced stare and turned back to the figures.

"This writing from last month is different to the more recent entries; I can tell you did the more recent work, William, so who did the earlier work?"

Nobody spoke.

Mr Wetherby looked around the three of them as they each stared at the floor. "I'm waiting. I knew there was something going on here. Who's been doing the books?"

"It was me, Mr Wetherby. I'm sorry." William-Wetherby's face was red.

"William, are you letting a boy barely out of

school do the accounts? I thought you were doing them."

"I-I was, but William-Wetherby needs to learn and so I sat with him while he wrote the entries."

"Didn't you check his work? It's clear that he's made mistakes."

"I wasn't aware of any mistakes. All the work was accurate when we finished and the entries balanced."

"So why did Thomas need to make changes?"

Again nobody spoke.

"All right, if you can't tell me the truth, I'll ask Mr Carlton to help me out. He'll be here shortly and mark my words he'll tell me what's been going on. Now get out of my sight, all of you, I need time to think."

Chapter Sixty-One

William followed William-Wetherby and Thomas into the court and closed the door behind him before turning to Thomas.

"There was nothing wrong with those figures when we left the books with you the other day. Why did you change them?"

"Clearly there was, otherwise I wouldn't have touched them."

"That's a lie." Conscious that the residents of the court were staring at them William tried to keep his voice down. "I think you're trying to hide something, that's why you didn't want me or William-Wetherby helping you."

Thomas pushed William on the shoulder. "I resent that."

"I don't care whether you resent it or not, it's the truth, isn't it? You worked into the night on several occasions and wouldn't tell us what you were doing. And why did you change the suppliers? I told you months ago that the quality of the new materials was below standard, but you said Mr Wetherby had agreed it."

"Father, watch out." William-Wetherby pulled his father to one side as Thomas slung his fist around to meet William's face. William saw it at the last second and managed to move out of the way.

"We're not on a ship now," William said. "Is that what they teach in the navy? When you haven't got an answer, resort to violence?"

Before William could move, Thomas surprised him with a left hook that caught him full on the chin.

"That's enough." William-Wetherby stood in front of his father. "What on earth's got into you? This isn't going to sort anything out. Mr Thomas, I think you'd better tell us what's going on so we can try and explain it to Mr Wetherby together."

Thomas backed away and appeared ready to run.

"Well?" William said. "Running away won't do you any good. For a start, you're going to have to give me a reason to explain this. I can't tell Mr Wetherby my chin started bleeding of its own accord."

Thomas leaned against the side of the building and slid down to sit on his heels. "I borrowed some money. I didn't think he'd notice."

"Borrowed or do you mean helped yourself to?" William said. "Have you been stealing from your own brother?"

Thomas glared up at him. "I was going to pay it back."

"Haven't you got enough money? He pays you well enough for what you do. What did you need it for?"

Again the question was met with silence.

"We can't help you if you won't tell us the truth," William-Wetherby said.

Thomas sighed. "A few months ago one of the suppliers gave me a tip for the Derby, a horse that had won his last six races, it was a dead cert."

"Don't tell me, the thing didn't win." William wiped the blood from his chin.

"It didn't even come in the first three and I'd put a week's wages on it. I knew I was in a mess and so I borrowed the money until my luck changed. I was going to pay it back."

"But let me guess. You've been on a losing streak ever since." William was out of patience. "So, how does it work? Every week you help yourself to a second wage and hope nobody notices?"

"I took it from the petty cash."

"So why did you have to change the books?"

"I had to keep withdrawing cash from the bank to replace it and so I created invoices to cover it and logged it as more stock. They hadn't been entered into the books."

"My God, man, are you trying to get us all into trouble? It'll look like we've missed at least one invoice a week, which is going to get William-Wetherby into trouble. Do you think of no one but yourself?"

William-Wetherby interrupted. "If Mr Wetherby thinks we've ordered more stock, he's going to wonder where it is. We're not carrying a lot at the moment and he's bound to notice."

"Could we say we used it?" Thomas asked lamely. "Tell him we thought we'd be making a cost saving on the material but ended up using twice as much?"

"He's not going to buy that. He saw some of the buttons we've been turning out and they're rubbish," William said. "To be honest, I think the best policy would be for you to own up. You're his brother and he thinks a lot of you. He might stamp his feet and shout, but I think he'll forgive you. More than he'd forgive me or William-Wetherby, at any rate."

Twenty minutes later, Mr Wetherby asked them

to join him. The accountant had arrived and Thomas reluctantly explained what he'd been doing. As he spoke, Mr Wetherby's face paled until he could bear no more.

"Thomas, stop there. I can't believe what you've told me. Mr Carlton noticed there were some late entries, but please don't tell me you wasted over fifty pounds on the horses."

Thomas could only nod as Mr Wetherby paced the office, his head bowed.

"William and William-Wetherby, will you leave us. I'll speak to you tomorrow but rest assured I fully acknowledge you're innocent of any misdemeanour. Mr Carlton, could you stay with my brother and I, and talk me through the full implications of this lunacy?"

As William reached for his hat, he saw Thomas sink into a chair and put his head in his hands. He was shaking his head as he and William-Wetherby rushed from the office. It was only when they were two streets away and clear of any passers-by that they spoke to each other.

"What do you think will happen to him?" William-Wetherby asked.

"I fear the worst, judging by the expression on Mr Wetherby's face," William said. "I expected him to fly into a rage but his reaction was much more sinister."

"Do you think we'll see Mr Thomas again?"

For the first time since they left the office William looked directly at his son. "If I'm being honest, no I don't think we will."

THE FOLLOWING MORNING, Mr Wetherby was waiting for them. He waited for William to get the workshop up and running before calling him into the office.

"I won't beat about the bush," he said. "I wanted to tell you that Thomas won't be troubling you any more. He accepted his behaviour was completely un-acceptable and that he'd given me no choice but to dismiss him. Once we got underneath Thomas's writ-ing, Mr Carlton could see the books had been right and so I'm going to leave you in charge from now on. I've spoken to our suppliers and we'll switch back to the original firms with immediate effect. Thomas ad-mitted he'd switched because they'd offered him some money and therefore I had no hesitation in telling them their contracts were terminated. I've also de-manded that they take back any remaining stock and provide us with a refund. This batch of buttons the men are working on should be the last with these materials and we'll sell them at half price on the market. I won't have my reputation ruined by shoddy goods."

"May I ask what prompted your suspicions?" William asked.

"Occasionally I call into the office and I'd noticed a discrepancy between the books and the bank statements, something that should always be checked before the books are signed off. If I'm being honest, I suspected it was you who was up to something. I'd also noticed the change in handwriting and that raised my curiosity. At first I thought it belonged to a woman, which would have explained the mistakes."

"Mother would never make mistakes like that," William-Wetherby said. "She's too good a bookkeeper."

"What did you say?" Mr Wetherby spun around to face William-Wetherby.

"N-Nothing ... I mean, I was just saying ... it couldn't have been Mother because she wouldn't make mistakes like that. That was all."

"That's right," William added. "Of course Harriet wouldn't be doing them."

Mr Wetherby's eyes were like slits as he glared from one to the other. "I'm glad to hear it."

Chapter Sixty-Two

Handsworth, Staffordshire

Harriet stood at the back of the room amazed at how busy it was. Spotting an empty seat three rows in front of her she squeezed past a number of women to sit down. She studied the faces of those watching her, hoping she didn't see anyone she knew, and was surprised by what she saw. There were women of all ages and from all walks of life. She'd expected the younger ones to be here. They were part of the new generation who wanted women to have the vote, but the number of older women was a revelation.

She turned to her right and an elderly woman smiled at her. "This your first time?" the woman asked. Harriet nodded. "I thought so, you look terrified. Don't worry, we won't bite and we won't tell no one you were here either, keep your name to yourself if you want to. We're all here for the same reason. For what it's worth, I'm Mrs Hillier. I've been coming every week for the last couple of months but to be honest things have gone off the boil recently."

Harriet nodded. "Why?"

The woman shrugged. "We had an excellent speaker a month or so ago. She was going to London to hand a petition to parliament, but we haven't heard from her since. The woman who's speaking today knows her and so I'm hoping she'll give us an update."

"Do you think we'll ever get the vote?"

"Maybe one day, but not in my lifetime. Everyone's too polite to make a difference. If you want my opinion we need to be more assertive but the women here are scared they'll end up in prison."

Harriet's eyes widened. "Is that what could happen if anyone found us here?"

"No, not for being here, but if we started to stand up for ourselves ... well, they wouldn't like it, would they?"

"Does your husband know you're here?" Harriet asked.

The woman laughed. "Doesn't know, doesn't

care; as long as his tea's on the table when he gets home."

"So why do you come?"

"To support the young 'uns. I know what it's like to be a prisoner in your own home with no way out. I was lucky, my first husband died, but that won't happen for a lot of you. All you youngsters need encouragement to make things happen."

Harriet was about to respond when the chairwoman walked onto the stage and introduced the speaker for the meeting, a woman Harriet guessed to be in her mid-thirties but who had more confidence than anyone she had ever seen before. She made her way across the stage in a formal navy blue dress with white collar, and held her head high as she placed some notes on the stand. She spoke with a calm, clear voice to give an update on the petition that had been taken to London. The room broke into spontaneous applause when she announced there would be a debate on the issue in the next parliament. In the meantime, she encouraged the women to continuing reading and studying so they could appear intelligent, polite and worthy of the cause.

Harriet felt as if she was floating when she walked home. For the first time in her life she'd met other women who felt the same as she did. Not only that, several had asked her to join them again next week.

As it was, she didn't need any invitation to work out that this was a cause she wanted to support. The opportunity to have this new circle of friends was beyond her expectations.

The following week she arrived a little earlier and stayed a bit longer at the end. She was even tempted to ask the speaker a question but her nerve had failed her at the last moment. She realised that many of the women fell into one of two groups: those who, like her, fundamentally thought it was wrong for men to have so much power when women had none; and the others had husbands they wished they could be rid of. The women genuinely believed that if they had the vote, they could make a difference. How she hoped they were right.

On her sixth week, she was so engrossed in a conversation about travelling to London to support the parliamentary debate that she didn't notice the time. As soon as she realised, she said goodbye and raced home to put some food on the table before William arrived home. She didn't think he would mind her going to the meetings, but she hadn't told him and would rather pick her moment than be rushed into it.

She'd just put the last plate on the table when she heard William and William-Wetherby arrive home. She pulled out William's chair to allow him to sit down, but when they came in both men slumped in their chairs by the fire and put their heads back.

"What's the matter?" Harriet asked.

William answered. "We have a problem,"

"What sort of problem?"

"Mr Wetherby was in the office again today checking up on us. Everything was going well until he asked William-Wetherby to show him the invoice he was working on. It was of no consequence to him, but as soon as he saw it he commented that William-Wetherby's handwriting was different to the writing he'd seen in the books."

"Well, it would be, I did the ... oh no." Harriet's eyes were wide as she put her hand to her mouth.

William closed his eyes and took a deep breath. "We didn't tell you at the time because it felt unimportant, but when Mr Wetherby noticed it wasn't my writing in the books, we told him William-Wetherby had been doing them. He seemed to accept it at the time, but now I'm beginning to wonder."

"Was he angry?"

"No, that was the strange thing, he wasn't; but after the way he was with Thomas I'm worried that he's at his most dangerous when he goes quiet."

Chapter Sixty-Three

With Sunday dinner over and the younger girls at Sunday school, Harriet sat at the dining table with William and William-Wetherby working through the accounts. With Mr Wetherby once again taking an interest in the office, William-Wetherby held the pen. It wasn't wise for Harriet to continue.

"I'm sure it won't be for long," William said. "The slum clearance is taking up so much of his time, he'll only be around for a few weeks before he gets distracted again."

"Maybe, but unless I can change my handwriting I'm going to have to hand the job over to William-Wetherby. The sooner you start your own business the better. I'm tired of you saying you will and doing nothing about it."

William was about to respond when there was a knock at the door.

"It's probably for me." William-Wetherby put the pen down and stood up. "I said I'd go for a game of dominos and the lads must be here early. I think we're finished here. Can I go?"

"I think so." Harriet spoke as Mr Wetherby walked into the back room.

"Mr Wetherby." William jumped from his chair, almost knocking it over.

"Please, don't let me interrupt," he said as he stared down at the table. "Carry on with what you're doing."

"We're not doing anything," William said. "What are you doing here? Is everything all right?"

"That's what I'm here to find out."

William-Wetherby closed the door and came back into the room. "Father and I were going over this month's figures. I wanted to check he was happy with them."

Mr Wetherby turned the book towards him. "You've changed your handwriting again."

William-Wetherby stared at the floor. "It must be the different nibs."

"Or perhaps it's because a different hand's been holding the pen?"

Nobody spoke as Mr Wetherby studied each of them in turn. "I would suggest that the reason for the different handwriting is because it isn't you who's been doing the books at all. It's your mother." Mr Wetherby glared at Harriet.

"Would it be so terribly wrong if it was me?" Harriet asked. "After all, you were happy for a seventeen-year-old boy to do them, would it be so much worse if it was me?"

"Harriet, please stay out of this," William said. "Of course you didn't do them."

"But Mr Wetherby thinks I did. The books his accountant passed, once the fraudulent entries of his brother were removed. Would it be so wrong if I was the one who'd balanced the books?"

"The information in those books is private and confidential," Mr Wetherby hissed at her. "They're no concern of yours."

"But you haven't answered my question. Would it be so wrong if I'd done them? If I'd worked through everything to give you a set of accounts that would have passed the audit first time round had it not been for your brother? In fact, would it be equally as wrong if Charlotte had done them?"

"Don't bring Charlotte into this; she's an educated woman."

"And so it would be all right for Charlotte to do them, but I'm incapable, is that what you're saying?"

Mr Wetherby straightened up and walked to the window. "It appears that you're talking yourself into a whole lot of trouble. When I arrived here this afternoon I couldn't be sure who was doing the books, but now I'm convinced it's you. You've been prying into the workings of my business and you had no right to. William, I'll speak to you tomorrow, but in the meantime I'll take these with me." He stepped forward to collect the books from the table but Harriet beat him to it.

"If I'm not capable of doing your bookkeeping, you needn't take them with you." Harriet grabbed the books closest to her. "If you want one of the men to do them, feel free, but they're not copying out of these." Turning to the fire, she threw them on, one by one.

Mr Wetherby ran around the table and grabbed the top of her arm. "Stop, you stupid woman, that's my property. William, take those off her now. I'll see you locked up for this."

Harriet pulled her arm free, throwing the last of the paperwork onto the fire. "You didn't want your books being done by an uneducated woman and so

I'm helping you get rid of them. You can find someone else to do them now."

"Harriet, stop," William said. "Go to the morning room. Now."

Mr Wetherby dropped to his knees to retrieve his books. "You'll pay for this. You see if you don't."

Harriet glared at the back of his head, but before she could respond, William took her arm and pulled her to the door. "Go."

Harriet stormed into the morning room and threw herself onto a chair. That was it. Who did he think he was? If he thought William was going to carry on working for him any longer, he could think again. Let him leave William Junior in charge of everything, then he'd appreciate everything they did. He should be thanking her for acting as his unpaid bookkeeper, not criticising her. She would show him.

It was over half an hour later when Mr Wetherby left and William came to find her.

"What on earth were you thinking?" he asked.

Harriet looked at him, her eyes red from tears of frustration. "I've had enough of him. You know I'm capable of doing the bookkeeping."

"That's beside the point, they're his books and he could have you arrested for damage to his personal property."

"Were they badly damaged?" she asked, her voice softening.

"Fortunately the binding on the books saved most of them, but a lot of the invoices and other papers are beyond repair. That was one of the most stupid things you've ever done."

"I'm sorry, but he made me so angry."

"Well, let's hope that's a good enough excuse if you're sent before a judge."

Chapter Sixty-Four

Birmingham, Warwickshire

William's stomach churned as he travelled to Birmingham the following morning. He'd prepared a few words in Harriet's defence, but he knew what Mr Wetherby was capable of. It didn't make for pleasant thoughts.

"What do you think he'll do?" William-Wetherby asked as they sat in the carriage.

"I've no idea. We might both lose our jobs, or he might try to have your mother arrested. If she's lucky she might get away with just paying for the damage."

"What if she's not lucky?"

William shook his head. "I don't want to think

about it. I just pray he'll accept her apology and forgive her."

When they arrived at the workshop, William was surprised to find it empty. "Is that good or bad?" he asked when he had checked the office.

"Maybe your prayers have been answered and now he's had time to sleep on it, he's not going to do anything."

"We can but hope, but I suggest that until we know for sure, you contact the suppliers and ask for copies of their invoices. I'll get the machines moving."

It was almost five o'clock and the men were packing up for the night when Mr Wetherby arrived.

"Have you had a busy day?" William greeted him with a smile. "I was beginning to think we weren't going to see you."

"I have as it happens, which wasn't helped by the fact that I spent almost an hour with my solicitor this morning." The smile fell from William's lips. "I went to see him about your wife. In part to talk about the legality of a non-worker having access to such confidential information and of course the small matter of her trying to destroy my property."

William took a deep breath. "She didn't mean it and was extremely sorry. When I found her, after you'd gone, she asked me to apologise and pleaded for forgiveness. She said she didn't know what had come over her."

"That's as may be, but I still plan to serve notice on her for compensation."

William went white. "What sort of compensation?"

"Financial of course. I'm going to have to pay for someone to rewrite all the damaged documents."

"I've already started," William-Wetherby said. "I've spent all of today going through them, sorting out what needs replacing and what can be rewritten. I could have them finished in no time."

Mr Wetherby scowled. "And what of the work you should have done today? When will you do that? I don't intend to pay you for something you shouldn't be doing. That's where the compensation comes in. If it takes you two days to rewrite those documents, then I want her to pay your wages for two days."

"She doesn't have the money for that," William gasped.

"Well, she'll be going to prison then."

"You wouldn't do that, Mr Wetherby, please. She was only trying to help," William-Wetherby said. "I'm sure she'd redo them for you."

"I don't want her going anywhere near those documents again, do you understand? She will certainly not be the one to rewrite them."

"Let me do them," William-Wetherby said. "I'll do them at home in the evening so it doesn't stop me from doing my other work. If you don't pay me for today it won't have cost you anything."

"I'm sure that's very generous of you," Mr Wetherby said, "but my solicitor has already sent the letter to say your mother owes me ten pounds."

"Ten pounds! I don't earn that much money," William-Wetherby said.

"It's not just for your time, it's compensation for my wasted time, as well as solicitor's fees and the cost of replacing the damaged books. Maybe it'll teach her a lesson."

William sat down and wiped his brow with a handkerchief. "Mr Wetherby, please give her another chance. I've just bought three more properties. Until the rents start coming in, I haven't got that much money to spare. She's not a bad person, please, can you stop the notice?"

"The letter was sent at midday today and so she may have received it already."

William-Wetherby jumped to his feet. "We need to get home. It'll frighten the life out of her if it's delivered before we're there. Please, Mr Wetherby, will you withdraw it?"

"If I do that, I want proof that she understands what she's done and that she's truly sorry. Perhaps I'll travel with you and see for myself. If I see fit, then I'll take the letter back."

~

Handsworth, Staffordshire.

HARRIET STOOD at the kitchen sink rinsing her face with cold water. It was a long time since she'd been physically sick, but after reading the letter from the solicitor she'd been unable to stop herself. Even now, when there was nothing left inside her, the retching continued.

The letter had arrived in the late post. It said she owed him ten pounds and if she didn't pay, she would be remanded in custody. They didn't have that much to spare at the moment. *I have to get out of here*, she thought as she dried her face. *I'm not being locked up. The asylum was bad enough; I'm not going to prison.* She stared at the horse in the stable and wondered about setting up the carriage, but shook her head. William would be home soon and she needed to be gone before he arrived. There were often private carriages on Livingstone Road; she would be able to hire one of those much quicker.

Not knowing where she would go, or for how long, she packed up a few belongings before going onto the street to find a carriage. Within a minute she had hired one and directed the driver to the house before asking him to load her luggage. She wanted to take whatever items of personal property she could. She wasn't leaving anything of value in case they sold them to raise the ten pounds. *Mr Wetherby has enough money without taking my things.*

With most of her items stowed, she walked into the front room and saw a couple of chairs she was especially fond of as well as several pictures and a mirror. She placed them in the hall for the driver to put in the carriage. She then went back for a final look around and saw her silver candlesticks. They were a wedding present from her aunt and uncle. *I'm not leaving them.*

By the time she returned to the street the driver had loaded everything into the carriage and was holding the door open for her. She was about to climb in when she saw William and William-Wetherby hurrying towards her. Mr Wetherby was close behind. For an instant she froze, transfixed by the sight before her, but her trance was broken by the sound of the candlesticks clattering to the road beneath her. She immediately fell to her knees to pick them up before she jumped into the carriage and slammed the door.

William ran towards her. "Harriet, stop. What are you doing?"

Harriet glanced over her shoulder before screaming at the driver, "What are you waiting for?"

"The gentleman wants a word with you, madam," he said.

"I don't care, I'm in a hurry ..."

Harriet didn't finish the rest of the sentence before William reached the carriage and opened the door.

"Where are you going?" he asked.

Harriet sat back in her seat and stared straight ahead. "For a drive, I needed some air."

"We have our own carriage, why are you using this one? And why are you taking the furniture?"

Harriet looked at the furniture as if she was seeing it there for the first time.

"I think you'd better come back into the house." William held out his hand to help her down.

Harriet hesitated, but when she saw William-Wetherby watching her, she relented and stepped down. William gave the driver a penny for his trouble and asked him to help William-Wetherby unload the furniture and take it back into the house.

~

BY THE TIME they got inside, Harriet's whole body was shaking. William sat her in front of the fire to warm up.

"She needs help," Mr Wetherby said. "She's hysterical."

William ushered him back into the hall and pulled the door closed. "I think it would help if you told her you didn't mean to send the letter and she won't be going to prison."

Mr Wetherby hesitated. "She needs to be punished."

"But not like this, please. She knows she's done wrong."

Mr Wetherby nodded. "Very well, she's clearly not herself. Let me see her."

When they returned to the back room, Harriet jumped and leaned back in her seat, her eyes wide as she stared at the two men. Mr Wetherby pulled up a chair and sat beside her.

"William's told me you didn't mean to damage the books and that William-Wetherby is going to make everything right again."

Harriet's chest rose and fell with each rapid breath.

"If you promise never to do anything like that

again, I'll take the letter away and won't press any charges. Do you promise?"

Harriet struggled to speak but nodded her head.

"Thank you so much." William let out an audible sigh. "I'll make sure nothing like this happens again. You have my word on it."

Mr Wetherby stood up. "I'll leave you for now. I would suggest you give her a stiff drink, and make sure the doctor sees her."

"No." Harriet jumped up, but immediately reached for William as her legs collapsed beneath her. A moment later she hit the floor.

Chapter Sixty-Five

Although it was dark, Harriet lay in bed, her eyes staring towards the ceiling. There was no point closing them, she wouldn't sleep. As soon as she heard the birds chirping she climbed out of bed and slipped on her clothes. The rest of the house was quiet as she crept downstairs and put the kettle on, before pacing the hall. *Would he really have sent me to prison? Yes, of course he would. If they hadn't found me trying to leave, he wouldn't have withdrawn the letter. He'd have smiled as the police led me away. He wants me out of the way.*

By the time William got up, Harriet had finished two cups of tea and was dozing in the armchair.

"Didn't you sleep?" William asked as he walked in.

Harriet stared at him. *What do you think?*

"I thought the laudanum the doctor gave you last night would help, but you still seem tired. I'll ask Violet to make sure the girls get to school so you can have a rest. You had a shock yesterday, but it's over now. Forgotten."

No it's not. Your stepfather was going to send me to prison. I'm not going to forget that.

"I need to be going, but I won't be late home tonight."

~

WHEN WILLIAM and William-Wetherby arrived home that evening there was no food on the table, no sign of Margaret and Florence, and Harriet sat staring into the fire.

"Harriet, what's the matter?" William bent down in front of her and took her hands.

"What are you doing home?" Harriet's brow creased as she stared at them.

"It's turned six o'clock; we've finished for the day."

She glanced at William-Wetherby and then at the clock. "I'm sorry, I didn't realise the time. I must have fallen asleep."

William turned to William-Wetherby and nodded to the door. Once they were alone, William tried again.

"Harriet, what's the matter? It's not like you to fall asleep or forget the time."

"Nothing's the matter. I didn't sleep last night and I've been tired all day. I'll get you some tea. Where are Margaret and Florence?" She glanced around the room.

"I was hoping you might tell me."

"They must be with Mary-Ann," she said as she stood up. "Will you go and get them?"

ONCE THEY HAD EATEN, William and William-Wetherby sat in their usual chairs by the fire while Harriet helped Violet tidy up before she took the girls upstairs. An hour later she sat down without a word and cast her eyes towards the fire. William offered her one of her magazines but when he got no response he put it down again. By the end of the evening, when she still hadn't spoken, William knelt in front of her and looked directly into her blank eyes.

"Harriet, what's going on? You've not said a word all evening, even when we've tried to speak to you."

Harriet's head twitched. "I'm sorry, I didn't re-alise you were still here. I'm thinking."

"They must be deep thoughts. Is there anything you want to tell us?"

She shook her head. "Nothing you'd be inter-ested in."

"Mr Wetherby called into the office today to ask how you were. He's concerned about you."

Harriet's frown returned. "Why should it con-cern him? Was it his guilty conscience?"

"Not at all ..."

"I don't trust him, William, not one bit. He won't be happy until he's got rid of me. He thinks I know too much."

"Now you're being silly. He wants you to get well again. We all do."

"There's nothing wrong with me. It's only the sight of him that upsets me."

"I think you're still tired." William stood up and offered her his hand. "Why don't you come to bed? Things will seem better after a good night's sleep."

"I keep telling you, there's nothing wrong with me but I will go to bed. That way I can do some thinking in peace."

∾

THE FOLLOWING morning Harriet was up early again. She had a lot to do today. By the time William and William-Wetherby arrived downstairs she had prepared them a breakfast of boiled eggs with bread and butter and a pot of tea. As they ate, she paced the morning room, willing them to hurry up, until William ordered her to sit down.

"Do you have any plans for today?" he asked as William-Wetherby went for his coat.

"Today, why do you ask?" Harriet snapped. "What's special about today? You never normally ask me what I'm doing."

"Nothing, I only wondered. You're on edge again, didn't you sleep last night?"

Harriet stamped her foot. "I'm not on edge and there's nothing wrong with me. Can't you leave me alone?"

"Harriet, will you stop telling me to leave you alone. You've not been yourself for the last couple of days and I'm concerned. I'll ask the doctor to call round later and give you a proper check-up."

"Stop it! I don't want the doctor here, besides, I'll be out and so he'll be wasting his time."

William stared at her. "Where are you going?"

Damn. "Nowhere, I've changed my mind ... but I might go for a walk."

William shook his head and got up from the table. "I don't want you going anywhere today, do you hear me? You're not well and I don't want anything happening to you. I'll see you tonight, by which time I want to have a sensible conversation. Is that clear?"

Chapter Sixty-Six

As the morning wore on, William's concentration left him. What was Harriet up to? She'd said she was going out. *What if she's going to leave? This time there'll be no one to stop her.* He glanced at the clock on the wall. It was still only five past ten, not ten minutes later than when he had last looked. He needed to focus on what he was doing.

By midday William's heart was pounding. He had to go and check on her. Leaving William-Wetherby to supervise the workshop he went to his carriage and hurried back to Handsworth.

"Harriet," he shouted as he walked into the hall-way. "Where are you?" When he got no answer he went first to the back room and then the morning room, but there was no sign of her. He popped his head into the front room before running upstairs. "Harriet, where are you?" He moved from bedroom to bedroom but they were all empty. *Where is she?*

He returned to the morning room, which was in a terrible mess. She hadn't washed any of the breakfast dishes and the bread and butter were still on the table. She would never normally leave the place like this. And, where was Violet? With hundreds of questions running through his mind, William put the food into the pantry and left to go and find her.

As he drove down Church Lane he saw a group of women deep in conversation. He paid them little attention until he got closer and saw Harriet was amongst them. He pulled his hat down over his forehead and flicked the reins of the horse to speed past them. A row of cottages stood a short distance up the road and as he reached the end of the row he turned the horse off the carriageway and came to a halt. *What on earth's she doing?*

William returned to the corner of the houses and peered back down the road. They were entering the church hall. Once the road was clear, he moved closer to the building but was disappointed to find nothing outside telling him what the event was. Glancing around to check he was alone he crept to the door and opened it a couple of inches. At first there was little to see other than about sixty women taking their seats. He was about to close it again when one of the group went to the front of the room and announced the day's agenda. William felt his stomach drop as bile rose to his throat. What on earth was she doing at a meeting like that? She must be ill.

He closed the door quietly and made his way to the road, his legs shaking. When he reached the carriage he sat down, grateful that he hadn't walked from home. Ten minutes later he felt calm enough to continue his journey and went straight to the doctor's surgery to arrange a visit. As he left, he looked at his pocket watch. He needed to get back to the workshop, but perhaps he had time to find Mr Wetherby before he did.

THE FOLLOWING MORNING, once William-Wetherby had left for work, William returned to the morning room where Harriet was tidying the table. She froze when she saw him.

"What are you doing still here? Why haven't you gone to work?"

"I'll go in later. I've arranged for the doctor to call and I want to speak to him."

"Are you ill?"

439

"He's not coming to see me ..." William went to take her hands, but she pulled away.

"He's coming to see me? I've told you, there's nothing wrong with me. Just because I've spent a lot of time thinking, why does everyone assume I'm ill? We are allowed to think, you know, or has Mr Wetherby stopped that as well?"

"Mr Wetherby's got nothing to do with this. I asked the doctor to call because you're acting strangely and I'm worried about you. Is that so wrong?"

Harriet said nothing, but went into the back room and closed the door behind her.

When the doctor arrived, William showed him into the front room.

"She's living in another world. She thinks we all want her out of the way and won't talk to us. It's not like her. Sometimes she doesn't seem to be aware that there's anyone in the room with her. When you ask her if she's all right she becomes hysterical."

"Have you any idea what could have brought it on?"

William hesitated.

"You need to tell me." The doctor held his gaze. "What is it?"

William explained about the argument with Mr Wetherby.

"I'd better see her," the doctor said. "I suspect she'll need more than a sleeping draught."

William went to the back room and offered Harriet his arm. "You need to come with me to the front room. The doctor would like to speak to you."

Harriet shot William a venomous glance before she walked past him into the front room.

"Now then, Mrs Jackson," the doctor said. "I understand you've had a shock that induced a marked case of hysteria. Can you tell me about it?"

Harriet sat down and stared straight ahead of her, her hands twitching in her lap.

"I can understand you were upset, but Mr Wetherby was entitled to compensation after what you did. You should be grateful he dropped the charges."

Harriet said nothing and didn't appear to notice the tears rolling down her cheeks. Even the offer of William's handkerchief was ignored as she fixed her gaze on the wall ahead.

"Mr Jackson, can we step outside?" the doctor said after a couple of minutes.

William guided the doctor into the hall and closed the door.

"You told me earlier that you have the money for your wife to be treated as a private patient."

William nodded. "I do."

"May I ask if it would be enough to cover an in-patient stay, say for a month or two?"

"It would, sir."

"In that case I suggest we take your wife to Winson Green. She'll get the best treatment there. If it suits you, I could travel with you this morning and secure a second signature on the admission papers."

William's shoulders dropped. He had been afraid this would happen but what else could he do? If it brought his wife back to her senses, it would be worth it.

∽

It wasn't until they were going up the sweeping driveway towards the hospital that Harriet realised where they were going. Fear flashed across her eyes as she stared at the building drawing closer.

"No, William, what are you doing? I'm not going here again, I won't." She tried to stand up but William held her back.

"Harriet, listen to me; it's for your own sake. It won't be like last time, I promise. You'll be a private patient and as soon as you've had a rest you'll be home again."

"We haven't got the money for me to be a private patient."

The doctor looked up, but William reassured him. "Don't worry; it's all taken care of."

Harriet's eyes widened. "It's Mr Wetherby, isn't it? He's paying to have me locked up. He might have dropped the legal case but he still wants me locked up. Let me out of here." She lunged for the door handle.

"Harriet, please, it's not like that. He wants you to get well again. We all do."

Harriet struggled to shake William off. "No he doesn't, he's lying." Her screams filled the carriage. "He's lied to you for years. Can't you see it? We have to get away from him ... he'll be the ruin of us."

Chapter Sixty-Seven

M r Wetherby sat in the morning room and pulled the newspaper away from the table while Sarah-Ann put some softly boiled eggs down in front of him.

"You were up early," she said as she took the seat opposite.

"I've a lot to do today. I've got to be in Birmingham this afternoon for an Artisans company meeting, but I need to go to Frankfort Street first to see William, and call in on my solicitor before I get there."

"Have you heard how Harriet's getting on? Is she showing any sign of recovery?"

Mr Wetherby shook his head. "The last thing I

heard was she'd stopped eating. Goodness knows what they'll do to her."

"I can't imagine what must have put her into such a state. She's usually so forthright ... too much so, if you ask my opinion."

"No one knows what goes on inside that head of hers. Certainly not me." Mr Wetherby spooned some sugar into his tea and stirred it.

"I'm afraid I can't help you there," Sarah-Ann said as she took the top off her egg. "What time will you be back tonight?"

"Not until late. I'm chairing a Conservative Association meeting this evening. Don't wait up."

"Don't you ever get tired? You never stop."

Mr Wetherby smiled. "Occasionally, but that's why we have Sundays. Our day of rest. It helps that I enjoy what I do."

As Sarah-Ann stood up to pour some more boiling water onto the tea leaves, she heard the postman knock and went to meet him.

She came back with a selection of letters, but one stood out from the others. She passed it to Mr Wetherby. "That looks important."

Mr Wetherby turned the package over in his hands, studying the thick embossed envelope. "It does." He took the letter opener from the holder, removed the letter from its envelope and skimmed the contents before he paused and read it again.

"Aren't you going to tell me?" Sarah-Ann asked.

"I'm going to have to change my plans for today." Mr Wetherby rubbed his beard. "The Liberal's budget bill has been defeated in parliament and Prime Minister Gladstone's resigned. The Conservatives are planning to form a government with the Marquis of Salisbury in charge. Not that it'll last. We'll have to prepare for another election sooner than we thought."

Sarah-Ann groaned. "When will it be?"

"That's the key question. We're in the middle of finalising boundary changes and it could take months to pass the legislation. When it is called, we need to be ready."

"Well, please don't try and solve it single-handedly." Sarah-Ann smiled as she spoke, but Mr Wetherby failed to notice.

"Somebody has to do something. The Liberals haven't got a clue and they can't carry on in government. We have to make sure the Conservatives are elected." Mr Wetherby scanned the letter again. "They've decided Birmingham Central is such an important constituency, Lord Churchill's going to stand for us. We have to capitalise on that. He's a big enough presence that it should have a knock-on effect in our ward. It'll give us the best chance we've had of winning for years." Mr Wetherby stood up. "I've got work to do."

Chapter Sixty-Eight

A carriage pulled up outside the front door of the asylum and William climbed out before turning to offer his hand to Mary-Ann.

"Thank you for coming with me," he said as they walked up the steps. "I realise it's not the sort of place you'd choose to visit, but I've no idea how else to get through to her. You're my secret weapon."

Mary-Ann smiled. "I hope I can help. I miss having her next door."

"She's on ward five; not too far. Every time I come I pray I'll be greeted with a smile, but most of the time she barely registers I'm there. She rarely speaks and when she does it takes a great effort to hear what she says."

"Do you think she's still mad at you for admitting her? It has to be said that she is one for holding a grudge."

William sighed. "I thought bringing her here would be for the best. I know last time she was admitted she was understandably angry, but I believed that being a private patient would help. It looks like I was wrong."

Mary-Ann slipped her arm into William's. "Come on, let's go and see if I can talk some sense into her."

William and Mary-Ann walked into a small ward with only eight beds, each with curtains to give them some privacy and enough room to allow several visitor chairs.

"She's in the third bed on the right-hand side," William whispered as they went in. "Things are looking hopeful, she's sitting in a chair."

"Good afternoon, Harriet." William bent to kiss her forehead. "Look who I've brought with me." Harriet's eyes didn't move and William shrugged at his sister.

"Don't be like that." Mary-Ann took a seat next to Harriet. "I came to talk to you, not to be ignored. I've missed having you next door."

Harriet watched her hands as she twisted them on her lap.

"Keep talking," William whispered.

Mary-Ann hesitated before she spoke about everything that was happening at home and how her daughters enjoyed Margaret and Florence staying with them. She continued with tales from the school playground and anything else that came to mind. William sat with his mouth gaping.

"I had no idea all that was going on," he said. "I should listen to your conversations more often, I feel like I'm missing out."

Mary-Ann laughed. "I hope Harriet will be able to tell you everything herself soon. Are you listening to me, Harriet?" Mary-Ann took hold of her hands to keep them still. "I want you back. You're my best friend and Margaret and Florence have told me I don't make as good a mother as you. And then there's William. He's missing you dreadfully. He's practically moved in with us at the moment; either that or he has young Sidney Storey staying with him."

"Don't say it like that," William said. "Sid's a decent lad and he likes coming up to Handsworth to visit his brother. He's good company and he gets on well with William-Wetherby too."

At the mention of William-Wetherby, Harriet looked at William and tried to speak. Her voice was faint and William offered her a glass of water before he leaned in to hear what she was saying.

"Take me home."

William rested his hand on her arm. "My dear, there's nothing I'd like more, but you're not well. The nurse told me on the way in that you're not sleeping and you haven't eaten any proper food for almost three weeks. If you could do both of those things, I'm sure the doctors would let you come home. Will you do that for me?"

Tears welled in Harriet's eyes. "Will you leave Mr Wetherby?"

"We'll talk about it once you're home. Just stop worrying about him and concentrate on getting better."

"You'll leave him." Harriet's eyes pleaded with him.

William wasn't sure if it was a question or a statement and was less sure how to answer. "You're tired," he said after a moment. "Try and sleep and I'll be back tomorrow. I need to take Mary-Ann home."

William stood up and kissed her again before Mary-Ann squeezed her hands.

"See you soon," she said as Harriet's tears overflowed. "Things are going to work out, you see if they don't."

HARRIET WATCHED them walk down the ward until they disappeared from view. Why hadn't she acknowledged Mary-Ann? For the first time in weeks, her curiosity had been roused, but she'd let her questions go unsaid. She put her head in her hands. What was the matter with her? Her whole life had been a struggle against those who wanted to control her. What was the point of carrying on?

Not that she could do anything but carry on. Even when she had stopped eating, the doctors had ordered the nurses to force food into her. At first she had fought with them, but now she no longer cared. They seemed to enjoy forcing a disc into her mouth and pouring liquid into her stomach through a tube. It had gone on for days, and she gagged just thinking about it, but perhaps next time she'd choke on it. She could hope.

Her thoughts were disturbed by a nurse standing beside her with a selection of medicines on a trolley.

"You've a new one tonight," she said. "It's usually reserved for difficult patients but your husband wants you home and so the doctor said you can have it."

Harriet's initial thought was to throw it on the floor, but as she watched the nurse put a small amount into a dropper, the image of Mary-Ann came to her mind. How she wanted to see her friend again.

WHEN WILLIAM VISITED several days later, he smiled and took her hands as he sat down.

"The nurse said you've started eating again. I can't tell you how happy that makes me."

Harriet's eyes filled with tears. "Take me home."

"I will as soon as you're well enough. You need to eat and you need to sleep. Will you do that for me?"

Harriet wiped her eyes with the back of her hand and nodded.

"I'm sorry I had to bring you here," William said. "I know you're angry with me, but tell me honestly, what's been the matter? We have a nice house, we all have our health, Charles and Eleanor are doing well at school, William-Wetherby and I have jobs and we have more money than we need."

"Mr Wetherby."

"Why are you so bothered about him? I can understand that he gave you a fright with the letter, but he withdrew it within a couple of hours and he hasn't mentioned it since. To be honest with you, he's too busy worrying about the next election to have anything else on his mind. I don't suppose you've heard about that, have you?"

Harriet nodded. "A few of the women were talking about it yesterday, but it doesn't change anything. The election will be over soon enough and he'll be back to his usual ways. He's always there and has to be in control, he can't help himself. As long as he has control over any aspect of our lives he'll cause us trouble."

"But what am I supposed to do? I'm a partner with him in the business, William-Wetherby works for him, he's paying for Charles to go to school..."

Harriet's shoulders slumped. "Isn't that the point? We've been talking about you running your own business for years, and you've always made excuses. I can't wait any longer. When I say I want you to set up your own business, I mean it. One where you're in charge, where I can do the bookkeeping without fear of being imprisoned, and William-Wetherby can work for you."

William felt beads of perspiration breaking out on his forehead. "Where would I get the money from?"

"From Mr Wetherby. Half the business is yours. Ask him to buy you out of your share. That should give you plenty to start with."

"You've been thinking about this, haven't you?"

Harriet shrugged. "I've nothing else to do."

William took out his handkerchief and wiped his

brow. "What if he hasn't got that much money to spare?"

Harriet glared at him. "Stop making excuses. He has."

William was about to ask how she knew, but stopped. Of course she knew.

Chapter Sixty-Nine

William-Wetherby sat at his desk in the office, writing out cheques to pay their suppliers. He was so engrossed in his work that he didn't hear his father come in.

"An errand boy's called to say Mr Wetherby is on his way over and he wants to see all the completed books and invoices now they've been rewritten. Have you got them?"

"I have." William-Wetherby patted the two piles on his desk. "They've been ready for weeks. I wondered when he'd want to see them. Are you happy to take him through them?"

"Why don't you? You're the one who's done all the work, after all, and you need to learn how to deal with him."

Thirty minutes later Mr Wetherby arrived and took a seat. "Have you got everything ready for me?"

William-Wetherby stood up and put the papers and books in front of him. "Everything's in here. We managed to get copy invoices off all the suppliers and there was nothing in our books so badly damaged that I couldn't copy it out again. You should find it all in order."

Mr Wetherby smiled as he flicked through the pages. "You've done a good job. I'll pass the books to Mr Carlton for him to run his expert eye over, but I don't think there's any major damage done."

"What a relief," William said.

"It is. So, what's troubling you?" Mr Wetherby got to his feet. "You look like you want to say something."

William hesitated and glanced at William-Wetherby.

"Before you two talk, can you excuse me?" William-Wetherby said. "I've written out some cheques and I'd like to deliver them myself before the end of the day."

Mr Wetherby nodded and waited while William-Wetherby picked up his papers and hat and closed the door behind him.

~

As he watched William-Wetherby leave, William cleared his throat, struggling to find the words.

"Come on then, out with it," Mr Wetherby said.

"I-I've been thinking ... I'd like to start my own company and wondered if you'd buy out my half of this one. The part Mr Watkins passed to me."

Mr Wetherby stared at William before he turned and walked across the office. "Has Harriet put you up to this?"

"No ... of course not. I've told her naturally and she thinks I should."

"You never were a good liar. Of course it's come from her. Is this so she can do your bookkeeping?"

"Yes ... no, it's not that. I want a chance to run my own business."

"Do you think all this came easy to me?" Mr Wetherby glared at him as he swung his arm around the room. "Do you think you're going to leave here and overnight you'll have a business like this?"

"No, of course not ..."

"I'll tell you now, you won't. Things have got a lot harder since I started off and you think you can do it all with the help of your *wife*?"

"I'd hire qualified men ..."

"And how would you pay them before you start

taking regular orders? You expect me to give you half the money from my business so you can set off on some hare-brained scheme that's bound to end in failure?"

William took a deep breath. "You wouldn't have a business this size if I hadn't let you take Mr Watkins's business from me. I'm entitled to it."

"You're entitled to nothing." Mr Wetherby spat his words out. "I've built this business myself and given you everything. You haven't had to put yourself out for any of it, you just expect me to keep paying."

"That's why I want to do something for myself, to prove I can do it."

"Well, you can go and find the money from somewhere else, because it's not coming from me."

HARRIET SAT in a chair by the bed waiting for William to arrive. She'd no idea what was in the new medicine, and it tasted horrible, but she felt so much better. Her general apathy and listlessness had passed and she was now able to walk and do menial tasks on her own. It had also set her mind racing.

She stared down the ward again, willing William to appear. He'd promised to be here by six o'clock, but it was now quarter past and there was still no sign of him. It was another five minutes before he walked onto the ward and as soon as she saw him, she knew there was a problem.

"What's the matter?" she asked as he sat down.

William put his head in his hands before he looked up at her. "He won't give me the money. I asked him this afternoon."

Harriet's mouth dropped open. "Won't give it to you? He has to."

"He says he doesn't have to do anything. He said he's built the business up himself without any help from me."

"He did not! He wouldn't have the Handsworth workshop to start with if it weren't for you. Did you tell him that?"

"He didn't give me a chance."

"Well, you need to go back and tell him you won't take no for an answer."

"Please, Harriet." William ran his finger under his collar. "You know what he's like. He won't hesitate in forcing me out of the business if I cause trouble, but that won't help me get the money from him."

"So we'll have to do something to bring him to his senses." Harriet turned round and picked up a small notebook from a table by the side of her bed. "I've had a lot of time to think while I've been here and I've been making notes. Do you remember when he had the fight with Mr Flemming? Well, he's still no idea that I saw everything that happened and can prove that Mr Flemming didn't die because of lung problems."

"We can't prove that. Remember, it's on the death certificate."

"But Mr Wetherby knocked Mr Flemming to the ground and beat him around the head. He somehow managed to get the police to drop their investigation. What if he did something similar with the doctor and had the certificate changed?"

"A death certificate's a legal document, you can't make up the cause of death."

Harriet cocked her head at William. "Maybe it depends on what's at stake. Mr Wetherby could have been charged with manslaughter if the head injuries had been given as the cause of death."

The colour drained from William's face. "You've no evidence that Mr Wetherby saw the doctor, you can't go making accusations like that."

"I'll tell you how we find out. I wrote everything down the day I saw the fight and we should tell him we're prepared to go to the police with the evidence if he doesn't give you the money. If he's guilty he won't want the investigation opened again."

Beads of sweat rolled down the side of William's face. "It's not that simple. It was over five years ago, and Mr Wetherby has a lot of influence with the police. They won't do anything to upset him."

Harriet's shoulders slumped before she sat up straight again. "Perhaps the local leaders of the Conservative Association might be interested. No, better still. The Liberals! The Conservatives won't want a story about Mr Wetherby's violence reaching the newspapers, but the Liberals'll be delighted."

William's eyes were wide. "There's an election coming up. We can't jeopardise the Conservatives' chances of winning."

Harriet raised an eyebrow. "Can't we? It's exactly the sort of thing that would make him take notice. In fact, even better." Harriet's eyes were sparkling. "Why don't we tell him I've written everything in a letter to the Marquis of Salisbury and I'm prepared to post it unless he splits the business fairly? That should make him stop and think."

William gasped for breath as he wiped his forehead. "I can't do that. What if he calls my bluff and I lose my job?"

"I don't think he will, he's got too much to lose.

Even if there's a small chance of his being found out, he won't risk it."

William put his hand over his heart as if trying to quieten it. "I can't do this."

"Of course you can. He's not getting away with it … and if you won't do it, I will."

Chapter Seventy

With her plans made, Harriet was determined to get herself out of hospital. She could do nothing while she was confined. Within a week she was allowed home for a four-day trial, but once home she had no intention of going back.

"Please promise you won't ever do that to me again." She had only been home for ten minutes but was sitting in the back room with a cup of tea.

"I only did it because I was worried about you. You'd gone into a world of your own and I couldn't get any sense out of you."

"Have you any idea what it's like to receive a letter telling you that unless you pay money you haven't got, you'll be sent to prison? I'd never been more frightened in my life ... except for the time my uncle sent me to Winson Green."

"But Mr Wetherby withdrew the letter. He told you himself that he wouldn't follow through with it, but it made no difference."

Harriet shook her head. "It wasn't as simple as that. Every time I closed my eyes, I could see the letter with Mr Wetherby's crooked smile behind it. It was like a bad dream that wouldn't leave me alone. I needed some time, but you went and sent me *there*."

"I couldn't leave you here on your own, I was worried about what you might do."

"I wouldn't have done anything out of the ordinary, but as it was, I felt ... worthless. Once I was in there, every day was worse than the one before until ... I stopped caring." Tears formed in Harriet's eyes. "I got to the point where I thought it would be better to die than stay there for another day, but they wouldn't let me die. They kept forcing food into me."

William walked to Harriet's side and crouched down beside her. "There, there, no more." He put his arm around her waist. "You're home now and well again. We need to put all this behind us. Promise me you'll try."

Harriet nodded. "I might never have seen the children again."

William passed her his handkerchief. "Here, wipe your eyes. From now on I'm going to take more care of you, and there'll be no more sneaking off to those meetings. They won't have helped."

Harriet lifted her face from the handkerchief and glared at William. "What are you talking about?"

"I saw you, the day before you went to the hospital ... at a *suffrage* meeting. That's when I knew you were ill."

Harriet sat with her mouth gaping, while she thought of what to say. "How did you find out?"

"I was worried about you that day and so I came home to check if you were all right. When you weren't here, I went looking for you ... and saw you outside the church hall."

"But how did you know what the meeting was about? There were no signs up."

"I poked my head through the door and saw the leader introduce the meeting. What were you thinking? You should be happy with everything you've got and not be mixing with troublemakers like that."

A flash of anger crossed Harriet's eyes. "They're not troublemakers, they're women who want to make their voice heard. Like I do. The leaders encourage us to read as much as possible and educate ourselves so we can give a good account of ourselves. I've told you how worthless I felt in the hospital, well put yourself in our shoes. We have no rights of our own, we're not allowed the same education and once we're married we lose our identity and our possessions. Men can beat us or lock us away, as and when they feel like it, and legally there's nothing we can do. If we had the vote, we could elect people who would represent us and start to change things."

William raised his eyebrows in disbelief. "Do you seriously believe that?"

Harriet threw William's handkerchief back at him and stood up. "Why shouldn't I? Women shouldn't be treated any differently to men. At least the University of London now treats us as equals and we can have our own property, but I hate the injustice of everything. Men are entitled to anything they want while we can have nothing. Unless we petition for the vote, nothing will ever change. Don't you see?"

"Come on now, sit down again. You know we have separate roles in life and you shouldn't worry about taking care of yourselves. That's what we're here for. That's how it's always been, is it so wrong?"

"If that's not what we want, then yes. We should be able to choose how we live, not be expected to conform to men's ideals. And what of those poor women trapped in unhappy marriages? They can't leave their husbands because they have no money and no other way of looking after themselves. It's like being in prison and the only way out is if their husband dies. Even then, unless they're left some money they're likely to be thrown onto the streets because they can't pay the rent. Men wouldn't put up with it and it's about time women started to stand up for themselves."

William shook his head. "I don't know what to say."

"You don't need to say anything."

"But how long have you been going to the meetings?"

"I'd been going for a couple of months before you had me locked up."

"I don't want you to go again ..."

Harriet glared at him. "Why? In case I get any ideas? Doesn't what you've just said prove my point? It should be my decision. Women need to have more say in how they live. You've no idea how angry I was after the incident with Mr Wetherby."

"Please, don't upset yourself again. We need to put all this behind us ..."

"You've not heard a word of what I've said, have you? If you don't want to discuss it, I'm going to talk to Mary-Ann and collect the girls. I won't have time to visit her tomorrow, I'm going to be busy."

The side of William's face visibly twitched. "What are you doing tomorrow? It's Sunday."

"I'm going to see Mr Wetherby. I've had enough of everyone telling me what to do. It's about time I did something about it."

Chapter Seventy-One

It was a bright, warm day as Harriet and William left home to walk the girls to Sunday school. It was the last time they would be going for a few weeks and despite her argument with William, she wanted him to walk with her. Once they had dropped them off they made their way towards the park.

"I expect there'll be a band playing this afternoon," William said. "It's a lovely day for it."

"Probably." Harriet wasn't interested in any band, and had no intention of staying in the park.

"There are plenty of people heading that way. I hope they have enough seats."

"Aren't you coming with me?"

Furrows appeared in William's brow. "Where to?"

"Wetherby House. Weren't you listening to me last night? Or are you pretending it didn't happen, like you do with everything else that troubles you?"

Despite the weather, William visibly shivered. "You can't go barging into Wetherby House on a Sunday afternoon. They might have guests."

Harriet shrugged. "It's one of the few times in the week he's sure to be at home. I think it's the perfect time."

"If they don't have visitors, they may go out for a walk."

"Well, if they do, let's hope they take a stroll in the park. It'll save my legs." Harriet walked away as William stopped, his mouth open. Seconds later he chased after her.

"Harriet, please, don't go causing any trouble. I've got to work with him."

Harriet's glare stopped him dead again. "That's the whole point. You shouldn't be working with him; you should be working for yourself. That's what I'm about to see to."

As she left the park she turned back to see if he was following her. When he caught her up, he was breathless.

"I can't do this, Harriet. I don't want to fall out

with Mr Wetherby and I can't run a business by myself."

"You won't be running the business by yourself. I'll be there and as soon as you're bringing in some money, William-Wetherby can join you. Nobody's asking you to do it alone."

"Please don't argue with Mr Wetherby. Promise me."

Harriet sighed. "All right, but I'm still going to write to the Marquis and the Liberals if he won't buy you out. We should accept nothing less than the value of my uncle's business."

William nodded and took a deep breath. "All right then. Let's go."

As they waited at the front door, Harriet smoothed down the front of her new dress and adjusted the layers of material that swept around the sides and into the bustle at the back. As she was still fussing a new maid opened the door and showed them into the front drawing room.

"I'll tell Mr Wetherby you're here," she said as she walked out and pulled the door behind her. A minute later Mr Wetherby entered.

"William," he said before he turned to Harriet. "So you're home I see. Are you feeling better? Perhaps you should wait in the morning room."

"No, that won't be necessary. I'm the one who's come to see you."

Incomprehension crossed Mr Wetherby's face as he turned to William before looking back at Harriet. "You?"

"I understand William's spoken to you about running his own workshop but you've refused to give him anything for his share in your business."

"This is most irregular. William, why have you brought your wife to talk about the business?"

"He didn't bring me, I brought us," Harriet said before William could answer. "You seem to have forgotten that when my uncle retired, he left his business to William. Unfortunately, at the time I was otherwise engaged and before I knew anything about it, you had taken over the running of it. Over the years you've conveniently forgotten to treat William as the partner he should be, and now you're under the delusion that William has contributed nothing to your business."

"I think you're the one who's deluded here. Haven't you recently come out of a lunatic asylum?" Mr Wetherby turned to William. "I think you need to consider taking her back."

"It's too easy and convenient, isn't it? If the little woman doesn't behave, lock her up, call her hysterical, call her a lunatic, any other name you like to make sure the world thinks she's mad. Well, I'm afraid it won't work any more ... not with me."

Mr Wetherby continued addressing William. "Will you take control of your wife? This is intolerable."

Harriet ignored him and started pacing the room. "You won't appreciate that when you're in these hospitals, you have a lot of time to think ... and I took full advantage of it. There was one particular thing I thought about a lot. It was an incident on Easter Monday several years ago. I was in the bedroom, doing a bit of housework, when I noticed you and William talking on the street below."

Mr Wetherby's eyes flicked to William but he remained silent.

"I was about to turn away when I saw Mr Flemming walking towards you. Well, I say walking, it was more of a stagger, and he was shouting at you as well. Something about his wife, I think it was."

The colour drained from Mr Wetherby's face.

"I could only hear the conversation when your voices were raised, but the next minute I saw you hurl yourself at Mr Flemming, sending him spinning to the ground. It really was a nasty bang on the head." She stared at Mr Wetherby through narrowed eyes before she continued pacing the room. "I think he was probably unconscious at that point, but you mustn't have been sure, because the next minute you were sitting astride him, beating him around the head. I believe it was only William pulling back your arm that stopped you killing him there and then. The business wouldn't have done so well with you in prison, would it?"

Mr Wetherby glared at William. "Did you put her up to this?"

William shook his head. "N-no ..."

"No, he didn't. As I said, I saw it all and I took the time later that day to write it all down. While I was in hospital, I went over everything I'd written. I don't think I missed anything..."

"You've no proof. The police were satisfied at the time that there was no wrongdoing and the doctor determined he died of emphysema."

"Yes, I'm glad you brought that up. I wondered how you'd bribed the doctor to change his findings."

"I didn't do anything of the sort. William, tell her."

"She's put it in a letter ..."

Mr Wetherby's face changed from white to red. "Who to? Have you no control over your own wife? If she belonged to me she'd be back in the asylum with no prospect of getting out."

"I did wonder who to send the letter to." Harriet ignored him as she walked to the window. "At first I thought the police, but you've already bought their loyalty, so then I considered the local Conservative Association."

"You can't do that ..."

'No, you're right. I decided that wasn't enough, which was when I thought your friend the Marquis of Salisbury might be interested ... especially if I mentioned I would also send a copy to the local Liberals."

With a face like thunder, Mr Wetherby walked across the room and grabbed hold of her arms. "You do anything of the sort and I'll see you never see the light of day again."

"If you're charged with manslaughter, there won't be much you can do. What I suggest is that we reach some sort of amicable compromise." With as much effort as she could muster Harriet smiled and pulled her arms from his grip. "If you give William enough money to buy him out of the business, I'm sure I can forget all about it. I might even throw the notebook with all my memories onto the fire. I'm sure with time I'll forget the finer details."

Mr Wetherby turned to William. "How much do you want?"

William shrugged. "We need to get the business valued, but I would say several thousand pounds, taking into account the original value of the business and something for goodwill."

"Goodwill! You can forget about that ... and where do you think I'm going to get that sort of money from?"

"You can take it from whichever account you want," Harriet said. "We really don't mind."

Chapter Seventy-Two

Harriet sat at the dining table in the back room of Havelock Road, with a stack of papers in front of her and a smile on her face. Wasn't this what she had always wanted? For her and William to run their own business? Well, now it was happening. She picked up the sheet of paper on the top of the pile and sat back. The contract to buy their own premises. William had found them for a reasonable price and now the money had come through from Mr Wetherby, they could move forward with the purchase. Not only that, they had started to buy the equipment they would need. They'd never had so much money to spend in their lives and she was loving every minute of it.

She entered all the figures into her new ledgers,

and as she collected up the invoices William walked in.

"How did you get on?" she asked.

William smiled at her. "It was a lot easier than I expected. The solicitor was extremely helpful and now we have the money he said it should only be a matter of weeks before the premises are ours."

Harriet clapped her hands before she bounced up to kiss him on the cheek. "This is so exciting. The next thing to do is recruit some men. Will you advertise?"

"I already know a couple who might be interested. I'm going to talk to them later in the week and hopefully they'll suggest a few others who'll join them. We only need three or four to start with."

"Hopefully it won't be long before your reputation precedes you and you have men coming asking you for work."

William took her hands, causing her to stand still. "Don't get carried away. There's a long way to go yet."

As William leaned forward to kiss her forehead, Charles burst into the back room. As he saw his parents, he stopped in his tracks. "What are you doing?"

William released Harriet's hands and took a step back. "What are you doing in here? I thought you'd gone out for the day."

"I came to tell Mother where I was going, but it doesn't look like you're interested. I'll be back in time for bed ..."

"Charles, come back," Harriet called after him the second the door slammed shut. A moment later the front door banged with equal ferocity. "That's all we need, him getting upset with us. He's been so good since he came home from school too. I'll have to speak to him when he gets in. It'll be so much easier when they're back at school."

William put his arms around her. "You won't know what to do with yourself come September."

Harriet smiled. She knew exactly what she would be doing in September.

SEVERAL WEEKS LATER, Harriet stood at the bottom of the driveway and waved to the carriage as William, Eleanor and Charles set off for Birmingham. Once William had dropped the children off at school, he would return to Lozells and his new business, making rivets and eyelets. As soon as the carriage disappeared from view, she hurried back into the house to finish her chores. She wanted to be out again by one o'clock.

It was almost four months since she had been to a suffrage meeting and as she walked down Church

Lane she could feel her heart pounding. What if they didn't remember her, or if the meetings had changed venue or time? She hadn't had a chance to check the details with anyone and wished, once again, that she could persuade Mary-Ann to join her. The street was empty when she arrived and she tentatively went to the door of the church hall and peered in. There were women inside, but none she recognised. She was about to leave, when she felt a hand on her shoulder.

"Mrs Jackson, is that you?"

Harriet turned to see the local leader arriving with a group of women.

Harriet gave her a weak smile. "Yes ... I was checking if the meeting is still on."

"It most certainly is but where have you been? We've missed you. In fact you were an agenda item at the last meeting while we discussed your where-abouts. Come in and tell us all about it."

Harriet followed the leader inside and her smile broadened as many of the women welcomed her back. For a moment she was overwhelmed to the point where she couldn't speak, but within minutes she'd generated a great deal of sympathy, describing the difficult time she'd had with her husband.

The speaker for the day was a Liberal Member of Parliament, sympathetic to the women's cause. He talked for an hour on how to lobby MPs into setting up a Private Members' Bill and as she listened, the smile on her face grew broader. *We're going to do this! We'll present such a case that parliament can't argue with us.* By the end of the meeting, she was so excited she called on Mary-Ann before she went home.

"I wish you'd come with me," she said as Mary-Ann poured her a gin. "The whole meeting was a revelation. You've read in the paper of course about meetings, but to be there and hear what they have to say, it's liberating. You can't be happy with the way things are, surely?"

"Does it matter what I think? Nothing's going to change and so is it worth the effort?"

Harriet banged her glass down on the table. "What a terrible attitude. If we all felt like that, nothing would ever change. Anyway, the Member of Parliament who came to talk to us thinks it's worth fighting for. He said he had a number of colleagues who were in favour of women's voting rights and that we should keep lobbying them."

Mary-Ann raised an eyebrow. "I bet he wasn't a Conservative."

"No, but that shouldn't change anything. The Liberals are very popular."

"They might be popular around the country, but they're not around here. Can you imagine Mr

Wetherby's reaction if he knew you were lobbying Liberal MPs?"

"It's got nothing to do with him. When we get the vote, I'll vote for anyone I want."

Mary-Ann took hold of Harriet's hand. "It might have nothing to do with him, but if he finds out, he won't let it rest. Please be careful."

Chapter Seventy-Three

Harriet was about to lift out this week's invoices when she heard the front door open. She looked up to see William walk in.

"What are you doing here?" she asked. "It's not two o'clock yet."

"Mr Wetherby sent a message to say he was in Handsworth and wanted a word with me. He didn't want to talk at the workshop and so I suggested he came here."

"Mr Wetherby. What does he want? And why is he stopping you from working? Is he trying to sabotage the business before it starts?"

William sat in his chair by the fire. "He didn't say. He probably wants to know how I'm getting on."

"I doubt it. Why would he send you a message just for that?"

"We'll find out soon enough." William stood up when he heard a knock on the front door. Within a minute Violet showed Mr Wetherby into the back room.

"Good afternoon, Mr Wetherby," Harriet said. "This is an unusual time to visit. On a Tuesday as well."

Mr Wetherby glared at her but didn't reply. Instead, he turned to William. "Are we able to go somewhere private? I'd rather we weren't overheard."

Harriet tensed as he spoke. "I'm sure if you've come to discuss the business, you can talk in front of me."

"William." Mr Wetherby spoke with a conviction that was unusual even for him.

"Yes, of course." William gave Harriet a slight shrug as he walked to the door and showed Mr Wetherby into the front room.

ONCE THE DOOR WAS SHUT, Mr Wetherby declined William's offer of a seat.

"Is everything all right?" William asked. "It is an unusual time for us to meet."

"Do you think everything's all right?"

"Yes, I think so, for me at any rate. The business is going well and I've managed to secure several bigger orders this week. Most are from new customers, but Porters have put in a repeat order, which is double the size of the last one. That should keep the men busy for a few more weeks."

"I'm glad to hear it, but that wasn't what I meant."

William's brow creased as he waited for Mr Wetherby to continue.

"How would you say your wife's state of mind is at the moment?"

A smile broke out on William's face. "Absolutely fine, in fact I've never seen her so happy. She's helping me with the business, doing the accounts and making sure I keep under budget; it's given her a new lease of life."

"You've obviously not been privy to some of the conversations I have. Over the last few days I've heard some particularly disturbing news about her."

William's frown returned. "About Harriet? Idle gossip I shouldn't wonder."

"That was my first thought, but it was too much of a coincidence when I heard it from two other sources."

"What have you heard?"

"Are you aware of the women's suffrage movement in Handsworth?"

William's face paled and he walked to the window. "What's that got to do with Harriet?"

"I've been led to believe your wife has become a regular attendee at these meetings. Were you aware of this?"

"No ... well ... yes, perhaps."

"Would you care to explain yourself." Mr Wetherby's eyes narrowed as he glared at William.

"Back in May, the day before she went into hospital, I saw her going to one of the meetings. I mentioned it to her when she came out of hospital and said I didn't want her going to any more."

"Well it would appear she's disobeyed your wishes."

"How can you be so sure? Maybe your sources saw her when I did."

"I've only heard about it recently. First was from someone Sarah-Ann invited to Wetherby House. Not a woman I've ever taken to, if I'm being honest, a bit too forthright, but she mentioned to Sarah-Ann that she'd seen Harriet at a meeting."

"That could have been before she was in hospital."

"It could have been, although I was led to believe it was only a couple of weeks ago. In addition, a second friend of hers also mentioned it to me last week."

"That still doesn't prove anything, but even if she did, why's it of such concern?"

"Why is it of such concern? William, listen to yourself." Mr Wetherby's voice grew louder. "Women are not capable of understanding politics and shouldn't be encouraged to do so. I've no idea what propaganda they give them at these meetings, but it's not right. Can you imagine what it would be like if women did as they pleased? This country would be the laughing stock of the world. Haven't you heard the Marquis of Salisbury talking about it? He makes a splendid case for keeping things as they are."

"But they're not going to change anything, are they? It just lets them get together and have a cup of tea. Most probably it's an excuse to sit and talk for an afternoon."

"Don't you be fooled. The third person I heard it from, and the reason I'm here, was a Liberal councillor in Handsworth. Apparently they had a Liberal Member of Parliament at last week's meeting. A Liberal, William, are you listening? Goodness knows what he told them, but you can imagine the delight of the councillor when he told me a member of my own family was fraternising with the Liberals. How do you think I felt? Not only that, it's the Liberals in parliament who are encouraging this nonsense. Can you imagine if millions of women started voting for the Liberals? It could be the end of the Conservative party. Don't you understand? We can't let that happen."

William laughed. "Harriet's not going to do that by herself; we'd have to stop them all from attending."

"You have to start somewhere and Harriet's the sort of person who'd encourage others."

"That's unfair. She's not one of the leaders."

"Not at the moment, but if she gets the chance to make a nuisance of herself then she will. If I'm being honest, you've become far too soft with her and this sort of behaviour suggests to me that she's still ill. If you want my opinion she has to go back to the asylum until she learns her place."

"No, absolutely not, it'll be the end of her."

"I tell you, I will not tolerate this sort of behaviour in my family. If you won't take her, I'll get her certified myself."

"That's a complete overreaction and quite frankly, it's a decision for me to take, not you. She doesn't need to go back. If it's the Liberals you're worried about, I'll talk to her and explain the situation."

Mr Wetherby was about to respond when they heard a noise that sounded like the front door.

"What was that?" William walked over to the door and peered into the hall. "Nobody there. It must have been outside." They both went to the window but the street was empty. Perhaps it was Violet and the wind caught the door. Anyway, where was I? I think you're completely overreacting. There must be a more effective way to sort this out."

"Have you any suggestions?"

William thought for a moment. "We need to find out what's going on. Until we understand how much of a risk they pose, we can't hope to act effectively. It might be better if I encourage her to go to the meetings and talk to her about what goes on. That way we'll know what we are up against and we could take the information to the Conservative Association for discussion."

Mr Wetherby paused. "What makes you think she'd tell you?"

"Because she loves talking. She won't tell me anything at the moment because I've asked her not to attend the meetings, but if I pretend to come round to the idea and show an interest, she'll tell me all we want."

Mr Wetherby stroked his beard as he paced the

room. "It could work, but I still don't like the idea of her being there. She never does anything by halves."

"Maybe we should encourage her. The closer she gets to the leadership the better, and the more we could find out."

Mr Wetherby continued pacing. "All right, let's try it your way, but if things get out of hand or she starts causing trouble, we know what the alternative is."

"I'm not sending her back when there's nothing wrong with her. She'll be fine, we need to trust her."

William escorted Mr Wetherby into the hall and offered him his hat before he opened the front door. Mr Wetherby was about to leave when a thought occurred to him. "Perhaps I'd better say goodbye to her. I haven't spoken to her since her *visit*, but if I'm to regain her trust, I need to make an effort."

William smiled. "I'm sure she'll be delighted."

William closed the front door and walked to the back room. "Harriet, Mr Wetherby's just ... that's strange, she's not here." William tried the morning room and then the kitchen.

"Was she due to go out?" Mr Wetherby asked.

William shook his head. "Not that I'm aware of. In fact, she can't have gone far, her hat and cape are still on the stand. Don't worry about saying goodbye,

I'll check upstairs once you've gone. There's probably a simple explanation."

"I'm not in a hurry, you go and check and I'll wait here."

William shrugged as he left Mr Wetherby and went upstairs. The bedrooms were empty. *Where is she?* He came back downstairs and went into the garden. Still there was no sign of her.

"I'm going to go next door to check if she's with Mary-Ann," William said as he came back into the house.

Mr Wetherby followed him into the street, but they both stopped when they saw Margaret and Florence walking home with Mary-Ann's daughters. Of course, William thought, she'd gone to school to walk home with the girls.

"Where's Mother?" he asked Margaret as they approached.

"We've not seen her. We come home by ourselves nowadays."

"So you haven't seen Aunt Mary-Ann either?"

Both girls shook their heads. "No, but she's usually with Mother. If they come to school, they generally come together."

"Yes, of course, I was going to your aunt's house, why don't you come with me?"

Florence took her father's hand as the three of

them walked up the driveway and knocked on the front door. William didn't wait for an answer, and let himself in.

"Mary-Ann, are you there?" he shouted.

"Yes, in the back room," Mary-Ann said. "What are you doing here?"

William glanced around the room. "Have you seen Harriet? She's not at home but she didn't say she was going out. I was talking to Mr Wetherby and when he went to say goodbye she'd disappeared."

Mary-Ann hesitated when Mr Wetherby walked into the room. "No, I haven't. Perhaps she's gone to visit her aunt and uncle."

William shook his head. "I don't think so. She didn't take her hat and cape with her."

Mary-Ann glanced again at Mr Wetherby. "Are you sure you've looked properly? She may have gone upstairs for a lie-down."

"I think I would notice my wife if she was lying on the bed. Can the children stay here while I go back and check again?"

Mr Wetherby followed William as he went back to the house and double-checked all the rooms.

"There's no sign of her anywhere." William went into the back room.

"You said she'd been in good spirits since she'd

come out of Winson Green. Are you sure she wasn't pretending?" Mr Wetherby asked.

"I'm certain. If you'd seen her in the hospital compared to how she is now, there's no comparison. I'm going to see if she's at her aunt and uncle's. Are you coming?"

Chapter Seventy-Four

It was a short walk to Grosvenor Street but what should have been a pleasant stroll in the fine weather was more like a route march. By the time they arrived, both men were breathless. Mrs Watkins was delighted to see them and insisted they stayed for some lemonade.

"I've not seen Harriet for a few days," she said. "As you know, we see her every Thursday and so it would be Thursday of last week when we saw her. She was in such high spirits, but she wouldn't say why she was so excited. I blame her uncle. If he hadn't sat with us all afternoon she might have told me."

"Did she seem ill or hysterical?" Mr Wetherby asked.

"Not at all. In fact I'd say she was as well as I've seen her for a long time."

William listened to Mrs Watkins for as long as he could, but as soon as he was able he excused himself. As he left, Mr Wetherby insisted on walking back to Havelock Road with him.

"You didn't have to come back with me," William said as they walked. "I'm sure she'll turn up soon enough,"

"We need to know where she's got to. I can't help thinking she's up to some mischief."

"Why do you always think the worst of her?"

Mr Wetherby stopped in his tracks. "Might there be another suffrage meeting going on?"

William shook his head. "I don't think so. When I got home earlier she was about to do some book-keeping. She wouldn't have done that if she'd been going to a meeting. Besides, it's almost six o'clock. It would be finished by now."

They arrived at the house as William-Wetherby was returning from work. He waved as he saw them. "What are you two doing here at this time of day?"

"We've lost your mother," Mr Wetherby said before William could answer.

"Lost her? What do you mean?"

William opened the front door and let his son and Mr Wetherby enter before him. "Mr Wetherby and I were talking in the front room earlier this afternoon, and when Mr Wetherby went to say goodbye, she'd gone. I don't suppose you've seen her, have you?"

"No, why would I have seen her? I presume you've been next door?"

"Yes, and to her aunt's house, but there's no sign of her."

William-Wetherby frowned. "That's not like her. Didn't you hear her go?"

"No, we ... oh wait, the front door." William turned to Mr Wetherby. "Do you remember? We thought we heard the front door, but we couldn't see anything. That could have been her."

"I suppose it could have been."

"What time was that?" William-Wetherby asked.

William shrugged. "I'm not sure, three o'clock, half past three? Mr Wetherby and I were talking and didn't take much notice."

"What were you talking about?"

William looked at Mr Wetherby.

"It was a private conversation," Mr Wetherby said. "Of no concern to you."

"It might not be of concern to me, but if Mother overheard you ... Can you remember what you were talking about?"

"She couldn't possibly have overheard us,

without her being stood listening at the door ..." Mr Wetherby said.

William-Wetherby put his hands on his hips. "Which is quite likely what she was doing if she thought she was missing something. She's not the sort of person to let a door get in the way of some interesting information."

"Oh God." William put his hand to his head and sat in the nearest chair. "I don't think this is an accident; I think she's run away."

William-Wetherby stared at him. "What on earth did you say that would cause her to leave and stay out for so long? It'll be dark soon."

"William-Wetherby, run and fetch the police. I need to speak to Mr Wetherby."

William-Wetherby glared at his father. "Don't cut me out. I want to find her as much as you do, but if I don't know why she left ..."

"Go now," William shouted. "I'll tell you later."

William waited until he heard the front door close behind William-Wetherby before he turned to Mr Wetherby. "It's about Winson Green. You said she had to go back, and if there's one thing in the world that would make her disappear, it's that."

Mr Wetherby paled but said nothing as William put his head in his hands.

"When she came out the other month, I

promised I'd never send her there again. If she over-heard us she's probably terrified I'll break my promise. What do we do?"

Mr Wetherby walked to the window. "She'll come back, I'm sure of it; and when she does you can tell her we didn't mean it. She has no money and no hat or cloak. She probably has nothing but the clothes on her back and so she'll either come back here or she'll go to one of her friends. We're sure to find her."

William nodded and took a deep breath. "I hope you're right, but I'm not sure I know all her friends. Since she joined that damn group, she could be any-where. What are we going to tell William-Wetherby? We can't tell him the truth."

"Tell him we were talking about getting an order from a firm in Winson Green and she must have got the wrong end of the stick."

"Yes, I'll do that." William glanced at the clock. "Where is he? He should be back by now. The police station's only round the corner."

It was another ten minutes before William-Wetherby arrived with two police constables. It didn't take long for William to tell them as much as he could. As he finished, one of the constables took out his pocket watch.

"It's coming up to seven o'clock now and you say

she could have gone out as early as three. In four hours she could be over ten miles away."

"I don't think she'd have walked away directly," William-Wetherby said. "If she went on an impulse, she wouldn't know where she was going for a start. I'd say she's stayed locally and will try to come home."

"I hope you're right, laddie, but let's keep our options open," the constable said. "Now which way would she be likely to go?"

The five men went out into the street and surveyed the area.

Mr Wetherby pointed to their left. "If she went out that way, she could have turned left again and walked through the allotments, possibly heading for the woods."

"She could have gone to the woods if she'd turned right and gone up Havelock," William said.

William-Wetherby nodded. "She's unlikely to stay in the woods overnight, it'll be too cold, but if she's gone to the allotments she could be hiding in one of the sheds. That would keep her warm enough."

"Its possible," the police constable said. "Perhaps we should start there."

"Before you do, what if she turned left out of the

house and right into Livingstone Road? She might have gone to the workshop," William-Wetherby said.

"It's down in Lozells," William said, seeing the constables' puzzled faces. "She'd have walked past a lot of people if she'd gone that way and so we could ask around to see if anyone's seen her."

"We could make some missing person posters and put them on the trees," William-Wetherby suggested. "She'd have walked past people whichever way she went. I'll start on them tonight if we don't find her on the allotments."

"We're going to have to hurry," the older policeman said. "It'll be dark soon. Mr Jackson, you go with my colleague and walk to your workshop. I'll accompany your son to the allotments. Mr Wetherby, if you're going home, keep an eye out for her on Wellington Road."

Chapter Seventy-Five

Harriet turned the corner into Havelock Road and stopped. All she needed to do was walk down the road and back through her front door, but her heart was pounding and the knot in her stomach made her feel sick. Her pace was slow as she set off again, but as she approached the house she saw William walk into the street with two policemen. A moment later, her son and Mr Wetherby followed them out. *Why's he still there?* Harriet jumped into the nearest driveway and pressed herself against the pillar of the gatepost. *They've reported me missing.* She peered out from her hiding place to see Mr Wetherby pointing in the opposite direction.

Without thinking she began to back away up the street. They hadn't seen her, but she needed to get out of Havelock Road. As the men walked away from her to the other end of the street, she turned and ran. She made it to the end of the road and darted round the corner before stopping, gasping for breath. She peered back around the corner; it was difficult to see them now, but they were splitting up. One of them was coming towards her. Mr Wetherby! She needed to move, but where to? She spun around, searching for a way of escape. The light was starting to fade but if Mr Wetherby was heading for home, he would walk straight past her. He was bound to see her.

"Please help me, God," she whispered, continuing down the street, moving as quickly as she dared. With every other step she turned her head to glance over her shoulder. No sign of him yet, but it wouldn't be long. She wanted to run, but she had one of her old skirts on with layers of petticoats that liked to tangle themselves around her legs. As she hurried past the gateposts of another house she noticed the hatch to the coal cellar was open. After checking to see that nobody was watching, she slipped down the side of the house and crawled through the small door, thankful she wasn't wearing a hard bustle under her dress. Once inside the coal cellar, she peered through the hatch and before long saw the figure of Mr Wetherby walking past the end of the driveway.

As his footsteps faded, she let out a sigh of relief and sat back against a mound of coal. *What now?* Should she go home and hope she could reason with William? What if Mr Wetherby went back to the house? He wouldn't hesitate in having her locked up again. She'd heard him with her own ears. *If you won't take her ... I'll get her certified myself.*

Harriet closed her eyes and squeezed back the tears that were forming. Mr Wetherby would be in Birmingham tomorrow. It would be safer to wait, then she could slip back into the house while they were all out and act as if nothing had happened.

She glanced around the coal cellar. Despite the fading light seeping through the open door, it was almost pitch black, but the occupants of the house were unlikely to come for coal at this hour. It might not be comfortable, but she would be safe for the night. She shifted to stop the coals from digging into her back and then lay still as Mr Wetherby's words filled her mind. *She has to go back ... I'll get her certified myself.*

She stared into the blackness, as tears of anger

and frustration rolled down her cheeks. *What gives them the right to treat me like this? Well, this time they've underestimated me. I am never stepping foot inside that asylum again.*

Chapter Seventy-Six

Harriet was woken abruptly by a noise outside and her heart raced as she strained to listen. She had no idea of the time or how long she had slept, but her limbs and back felt like lead as she eased herself into a crouching position. She moved towards the hatch and peered outside. The light was faint and she wondered if she had slept through the night or whether the sun was still setting. Staying as still as she could, she listened for any hint of people approaching, but heard nothing. After what felt like an age she heard the birds singing and when she peered out again the light was indeed getting brighter.

She knew she had to leave before the sun came up

and so she fixed her hair and with a great effort hauled herself out of the cellar, closing the door behind her. Her hands and clothes were filthy but at least the dirt had covered the bright blue of her dress and would help her stay concealed in the dull light. The air was cool and she rubbed her arms briskly before setting off. It was still too early to go home but she couldn't head towards the woods. They were bound to look for her there. Instead, after a moment's thought she found herself heading out into the countryside with nobody but the birds for company.

There were few clouds in the sky and as the sun rose she walked close to the hedgerows to conceal herself from prying eyes. They were full of berries and she picked at them as she walked. Occasionally, when she spotted a farmer she would change direction, but for the most part she saw nobody.

WHEN THERE WAS STILL no sign of her, William refused his breakfast and instead paced up and down the hall.

"Where on earth could she have got to?" he said to William-Wetherby. "It went cold last night and she'd have needed shelter. I need to ask Mary-Ann if she'll call on her friends; she should know most of them."

"Before you go, what do you think of this?" William-Wetherby held up a piece of paper. "It's a missing person poster. If you like it, I'll copy it out as many times as I can."

William read it aloud. "Missing person. Mrs William Jackson, forty-three years old, about 5 foot 4 inches tall, medium build with greying fair hair and blue grey eyes. Do you think it says enough? It could cover half the women in Handsworth."

"But what else do you say? She hasn't got any distinguishing features."

As William sat down to think he heard Mr Wetherby at the door.

"Any sign of her?" he asked as he walked in.

William shook his head. "William-Wetherby's done this poster, and we were wondering what else to put on it. What do you think?"

Mr Wetherby stroked his beard as he read. "It doesn't say what to do with her if anyone finds her."

"You're right." He turned to William-Wetherby. "We need to put our address on."

"Is that wise?" Mr Wetherby said. "If they bring her here while you're out she could disappear again. Why don't we suggest that whoever finds her takes her to the police station? They'll keep her until one of us arrives."

"That could work if one of us calls into the police station every couple of hours." William said. "I'm worried about how she'll be though. She's bound to be frightened and so perhaps we need to warn people to be careful with her."

Mr Wetherby took the pen from William-Wetherby and thought for a moment. "Here, how's this?" he said once he'd finished.

William read the postscript. "Approach with caution, this woman may be suffering an attack of insanity. If found please take to Handsworth police station."

"You don't think it makes her sound like a madwoman, do you?" William said.

"Not at all. I was thinking she may be hysterical by now and if anyone approaches her they need to make sure they don't frighten her off."

William nodded. "I see your point. All right, you start copying it out, William-Wetherby, and then attach them to as many trees as you can. I'm going to see Mary-Ann and then I'll take a walk and hope I can find her."

～

As the sun rose in the sky, Harriet turned to head for home. She had nowhere else to go and nothing but the clothes on her back; besides, she needed to speak to William. He had stood up for her at the suggestion of her going back to Winson Green and she had nothing to fear from him other than his anger. Taking a deep breath, she made her way towards the houses, but as she reached Wellington Road she noticed papers attached to the trees, which hadn't been there before. She stopped to read one and felt the bile rising in her throat.

MISSING PERSON

Mrs William Jackson
43 years old, about 5 foot 4 inches tall,
medium build with greying fair hair and blue
grey eyes
Approach with caution.
This woman is likely to be suffering an attack of
insanity.
If found please take to Handsworth police station

It was William-Wetherby's writing, but the last two lines sent a shiver down her spine. The handwriting was unfamiliar; it must be his. Mr

Wetherby's. Tears started to fall down her cheeks. William knew those words weren't true; only one person thought she was mad, but he seemed to be in charge. He was always in charge. She leaned her head on the tree, and pulled a sleeve over her hand to wipe her eyes. After a few moments she tore the leaflet from the tree and retraced her steps back to the fields. She couldn't go home now. She needed a plan.

As darkness approached, she walked towards the nearest farmhouse and spotted a barn close by. There didn't appear to be anyone around. Creeping to the door she peered in. There were stacks of hay across the back wall and it seemed dry and comfortable enough to spend the night.

Once inside, she clambered up a stack of hay in the far corner and hid as best she could. It was warm here and a lot more comfortable than the coal cellar. She lay down and started to rethink what she would do. Images of the children filled her mind. She desperately wanted to see them but she had to forget them for now. If she went back, and they locked her away, she might never see them again. She had to put herself first, at least for a few weeks, until all this blew over.

As she lay under the rafters, the sky turned from grey to black and her thoughts moved to William and how he would manage without her. If there was anyone she was worried about it was him, but William-Wetherby would support him. He was a good lad, and bright too, she hoped the new business wouldn't be too much for him. *Why has this happened now of all times?*

~

As NIGHT DESCENDED, William made his way back to Havelock Road. He needed to collect his young daughters, and Mary-Ann and Mr Diver had just sat down for the evening when he arrived.

"I visited about a dozen of her friends, but nobody's seen her," Mary-Ann said as William took a seat. "She still has friends in Birmingham but I didn't get that far. Other than that I'm struggling to think where else to go."

"What about women from the suffrage meetings? Have you met any of them?"

Mary-Ann shook her head. "No. She kept trying to persuade me to go with her, but I never did. I've no idea who she met there."

As she was talking, the maid brought Margaret and Florence into the back room.

"Has Mother gone back to the hospital?" Margaret asked.

William looked at them. What did he say? Was it

better for them to think she was in hospital or to tell them she had disappeared? He turned to Mary-Ann but she remained silent.

"Yes ... yes she has," he said eventually. "She won't be there for long this time, in fact she might be back by tomorrow."

"I hope so." Florence clung onto William's arm. "I miss her. Tell her to come home soon ... and tell her that if she's sad, I'll make her happy."

A lump reached the back of William's throat and he pulled her into an embrace. Moments, later, without a word, he took hold of the hands of both daughters and took them home. Once he had sent the girls upstairs to bed, William-Wetherby joined him.

"I don't suppose she's here?" he asked.

"No, I'm afraid not. Where've you been?"

"I've been down Havelock, Livingstone, Westminster, Putney, Hutton, Grosvenor and Wellington Roads putting up posters," William-Wetherby said. "I've also been back to the allotments. I stopped everyone I saw to ask if they'd seen her, but nobody had. How can someone become so invisible?"

"I don't understand why she hasn't come back," William said. "How's she living? She must have a friend we're not aware of."

"What about her friends in Birmingham?"

William-Wetherby said. "What were they called? Mrs Booth I think one of them was."

"Yes, Mary-Ann mentioned her and Mrs Kent. Hopefully she'll be there and if so, she'll be safe for tonight. Mary-Ann didn't get there today and so I'll go first thing in the morning if she hasn't come back. What will you do? Does Mr Wetherby expect you in the office?"

"No, he said I can take some time off and so I'll stay around here. We haven't gone out into the farmland near to the woods yet and so I'll go up there. She could be hiding in one of the barns."

William shook his head. "You amaze me with all these suggestions you keep coming up with."

"Well, if it was me, they're the sorts of places I'd go to. You always say I take after her and so hopefully I can second-guess her."

William studied his son. "You miss her, don't you?"

"Of course I do. I don't think I'd be in the position I'm in today if it wasn't for her."

"I think we can all say that. She pushes us, but she gets the best out of us. We'll find her tomorrow, I'm sure."

Chapter Seventy-Seven

B oth men were up early the following morning and as William left for Birmingham, William-Wetherby made his way towards the farmland beyond Wellington Road. It was market day and he studied the carts passing by to make sure his mother wasn't hiding amongst the produce.

After walking for fifteen minutes, he stopped and looked around. He hadn't been up here since his childhood when he'd played amongst the corn. It hadn't changed much, except that the corn had been harvested and for now there was nowhere to hide other than in the hedgerows. There were barns dotted on the landscape and he decided to start with those on the right-hand side nearest to him.

The first three barns were empty of everything except farm equipment and so he continued on to the next one. Unlike the first three, this one was dry and there was a pile of haystacks away from the door that looked comfortable enough to sleep on. He couldn't put his finger on why, but somehow he sensed his mother had been here. He climbed up the haystack, searching for any sign of her, but when he found nothing, he turned and jumped onto a hay bale that was sticking out beneath him. At first it held his weight, but within a second it slipped and he crashed to the floor. He pushed himself up, but when he put his weight on his right foot a pain shot through his ankle and up his lower leg causing him to fall back to the floor. Cursing his luck, he rubbed his ankle before easing himself up again. He couldn't go any further and so with a final glance around, he turned and began his slow journey home.

SITTING in the shade of the hedgerow, Harriet pulled at the stray ears of corn that had been left from the harvest. What was she going to do? She wanted nothing more than to go home, but if it meant she would be locked up in the asylum, it was something she couldn't consider. Not that she could stay here either. She was trapped with no home, no food, and no money. Why now? she thought for the thousandth time.

As the day wore on, she realised that going to Birmingham was her best hope for starting a new life. She had always dreamed of going to London, but had no idea how to get there. If she could make it to Birmingham it would be a start and then she could think about London once she had some money. She watched the sun as it slipped closer to the horizon. It was too late in the day to start the journey now. She would forage for as much food as she could find and spend a second night in the barn. The best time to set off would be in the morning.

Back at the farm, an empty trailer sat in the middle of the barn but there were no signs of the farmer. She made for the corner where she had spent the previous evening, but noticed one of the hay bales had been dislodged. Lines formed on her forehead. She didn't remember doing that, but maybe she had. She stopped and listened; there was nobody there. She waited for a minute to be certain before she returned to her hiding place.

By the time his father got home, William-Wetherby was sitting by the fire with his foot on a stool.

"What have you been doing?" William said as he poured them both brandies. William-Wetherby was about to answer when they heard Mr Wetherby at the door.

He accepted the glass of brandy William offered him. "I've come from the police station. They've had no joy searching the woods despite having half a dozen men searching for her. I take it neither of you have had any success?" When William and William-Wetherby shook their heads, Mr Wetherby continued. "The officer in charge said they were going to move to the canal tomorrow."

"The canal. Why didn't I think of that?" William-Wetherby said.

"She wouldn't have gone on a barge," William said.

"She could be walking down the towpath though. If she's decided to go to Birmingham, it'll take her straight there. It's secluded too. That could explain why no one's seen her."

"If she set off down the towpath on Tuesday afternoon, goodness knows where she could be by now," Mr Wetherby said. "She'd have been travelling for over two days."

Chapter Seventy-Eight

The following morning William-Wetherby was woken by the sound of rain. He climbed out of bed and put his weight on his ankle. It still hurt, but it was bearable and he couldn't let a bit of pain stop him from finding his mother.

His father was in the morning room eating breakfast when he got downstairs.

"Are we going to the canal today?" William-Wetherby asked.

"Are you up to it? Have you seen the rain? It might be as well if I go on my own."

"I'm fine. I can't sit at home all day worrying. I'll be better with something to take my mind off things."

As soon as breakfast was over, they both donned their heaviest coats and set off for the canal. It was busier than they'd expected, but they hoped it would increase the chances of someone seeing her. The towpath had been turned to mud by the footsteps and the horses pulling the barges, and as they made their way towards Birmingham, every footstep squelched. Not that it would stop them. Whenever they saw a barge coming towards them they spoke to the horse handler and asked if he had seen Harriet. Throughout the morning the answers were negative but by early afternoon several people said there was a lone woman not far ahead of them.

With their spirits lifted, they increased their pace until they saw the sight they wanted. A woman walking alone, no more than a hundred yards ahead. She had a shawl pulled tightly over her head, making it difficult to see her features, but she was the right height and build. With his ankle throbbing, William-Wetherby clenched his teeth and hobbled up behind her.

"Mother, Mother, is that you?" he shouted. The woman continued walking, but a minute later, he caught her up and put his hand on her shoulder.

"Mother, it's me, where are you going?"

The woman turned to face him and in an instant his whole world came crashing down.

"I'm not your mother, laddie, be off with you." She pulled her shoulder from under his hand and continued on her journey.

William-Wetherby turned to face his father. "It wasn't her." He blinked back the tears threatening to fall. "Oh Father, what are we going to do?"

"Come on, let's turn back for today. I'd better hail a carriage, you're struggling on that ankle."

"Why, oh why did she have to leave?" William-Wetherby spoke to himself but immediately turned to William. "You were going to tell me why she left. The afternoon she went missing, you remembered what you were talking to Mr Wetherby about when you heard the front door."

William avoided his son's gaze.

"Don't ignore me," William-Wetherby said. "You sent me to the police station and said you'd tell me later. Don't pretend you don't remember. Come on, what was it?"

William took a deep breath. "We were talking about orders for the business and Mr Wetherby suggested I go down to Winson Green ... I wondered if she misheard and thought he wanted to send her back there."

"Why would she think he was talking about her? Are you sure he didn't mention her?"

"Why would he be talking about her?" William answered a little too quickly.

"I don't know, but it would explain why she left." William-Wetherby blinked back his tears. "If Mother thought she was going back to Winson Green she could be miles away by now."

Chapter Seventy-Nine

After a day spent huddled in the barn, Harriet woke to find the sky was once again clear and she knew that today was the day she needed to leave. She moved down the hay bales, and paused by the door to the barn, checking for the farmer or his labourers. When she saw no one, she stepped outside and headed back along the track she had walked up two days earlier. As she neared its end, she kept her head down and walked as fast as she could. People would know by now that she was missing and she needed to keep away from the houses as much as possible. She turned left out of the track and realised she was heading for the canal. A thrill coursed through her body as she realised it would take her towards Birmingham.

The bank to the canal was steep and after the rain of the previous day, it took all her concentration to keep herself from slipping, but once at the bottom she glanced around and started walking at a steady pace.

~

WILLIAM-WETHERBY SAT at the breakfast table waiting for his father. When he saw him, his mouth dropped open.

"You're in your Sunday clothes. Aren't you coming out to look for Mother?"

"I will, but we need to go to church first and pray for her safe return. We should have done it days ago, it's no wonder we can't find her."

"We can't waste most of the day at church, she might be injured or lost and we haven't got time to go all the way down to Grove Lane."

"The day won't be wasted. The police constables are going back to the canal today and we'd do far better asking for the Lord's help. We can't do it by ourselves. We can go to the Parish Church to save time if that makes you happy."

"It doesn't matter where you go, I'm not joining you. I'm going back to the barn where I hurt my ankle. I had a sense she'd been there and I want to check if she went back."

"I don't think you should. You couldn't walk properly on it yesterday."

"I'm not sitting here and doing nothing, it'll be fine once I start moving it."

William reluctantly agreed and as soon as he'd eaten, William-Wetherby grabbed his hat and coat and set out for the fields. The rain of the previous day had made everything wet and muddy, and it took him longer than he expected to reach the barn. When he got there he found the farmer in the yard.

"What can I do for you?" he shouted to William-Wetherby when he saw him.

"Is this your barn?" William-Wetherby asked, pointing behind him.

"What is it to you?"

"Do you know if there's been a woman sleeping in it this week?"

The farmer looked William-Wetherby up and down. "Funny you should say that. We saw a woman here this morning and I asked the lads if they thought she'd been sleeping here. She was in the fields the other morning as well but I didn't think much of it at the time."

William-Wetherby gave the farmer a full description of his mother.

"Yes, that could have been her," he said after a moment. "I remember thinking she was well-dressed, even if her clothes were dirty and she had no hat and coat."

William-Wetherby knew this was her. He hadn't told the farmer about the lack of hat and coat and the chances of there being two women in the same predicament seemed unlikely.

"What time did you last see her?" William-Wetherby asked.

"Not long after sunrise this morning I would say, maybe about seven o'clock."

"So she was still here this morning? Praise the Lord. Can I check she's not in any of your fields?"

"You can if you like but I last saw her walking down the track so I don't think she'll be around."

William-Wetherby hesitated. He wanted to check the barn and fields again, but if the farmer thought his mother had gone, surely he should try to catch her up. He thought for a moment before deciding to go and check the barn one more time.

It was pretty much as he had left it with the hay bale still on the floor, and no sign of his mother. As he turned to leave, he saw some footprints in the mud that couldn't possibly belong to the farmer or any of his labourers. He looked around to check if there were any others and he noticed there was only one set leading away from the barn and down the track. Suddenly excited, he started to follow them, ignoring the pain that was now constant in his ankle. The footprints were still visible when he reached the road, and he continued to follow them until he realised he was heading for the canal. He'd been right about that at least and so if she was walking towards Birmingham the constables should find her. *But what if she's not going to Birmingham?*

Once he reached the canal, his hope faded. There had been so many people passing that way, there was no chance of making out any footprints and he had no way of knowing which way she would have turned. As he went down the steps he decided to head north, away from Birmingham, knowing that the police were further south. He walked for about fifteen minutes, asking everyone he saw whether they had seen anyone answering his mother's description. Several people thought perhaps they had and so he continued on his way. With his ankle throbbing, every step felt like a knife cutting into him, but he couldn't stop. He had to try to blank it out so he could cover as much ground as possible before the sun set.

MR WETHERBY HAD BEEN restless all afternoon. Sarah-Ann had invited William Junior, Olivia and Henry for Sunday dinner, but since they had seen William in church all the talk had been about Harriet. It annoyed him that Charlotte and Olivia were so fond of her and could speak of nothing else. At the same time, he was frustrated that William-Wetherby had now taken four days off work. The election could be called at any time and he needed him back. As soon as the dinner broke up, he excused himself from Sarah-Ann and Charlotte, and walked to Havelock Road. When he found nobody in, he continued to the police station to get a progress report.

"We've had a disappointing day, sir," the sergeant said. "I had a group of lads start out at Marsh Hill this morning. Two went north and two south. I sent Mr Jackson off to join those going south earlier this afternoon but so far I've heard nothing from them."

"Why would they go north? There's nothing up there."

"It might be an ideal place to go if you want to hide, and who knows what goes on inside the head of a woman," the sergeant said.

Mr Wetherby nodded. "That's true, but I still think it's a mistake. I might as well walk up there now and tell them not to bother going any further, I'm certain she'll have headed for Birmingham."

"As you wish, sir, but they'll be calling it a day shortly."

"Nevertheless, how far do you think they'd have travelled?"

"After the heavy rain yesterday they expected it to be slow-going, but we said this morning that they should aim for Tower Hill before nightfall. They shouldn't be far from there by now."

Mr Wetherby bid the officer farewell, cursing him silently for wasting time on that stretch of the canal. Tomorrow, he would make sure they went south.

THE THICKNESS of the clouds meant the light had been subdued all day, but as the afternoon wore on, darkness loomed sooner than it should. Harriet knew she hadn't gone nearly as far as she'd hoped, largely because she'd stopped to hide from every barge she had passed, but despite that, she needed to find somewhere to spend the night. At the next set of steps, she would leave the towpath and search for another barn.

She was contemplating how far she might have to go when she heard a noise behind her that sounded like grass being beaten. She stopped and turned in a full circle but she couldn't see anything. Instinct told her to keep going, but curiosity got the better of her and she turned back expecting to see something round the previous bend. She didn't have far to walk before the canal straightened out and she saw two policemen beating the grass with their truncheons. It was clear they were searching for something but they had their backs to her and she couldn't tell if they were the same men she had seen outside the house days earlier. Her heart skipped a beat. *Are they looking for me?* Whether they were or not, she didn't intend to stay and find out. She turned on her heel and headed down the towpath, praying that the bridge, and its steps to safety, were not far ahead.

Within a minute she saw the bridge and breathed a sigh of relief. She increased her pace and in her haste she started to climb the bank before she reached the steps. The weeds grabbed at her ankles but with a new burst of energy she soon felt the sturdiness of the steps beneath her feet.

As she approached the top she glanced up to get her bearings and her heart stopped. Staring down at her with an unreadable expression on his face was the last person in the world she wanted to see. She hesitated, feeling trapped from both sides, before she turned and ran back down the steps. She hadn't gone far when she lost her footing and fell, her body crumpling and hitting the hard edges of the remaining steps as she did.

By the time she reached the towpath she was travelling too quickly to stop and plunged into the canal. She had never learned to swim and the shock of the icy water in her nose and mouth paralysed her and forced her under the surface. She emerged moments later and gasped for air but before her lungs were satisfied, the water took her again. Her heart and chest felt as if they would explode as she struggled to break the surface, desperate for another breath, but there was so little time. She couldn't breathe. She pushed her arms down again but they were numb; all she could feel was the pounding of her heart as it beat, faster, faster. She had to fight, to give herself time. She couldn't stop; she needed to breathe. Her head was throbbing now; the blood was fighting to escape. She needed to breathe. Why wouldn't her body respond? She surfaced again and gasped for air. There was so little time.

With every fibre of her being she fought to stay above the water, but the noise deafened her ears, it was too loud, but she couldn't stop. She had to fight. She had to breathe. She sank beneath the water again as spots of colour grew before her eyes and then faded as the blackness started to close in on her.

~

AS THE DAYLIGHT RECEDED, William-Wetherby was close to tears. All he wanted was his mother to come home, but his ankle was on fire and there had been no sign of her all day. There would be no full moon tonight and so he would have to head home as soon as he found the next set of steps. He tried to quicken his pace but with every step his ankle screamed at him until he had to sit down. Throwing himself onto the bank, he lay with his eyes closed, unable to focus on anything but the searing pain. He hadn't been there long when a sound permeated his consciousness and he sat up, trying to fathom what he was listening to. It was a minute before he realised it was the sound of grass being thrashed. He eased himself up and made out the figures of two policemen searching in the undergrowth ahead of him. He staggered up again, causing them to stop as he approached. They were about to send him on his way when he asked after his mother.

"No, sorry, son, we've seen no sign of her all day. The steps at Tower Hill are beyond the bend and once we reach them we'll be stopping. It's as if she's vanished into thin air."

Almost collapsing with disappointment, he thanked the officers and continued along the towpath until he saw the steps in the distance. He let out an audible sigh of relief and tried to quicken his pace, but as he did he heard the sound of water being thrashed somewhere ahead of him. Seeing no one he took a deep breath and hobbled as fast as he could towards the noise. As he approached the steps he saw Mr Wetherby staring down at him.

"What happened?" William-Wetherby shouted. When he got no reply he followed the direction of Mr Wetherby's gaze. In that instant he froze. No more than six feet from him, the body of a woman broke the surface of the water. It was his mother. With the pain from his ankle forgotten he jumped into the canal without any care for its depth. He wasn't a strong swimmer but he reached the body in a couple of strokes. His first priority was to turn her onto her back, to allow her to breathe, but her clothes were heavy and pulled her away from him. Several times he slid under the water but pushed himself up as his feet connected with the bottom of the canal. After what felt like an age he scrambled back to the bank and screamed to Mr Wetherby for help, but when his eyes reached the top of the steps Mr Wetherby had gone.

Chapter Eighty

As the light faded, William and the police constables climbed the steps from the canal, letting their eyes search for the police carriage they were expecting. Within a minute, they saw it coming towards them. William gratefully climbed into the back to be transported back to Handsworth. *Where is she?* They'd reached the point where she would have had to leave the canal to travel into Birmingham, but there was no sign of her.

"We'll start again at first light," one of the constables said.

"But where? If she's left the towpath to head for Birmingham she could be anywhere, or she could be on her way to Tamworth if she didn't realise where she was."

"Don't worry, Mr Jackson. We'll find her. As soon as we're back in Handsworth we'll go to the station and get our next instructions."

William nodded and let his head rest on the hard back of the carriage causing him to stare at the roof. *We must find her. She can't leave me. What about the children ... and the business?* A cold shiver ran through his body and his heart thumped as if it were trying to leave his chest. *I can't manage either without her. Please God let me find her.*

The journey back to Handsworth took over half an hour and as they pulled up outside the police station, the place looked eerily empty.

William sat up straight and turned to the constables. "Where is everyone?"

The constables exchanged glances before the older one spoke. "I would say that something's come up that required assistance. Don't forget, it's Sunday and there's not as many men on duty as usual."

William's eyes sparkled. "Do you think they could have found her?"

"I would say that's a distinct possibility," the constable said. "All we have to do now is wait for everyone to come back and find out what's been going on."

~

Thank you for reading *When Time Runs Out*.
I hope you enjoyed it.
If you did, I'd be delighted if you'd share your
thoughts and leave a review on Amazon

~

I'd love to keep in touch with you!
I send out regular newsletters with details of new
releases and information relating to The *Ambition &*
Destiny Series.

By signing up for the newsletter you'll also get a
FREE digital copy of *Condemned by Fate*, a short
story prequel to the series.

To get your copy and keep in touch, visit:
www.vlmcbeath.com

The Next Installment...

Only One Winner

A family divided, with no signs of reconciliation. Will Lydia rue the day she met them?

Keen to get away from her abusive father, Lydia happily accepts the post of housekeeper at the Jackson family home.

But when William senses romance in the air between Lydia and his son William-Wetherby, he is determined to put an end to it... For good.

As a feud erupts between father and son, Mr Wetherby is still furious about Harriet's betrayal.

And he's going to make sure someone pays...

To order your copy visit:
mybook.to/OnlyOneWinner

Also by VL McBeath

The *Windsor Street Family Saga*
The full series:

Part 1: *The Sailor's Promise*
(an introductory novella)

Part 2: *The Wife's Dilemma*

Part 3: *The Stewardess's Journey*

Part 4: *The Captain's Order*

Part 5: *The Companion's Secret*

Part 6: *The Mother's Confession*

Part 7: *The Daughter's Defiance*

The *Ambition & Destiny* Series
The full series:

Short Story Prequel: *Condemned by Fate*

Part 1: *Hooks & Eyes*

Part 2: *Less Than Equals*

Part 3: *When Time Runs Out*

Part 4: *Only One Winner*

Part 5: *Different World*

A standalone novel: *The Young Widow*

Eliza Thomson Investigates

A Deadly Tonic (A Novella)

Murder in Moreton

Death of an Honourable Gent

Dying for a Garden Party

A Scottish Fling

The Palace Murder

Death by the Sea

A Christmas Murder

To find out more about visit VL McBeath's website at:

https://www.valmcbeath.com/

Author's Note and Acknowledgements

Writing certain parts of this book was difficult. It is never nice to write about the death of one of the main characters in a book, but as this whole series was inspired by a true story, the storyline was, unfortunately, inevitable. With the benefit of hindsight, I believe that Mary's death was a pivotal point in the destiny of the rest of the family. Had she lived for longer, my guess is that things would have turned out very differently.

Harriet, on the other hand, was a great character to bring to life. Did she really get involved in the suffrage movement and cause the trouble I attributed to her? In truth I've no idea, but I like to think that she was a strong woman struggling to live within the repressed role society expected of her. It's true that she spent a second period in the asylum, and I know that the strange behaviour where she threw books onto the fire and packed up a carriage with furniture are also true. Was Mr Wetherby the cause of her anger?

Again, I don't know, but for reasons that will become apparent, he isn't my favourite character and so I decided that Harriet could dislike him for me!

Once again I have family and friends to thank for being supportive of my work and for reading and providing comments. As always, thanks go to my husband Stuart who seems to relish his role as unofficial proofreader, friends Rachel and Marie for their comments, as well as my mum and dad, and brother-in-law Dave. Your help and support is also really appreciated!

The story takes a bit of a turn in Part 4, *Only One Winner*. I hope you'll join me and continue the journey.

About the Author

Val started researching her family tree back in 2008. At that time, she had no idea what she would find or where it would lead. By 2010, Val had discovered a story so compelling she was inspired to turn it into a novel. Initially writing for herself, the story grew beyond anything she ever imagined.

Prior to writing, Val trained as a scientist and has worked in the pharmaceutical industry for many years. In 2012, she set up her own consultancy business, and currently splits her time between business and writing.

Born and raised in Liverpool (UK), Val now lives in Cheshire with her husband, youngest daughter and a cat. In addition to family history, her interests include rock music and Liverpool Football Club.

For further information about The *Ambition & Destiny* Series, Victorian History or Val's experiences as she wrote the book, visit her website at: vlm-cbeath.com

Follow me

at:

Website:
https://valmcbeath.com

Facebook:
https://www.facebook.com/VLMcBeath

Amazon:
https://www.amazon.com/VL-McBeath/e/B01N2TJWEX/

BookBub:
https://www.bookbub.com/authors/vl-mcbeath

Made in the USA
Columbia, SC
08 March 2024

32879843R00336